A ROBOT
WHAT A ROI

Seven was about to pull ..

ship when Keeko's image appeared.

"Hello," it said.

"My analysis shows you've sustained significant damage. What the hell is going on?"

"I encountered one of the persons who killed my origin family. She had returned to reactivate the mine. I proceeded to administer justice, but was denied the opportunity by her security drones. By the time I dispatched them, she was gone."

"Did you get her coordinates?"

"Yes."

"Good. You know where she's going, and she'll be expecting you. Come on back, and I can get you fixed up for the showdown."

"That will not be necessary," Seven said.

"Look, I gave you the best I got," Keeko replied, "but that's not going to be worth a damn if she's got military-grade drones or freelance cyborgs protecting her. You won't make it."

"My 'making it' is not the priority," Seven replied. "My objective is justice. I performed a proper burial for the miners. I will now follow the murderer to her current location."

"Seven, listen to me. If you pursue whoever this is, it's going to be a one-way trip."

"I am aware of the possibility. The military protocols you coded into my core advise that the sooner I follow, the less likely my enemy will be prepared."

Hearing no further objections from Keeko, Seven set a course to follow the woman's ship.

—from "Justice and Prosperity"
by Milton Davis

BAEN BOOKS edited by DAVID BOOP

Straight Outta Tombstone
Straight Outta Deadwood
Straight Outta Dodge City

Gunfight on Europa Station
High Noon on Proxima B
Last Train from Kepler - forthcoming

HIGH NOON ON PROXIMA B

Edited by
DAVID BOOP

HIGH NOON ON PROXIMA B

A Baen Books Original

Baen Publishing Enterprises
P.O. Box 1403
Riverdale, NY 10471
www.baen.com

ISBN: 978-1-9821-9335-5

Cover art by Dominic Harman

First printing, February 2023
First mass market printing, April 2024

Distributed by Simon & Schuster
1230 Avenue of the Americas
New York, NY 10020

Library of Congress Control Number: 2022051589

Printed in the United States of America
10 9 8 7 6 5 4 3 2 1

To the readers, authors, and editors
we lost in 2019–2023, all much too soon...
but especially to my friends,
Stephen Vessels, Stacy Vowell, Bruce Taylor, and
John Betts.

Missing you guys.

CONTENTS

FOREWORD

"Knowledge is a commodity to be shared.
For knowledge to pay dividends, it should not
remain the monopoly of the select few."
—Moutasem Algharati

"Write what you know" is bullshit, pure and simple. We have long left this idea behind in the days of instant research. Why go to China to tour and take notes for a novel, when you can jump online and get 360-degree views of the Great Wall from the comfort of your own home...in your jammies...while listening to Bob Dylan in the background? (Dylan is famously banned in China.) And sure, you could write off that trip on your taxes as a business expense, but in our pandemic society, why mess around with all the things that come with international travel?

"Write what you can thoroughly research" is a much better mantra to work from. When writing weird westerns, historical paranormals, or retro sci-fi noirs, I do an exhausting amount of research to get facts right. I have maps all over my office, and shelves filled with essay collections, biographies, and encyclopedias dedicated to famous people, dead languages, and lost civilizations. Why? Because more often than not, someone reading an anthology like this is an armchair historian or expert on something, and they'll call me or any author out on incorrect "facts."

(You know you do. Don't sit back there and say you don't.)

And that's not actually a bad thing. It's important to get facts right, even when playing with historical fiction. Saying it's an "alt-history" or "secret history" can only take an author so far before they lose credibility. Some books paint history with a light brush; others make sure every detail is as accurate. As an editor, I have to trust authors did their homework, but often, I will challenge a historical "fact." (This gets scary when you're editing your idols.)

But this idea of researching for accuracy becomes a slippery slope when you're no longer talking about the past, but the future. How does one research that which is not known or not yet created? This is what every science fiction writer must contend with when they sit down to build their future societies and technology.

As a reader, I'm sure you've wondered where authors come up with all their details about planets and space travel and science-y stuff. (No? Just me?) Well, *I* wondered right up until I became a writer myself and had to start coming up with imagined facts. I discovered early on there are three main sources for acquiring "future facts." Hitting the books, whether physical or digital, is usually an author's first go-to. Next, turning to other authors who write in a similar genre you do. Finally, seeking out scientists and the like who have an expertise that you can tap into.

I began my future research with the short story "The Devil You Haven't Met," my first attempt to write hard science fiction. In it, I wanted to create my own form of space travel based off ideas the science community was exploring at the time. When I googled "warp drive think tanks," I found blogs for the Radcliffe Institute for Advanced Study at Harvard and another at UC Berkeley; both seemed to be tackling the theoretical concepts of warp technology from different directions.

Dr. Katherine M. Benson, at Radcliffe, was exploring "M theory," which, according to her bio, is "an intrinsically eleven-dimensional understanding of forces [that] can lead to our known forces in four-dimensional spacetime." Meanwhile, on the other side of the country, Dr. Raphael Bousso's bio lists him as working on "a surprisingly strong and counterintuitive relation between quantum-mechanical information and the geometry of spacetime." I thought to myself, *What if these two kids got together and built a type of trans-space engine?* The Putnam Engine strips all matter around it, leaving only time. Without matter to slow it down, the engine moves quickly along the timeline like a bullet train. I'm obviously no scientist, and I have no idea if anything these two were working on would actually create the engine I theorized, but I loved the process of being inspired by *real* science and the possibilities it contains. I've never met either of them, nor discussed my story with them, but I did attribute them in the story as the "creators" of the Putnam Engine.

Being a new writer at the time, I had yet to build up a collection of scientists to review and critique my ideas. But I did know an author/editor/scientist-type person I could add to my cadre of experts. David Lee Summers is a Senior Observing Associate at Kitt Peak Observatory in Arizona. Summers—as I've mentioned in my previous introductions—edited *Tales of the Talisman* magazine, but I also discovered, as an astronomer, he was a great source for running ideas by. He can often see things from both the scientist's and the writer's perspective.

Authors who are—or were—scientists are not an uncommon occurrence. They can be a great resource when it comes to making sure your future facts are correct. Author Alan Dean Foster told me of one he often consults with:

"When writing the novelization of *The Chronicles of Riddick*, I was concerned how the extreme rise in temperature on the planet Crematoria would affect the atmosphere that the characters would continue to breathe. So I reached out to Gregory Benford, [science fiction] writer and astrophysicist, to confirm my suspicions that the heat indicated in the film would likely not only be unbreathable but possibly destroy the atmosphere itself. Which he did."

When I started writing the titular story for *Gunfight on Europa Station*, my previous Baen space western anthology, I consulted a couple of my peers, including Summers and fellow author C. Stuart Hardwick, for information on Europa. Summers sent me some amazing links such as to solarsystem.nasa.gov/moons/jupiter-moons/europa/overview/ and solarsystem.nasa.gov/moons/jupiter-moons/europa/in-depth/ while Hardwick made sure I knew the all-important facts like "radiation on the surface of Europa would kill a human in about a day." Both helped me lay the foundation of my story, but I needed more. I needed an actual specialist on Europa research.

Luckily, I'd met one such researcher at a con in Denver.

Spaceflight Historian Hugh S. Gregory has a long

pedigree when it comes to all things non-terrestrial. Among his many and varied credentials, Hugh's bio lists he was "the Mars Society Engineering Team's Chief Training Documents Editor, Chief Cartographer and Waypoint Database Curator for both the MDRS and FMARS research stations." But when I first met him, he was just a guy who gave my son some amazing—and very exclusive—highly detailed photo prints of nebulae, taken with the Hubble telescope, for him to bring to his elementary school's science class show-n-tell. (Believe me when I say these were not photos that just anyone could get at that time.) I've run into Hugh at many cons, and he always has new space exploration stuff to talk about. He was the guy I needed to chat with about Europa.

He, in turn, introduced me to Daniel D. Dubrick, Aerospace Historian. Together, the three of us created an email chain about everything known and/or suspected about Europa, one of Jupiter's moons. They provided data on salinity to ice ratios on Europa's surface and what "seasons" on the moon would look like: "Being 75 million miles closer to the Sun in its Summer, Jupiter would see a tiny increase in the solar radiation received and the Sun would be marginally brighter as a result. . . . This translates into watts received per meter square at the equator on Jupiter or one of the Galilean to 55.8 W/m2 in the Summer and 45.9 W/m2 in the winter." I cannot express my gratitude at how much better my story turned out due to their efforts, and the efforts of those mentioned above.

It's also pretty obvious that I am far from the only author who can make this claim. The idea for this topic came from conversations I had with Cliff Winnig, one of the authors in the anthology you're about to read, *High Noon on Proxima B.* He had been exulting on the research he did for the anthology's titular piece. He cited astronomer Ruslan Belikov of NASA Ames "for many discussions about Proxima Centauri and the Alpha Centauri system and their potential habitability." Cliff said, "Rus has been a terrific source of information on what is known and what is possible." He also accredited "the SETI Institute of Mountain View, California, for the many years of science talks they've hosted, which have included more than a few talks by planetary scientists."

These future facts aren't just related to technologies. A futurist, such as the likes of David Brin, will often start with the past, see where things floundered, and imagine a world where such things could be corrected. He writes in his novel, *The Postman*, "Of course we can establish constitutional checks and balances, but those won't mean a thing unless citizens make sure the safeguards are taken seriously. The greedy and the power-hungry will always look for ways to break the rules, or twist them to their advantage." Such can be said of authors writing religions, governments, and alien races. One of my favorite series is the Well World books from the late Jack L. Chalker. In it, Chalker created over three hundred races, each with a different society. No two are alike, but each can be traced back to a system of rule we, as a people, have tried on our little blue marble—theocracies, dictatorships, rule by combat, or complete lack of any central government. Just from a sociology standpoint, it's a fun series to explore. For many a science fiction author, building a future society is sometimes more fun (and takes longer) than writing the actual novel.

As the epitaph above states, information wants to be shared and should. For what is the point of accumulating knowledge just to sit with it and never pass it along to others? This is what infuriates me about movies or shows. There's not a scientist alive who doesn't pick apart every science fiction work to determine which writers actually did their research and which ones just pulled the proverbial string theory from their asses. The same can be said about shows featuring soldiers, police officers, FBI agents, doctors, and yes, even writers. Nothing upsets me more than seeing portrayals of authors where someone sits down and "births" a best-selling novel. Just like the famous commercial said, "That's not how it works; that's not how any of this works."

So, authors should take great care when they write our future facts, and be sure that they're investing the time to build our plausible worlds on known science. Not just because they want to show off how smart or creative they are. Not because they got various degrees in engineering, physics, sociology, psychology, or a plethora of other fields before finding their calling as scribes. They should ultimately take care because readers ask it of them. Demand it even, at times. And readers deserve the best future authors can give them, or they'll post a negative review faster than my proposed Putnam Drive.

(You know you will. I see you there with your finger hovering over the "enter" key. Don't think I can't.)

Faithfully Submitted,
DB
12/22/21

JUSTICE AND PROSPERITY

Milton J. Davis

Asteroid 11-471 was one of millions of rocks trapped in the sun's orbit, but to the Dobbins family, it was hope. Ben and Tonya Dobbins spent all their savings and sold all their belongings for a chance at a better life not for them, but for their four children. Their future was in the stars, and they were determined to make the best of it.

Ben Dobbins laughed as Tonya squeezed his butt through his A-suit. The mine shafts had been secured and oxygenated for months, but old precautions were still taken. He turned to face his wife, her honey-brown skin glowing. He swept his hand over her braided hair, and they kissed.

"I wish I was going with you," she said.

"No, you don't," he replied.

Tonya patted her plump belly. "I'd rather be working than pregnant, especially on this rock. It's all your fault."

"I remember someone else involved, as well."

Tonya punched his stomach. "Get out of here."

Seven, their service bot, joined them at the door. It held up his lunch cannister.

"You forgot this, Mr. Dobbins."

"Thank you, Seven. At least something around here has a memory."

"You're welcome, sir," Seven said. "I'll attend to breakfast."

The couple watched Seven stroll into the kitchen.

"It was expensive but worth it," Tonya said.

"I wouldn't say all that," Ben replied.

Tonya pushed him toward the door.

"Get out of here before you make me mad."

"Love you," Ben said.

"Love you, too."

Ben walked down the corridor to the main tunnel. Five minutes later, the work sled appeared, packed with his shift members. They greeted him with grunts and waves as he climbed into the sled.

"It's gonna be a great day," he said.

Marcus Delany chuckled. "You have to say that. You're the supervisor."

Ben patted the blond man on the back. "We work for ourselves, remember? I feel like we were close to another vein yesterday. All the signs were there."

Sherry Rosenstein nodded in agreement. "One more and we're off this piece of shit."

"Cluster, here we come!" Yuri shouted.

"Hey!" Ben said. "Don't talk about home like that!"

They all laughed. The covert colony had collected enough rare metals to pay for jump-ship transit and recolonization documents to the Cluster. Another good strike would set them up for life. They voted to extend their time for that very reason, despite increasing their chances of detection. It was all or nothing.

The shuttle sped down the corridor until it reached the drop shaft. It hovered and its passengers prepared for the descent. As the craft made the final adjustments, there was a flash from above. The shuttle exploded.

Seven was prepping the dishes for the washer when it detected motion at the entrance. Determining it was probably Mr. Dobbins returning for some forgotten item, it placed the dishes down and proceeded to the door. It was almost there when the door burst inward, slamming against it with a force that knocked it to the floor. Seven attempted to rise but its leg joints were damaged and it was pinned under the door by trampling boots. Its sound sensors picked up noises of distress followed by weapon blasts. The blasts continued until the screaming stopped. Seven sent out a distress signal and struggled to stand. The door was lifted and two humans in atmosphere suits looked down on it, their faces obscured by their shields.

"What is that?" one of them said.

"Server bot," the other replied. "Must be a wealthy colony if they can afford that."

"Hey," another voice said. "We hit the jackpot!"

"The fuck you talking about?"

"They're mining rare earth metals! They have a shitload of it!"

"Bingo!" one of the humans said. "I told you prowling the Belt would be worth it. Let's find the cache then sprint."

"What about the bot?"

"What about it? We got minerals."

"Never leave anything to waste."

A human reappeared. It extended a tubelike object. There was a flash, and Seven's sensors went dead.

Danforth Anderson sat at the small dining room table, then took off his helmet, revealing his grizzled face. He removed his gloves, then rustled his straw-blond hair with a calloused hand before gazing around the cramped space. A frown formed on his face, and he spat on the cheap tile floor. He'd spent most of his life living in shit quarters like this, hewing rock for the Corpos before he got smart and stole an old transport ship and changed his life. Ever since then, he'd been a pain in the ass for them. But even revenge gets old. It was time to move on, to get back to living. This was a big step.

He stood, then walked through the quarters. He passed the little bedrooms, then entered the family space. The woman lay there dead with the children, their blood spattered on the walls and pooling on the floor. Dan squatted to get a closer look at them. Dead people stopped bothering him a long time ago, especially since he was the one who killed most of the ones he'd seen. He grabbed the woman's hair, then looked into her lifeless eyes.

"Pretty," his said with a gravelly voice. "Too bad."

He stood, then left the room. As he entered the main room, Skyles hit him on the comm.

"Talk to me."

"We found a hauler," she said.

"Can it fly?"

"Yep."

"Good. Have the boys gather the rich rock and take

it to *Blade*. Once y'all get it all secure, meet me at the living quarters."

"Will do."

Danforth took a tour of the illicit base while his boys loaded the ship, his countenance hardening with every corpse he passed. It wasn't the carnage that bothered him; it was the unnecessary use of it. These people had been defenseless. It would have been just as easy to round them up, take the rich rock, then fly away. It was an illegal dig, which meant they couldn't report what happened even if they'd wanted. He shouldn't have put Kelly in charge of the landfall. The man was a murderer. Toby and Matt did whatever Kelly told them to do. Danforth decided he'd make better decisions next time.

He worked his way back to the main chamber. His comm clicked again.

"Talk to me."

"We're here."

"Good. On my way."

Danforth ducked his head as he entered the main chamber. Kelly, Toby, and Matt stood shoulder to shoulder, their suits decorated with clothing and other items they'd taken from the people they killed. Skyles sauntered up to him, a smirk on her face.

"This is what we've been waiting for," she said.

"Yes, it is," Danforth replied.

Danforth smiled before he addressed them all.

"Boys!" he said. "We've been scouring these rocks for five years hoping to hit the jackpot. Well, here it is!"

The chamber echoed with cheers.

"Y'all have made me a rich man," Danforth said.

Kelly's face went from jovial to stone cold.

"You? What about the rest of us?"

Danforth answered him with a bullet to the forehead. Skyles shot Toby through the neck; Danforth emptied his gun in Matt's back as he attempted to run away. Skyles put an extra round into each of them before standing by Danforth.

"Should have done this a long time ago," she said.

"Better late than never," Danforth replied.

"We'll have to get a new crew," Skyles said.

"We will, once we jump to the Cluster."

Skyles grinned. "Prosperity is one step closer."

Danforth patted her shoulder.

"It is."

Keeko peered at the damaged circuit board through his magnifier, the hot soldering iron quivering in his left hand. The medicine was wearing off, and the trembles had returned.

"Fuck!" he hissed.

He placed the soldering iron down and groaned as he stood then scratched his ass. Fluffing back his salt-and-pepper Afro with his fingers, he shuffled across the repair room to his medicine box. He opened the container, then frowned. He was down to his last two. Keeko shrugged as he took the bottle from the box, popped open the lid, then dumped the pills into his mouth. He ambled to his fridge, took out a water bottle, and washed the bitter medicine down his throat. He held out his hand, watching it until the trembling subsided. Keeko trudged back to his workbench and was about to pick up his soldering iron when the entrance door slid aside. Mario strode into the shop, a bot draped over his shoulder. Keeko's eyes went wide. He jumped to his feet, waving his hands.

"Mario! Don't—"

Mario dumped the bot on to Keeko's workbench, shattering his magnifier and the circuit board.

"You dumbass!" Keeko shouted. "Look what you did!"

Mario looked at the workbench, then shrugged.

"My bad. Hey, boss wants you to harvest this bot's core. He's got a buyer for the body."

"Might as well give him the core," Keeko said as he lifted the bot to get what was left of the board and his magnifier.

"Nothing's free," Mario replied. "You should know that by now."

Keeko scowled. "How soon does he need it?"

"Tomorrow."

Mario didn't wait to ask if tomorrow was possible. Bossman's word was law; if he wanted it done the next day, it would be done. Keeko didn't need another month added to his indentured contract.

Keeko perused the bot before cracking it. This was a quality unit, definitely not salvage. Whoever brought it in stole it. If it was raiders, the owners were probably dead, too. The number 7 was etched on its left breast, another sign of a high-quality job. Now here it was, resting on the tabletop of an indentured repairman's workbench. Couldn't get any lower. He probed the cranium until he located the seam. He popped it opened, then extracted the core. Keeko tossed it, then caught it. It was dense, which indicated high-level programming. Procedure called for him to wipe and recondition it, but Bossman said the shell had to be ready by tomorrow.

He placed the core on a nearby shelf, then cleared his workstation. There was a buyer's holotag on the body. They wanted the shell to be converted into a pleasure bot, which meant he'd have to do a lot of wet work. That also meant sealing off the frame to make sure there would be no seepage before dunking the shell into a skin vat.

Keeko went to work, changing his soldering tip and switching to an appropriate solder for the task. All the while he worked, he kept glancing at the core. It wasn't often that he had access to a unit that interacted with humans as a domestic. He was curious about what images it stored, what secrets it contained that he could harvest and sell on the Mesh. The thought made him hurry; he completed the sealing in half the time. He rolled the shell onto a cart, then pushed it through the clutter to his skin vat. He grimaced; it had been so long since he used the thing that the solution had soured. It took another hour to drain the vat and replace the elixir, which luckily had not gone bad as well. As the solution warmed, he slathered nano paste onto the shell. The prep alarm rang, and Keeko submerged the shell into the vat. It would take ten hours for the skin to form, and another three hours for it to cure. That gave him enough time to finish his board repair, then dive into that server core.

"The hell with it," he said. "I deserve a break."

Keeko got the core from the shelf, then placed it on his table. He went to the fridge again, this time for bread and meat paste. He made a quick sandwich, grabbed his water, then ambled back to his bench. Keeko pulled open his bench drawer, then took out his Ocs. He put them on, then linked to the core.

"Okay, let's see what you got," he whispered.

He tapped the on button and the app intro started. Keeko skipped it with the twitch of his head.

"Last entry," he said.

The image swirled, then he was standing at a kitchen counter, prepping dishes. Keeko felt the wetness on his fingertips, then shut off the neural sensors. He wanted to see the last minutes, not feel them. He had no idea what was about to go down.

There was a banging on the door.

"Oh shit," Keeko mumbled, his mouth filled with sandwich. Seven went to the door. There was an explosion, and the door slammed into the bot. The rest was carnage. Keeko stopped eating. He watched until the recording went dead, then took off the Ocs. There were tears in his eyes. He knew shit like that happened all the time in the Belt, but to see it was another thing. He waited for a few more moments before putting the Ocs on again. He gestured with his hands as he fast-forwarded through the grim parts and uploaded the faces of the raiders. He linked to the Mesh to transfer the images, then stopped. Who was he kidding? Even if he was able to find the bastards, who would go after them? The law was too busy trying to keep "undesirables" from jumping to the Cluster. Nobody gave a damn about a bunch of murdered squatters.

"File it away, Keeko," he said. "Ain't nothing you can do."

Skyles maneuvered *Blade* as close to the ship before them as she dared. Danforth looked ahead to the transition gate and smiled. The line wasn't as long as he remembered from ten years ago. It was getting more and more expensive to buy passage, and the means to getting enough crits were getting fewer. Finding that squatters camp was a true blessing.

Skyles set the ship on auto, then pulled up her holoboard. Her well-manicured fingers flashed across the keys as she prepared them for inspection. Danforth looked at her with a frown.

"You sure this is going to work?"

"You better hope it does," she said. "Just get ready to do your part."

"I'm always ready," Danforth said.

Twenty minutes passed before they were next in line.

"Hook up," Skyles said. "We're on."

Danforth linked his comm to the system. There was a brief moment of painful static before the link connected.

"Access," a metallic voice said.

Skyles opened their system to the gate. She looked at Danforth and winked as they waited.

"Welcome to the Gate, Goliath Enterprises," the voice said. "Your documents check out. A passage fee of twelve million crits is required."

"Twelve million! Since when?"

"Since right now," the metallic voice replied.

"I request barter," Danforth said.

There was no response. Danforth looked at Skyles and she shrugged.

"Prepare for boarding," the metallic voice finally responded.

"I'll get the hatch ready," Danforth said.

He worked his way to the rear of the transport

and sealed the hatch. A few minutes later, the ship shook as the Gate shuttle contacted and attached. Danforth closed the chamber before opening it to the shuttle hatch. The hatch opened and the Unity gatekeeper stepped into the void. He was Clusterone, thick at the shoulders and hips, narrow everywhere else. He waited until the atmosphere cleared before removing his helmet. This one was bald, which was rare. Clusterones were vain about their appearance, especially their hair. Danforth forced a smile to his face before opening the chamber.

"What are you bartering?" he asked.

Not one for conversation, Danforth thought.

"Rich rock," he said.

The Clusterer's eyebrows rose.

"Let's see it."

Danforth led him to the cargo hold. He punched in the access code and the door slid aside. The officer followed him inside.

"How many tons?" he asked.

"Five hundred."

The agent went to the ore. He took a mineral analyzer from his pocket, then scanned it. He cut a side eye at Danforth as he put the analyzer back into his pocket.

"Where did you get this?"

"Goliath Enterprises," Danforth said.

"Bullshit," the agent retorted. "Goliath doesn't have rich rock this pure. Nobody does."

Danforth's smile faded. The game was over.

"I won't tell you where I got it," he said. "The only thing we need to decide is how much of it I need to give you to get through the Gate."

"Half," the agent said.

"That's not going to happen."

"Then there's nothing else for us to discuss."

"Yes, there is."

Skyles pressed her gun against the agent's head.

"You don't leave this ship until we make a deal."

The agent cut his eyes at Skyles.

"You must be crazy. Both of you."

"Maybe," Danforth replied. "So, this is how it's going down. You're going to approve our passage. You'll stay with us until we're secured. We'll transfer one ton of ore to your shuttle and send you on your merry way."

"Or?"

"My friend puts a hole in your head, and we run to fight another day."

"So, you can be either rich or dead," Skyles said. "Your choice."

The agent tapped his comm.

"Authorize passage for the *Blade*," he said. "I'm staying with the ship until they reach the worm pad."

"Affirmative," the metallic voice replied.

Skyles gestured with her gun. "Come with me."

Skyles and the agent walked to the cockpit while Danforth cleared the passage between the ships. He activated the transfer pod, then watched as the robotic device moved exactly one ton of rich rock into the shuttle. By the time it was complete, they'd reached the worm pad.

"Done!" he yelled.

Skyles led the agent back to the passage.

"Nice doing business with you," she said. She shot him in the head.

Danforth dragged the agent by his feet into his shuttle. He activated the robot, then transferred the rich rock "payment" back into their ship. He returned to the *Blade*, and Skyles disconnected the vessels. He joined Skyles in the cabin.

"How long?" he asked.

"Guiding the shuttle clear now."

Danforth pulled up the visual. He watched the shuttle drift until it was a safe distance away. He hit the comm.

"This is the captain of the *Blade*. We are prepared for jump."

"Jump sequence initiated," the metallic voice said. "One minute before transition."

Danforth and Skyles strapped in. Skyles reached out and grabbed his hand.

"We did it," she said.

"Yes hell, we did," Danforth replied.

"Hey, Steven, come over here and give me a hand."

Steven rose from its seat, then wormed through the clutter to the heavy lifter. It squatted near the vehicle, then peered under its massive frame.

"How can I help?" it said.

"You can slide the large Philips tip under here," Keeko said.

Steven stood, then went to Keeko's toolbox. It was reaching for the tip when blackness swallowed its vision and was replaced by the scene that had plagued its core ever since Keeko rebooted it. The door slammed into it, knocking it to the ground. The shots and the screams, then nothing.

"Steven? Steven!"

Steven's optics cleared and the tip returned to focus. But it did not move.

"Steven?"

It felt weight on its shoulder, then turned to see Keeko standing next to it.

"What's wrong?" he asked.

"A minor glitch," Steven said.

"Same as before?" Keeko asked.

"Yes," Steven replied.

Keeko pulled up a chair, then sat beside Steven.

"I tried everything to clear that data from your core, but nothing has worked," he said. "It's as if you're holding on to it. Like you don't want to let it go."

"Why would I do that?" Steven asked.

"I don't know," Keeko answered. "Maybe you have some unfinished business."

"I'm a server," Steven said. "The people in the image no longer exist."

"But something inside you does," Keeko said.

He stood, then went to his Ocs.

"Let's link," Keeko said.

Steven watched as Keeko placed the Ocs over his eyes. Moments later, he felt the power surge of linkage. Keeko materialized, a smile on his brown grizzled face. A room similar to the one they occupied appeared, also much neater. Steven's programming did not allow randomness.

"Let's look at this again," Keeko said.

A chair appeared beside him. Keeko patted the seat.

"What does that mean?"

"It means come sit with me."

Steven took a seat. A blank screen appeared before them. Moments later, images appeared.

"Wow," Keeko said. "Never saw those before."

Steven remained silent. This was old data, images impressed over the years of its service with its first family. Something stirred within it, something that Steven had never experienced.

"What's going on, Steven?" Keeko asked.

"Don't call me that," it said without thinking. "My designation is Seven."

"Interesting," Keeko said. "How do you feel, looking at the images?"

"Feel?"

"Bad choice of words," Keeko said. "What do you think?"

Seven looked at the images five more times before answering.

"The people I served. They did not deserve this."

Keeko nodded. "What about the people who did that to them?"

"They deserve justice," Seven replied.

Keeko laughed. "I think so, too."

"Will that happen?" Seven asked.

"No," Keeko answered.

"Why?"

"Because the universe sucks, that's why."

After disconnecting, Keeko went back to the hauler, then slid back under it with his tools.

"People die every day just like that," he said as he worked. "Other people spend most of their lives working off debt just because they made a bad decision. Then some folks just take and keep taking until there's nothing left. Then they find somewhere else to take it from."

"What does that have to do with these people?" Seven asked.

"It means if you want justice, you have to do it yourself. Now slide me that wrench."

Later that day, after Keeko took his required rest, Seven linked to the Mesh.

"Define justice," it said.

"I think I have just what you're looking for."

Danforth and Skyles held hands as the property manager flipped his hand across the holoscreen. A small planet appeared, its surface pockmarked with brown, green, and blue.

"Planet 2211-E," he said. "Formerly owned by the Yuan Collective. It was five years from optimum terraforming before the Collective dissolved. I estimate an intense investment could make it operational in three."

"What kind of investment?" Danforth asked.

"One billion Ucoin," the manager said.

"Can we have a few minutes?" Skyles asked.

"Of course."

The manager shut down the holo, then exited the conference room. Skyles activated her dampers before speaking.

"That's almost all we got," she said.

"Almost," Danforth replied.

"It's a hell of a risk."

Danforth grinned. "You getting soft?"

"Shit, no. Just cautious."

"Look, rich rock is more valuable than we thought. Plus, there's more where that came from."

Skyles stood, then walked to him.

"Still . . ."

"This is it, Skyles. This is what we've been working for."

Skyles bit her lip. "You sure about this? We could just drift. We have enough to do it for the rest of our lives."

"We can be players," he said. "Prosperity is just the beginning. We could end up with a section. Hell, we could have our own cluster!"

"Calm down, jockey," Skyles said. "One step at a time, remember?"

"So, you with me?" Danforth asked.

Skyles smiled. "I'm with you. You couldn't do it without me."

"Damn right, I couldn't. Let's get this manager back in here and make this deal."

"How's that?"

Seven gazed at the new appendage, the design similar to a human limb. Its entire body had been refashioned over a period of three standard years, Keeko working on it between his regular assignments.

"It is acceptable," Seven said.

Keeko frowned. "Acceptable! It's a fucking work of art!"

"I don't understand," Seven said. "I asked you to help me find justice. I didn't ask you to make me a work of art."

"Shut up and follow me," Keeko said.

Seven followed Keeko through the shop to the skin vat.

"Why are we here?" it asked.

Keeko grinned. "If you're out for revenge, you have to look the part."

"I don't understand."

"Revenge. Payback. Comeuppance."

"I didn't ask for those things," Keeko said. "I asked for justice."

"There is no justice," Keeko said. "Unless you make it yourself."

Keeko activated the skin vat.

"See, Steven—"

"Seven," it corrected.

Keeko rolled his eyes. "How did I get stuck with a hard-headed bot? Anyway, a long, long time ago, there was such a thing as punishment. You did wrong, you got arrested, you went to trial, and you were sentenced."

"I learned as much on the Mesh," Seven replied. "That is why I require your assistance."

"Be careful. Everything on the Mesh ain't true," Keeko said.

"Then why would it be there?"

"That's another story," Keeko said. "The truth is, justice ain't never been fair. Those with money have used it to influence the folks running the government. It was bad before the collapse; it's worse now. Government folks have kissed Corpo ass for centuries. Now they're licking it. So, if you want justice, you have to do it yourself."

Seven's optics fluttered as it crawled the Mesh.

"I must become a vigilante," it said.

"Yep," Keeko said. "Now get in the vat."

Seven climbed into the nutrient-rich liquid.

"I'm shutting you down for a few hours," Keeko said. "Sweet dreams."

Seven's optics faded and its core went dormant. But it was still active. Memories repeated themselves, images and sounds from its former hosts. Seven recalled their names, their conversations, their sounds of happiness, sadness, stress, and relief. And then it was all ended abruptly by the attackers. Each time its resolution for justice became stronger. As Keeko reactivated it, Seven's actions had been considered and accepted.

"Let's get you out of here," Keeko said.

Seven climbed the chamber. Keeko stood before it, holding a body-length mirror.

"Well, what do you think?"

Seven studied its umber skin, its body structure, and facial features. It took a moment to process that this shell was created to resemble his former patron, Ben Dobbins.

"This is appropriate," it said.

Keeko chuckled. "It will scare the shit out of them if they know who he is. Fear will give you an advantage. Now comes the tricky part."

"What's that?"

"Recoding you," Keeko said. "Revenge requires a certain attitude."

"You mean I must be willing to kill humans," Seven said.

"Yep," Keeko replied. "And you have a shitload of protocols imbedded in you to keep that from happening."

"Then there is no reason for me to pursue this option."

"O, ye of little faith," Keeko said.

"What does that mean?"

"Don't worry about it. Sit down."

Seven took a seat. Keeko peeled back a section of flesh covering its external ports.

"Can't do this wireless," he said as he hunted for cables. "Too many eyes watching."

Keeko found the cables, then skipped back to Seven.

"This is going to take a while," he said. "I have to recode you manually. Can't risk any detection."

"Are you qualified for such a task?"

Keeko laughed. "If you were human, I'd cuss you out. I was a pretty decent hacker in my day. Besides, I don't have to build code for this. I just need to get rid of it. A lot of it."

Seven felt surge of energy, then a decrease.

"When you wake up, you'll be a different unit," Keeko said. "Night-night."

Skyles looked down on Asteroid 11-471 with a scowl. She hated returning to the scene of the crime, especially if it was a crime she committed. She was pissed when Danforth asked her to, but she understood why. Prosperity wasn't turning out as profitable as they hoped. Settlers trickled in, but not nearly as fast as they needed to complete the final stages of terraforming. They needed income, and what better way to raise cryptos than rich rock.

She did another circle of the surface before preparing the ship for landing. Once the coordinates were confirmed she switched the cameras to the cargo hold. The mining units were still as she had stored them, showing minimum shift. Each had cost a fortune, but it was worth the investment. If the remaining rock was as rich as the first haul, they would be set for the next century at least.

The ship landed with a soft thud. Skyles donned her atmosphere suit, then checked the specs one last time before opening the cargo door. She made her way to the units, activating them as she walked to her bike. Opening the hatch remotely, Skyles maneuvered the ship into the empty atmosphere. She shivered a few seconds as her suit adjusted, then linked to the mining units. They formed a silent train, rolling over the rough surface to the old mining camp. Skyles sent a reconnaissance drone ahead to make sure the mine was still uninhabited. She monitored the data as she received it, grinning when the drone confirmed there were no occupants. At least not living.

She led her caravan to the cargo entry. To her surprise, the security system was still active. It only took a few minutes to hack, and the hatch door slid aside. Skyles entered first, parking her vehicle as the others trailed in. She closed the door, then followed the drone schematics to the mine. She briefly considered restoring oxygen to the facility, but decided not to. She was fine in her suit. If she wanted freedom, she could return to the ship.

The mine was located a mile underground. Skyles found the old lift craft and reactivated it. She loaded the gear onto the craft, then they descended to the mining level. The barely decayed bodies of the miners greeted her. She frowned at the dismembered carcasses, remembering her dead former colleagues.

"Fucking maniacs," she said.

She set up the equipment, then activated it. Skyles watched as the mining equipment evaluated the rock, identified the area with the highest concentration of rare metal, then proceeded to dig and process. After a few minutes, she decided to return to her ship. She cruised across the bare rock and a grin came to her face. She grew up on a planet much like this, a dead sphere void of prospects. Now she was on the verge of becoming one of the richest people in the Worlds, something she'd never imagined.

A red light flashed at the corner of her eye. She pulled up security.

"Status," she said.

"Unidentified craft has landed near mining personnel facilities. Security drones are en route to investigate."

Skyles checked her weapons, then veered toward the buildings.

Memory data activated in Seven's core as it entered the cubicle that had once been its home. The small space came alive with images of the family going about their daily routine. Through the translucent remembrances, it saw their remains. There was some decay, but they mostly looked the same as they did when it last saw them.

Seven knelt beside the mother. It reached out, then touched her hair, and a strange sensation flooded its core. Seven felt weight upon its body, forcing it to sit down. Memories emerged again, slow and more defined. Seven linked to the Mesh.

"Grief," it said.

It would have to honor them. Tradition required either cremation or burial. Since there was no atmosphere to sustain fire, the only choice was burial.

Seven gathered the bodies of the children, then brought them to the main room. The father was missing; it would search the mines for his body. If it found him, it would bring his corpse to the cubicle. Seven departed for the mines, passing the bodies of the other unfortunate miners. The heaviness increased, but not as deeply as that for its "family." As it neared the mine shaft, it heard functioning equipment. Seven reached the edge of the tunnel, then peered into the darkness. It pressed the code for the lift, and the platform appeared moments later. It boarded, then rode the platform into the mines. Mining machinery was hard at work harvesting the ore. Someone else worked the asteroid. Another sensation entered Seven's core, one that dispersed the heaviness, replacing it with nervous energy. Its hand gripped the handles of its guns, then pulled them. Seven accessed the martial coding Keeko installed, and its senses became augmented. It picked up communication between a dozen security drones approaching its location. They were being led by a human. Seven attempted to link with the camp cameras, but they were inoperative. It followed martial protocol and found a secure place to hide and wait.

Skyles ran behind the security drones, gun in hand. There was always the possibility another party would happen upon the mines, but that chance was minimum. At least that's what she had thought. Someone else was in the camp with her mining equipment and that wasn't acceptable.

She sent the drones down the shaft, then activated her video feed linked to the first one. As the drone stepped on the platform, a man emerged from behind one of the diggers, a gun in each hand. There was a flash, and the video went dead.

"Fuck!"

Skyles switched to the camp camera feed. The man stood out in the open, exchanging fire with the drones. As she watched, her throat went dry. The interloper's weapons were synced with his dispersal shield, open only when he fired. The security drones weren't sophisticated enough to take him down. This wasn't a prospector or scavenger; this was an assassin.

Skyles shut off the link, then ran as fast as she could to her bike. She jumped on the vehicle, then sped to her ship. Once inside, she overrode launch protocols and lifted off. As soon as she breached atmosphere, she contacted Danforth.

"Skyles, talk to me."

"Mission aborted."

"Aborted? Bullshit! We need that ore, Skyles."

"Then you come get it," Skyles replied. "We had a visitor. An assassin."

"Assassin? How do you know? Are you okay?"

"Watched him take out our drones like they were puppets. He's augmented. Military-level cyborg most likely."

"Only a handful of people have access to that tech," Danforth said.

"Danforth, I don't think this was random," Skyles said. "I think he's looking for us."

"An assassin? Looking for us? Don't think so," Danforth said. "We don't leave trails. Besides, that shit camp wasn't worth anybody spending a corrupt crypto on. You probably stumbled on somebody else staking a claim."

"Maybe," Skyles said. "So, what are we going to do?"

"The only thing we can do," Danforth said. "Put our people to work."

"They're not gonna like that."

Danforth grinned. "Like they have a choice. Get your ass back home. We got work to do."

☆ ☆ ☆

Seven stepped through the wreckage that was once

the security drones. The human commanding them had fled the compound and the asteroid. It pulled the human's image from the compound cameras, then compared it to those in its memory. When its core found a match, Seven froze. It lingered on the image, and the surge of energy it felt earlier returned. Seven's ship would have automatically picked up the craft launch and calculated possible escape routes as it was coded to do. Keeko installed that feature just in case one of his "targets" went on the run.

Seven considered pursuing the ship, but there was no hurry. As long as it had the coordinates, it could pick up the trail. Seven had not come to the mine to fight looters; it had come to locate Ben Dobbins's remains. It left the mine, working its way down the corridor leading to the elevator. Ten feet beyond the lift were miner bodies. Seven ambled to the bodies then knelt. Like the others, the loss of oxygen and the subzero temperatures kept the bodies preserved, so it took Seven only a few inspections to find the remains of Ben Dobbins.

Seven carefully separated Ben from the rest of the corpses. It lifted the body onto its shoulders, then carried it to the cubicle with the others.

"Together again," it said.

Seven hacked the compound atmosphere and restored oxygen production. It used the compound data bank to identify all the inhabitants, then placed them with their families in the proper cubicles. Once that task was complete, Seven located the compound's explosives. It distributed the supply throughout the compound, placing the charges at strategic points based on the diagrams in its memory. Once the explosives were properly placed,

Seven rigged a remote, then returned to its ship. It waited until it was airborne, circling the facility, before it pressed the remote. The ground shuddered, then the surface rock collapsed into a wide crater.

"A proper burial," Seven said.

It was about to pull up the coordinates of the ship when Keeko's image appeared.

"Hello," it said.

"My analysis shows you've sustained significant damage. What the hell is going on?"

"I encountered one of the persons who killed my origin family. She had returned to reactivate the mine. I proceeded to administer justice, but was denied the opportunity by her security drones. By the time I dispatched them, she was gone."

"Did you get her coordinates?"

"Yes."

"Good. You know where she's going, and she'll be expecting you. Come on back, and I can get you fixed up for the showdown."

"Showdown?"

"Never mind. Just get your android ass back here so I can patch you up."

"That will not be necessary," Seven said.

"Look, I gave you the best I got," Keeko replied, "but that's not going to be worth a damn if she's got military-grade drones or freelance cyborgs protecting her. You won't make it."

"My 'making it' is not the priority," Seven replied. "My objective is justice. I performed a proper burial for the miners. I will now follow the murderer to her current location. It is a good possibility that the others will be present."

"Seven, listen to me. If you pursue whoever this is, it's going to be a one-way trip."

"I am aware of the possibility. The military protocols you coded into my core advise that the sooner I follow, the less likely my enemy will be prepared."

"Shit."

Hearing no further objections from Keeko, Seven set a course to follow the woman's ship. Once complete, Seven powered down for the journey.

Danforth was waiting when Skyles stepped out of decompression.

"Did you come straight here?" he asked.

"Yeah," Skyles replied.

"Fuck! Why did you do that? If it was an assassin, you probably led them here!"

Skyles glared at Danforth.

"Yes, I'm fine. Thanks for asking."

"Look, we don't have time for that polite shit," Danforth said.

Skyles pushed by Danforth.

"Let's pack up," she said.

"What do you mean 'pack up'?"

"This was a nice dream, Dan," Skyles said, "but I'll be damned if I stay here and wait for an assassin to take me out."

"We can't run!" Danforth said.

Skyles spun around, her eyes wide.

"We can't? Do you remember what we are? Running's in our blood. It's the only thing we do better than stealing."

"Not this time," Danforth said. "We worked too hard for this. This is our roots."

Skyles planted her fists on her hips.

"So how do you plan on keeping us alive to reap the benefits of our ill-gotten gains?"

Danforth shared a sly grin. "Come with me, and I'll show you."

Skyles followed Danforth to their main office. He sat before his screen, then folded his hand on his lap.

"Fortress," he said.

Danforth's screen shifted, highlighting three warehouses on the outskirts of their settlement.

"There are enough mercenary cyborgs in those warehouses to take over an Earth country...or defend a promising settlement."

"Why didn't you tell me about this?" Skyles said.

"I don't tell you everything," he said.

"So, what do we do?"

"Activate Shield Initiative," Danforth said. "The cyborgs have the vitals on every living and unliving thing on this planet. When our friend arrives, they will identify, pursue, and destroy. And we'll sit right here and watch it all."

Seven read the Mesh as his destination became visible. The planet was named Prosperity. It had been purchased by two individuals a few months after the massacre of the people he'd buried. The names were most likely false, but that didn't matter. Seven hoped all the perpetrators were on the planet, which would make administering justice easier for him.

According to data, the planet was sixty-five percent terraformed when purchased. Current upgrade levels were unknown. At sixty-five percent, humans would still require atmosphere suits in some areas. Population upon the purchase was one thousand. An additional five hundred arrived after the deal was approved. Most of the population was scattered about the planet surface except for one city named Opportunity. Seven calculated that this is where it would most likely find the woman it searched for. It set Opportunity as its destination, then worked to repair its damage based on the instructions Keeko had sent.

Seven landed its ship on the main pad. Military protocol advised against it, but Seven was not interested in stealth. It was here to carry out justice. It unbuckled its seat harness and was standing when a series of explosions rocked the vessel, knocking Seven to the floor. Seven secured its weapons, then crawled to the hatch.

"Open."

The door opened halfway before it was bombarded. Seven activated its shield, then jumped into the open. The bullets came too fast for it to fire back, the shield losing integrity with every impact. Seven reached the nearest cyborg, sidestepping its gun swing, then driving its fingerings into its throat. It jerked the assault rifle from the dying cyborg's hands, then turned it on its cohorts, gunning down three before they sought cover.

Seven rested as its shield regained full strength. It counted twenty-three security units between it and the main building. Seven calculated a fire pattern and assault path based on available ammunition and shield capability.

"For justice," it said.

Seven leapt from cover, guns firing. The security cyborgs returned fire, a round occasionally slipping through Seven's shield. Seven continued despite the mounting damage, eliminated the cyborgs one by one as it came closer to the main building. The cyborgs were as determined to destroy the threat attacking them as Seven was in reaching the building. The last cyborg threw its weapon aside and lunged at Seven. Seven fired both guns into its faceplate, destroying its control unit. The cyborg collapsed, its hand striking Seven's torso before sliding down its body to the ground.

A powerful blast struck Seven's shield, knocking it off its feet and reducing shield strength fifty percent. Seven rolled and another blast gouged the ground beside it. Seven fired three rounds in the direction from which the shots came before its guns emptied. As it attempted to reload, a round struck its shield, lowering protection to five percent. Seven turned its head toward the shooter and spotted the person from the mining planet running toward him, gun aimed.

It raised its gun to fire back, but the weapon didn't respond. The woman shot Seven in the shoulder, spinning it around, then onto its back. Seven's gun was recharging; it would take twenty minutes before it was functional. That was time Seven did not have.

The woman stopped to reload. Seven gripped its weapon with both hands, then threw it at the woman. She looked up, her mouth falling open in surprise just before the weapon struck her face. Seven heard a loud crack before the woman dropped to the ground, her head twisted away and bleeding.

"Skyles!" a male voice in the building shouted.

The ground around Seven erupted, the person firing round after round, their aim weakened by their emotion. The blasts tossed Seven about like a rag doll, its shield depleted, its body absorbing each blast. Seven landed beside the woman it now knew as Skyles. It grabbed her rifle; it was still loaded. It held onto the weapon as a round blew him over Skyles's body. Seven rolled onto its back, sighted, then fired eight rounds. It braced for another barrage, but there was none.

It stood, its left arm dangling, its right leg sending a moderate-damage report to its core. Seven hobbled to the dead woman, matching her face to the image in its memory. Satisfied, Seven trudged to the main building. It kicked opened the door, then entered, sweeping the rifle from left to right as it proceeded to the stairs.

Seven climbed to the second level. As it reached the top of the stairs, it saw the person from the window propped against the wall facing Seven. He bled from multiple wounds. The man lifted the large-caliber weapon to aim at Seven.

"You ruined everything," he managed to say. Blood trickled from his mouth with each word.

"You killed my family," Seven replied.

Seven and the man fired simultaneously. Seven's round found the man's forehead; the man's final round struck Seven in the chest, lifting it into the air. Seven crashed to the ground, sliding across the room until it slammed against the wall. Seven's systems registered catastrophic damage. Its vision fading, Seven studied the dead man lying against the opposite wall. The man's face matched that of the human who had led the others into its cubicle. A calm settled into its core, and Seven did something it had never done before. It smiled.

"This is justice," it said.

Seven's core shut down, and the world turned black.

☆ ☆ ☆

Keeko leaned back in his chair as he shut off the vid-link. Tears formed in his eyes, and he wiped them away.

"Why are you crying?"

He looked to his left. Seven sat beside him, a curious look on his face.

"I would think you'd be a little choked up, too, watching yourself die like that."

"But it was not me," Seven said.

"It wasn't, but it was," Keeko said.

"I don't understand."

Keeko stood, then stretched. "Never mind. So, what do you think?"

"I think justice was served," Seven said. "I am content."

"Good," Keeko said. "Let's get these bots repaired. We sell this batch, then I'm a free man."

"Then what?" Seven asked.

"We take a long trip," Keeko said. "I know a place where we can get us some rich rock and start a new life."

"Wouldn't that be considered desecrating a gravesite?"

"Not if you don't tell," Keeko said.

"We should go," Seven said. "I would like to visit as my true self and pay respects."

Keeko grinned. "Day's not getting any longer. Let's get about it."

Keeko sauntered to the pile of units waiting to be repaired. Seven glanced at the blank vid screen for a moment, then followed.

FIVE MULES FOR MADAME CALYPSO

Thea Hutcheson

The Queen of the Stars, the #1-rated bordello in colonized space, would arrive in four weeks at the prime viewing position to see a string of icy rocks—gleaming like diamonds in the light of the local sun—smack into HC-4280-6, a gas giant in the Hellat-Crisat system.

Three thousand people would party nonstop until then.

One thousand five hundred jades and jigs, both human and synthetic, would see to their pleasure.

One thousand crew members would make the party memorable and clean up the mess afterward.

And one monster planned to wreak havoc amongst them.

Thalia Jaltner didn't know about the monster as she moved down the concourse against what felt like a palpable wall of sound: the hum of people talking and laughing, dinging bells and whooping sirens of the games, and the bass thump of the music from the dance bar at the far end.

But she would. Very soon.

A mélange of food, booze, and perfume smells piggybacked the musk of the pheromones Madame Calypso insisted on pumping into the air system to encourage the customers to utilize the bordello's services.

Thalia was on a double shift that night, covering for the swing-shift maintenance lead who'd come up ill that morning. As she looked out over the crowd, assessing the room's needs, she worried whether the staff would survive until they reached their destination.

She tapped her ear bob. "NovaThirty, please pull down the maintenance schedule."

"Done," her assistant, a tiny sliver of the ship's AI, murmured. Thalia's tablet chimed.

As she walked through the concourse, the crew, jades, and jigs greeted her. She rarely saw these particular people because of opposite shifts and greeted them back enthusiastically.

Marella, a svelte jade with jet-black hair, touched her arm. "Thank you for suggesting I audition for that audio serial. I got the part!"

"You're welcome," Thalia said. "You have such a fine voice, and you're so clever creating storylines for your clients to role-play. It'll be a nice gig between ports."

Thalia's shoulders straightened, and her heart swelled at the news. She was always glad to help out her fellow crew members. The bordello had given her a home and a path to regaining her confidence after her dream job blew up, leaving her homeless, friendless, and jobless.

As Thalia made her inspection, she looked up to see several people leaning out over the eleven decks' worth of balconies that encircled the concourse, laughing and waving at her, their drinks in hand.

They didn't actually know her; it was a combination of inebriated gaiety, the pheromones, and the bordello's convivial atmosphere, which fell on her to maintain.

Thalia worked through the crowds of well-dressed guests, then jumped a little when a woman stumbled against her as she moved past. Thalia watched her leap at a man and throw her arms around him drunkenly. He looked harried, disentangled himself, and nodded his apologies. Thalia grinned at him in sympathy.

She inspected the floors, walls, and furniture, making notes about wear or deep cleaning needs. The staff's efforts had been Herculean: despite the huge number of guests, the chrome surfaces gleamed, the blue-and-cream-patterned laminate flooring shone, and the trees had been well-dusted and freshly watered.

Tumbull, one of the jigs for this section—who hailed from Dener 12, a Russian-descent mining planet in the Selter System—waved at her. Gay as a tulip in April, he always cracked her up with his descriptions of his johns. When she first came aboard two years ago, he'd asked her to sit with him in the staff commissary. "Just for company, *dorogoy*," he'd said in a drawling Russian accent, then winked. "You haven't got the right equipment for anything else."

Coming up to him, Thalia said, "Long time no see, my friend. Any action?"

"Steady stream of lookie-loos, but no real meat tonight," Tumbull lamented, flipping a hand dismissively.

"It gets better each night we come closer to the main attraction."

Thalia laughed and mock punched him.

"Not that arm, *dahlink*. I might need it if no customer appears," he said, making a loose fist and pretending to jerk off.

She made a crybaby look and walked on.

"Jalty, baby," someone said to her left.

Thalia froze, her heart suddenly pounding. She hadn't heard that voice or that wretched nickname in three years. She fumbled for her tablet now slipping in hands turned suddenly sweaty, the churning starting in her belly all over again.

Marcus Salfier—the monster who had destroyed what had been her dream job. *Here.* She wanted to sound the alarm, but instead struggled for calm so as not to frighten the guests.

A cloud of musky cologne overwhelmed the ambient smells as a hand grabbed her upper arm from behind and pulled her into a tight embrace, arms just under her breasts. Not affectionate, glad-to-see-you tight, but tight so she couldn't get away. Tight so she knew her situation.

Familiar futile anger and helplessness washed over her like her last two years meant nothing.

"What are you doing here, Jalty?" Marcus said in her ear before twisting her around to look at her.

She froze as his familiar minty breath swirled across her cheek. His words sent a shiver down her back, and her belly clenched as she walked away, her legs quivering.

This would be just like Hastings-Pfifer. He would steal whatever credit he could from his department, ride them all into the ground, blacken their names with the powers that be, and leave a path of death and destruction in his wake.

She couldn't let that happen to the *Queen*.

Thalia left a note with HR, citing the incident, her past work experience under him, and a link to the deaths on the station, but nothing happened. She talked to fellow crew members over the next week. The entire section was bitching about the extra hours he assigned, sabotaged work, insults, and public humiliation.

It sounded like she'd never left Hastings-Pfifer.

As she and her team came out of a briefing, he was in the corridor and made that stupid two-finger V from his eyes to hers. "Hey, Jalty baby, I'm watching you."

He looked her team over. "She's a shitty manager," he said. "She'll sell your ass for a good word from the folks upstairs. If you have problems with her, just come see me."

Thalia flushed and grasped for something to say in the dead silence.

But Bern, the hardware tech, spoke up. "Wayull, Mr. Salfier," Bern drawled. Thalia glared at him, but he ignored her. "Last time I looked, concourse staff cayn't do nuttin' fur maintenance. And . . ." the tech continued, "Thalia works hard and makes sure we got whut we need." He eyed Marcus like a spec of dirt. "And callin' her out, that's just rude. We dun do rude on the *Queen*."

Marcus smiled at the man, then took in everyone else, his perfect white teeth glinting in the corridor lights.

"Well, then pardon me for wanting to help. But the offer stands." He bowed and headed on his way.

"Thanks, Bern," Thalia said. "But you embarrassed him. You'll be in his sights now."

"Dun you worry 'bout me, Thalia. Bastards layk him see us all as sheep, and never see the mule mixed into the herd." When she looked confused, he said, "Mules're like hosses, but badass. There's a story in mah family about mah great-grandaddy watchin' one stomp shit outta a cougar once." He ambled off to schedule bot maintenance.

Two days later, she found an anonymous video in her inbox of Bern sleeping in the maintenance bay during his shift. With time stamps.

"I'm sorry, Bern," Thalia told him. "I'm looking into this, but I may have to put you on report."

"'S all right," the man said placidly. "A lotta fur is gettin' ruffled. Some mule'll be looking to stomp on Marcus Sal-Fi-Ay soon enough."

Thalia hoped so. The *Queen* was different from Hastings-Pfifer. There, everyone had been trapped in their own nightmares, and no one had talked about Marcus's reign of terror. Here, gossip ran like water through the corridors and staff commissary.

But Marcus strutted through it all, never getting swept up.

Nervous energy had propelled Thalia through her run, but it didn't do anything for the stress of constantly covering her backside. She might as well have never left Hastings-Pfifer, except that here she could commiserate. No one had any idea what to do about Marcus. Complaints went nowhere or were excused on the grounds of inexperience with the protocols, but people paid for their efforts in petty ways.

She headed to the showers. NovaThirty pinged her. "Alskar wants to see you when you clock on."

Thalia's nerves ratcheted up until even her fingertips tingled. And now her supervisor wanted to see her. She tried to breathe smoothly, but she trembled so hard her breath wavered.

As she entered the maintenance section, a wave of depression washed over her. Damn. She had always liked coming to work on the *Queen*, even when she was just an environment tech, washing filters.

She growled at the way it took Marcus just a few weeks to destroy the life she had so meticulously rebuilt.

Alskar caught her eye and waved her through to his office. The walls were covered with monitors so he could see any area. One showed a false-color image of the cometary string against star-studded space with a countdown showing six days left.

"Afternoon, sir," Thalia said. He gestured her to sit, and she laid her tablet on her lap. She bet this was about Marcus. Well, she'd tell him about Marcus's history, point him to all the staff complaints over the last month. Then maybe HR would have a little come-to-Madame meeting with him, and he'd be gone.

Gone to wreak his havoc elsewhere.

That's what he did. He moved in, destroyed people's lives, sucked everything down to the marrow, and moved on. She'd heard Hastings-Pfifer went bankrupt from the wrongful-death suit Sloan Station filed.

Alskar sat in his chair instead of on the desk's front edge.

Her heart sank a bit more.

"Tell me what's going on between you and Marcus Salfier," he said. "You used to work together."

"Yes. He stole credit for my work at my previous job."

Alskar lifted one eyebrow. "Funny. He never mentioned that. He said you were a sour grape looking for revenge. Then there's your inappropriate interaction with him on the floor when you did the double shift."

Thalia reared back, blinking as disbelief, then anger washed over her. "I would never behave inappropriately on the floor or off. He's the one who's been making rude and inappropriate comments."

"I don't know about that, but there's video that supports his accusation."

For a moment, Thalia couldn't get enough air and thought she'd pass out. Then she choked out, "Let's see the video."

Alskar's eyes flicked back and forth as he sought the file, then flipped his hand out and away. A video opened on a wall monitor.

The time stamp said 18:40 hours. The camera showed her walking her section, looking at her tablet and then the floor. She stopped and stared at the tile floor.

Thalia remembered. She'd seen a gouge in a tile near the server station.

The video showed her fiddling with her tablet, which went as she remembered.

But then, Marcus walked up behind her and she turned, throwing herself into his arms with a sappy expression. The look on his face was a mixture of embarrassment and irritation. He pushed her back, and Thalia saw him look right at the camera and clearly mouth, "Let me go or I'll call security."

Thalia seethed through her confusion. Had he gaslighted her again?

"No. That never happened," she said as much to

herself as Alskar. "The video is doctored. He grabbed me the first night I saw him. He made rude comments about me. I told *him* to let go of *me* or *I* would call security."

"That's a breach of protocol," Alskar said. "Why didn't you report it?"

She clenched her teeth. Marcus was going to ruin her. "I did. Nothing came of it."

"There's no record of any complaint by you."

"What about all the others?"

"I can only speak to this incident."

Of course.

"This never happened," she said flatly, staring at the video, frozen with Marcus's face outraged and hers a mess.

Alskar drummed his fingers on the workstation. "He suggested you had been drinking, but NovaThirty's vital checks don't agree. I interviewed all the staff on the floor; no one saw anything. This footage is the only record of what went on."

His mouth worked and he frowned. "Thalia, you've been a good employee on the *Queen*. You're prompt, efficient, creative, and kind to all your coworkers. But this is totally unlike you. He told us that he was your supervisor when you two worked together. He said his management records noted that you were surly and uncooperative, that you put off work on critical timelines until the last minute and then turned in shoddy work."

Thalia thought she might throw up. Or quit. "They did, but he lied. He was responsible for over a hundred deaths on Sloan Station. And if I hated him so much, why would I fall into his arms like this? He's disgusting."

"Thalia," Alskar said sharply. "That's enough."

She sat back, shocked that he would raise his voice to her. This was just like Hastings-Pfifer. No matter what the grunts who worked with Marcus said, it never made a difference because he'd already buttered the management side of the bread.

I quit was on the tip of her tongue when Alskar flicked the video closed and said, "My mentor always told me that in situations like these, the truth lies somewhere in the middle."

"But it doesn't, Alskar," Thalia said, trying to keep the whine out of her voice. "He lies up and down, backward and forward, and straight down the middle; whatever he needs to, and even when he doesn't."

"Enough," Alskar said. "Clearly there is tension between you. You're a good worker now, whatever you might have been before. We've all had issues in the past, or we wouldn't be on the *Queen*. He came very highly recommended, and he's been a model employee so far." He made placating motions with his hands when she rolled her eyes. "That said, I have limited choices: reprimand you and send you back to work, transfer you, or let you go."

"I'll take the transfer," Thalia said, opening up the jobs board and flicking through it. "Yes, the air plant. The tech five position."

"Thalia, that's a demotion. I was going to move you up to deck fifteen. Jase Willers is retiring."

Thalia stared at him, willing the stinging in her eyes to subside. "No. Clearly you're willing to believe Marcus over me, even with my work record. So, I'll take the transfer to a different department. Really, anything to get away from him. But I'm telling you, he's a monster. And I'm just the first of the people he's going to ruin."

Alskar blew out his breath. "Okay, then. I'll make the notations and get you new credentials."

She stood, trembling. Marcus had done it to her again, and all she'd ever done was be in the wrong spot at the wrong time. She clenched her fists, nails biting into her palms.

Something had to be done.

"I want a copy of that footage," Thalia said. "It's my right."

He shrugged and waved the file to her. Her tablet chimed as the file hit.

"Report to Environmental, Thalia, and stay away from the concourse."

She left, her ass tight with anger and humiliation, and headed for the service elevator. Marcus had doctored the file. Or gotten someone to do it. He'd never much cared for real work. He liked schmoozing with management and those whom he considered important to his well-being. Everyone else was fair game for his entertainment or his image.

Thalia's boots thumped through the pale sage passageway, and she consciously walked lighter. She jabbed the lift button and tried to not huff as she waited. Her chest felt tight and her head light and buzzy.

He'd clearly felt she was a danger to him. Except she hadn't been fired. Just moved. She raked the back of her index finger under her chin and flicked it outward. *Take that.*

She really needed a plan.

But Thalia couldn't do anything against him. She was no mule, just a sheep set up for slaughter, the way she had been before. She kicked at the elevator doorframe.

She needed help.

Space was big, but colonized space wasn't so big, evidently, that you could escape your past. What if Marcus had learned she was on the *Queen* and got the job just so he could pick up where he left off?

"That's crazy," she muttered as the elevator door opened, then whispered shut.

The elevator asked, "Thalia, are you heading for service level one?"

"Yes, please," she said, trying not to growl as the car hummed. The deck floor notices ticked softly as she dropped to the lowest level of the ship.

The elevator chimed and opened the door. "Have a good day, Thalia," it said brightly.

If only.

The air plant smelled moist, rotty, and full of growing things. Like coming home. What was she thinking choosing the air plant, the same kind of job Marcus had destroyed? *A bit of masochisism, then*, she imagined Tumbull saying.

Directional signs covered the unadorned ceramic corridors. She headed toward the supervisor's office. Diagrams, broken hydroponic parts, tools, and chemical packets clotted the cramped room. A single monitor on the desk showed the diamond necklace of icy rocks headed for the gas planet.

She tapped at the doorframe.

Woller Senson looked old and rail thin, and wore a buzz cut that left his silver hair a simple gleam on his skull.

"Hey, Thalia. Color me totally surprised." He stood, and offered his hand. Her hand trembled as she took it. "By your history, you're totally overqualified for this job. I'm not going to ask why you changed from a lead in maintenance to a lowly air tech, but I'm very pleased to have you."

She shrugged.

"Well, there're tables in the lab, I'm sure you know what to do."

"Thanks." The bench felt like a bittersweet homecoming. She'd loved her work at Hastings-Pfifer, loved the living puzzle of designing the best plant combinations for carbon dioxide and oxygen balance in different environments.

She'd been drifting for a year after she'd left Hastings-Pfifer when she'd run into a line manager Marcus had fired. Until they talked, she'd never known he'd been abusing others during his tenure. The man told her stories from three other people, but said there were more.

Discovering that others had been suffering in isolation, ostracized, or ignored by their fellow workers had made her angry.

And Marcus enjoyed every minute, like the director of his own personal entertainment series.

"If you're looking for a job," the manager said when she said goodbye, "the *Queen of the Stars* has postings." He flicked a link to her tablet. "It's a bordello ship, but the people are good. I added a reference."

She'd applied, gotten an entry-level maintenance job, and been happy.

Until now.

Thalia sat down at the bench and threw herself into the work, finding she enjoyed reclaiming her half-forgotten skills. At shift end, she headed up to the staff commissary. In the practically empty room, the conversation remained a low hum punctuated with cutlery and glasses clinking.

The monitor on the far wall showed five days and roughly twelve hours to go for the comet fragments' rendezvous with the gas planet.

Tumbull waved her over to his table and took her hand in his. "*Dahlink*, what happened? You didn't show for your shift, and King Dick said you got fired."

"King Dick got some doctored footage that showed me throwing myself at him."

Tumbull gaped incredulously. "Throw yourself at that grease sphincter? You had to have tripped, and he was the only thing you could find to grab." His mouth twisted in disgust.

His words sparked a memory but it was gone before she could grab it.

"I took a transfer."

"Hmmm, better than fired," Tumbull said. "Coincidence that someone had footage of Bern sleeping on the job? I smell some very fine deep-fake work, and I bet Tralley's fingers are all over it."

Tralley, a junior purser, had been a cameraman for some PR outfit before he'd come aboard the *Queen*. Clients often asked for video of their hijinx without releases, and he produced really fine footage that didn't impinge on image restrictions.

"Let me have it. I can get answers," Tumbull said, drumming his steepled fingertips together under a leering grin.

Thalia flicked the file to him and ordered a meal. Tumbull watched the footage, his mouth puckering like he'd tasted something bad.

A bot delivered her plate to the table. As she dug

in, Tumbull said, "You said you worked with King Dick before, where he berated you, stole work, and took credit for it."

"Yeah. It's what he does."

"Of course it is. When did you first see Marcus Salfier here?"

"About three weeks ago. Why?"

"Why didn't you tell someone then?"

"I did. The complaint disappeared."

"Trishy said the same thing. He dressed her down at the staff meeting three days ago because she didn't smile enough. She transferred out of his section. That's the fourth person in six weeks." Tumbull looked at her over his fingers. "What happened when you first saw him?"

"He grabbed me as I was looking at my tablet. He insulted me. I threatened to call security if he didn't let go. It should be on the security video."

Tumbull murmured to his AI assistant and stared at Thalia thoughtfully. "So he knows you. Or at least he did."

"What?"

"Oh, *dorogoy*, you've changed since you came on board."

She had? "How?"

"You stand up straight, for one. You used to act like you were trying to disappear into the scenery. Now, you take care of everyone around you. If he's the one who made you like that, he's a bastard, and I'm all for kicking his ass."

Warmth flushed her. She had friends; people who cared what happened to her.

☆ ☆ ☆

Two days later, Tumbull caught her at breakfast in the commissary.

He grinned wickedly and flicked a file at her tablet. Thalia almost felt sorry for his clients.

"Look at it."

She clicked the video and saw the concourse floor. The date was three weeks ago, at the beginning of her shift. By the angle, the view was from the aft-side bow camera. Beyond Thalia, a woman wove through the crowded room, grabbing on to people, tables, and android servers. She bumped into Thalia, and she watched herself wipe the spatters of drink off her arm and tablet.

The woman continued on, oblivious, toward a man a few feet away from Thalia. The clip ended as the woman threw herself at the man, who looked back at Thalia, embarrassed and apologetic.

"I remember this happening!" This explained why Marcus's complaint footage had looked familiar. And why Tumbull's comment about tripping sparked a memory.

"Yes, *dorogoy*."

The bot brought her order.

"Now, watch this." He flicked another file at her tablet. Thalia opened that video, saw it was the same night and about the same time. She saw herself standing on the concourse, bent over her tablet typing, the concourse in full swing around her. A few feet away, Marcus noticed her, did a double take, and, grinning like a kid offered a cookie, approached her. A few minutes later, she saw herself glance at the camera, saying, "Let me go, or I'll call security."

A rush of anger made Thalia grit her teeth. Her

mouth was dry. She lifted her cup and sipped the bitter, smooth coffee. It wet her mouth but had lost all its savor.

"Where did you get this?"

Tumbull looked at her sideways, the hint of a smirk on his lips. "The *Queen of the Stars* hosts a number of public and very private figures who trust us to protect them and their reputations during their visits. We take that trust very seriously across all aspects of the ship."

"It's from a separate archive."

"Yes, *dorogoy*. And because Tralley produced the original footage, he'll only be nursing his fingers, not mourning their loss."

"Oh, please don't hurt anyone. That's what Marcus does."

"*Dahlink*," he said, looking at her from under his eyebrows, "I never hurt anyone without their permission."

This time, she did feel sorry for his clients, even as a tendril of hope pushed its way up out of the cauldron of futile rage.

"We can't let him do what he did to Hastings-Pfifer," Thalia said. "He's a monster," she growled, shocking herself at the depth of emotion in her voice.

"So, King Dick is a power-grabber," Tumbull mused. "He intimidated Kandy, one of the jades up on the twelfth floor, into sleeping with him. But since he manipulated her into agreeing, there's nothing to be done. About that time."

Marcus hit on every woman at Hastings-Pfifer. At first, Thalia had been flattered. But then she realized it wasn't about her, or even the others. It was all about him getting his nut. When she tried to break it off, he threatened to share what they had done, what he had coerced her into doing. She doubted that management would have cared. No, it was the humiliation of the acts, and the knowledge that he had tricked her that kept her silent.

"He has it in for Bern, but so far it's only been reprimands. He's even tried to make me a pariah." Tumbull snorted at the thought. "Everyone loves me, though. This time he has chosen the wrong place to make his grab."

"How did he get hired?" Thalia barely kept herself from wailing in frustration.

"No one's perfect," Tumbull said. "Not even AIs, Thalia. Marcus slipped through the cracks. But, with Tralley's confession and the other complaints I've gathered, we have enough to get him fired."

"Fire him and let him just move on to the next unwitting employer?"

"Another choice is to keep him, and let the ship's HR department manage his behaviors. I found there's a lot of management psychology data focused on dealing with workplace psychopaths. They would have to develop a plan that uses his own self-interest to limit his negative behavior. We would have to be trained to protect ourselves from those behaviors."

Psychopath. That's what he was. A monster with a clinical name.

"There are reasons that HR would do this," Tumbull said.

"Like what?" Thalia asked incredulously.

Tumbull waved his hand idly. "He's smooth and engaging. Clients like him. He's also very effective at deducing people's desires and manipulating them in the direction of the most profit for the bordello. Sales in his section have gone up since he came on board."

Thalia ground her teeth. Yes, that sounded right.

"Of course, there have been a few instances where he embarrassed several jades and jigs when he offered services that were not actually available. We complained to Madame Calypso when he tried to coerce us into acquiescing."

A dry chuckle slipped out before Thalia could stop it. "And he pled ignorance because of his short tenure."

"Why, yes, he did."

Thalia sipped her coffee and twirled the cup on the table. "The effort to protect everyone from his predation feels exhausting." She lifted her lip in a half sneer, half growl. "And what's the point? He's a pox on humanity and not worth the effort or the income." Saying that out loud made her feel good.

"I *could* arrange an accident."

The idea of action felt better, but the notion of murder left her sick.

"So, it has to be subtler," Tumbull said, watching her. "Let him walk right to his doom, eyes open, greedy hands clutching for his heart's desire. Yes. That would be more satisfying."

"It's not a matter of satisfaction. It's necessity to protect everyone from him." Thalia added, "I wouldn't know what to do."

"Me either, *dorogoy*, I'm not so cunning."

"We need help."

Tumbull winked at her. "Leave it to me."

A few days later, Tumbull sent an invite to his suite. When she arrived, he took her ear bob.

"Why take the earpiece?" she asked.

"To be private from the ship's AI," Tumbull said.

"And taking earpieces will make us private?"

He shrugged and gave her a drink. "I have privacy mode engaged."

Bern, Kandy—the twelfth-floor jade Marcus had hit on—and Marella, the jade she'd helped get the audio gig, sat in the decadently orange seating area. Tumbull took a burnt orange chair that resembled a throne, and looked at everyone. "We're here to solve the King Dick problem." He sipped from his drink and looked around at everyone.

"Space him," Bern said. "Problem solved."

"No," Thalia said. "That's cold-blooded murder. But we can't just put him off this ship, either. He'll just go somewhere else and do the same thing."

"He humiliated me in front of a client and lost me my quarterly bonus. But killing him seems a little much," Kandy said.

"He killed more than a hundred people and destroyed many other lives and companies," Thalia countered. "He'll never stop on his own."

"Well, none of us have enough credit to get a lawyer to build a good enough case against him to send him to prison," Tumbull said.

"Yeah, and in the meantime, he's still mucking about with people's lives," Kandy said.

"I agree wit' Thalia," Bern said finally. "This is our jobs, our home. If we dun stop him, who weeyul?"

"So we are judge, jury, and executioner," Marella said.

Everyone nodded soberly.

Tumbull lifted his glass. "For the *Queen* and all aboard her."

They all clinked theirs with his and repeated his words.

"He likes power," Marella said after a moment.

"Yes, so we offer him what he wants," Kandy said.

Tumbull nodded. "It would have to be credible."

Kandy tapped one well-manicured finger against her chin. "He's always going on about how he could run the *Queen* better than Madame Calypso and the AI. He could get a recruitment offer. They could say they've been watching him, that he's wasted in his current position."

"I could do that part," Marella said. "He's never met me."

"Okay. Then what?" Tumbull said. "He'd still have to get off the ship."

Everyone fell silent.

"I got a ship in storage," Bern said. "I won it gamblin'. It ain't much, doesn't e'en run well. And it's costin' me a fortune in storage fees. I'd give it up for this."

"But you can't just get him off the ship and hope he runs out of air or goes into the deep," Thalia said. "He could be rescued or picked up for salvage. We have to be certain."

Kandy smiled wickedly. "Leave that to me. And Bern, of course."

Two days later, Thalia's tablet chimed at shift end. PRIVATE MESSAGE FROM TUMBULL, the screen read. A video link that said WATCH ME sat below the header.

She went out to the empty hydroponics lab. Once settled on a stool, she clicked the link.

The time stamp on the video was for 1200 hours today. A split screen showed Marcus and Marella, with carefully styled hair, wearing a navy business suit and white blouse, talking.

"We've noticed your work, Marcus," Marella said.

Marcus played it to the hilt, looking briefly appreciative before turning to full-on brash cockiness. "I'm pleased you've noticed. The *Queen* is a marvelous place. I think I can add a lot of value to the bottom line."

"I think you have already. Sales numbers are up in your section. You've gotten a lot of personalized compliments from guests."

He smiled, his bright, straight teeth flashing in the light.

"We think you could be better utilized, though." Marella leaned forward to create some intimacy—and show some cleavage.

"Yeah? How?" Marcus clearly envisioned a promotion and maybe a roll in her bed.

She lowered her voice. "There's a deal on a new bordello. How does general manager sound?"

Thalia marveled at the way Marella never actually offered the job. Marcus did a double take.

"General manager?" His eyes narrowed in suspicion. "That's a big jump."

"I was thinking you need something new to challenge you. Or did I misread your aspirations?"

He lifted his palms in a pushing movement. "No, you aren't mistaken. I just figured it would take longer to work up to that kind of position."

"Well, time is of the essence and a decision had to be made."

Marcus licked his lips. "And the pay?"

Marella flicked her hand dismissively. "How does seven hundred and fifty thousand for a base, and a bonus based on profits sound?"

"Plus stock options," Marcus said.

"I think that's reasonable."

Marcus grinned.

"Then we're agreed?"

"Yes."

Thalia watched his eyes flick back and forth as he thought, then he nodded sharply. "Count me in."

"Be at dock twenty-three-A at oh-four hundred tomorrow morning."

"That's really fast."

"As I said, time is of the essence, as is circumspection. Does that change your mind?"

"No, no, that's fine. And you can count on my discretion."

"Very good." Marella signed off.

A smirk curled on Marcus's cupid lips. "It was worth taking this shit job to climb that golden ladder," he crowed to the blank screen. "That bordello will be mine before that Calypso bitch knows what hit her. *Salfier's*. Yeah," he murmured.

The video ended.

The clock was ticking. They were doing it! Thalia's heart raced, fear dancing with trepidation in a beat that left her jittery.

A half hour later, Bern pinged her on their private group channel. "We got problems. Air handler's dead."

Trepidation changed the dance to a cha-cha of fear and disappointment.

"Get me video," she sent.

A moment later, she had a jerky shot of the shuttle's air module. It was old and a glance told her it had been poorly maintained.

"Press the master start controller."

She walked him through troubleshooting, her belly falling faster with every failure code.

"You're right. It's hosed. It's a private system, so we don't have parts for it on the *Queen*."

Her mouth squinched up so hard her lips hurt.

"Tumbull, that means we gotta scuttle the plan," Bern said.

"No." Thalia couldn't let go so easily. "If we quit now, Marcus will take Marella's offer as a joke on him and punish people in his frustration."

"I agree," Tumbull said and the other murmured agreement. "Work on the other issues."

"I got a shift in four hours," Bern said.

"I'll do the best I can," Thalia groaned. "Send the schematics over."

He signed off and a file notice chimed on her tablet.

She opened it and took a breath. The system was simple, just a big tank of air with nodules to manage pressure and flow based on consumption. Whomever had owned the shuttle before had been constantly wearing an EVA suit for awhile.

Frustration and the added stress of this problem made her feel lightheaded. She rested her head on her elbows and breathed.

Then she got to work.

Two hours later, her supervisor, Woller, put his head in the door. He glanced at the tank and control board spread out on the bench. "Hey, I didn't think that assembly on the ninth floor was that dated."

Thalia looked up and blinked at him. *Shit.* She was supposed to be rebuilding a control assembly for a service module.

"Just stuff I found in a bin."

He frowned. "It's probably recycling."

"Uh, yeah." She turned to the cabinet behind her, rummaged around, her heart pounding. She slammed that drawer and opened another, pulling out a board with wires hanging off it.

"Here's the assembly."

Woller took it. "Thanks. Recycle that stuff once you've finished, will ya?"

"Sure thing, boss."

He left and she sat there, her heart doing a two-step as sudden sweat trickled down her ribs.

Her hands shook as she reached out for the control board and hooked the tester to it. An hour later, she had a very primitive air system jiggered.

"Bern," she said when he answered her ping. "I have a very simple working system ready."

"Wayull, yer gonna have ta install it. The ignition up an' died. Plus, I still got a shift in a hour."

"No one would cover for you? I'll throw in some Istban drip coffee and some fudge from Calos Station to sweeten the offer."

He whistled. "Now that's incentive. I appreciate that. I'll ask Jer again."

"Good. I'll be there in an hour to install it."

Off shift, the board tucked safely in her carryall and a five-gallon tank bumping against her thigh, she headed toward the dock.

Marcus stepped through a service door and saw her, a sneer growing on his full lips.

Thalia took a breath of air that seemed sharp and suddenly too thin. She actually checked her atmosphere sampler, then realized it was nerves. Would he know what she was doing?

No, he couldn't. He knew so little at Hastings-Pfifer, she bet he barely recognized the parts.

"See, Jalty baby, I told you not to push me." He looked over the tank and her dirty coveralls, and nodded. "Yeah, you got shown."

She screwed up her resolve, met his gaze, pasted a smiled on her lips, and nodded as she pushed past him, his chuckle following after. Her back felt exposed, and the tank banged against her leg painfully. She took a shaky breath and let it out when she got into the elevator, her heart banging double time against her ribs.

Bern opened the shuttle hatch for her, letting out a puff of stale, sweat-laden air. She squeezed past him and the components scattered over the shuttle's table.

"I got it," the engineer said, waving a wrench over the pieces strewn around. "There's enough fuel ta start the engine an' get it goin' in the right direction. Planet'll do the rest."

Thalia clapped him on the shoulder and made her way to the air supply cabinet. She muscled out the old parts and stowed them. The new board and tank went in smoothly, and checked out. "Pressurize the cabin before you leave," she told Bern on her way out. "And flick the big green switch on the control board. That'll be an adequate air supply."

"Got it," Bern said, never looking up from the switch he was building.

At 1950 hours, the private group channel pinged. "Got another problem," Bern said. "Mah license is expired. Dock master won't approve leavin'."

"Crap," Kandy said. "What now?"

"I take it you've already run through the possibilities, Bern," Tumbull said.

"Yeah. But they'll allow an auto pilot's."

"Then file it that way and put a disable switch with a timer on the auto pilot," Thalia said.

"That'll work. I'm on it," Bern said, and clicked off.

After that, it was all bitten nails and tapping fingers until Thalia's tablet chimed. A cheerfully blinking lilac link said WATCH THIS.

She saw the empty dock. A moment later, Marcus stepped in, carrying his duffel bag. An android greeted him, checked his badge, and led him to a port access. The video shifted to show Marcus strapped into his seat in a small shuttle watching a countdown.

At zero, the screen blinked and switched to an exterior dock camera. Thalia watched the shuttle fall away from the bordello, the engines flare, and turn into a tiny pinpoint of flame lost against the swirling clouds of the gas giant.

The screen blanked, then brightened to show Marcus punching buttons on the bridge station. "Hey, anybody. What's going on with this ship? It's going around the planet."

"Marcus Salfier," Marella's voice said from the comm panel. "The ship is on course to the last icy rock in the string that is about to impact HC-246."

Marcus blanched. "What? You told me I was going to be the general manager of your new bordello."

"I never did." Marella sounded affronted. "I only talked about a new venture, and your hopes and dreams. You just obeyed my instructions, went to the dock, and boarded this ship."

Thalia felt her heart ping in sympathy as she watched Marcus work through Marella's words, and the conversation they'd had.

Sweat broke out on his forehead. "Turn the ship around. Right now."

"I'm afraid that's not possible, Marcus. The route is programmed and locked. No one can do anything, and the only thing that works on the ship are incoming transmissions and nominal life support. But don't fret. There are forty-five hundred people watching the show, and you'll be part of the final act, providing many people a great deal of pleasure. Especially some of the ones that you used and abused.

"But not Thalia Jaltner," Marella said. "Even though she knows that you're too dangerous to just fire and be allowed to move on to the next unwitting victim, she refused to allow you to be simply put out an airlock. You should take comfort in that."

Thalia could barely hear Marella for all Marcus's screaming. Foam flecked his lips and his face turned a brilliant shade of red as he pounded his fists on the workstation. He cursed, shouting out foul phrases against the *Queen*, and the "bitch" who tricked him. He ran down, then revved back up to call Thalia weak and idiotic, stupid, and useless.

Thalia's heart felt heavy. Justice was not always pretty and the right thing was often hard. But lots of people, here on the *Queen* and everywhere else, were now safe from him.

That made her happy. She caught the irony that she now had friends who knew her and cared about her, because Marcus had ruined her life. She decided to be grateful for that and leave the rest behind.

A chime sounded. "This is your ten-minute warning," a feminine voice said over the common loudspeaker. "Ten minutes to showtime!"

Thalia deleted the link and scrubbed the files before heading to the commissary.

HC-246, the gas giant in the Hellat-Crisat system, filled the wallscreen at the far end of the commissary, and likely also filled every screen on the ship. The countdown, laid over one corner of the ruby-red and desert-orange swirling clouds, indicated a bit less than five minutes when she arrived.

Conversational murmuring, laughter, and the clink of glasses and dishes filled the room pleasantly. She nodded, wending her way through the tables, her heart beating with guilt and satisfaction at Marcus's sentence.

Tumbull gestured melodramatically for her to join Bern, Kandy, and him at a four-top table. "Did you hear, *dorogoy*? There's a huge sex party across the entirety of deck fourteen, and all the attendees aim to get off as the string starts punching the planet. Marella's conducting one of the scenes and sends her regrets."

He poured her a beer out of the pitcher on the table. "No one can find Marcus. He failed to show for his shift. They're taking bets on how long it takes to find him and where he's hiding."

Thalia frowned at him. He shrugged and sipped his beer. Bern's and Kandy's faces were somber.

"I was the last to see him," Kandy said. "Security interviewed me. I stopped saying no and played sweet on him because I knew you needed the extra time, Bern. What a douche. He shut the door and *told me* to get naked and on the bed." She *tch*ed at the memory. "Then he kept asking me if I liked it." Pressing a hand to her chest, she drawled, "I should get an acting award for how much I showed him I liked his pathetic, boring efforts."

"Well, you took one for the team, and we appreciate it." Tumbull said.

She bowed graciously.

"The ship has been paging him all morning," Tumbull said.

"She's had bots searchin', too," Bern said. "I heard there was a camera failure in a bunch'a sections an' on one'a the dock bays."

Thalia couldn't bring herself to be pleased. But then she remembered Marcus was a monster, and that he had preyed on her friends. He'd had to be stopped. Permanently. She drank her beer. But she wasn't happy.

A chime sounded and everyone looked to the screen on one end of the room. The line of seven diamonds approached the planet, pulled in by its gravity. One side of the screen showed the various bets. The most general was how large the impacts would be, but the one that cracked Thalia up was how many people on deck fourteen would pop in synch with the impacts.

The first one hit, creating a blue-black bruise amongst the ruby-and-orange clouds.

Several people pointed at the screen suddenly, murmuring or sucking in breath as they watched a tiny black speck on an intercept course with the last diamond. It disappeared behind the rock and never reappeared. Thalia killed her beer and poured another one as the rocks continued to rain down, wounding the planet.

She lifted her glass as the last one disappeared into the ruby-rust clouds and turned into a star-shaped bruise a moment later.

"To the sheep'a the *Queen'a the Stars* an' the mules

what watch out for 'em!" Bern said, lifting his glass. Tumbull and Kandy joined him. Thalia frowned, but clinked her glass to theirs and drank.

It seemed the least she could do.

The next day, the ship's AI announced to the staff that the black spot, circled in white on an accompanying video, had been identified as an unauthorized shuttle stolen from one of the staff members by Marcus Salfier. "Madame Calypso and I regret that we were unable to help him through whatever emotional difficulties Marcus suffered from," the ship's AI said. "A memorial has been scheduled for fourteen hundred in the ship's Galactic Ballroom."

Only a handful of people showed up.

The staff buzzed with speculation that someone had drugged him and put him on board, to repay him for injuries he had perpetrated on them. The ship's AI instituted an investigation into the rumor.

Kandy, his last victim, had been released from consideration as a person of interest, and several people bought her drinks or sent her bottles of wine and bouquets of flowers for a week.

A full diagnostic was performed on the ship's security camera system.

The ship's AI pinged Thalia a week later just as her shift ended. "Woller Senson has recommended you be promoted to a second-level technician and take the lead on the new air plant design project," she said.

"But I don't want it." In truth, she was afraid to, still plagued by doubts about her abilities.

"Thalia, you saw fit to render rough justice aboard my ship. Consider this tit for tat."

All the blood rushed out of her face and her belly flip-flopped.

"You all covered your tracks well," the AI said, "but you forget, I *am* the ship. It takes more than Tralley tweaking my systems, or you all dumping your earpieces in a box, to conceal things from me. I know what you five did, and I know why."

The ship knew, which meant Madame Calypso knew. Thalia felt ashamed, but defiant. She had not done it out of revenge, but necessity.

Maybe that wasn't a real distinction, but she'd do it again to protect her friends.

"I'm sorry that Marcus slipped through the cracks," the AI said. "HR has undergone a thorough review of hiring and complaint processes as a result. I'm sorry that your complaint did not make it to my attention, and you felt forced to take matters into your own hands. Madame and I are sorry that we were unable to protect you and the others. That is a top priority, and we failed you."

"But even if my complaint had been heard, what would you have done?"

"Taken him off the ship."

"He would have just moved on the same way he did before."

"You must trust us, Thalia. We're all in this together. Which is why you succeeded."

"Why didn't you just tell us?"

"I wanted to see if you would go through with it, how well you would plan it."

"So you watched."

"Humans are interesting. They talk a lot, but often don't follow through. You and the others were truly concerned, not doing it for spite or to see a man die.

You felt it was necessary, so you did it. So Madame and I decided there would be no repercussions."

"But you just told me I had to accept this job. How is making me accept the job not a repercussion or a reason to trust you?"

The AI didn't answer for a long moment, then it said, "Because you're good at it. Or you were. I would imagine you're a little rusty, and you need to catch up on current technology. But isn't reclaiming what he took from you the best way to honor what you've done?"

"Oh." Thalia thought about that, looking around the hydroponics lab.

She did love it. And the chance to design a completely new system made her heart lift and feel lighter than it had for years.

Yes. She wanted this.

"Besides, Madame cannot afford to lose out on talent. Bordello ships are very competitive, and we need to use every edge we can hone."

"Thank you. I accept."

"Then you had best get to studying. I have downloaded texts and papers on the latest in air plant design. On your own time."

Thalia's tablet chimed.

"Yes, ma'am."

"I expect you will do your best as you always have." The AI paused. "And Thalia? It *is* good to have a few mules on the *Queen*."

Thalia grinned as she opened her tablet to scan the files.

PAST SINS

Dayton Ward & Kevin Dilmore

Sheriff August Jeffers never was much for fights, especially those that disrupted the atmosphere of the only place in town with food and drink he thought was worth a hot damn.

He entered the Alamo Saloon, the *ping* of the doorway sensor detecting the sheriff's sidearm and tipping Smitty the barkeep to his arrival. The older man looked up from his duties and silently pointed to the scuffle in the back corner. When Jeffers saw who was involved, he would have bet his badge right then and there that this wouldn't last long.

A broad-shouldered man wearing spacers' coveralls took a wide swing at a similarly dressed woman about a head shorter than he was. Her dark hair waved as she bobbed, deftly avoiding what looked to Jeffers like an ill-considered punch. With jackrabbit speed, she jabbed her fist into the man's throat.

He gagged, pitching forward as the woman grabbed his head and pulled it down to drive her knee up under his chin. He sputtered, grunting in pain before falling backward onto the saloon's dusty hardwood floor. The scuffle over, the woman took a look around the place until her eyes met Jeffers.

"Laying someone flat?" he asked. "Far as I've seen, Myla, that's a first for you." Crossing the room toward her, Jeffers smiled as the woman tugged a Windsor wooden chair from a mismatched square-topped table and sat down to a plate of eggs and fried potatoes that Jeffers could see was still steaming. "He get in the way of your breakfast?"

She spoke around a forkful of eggs. "Ask him, Gus."

Was it his imagination, or was she trying to hide... what? Nervousness? Agitation? Jeffers regarded the man lying on the floor, which bore a few spatters of blood from what the lawman figured was a bitten tongue or a split lip. Even though the poor lug likely would stay unconscious until Myla finished her meal, Jeffers pulled a pair of shock binders from his belt and cuffed the man's hands behind his back. That done, he gestured to an empty chair at Myla's table. She shrugged noncommittally, and he lowered himself into the seat.

"How're the eggs?"

"Runny," she said, prodding them with her fork.

Jeffers turned toward the saloon's long mirror-backed bar and hollered at the mustached worker behind it. "Smitty!"

The shout startled the older man, who set down the glass stein he'd been drying with a rag before hustling toward them. "Sheriff," he said, sidestepping the man on the floor, "whatever happened, I'd say he got what was coming to him."

"Thanks, Smitty, but I don't need you to vouch for

Myla." Jeffers pointed to her plate. "Just bring me some of what she's having. Just not so runny."

"Oh!" The barkeep started to reach for Myla's plate. "Miss, if you're not satisfied with—"

"It's fine." Myla waved off Smitty without looking up from her plate.

Something's bugging her this morning, Jeffers thought. The two of them had crossed paths plenty since her arrival planetside and in that time cultivated what he would call a friendship. Their interactions were pleasant albeit within bounds; he always suspected that what little he knew about her was exactly what she allowed. Myla tended to use words sparingly and kept to herself—qualities Jeffers wished more people around here might display. She would often hit the Alamo for a drink or a meal to close out her shift as a systems tech at the spaceport docks, and crossing paths typically amounted to little more than a respectful nod in passing.

The most significant conversations they ever shared had taken place after someone new to town reckoned they would get a little handsy. On those occasions, like today, Jeffers had seen the speed and skill with which she showed such newcomers the pained errors of their ways. Hell, his feelings about her over time were good enough that he tried luring her from her job on the docks with an offer to deputize her on the spot. He'd done it more than once. She never bit.

Jeffers watched Myla eat while shifting her focus between her plate and his face, shooting glances that he'd seen before—ones that felt like she didn't really want him around. He sensed she was eating not because she was hungry but more to make this all feel . . . normal? Jeffers decided to press into that.

"This guy's got you rattled some."

She kept her eyes on her plate. "No more than any others. You've seen enough of what happens around here."

"That I have," Jeffers said. "He didn't follow you in here from the docks or anything?"

She shook her head.

"So he's fresh off of a passing hauler or something and just put himself with you where he didn't belong." Myla stayed silent, pushing away her nearly finished plate, so Jefferes continued, "You don't like the cut of this guy, so maybe I don't, either. Ordinance says I can jail our out-of-towner for two days for disturbing the peace, attempted assault, and general assholery."

"Your call, Sheriff."

Jeffers reached into his pocket and then placed his hand closed-palmed on the table. He let go of what he'd been holding, a silver star-shaped badge. "Or you could pin that on, and we'll both run him in."

Myla slid her chair from the table. "This game isn't funny today, Sheriff. Excuse me." She rose and made her way at a brisk pace out of the Alamo.

Sighing, Jeffers retrieved the badge just as Smitty arrived at the table with a plate of eggs and potatoes as ordered.

"Thanks, Smitty. Hope I can eat in peace before our problem here wakes up."

"The lady has left us?" asked the barkeep.

"It appears so."

Smitty cleared his throat. "Then I'd like to report a theft of services, Sheriff."

Jeffers sighed again before taking a forkful of eggs into his mouth. "How about you just put her breakfast on my tab, and we'll skip the report, okay?"

On the job less than a year, according to the planetary calendar, Jeffers still wasn't entirely sold on the idea of his being the lead lawman in these parts. On the other hand, New Bandera's slower rotation meant longer days, and its slower revolution meant a longer year. By Earth standards, he'd held the badge for three years and change, and to him it sure as hell felt more like that.

His predecessor, Rosy Randall, had talked him into it. "*Gus, what I can't do is bring a good law enforcer to this shithole and teach him to love it here. What I* can *do is take someone with a good disposition who, for whatever reason, loves this place and teach him to be the kind of sheriff these people need. And you sure do seem to love it here.*"

That he did, so here he was.

The sheriff's office was pretty small and sparse, with half of the single-floor building devoted to Jeffers's living quarters. Aside from a pair of workstations with data terminals, a weapons locker he mostly opened to inventory its contents, and some chairs, its chief feature was a pair of lockups that saw more use as cooling tanks for drunk-and-disorderly off-worlders than for any other offenders. Jeffers sat across from the cells, absentmindedly turning a small magnetic fob over in his grasp while watching through the cell bars as the idiot from the saloon scuffle started to stir in his bunk. The man rolled over, coughing a few times while bringing his hand to his mouth to gingerly assess the swollen split he'd suffered to his bottom lip.

"There's some water in there for you," Jeffers said. "Just don't kick it over."

The man bolted up to a sitting position on the bunk and swung his feet to the floor. In doing so, he kicked a paper cup resting on the floor near his bunk, dumping its contents across the floor.

Jeffers snorted. "Well, your choices this morning aren't running for shit, sir."

Surveying his surroundings, the man met the sheriff's gaze. "Bars. How . . . nostalgic."

"You can't go wrong with the classics," said Jeffers. "Besides, fancy force fields use a lot of power. That said, those'll shock your ass if you decide you want to grab onto them. Feel free to test that theory, if you're bored."

The man massaged his temples. "Thanks, but I think I'll pass."

"Care to introduce yourself?"

"You know my name, by now. Didn't she tell you?"

"Myla didn't tell me anything," Jeffers said, noting how the man looked at him as he spoke. "Once I got you carted over here, it was pretty plain to see the syntheflesh puckering on the back of your neck. Myla must have snapped your head back pretty good to do that."

"My-la," said the man, as though trying the name on for size.

Holding up the fob in his hand, Jeffers said, "I peeled that back just enough to find this thing jammed up into your bioport. I don't know about this gizmo, but I do know that implant of yours is military hardware."

"You've just explained my headache, Sheriff. Now

you're going to tell me you have a law enforcement-grade scanner at your disposal."

Jeffers nodded. "Didn't take long to read your identity module, Sergeant Jarek Shaw."

"Nicely done, Sheriff," said Shaw. "Now, suppose I give you some insight into why I've made the trip to your small town."

This ought to be good, Jeffers thought. "I'm guessing we've got time, and neither one of us is going anywhere."

"You might rethink that when I tell you that your 'Myla' is not who she says she is," Shaw said. "I'm here because she's a fugitive from military justice."

Jeffers didn't try to hide his surprise. "Really?"

"Were you to run your scanner on *her* implant—and I assure you she has one just like mine—you'd learn she's really Sergeant Shanna McCall of the Colonial Defense Forces, wanted for war crimes on Malpaso. I'll spare you the details. Maybe you can get her to talk about them after we go and bring her in."

"We?"

"Why not?" Shaw asked. "I'll forgive you the misunderstanding at the saloon, and, for your help, I'll offer a split of the bounty on McCall's head, which you'll find surprisingly rewarding."

Jeffers had seen the breaking news bulletin about the war crimes exposé released late last night. Details were still coming in, and he'd not yet had time to absorb everything. He'd try to get caught up tonight, but for now? It was enough that this news had obviously expedited Shaw's identi-check, with the CDF responding that someone was already on the way to retrieve him.

"A split sounds good and all," he said, "but I'm just as happy to take all of whatever bounty the CDF might be offering for *you*." He reached over to the vid-screen on his desk and spun the arrest warrant bulletin it displayed so Shaw could see it. "Nice try with the whole 'project your own situation away from yourself and onto one of our people' plan, but as I said before, your choices today aren't runnin' for shit."

Shaw studied him for a moment. "You entered my name and arrest notice into the Colonial DataNet."

"Pretty standard procedure for a spaceport town, even one as small as ours." Jeffers stood and approached the lockup's barred door. "I expect the CDF will have people here pretty directly."

"That's a damned shame." Shaw once more massaged his temples. "Between that and your having removed my implant scrambler, I suppose there's nothing stopping me from connecting to your local DataNet hub." The smile spreading across the prisoner's face made the hairs on Jeffers's arms stand up.

"Shaw, what are you on about?"

"When it comes to choices regarding your office information network security, yours aren't running for shit, Sheriff."

Before Jeffers could react, the lockup's bars de-energized as its steel bolt clacked back into the door's lock assembly, and Shaw burst through the open cell door.

". . . bombshell report comes nearly five years after the alleged incident on Malpaso, a farming colony and the first settlement in Sector Eleven. Reaction to the exposé has been swift, with Colonial Defense Forces

security teams taking all but two members of the elite special operations unit into custody."

Transfixed, Myla stared at the small vid-screen on the wall of her cabin's main room. The Colonial Network News anchor, a middle-aged Asian man, shifted his attention from a data tablet in his hand and the camera, doing his best to convey information fed to him in real time even as he offered the breaking news.

"Efforts remain underway to locate and apprehend former sergeants Jarek Shaw and Shanna McCall. While security forces have some information on Shaw's last known whereabouts, McCall is listed as a deserter since shortly after the alleged crimes took place."

The anchor's face disappeared, replaced by two photographs. Studying Jarek's picture as she nursed a lukewarm beer, Myla shook her head, awash in conflicting emotions as she replayed encountering him at the Alamo. As for the other photo, despite the shorter haircut with military precision, fuller cheekbones, and skin unblemished by years spent in direct sunlight, the face on the screen was the same one she saw on those occasions she bothered to look in a mirror.

"Long time, no see, Troop."

"We're told these highly skilled soldiers are trained to conceal their identities and operate for extended periods under false personas. CDF officials believe McCall has utilized these skills to evade capture since her disappearance."

Finishing her beer, Myla tossed the empty bottle into a small waste receptacle in the corner of her austere cabin's compact kitchen. Like everything else in the modest abode she'd built well away from town, the emphasis here was on functionality, not luxury. It was a fallback position; a retreat in the event her house became unsafe.

Like now.

"Well, shit."

This backwater planet of New Bandera was among the more remote worlds in the United Colonies, home to an unimpressive agricultural operation that neither attracted nor deserved notice from the authorities. On the other hand, it had a reputation for being the sort of place anyone looking to cause trouble tended to avoid. Such an environment, far away from the soul-sucking tempo of the more developed colony worlds in the core sectors, appealed to Myla. After spending the money needed to fashion a new identity and take other steps to isolate herself from a life she'd come to loathe, she figured she could blend into LaGrange's quiet, unpretentious community. If she kept her head down, did the job she'd taken at the spaceport to the north of town, and avoided unwanted attention, perhaps the CDF might one day just forget about her.

Myla sighed. "So much for that plan."

A great deal of time, effort, and money had gone toward covering up the atrocities on Malpaso. She now thought herself foolish to think they might ever stop hunting her, if for no other reason than simple fear of her doing what someone else had accomplished: bringing the entire gruesome story to the public. With the other members of her old unit in custody, the efforts to find her would intensify.

Think it through, Shanna.

"Myla," she said, scolding herself for the mental

slip. "Your name is Myla Dynion. Don't go getting stupid, now." Long ago, training taught her to suppress urges to think of herself by her real identity while operating undercover, but even after five years there still were times when she let her inner defenses slip. A momentary loss of focus could be dangerous if not fatal. This was not the time for such weakness.

"Think it through, *Myla*."

Somehow, Jarek had tracked her to New Bandera, and so far as she knew he now sat in Sheriff Jeffers's jail. As a matter of procedure, Gus already would have run an identity check, triggering CDF monitoring algorithms throughout the Colonial DataNet. Security forces would be dispatched here. For all she knew, they'd already made planetfall.

Realizing she'd been caressing the patch of scar tissue in that hollow space near the base of her skull, Myla pulled her hand away and rubbed it on her pants leg. There'd been no breaking that habit. Her fingers, seemingly of their own volition, often found the spot where her CDF SpecOps implant still connected to her cerebellum, at one time interfacing her brain directly with the civilian DataNet, as well as the military's own network. Removing it had been impossible with the resources at her disposal; deactivating it cost her a large portion of the money she'd hoarded in her contingency fund. Is that what had brought Jarek here? Seeking help to evade capture as she'd done? It still didn't explain how he'd found her, but that was now a moot point. Jarek was here. CDF wouldn't be far behind.

Playing a hunch, Myla tapped the vid-screen and called up a status for the spaceport's inbound and outbound flights. One entry from the arrival itinerary caught her eye, its format different from the others on the list. Instead of a name, a ship recorded as having landed an hour ago bore a nondescript string of letters and numbers Myla recognized as a CDF transport identifier.

"Yeah. Time to get gone."

She had a plan for getting off-planet, but CDF security forces already on the ground complicated things. Supplies in the cabin could last several weeks. She could bide her time before sneaking onto an outbound hauler—but that presupposed Jarek not alerting the CDF to her presence just to save his own ass. Given the charges he faced, Myla harbored no doubts he'd give her up as part of some deal with prosecutors.

This place isn't safe. Just a few minutes with a public DataNet connection to forge the proper credentials, and I'm out of here.

The vid-screen squawked for attention and Myla looked up to see a local "Breaking News" banner flashing across the display. It cut to an older Latino woman with black hair cropped close to her scalp, staring into the camera with wide, dark eyes.

"We interrupt the Colonial News feed to bring you this important report of a jailbreak at the LaGrange Sheriff's Office. Sheriff August Jeffers has been injured, and there are unconfirmed reports of at least one unidentified fatality. We're awaiting official word on the escaped prisoner's identity and description, but sheriff's deputies caution the citizenry this fugitive is to be considered armed and dangerous. Notify local authorities if you see this individual. Again, a jailbreak has occurred—"

Myla deactivated the vid-screen, her mind swirling with the new information. She should've taken Jarek somewhere quiet to work out whatever problem he'd brought her way. Instead, she'd made him the sheriff's problem. Now Gus was hurt and someone else was dead.

This was her fault.

Any thoughts of eluding the CDF vanished as Myla entered the foyer of the LaGrange Sheriff's Office. Instead of facing one or more of Jeffers's deputies, she found herself before an imposing, dark-skinned man wearing an impeccable drab-green utility uniform bearing a colonel's insignia on the collars. His bald head reflected the office's low light, and he regarded her with cold, piercing eyes. Years of military training and discipline almost made her pull herself to a position of attention but she caught herself. She schooled her features, hoping she might pass off her shock at seeing the colonel as genuine confusion.

Any thoughts of bluffing her way through the next few minutes evaporated as soon as the colonel spoke.

"Sergeant Shanna McCall."

It was a declaration, not a question. The colonel exuded not doubt but confidence. His gaze never wavering, he made no effort to move toward her. Myla's initial shock at hearing her own name spoken by someone else was replaced by an impulse to flee. Then she heard footsteps before noting in her peripheral vision someone standing on either side of her. She didn't have to look to know they had to be CDF soldiers, each likely armed.

"Got me fluxed with someone else. My name's

Dynion. Myla Dynion." It was worth the effort, if only to observe the colonel's reaction. She wasn't surprised when he smiled. Rather than speak to her, he gestured to the soldiers flanking her.

"Search her."

The pair made short work of patting her down and finding the plazmag strapped to her right hip. The female soldier to her right removed the pistol from Myla's holster and tucked it into her own gun belt while her male counterpart extracted the hunting knife from the sheath on Myla's left side. They were thorough, even finding the second knife, folded in her back pocket.

"You could've just asked," said Myla. "I'm not looking for trouble."

Now the colonel did move to step around the desk, drawing close enough for her to read the name tag on his chest: THORNE. She also noted the diamond-shaped crest of the CDF's Security Forces, but nothing to indicate any affiliation with its Special Operations branch.

He's here because he was the closest CDF resource to New Bandera, she decided. *He only knows what he's been told.*

"Sergeant McCall," Thorne said, "you're under arrest for disobedience of lawful orders by a superior officer, insubordination, and desertion from the Colonial Defense Forces. You have the right to be represented by counsel provided by the judge advocate general, and to say nothing except on the advice and in the presence of counsel. With that in mind, is there anything you wish to say to me at this time?"

"How's Jeffers?" asked Myla, holding out her hands while the woman soldier placed restraints around her wrists. "And the person who was killed. One of the deputies?" She knew all of them by name. The thought of one of them dead at Jarek's hands sickened her.

The questions seemed to catch Thorne by surprise. Regaining his composure, he replied, "The fugitive killed one of my security officers. That individual's name is not being released, pending notification of their family."

"Damn." Lowering her head, Myla cast glances at each of the soldiers flanking her. "I'm sorry."

Another voice said, "As for the sheriff, I'm figuring he'll live."

Moving with a noticeable limp, Jeffers emerged from an adjacent office. Myla couldn't help grimacing at the large bruise on the left side of his face, and his right arm now nestled within a sling. The blue mesh of a bone-knitter cast stretched from elbow to wrist. Another cast sheathed his right foot to just above the ankle.

"What the hell happened?" She watched Jeffers shuffle toward his desk, with Thorne stepping aside to afford the sheriff access.

"Your buddy, Shaw." Jeffers released an extended groan as he lowered himself into his chair. "Managed to hack the lockup and let himself out before Colonel Thorne and his team showed up. He waited to make his move, then took out one of their soldiers and ran for it." He scowled. "Broke his neck. Kid never had a chance."

Myla flinched at the blunt recounting of the soldier's murder. What the hell was Jarek thinking, killing one of their own? Thorne and the entire Security Forces would hunt him down like a rabid animal.

"He was in our sights already," said Thorne, his voice

tight. "What your unit did on Malpaso is on every news broadcast across every colony world. There's no place for him to hide, and he didn't do a very good job covering his movements."

"You did the CDF a favor, stomping him the way you did," added Jeffers, before he held up his broken arm. "Can't say it did me much good."

"Sheriff," said Myla, "I never wanted anything like this. I just wanted—" She stopped herself, redirecting her gaze to Thorne. "I just wanted to be left alone."

"He didn't waste any time offering you up." Jeffers regarded her for a moment before adding, "I always knew there was something about you. I wish you'd told me."

Thorne eyed him. "You'd have been an accessory to her desertion."

"Maybe you work out your own problems before you go looking for others where you're not wanted. We were getting on just fine without all this dumbassery." Before the colonel could react to his comments, Jeffers turned to Myla. "When I processed Shaw, I found the implant. It was pretty sloppy work." He hooked a thumb toward Thorne. "I ran an identi-check, which rang his bell."

"Clearly his implant's still active," said the colonel. "We've picked up DataNet activity we think might be him, trying to arrange transport off-world. We'll have to hunt him the old-fashioned way. He's got my man's weapon and equipment. That and his training make him pretty damned dangerous. I was fine taking him back for trial, but now?" He stepped toward Myla, his expression going flat. "It's up to him, but I'm hoping he puts up a fight."

In her mind, Myla saw no other choice.

"I'll help you."

There was no time to second-guess her impulsive decision. In fact, she could feel a measure of relief welling up within her. This was the right thing to do.

His eyes narrowing, Thorne said, "If you're looking for some sort of leniency deal—"

"I'm not doing this for the CDF," said Myla, cutting him off. "Though I suppose I *am* doing it for you." She nodded to Jeffers. "And you, and the people of LaGrange. Nobody here's done anything to deserve any of this. Jarek's here because of me. He killed your man because he came looking for me. I don't give a damn about any military tribunal, but I can't leave here without making things right. So, let me help, then you can take us both back for trial."

Sounding unconvinced, Thorne asked, "Even if I agree to this, how do you suggest we find him?"

Myla could almost feel a not-quite-forgotten tingle at the base of her skull.

"I can find him."

Sitting on a stool and holding her hair away from her neck, Myla felt only the slightest sensation as Thorne, standing behind her, guided the scalpel along the scar tissue at the base of her skull.

"You know this is insane, right?" asked the colonel.

"Let the scalpel do the work." Myla had set the tool to cut no more than half a centimeter into her skin, which was already numbed thanks to a pain masker from the medical kit in Jeffers's office. "You've performed first aid in the field before, right?"

There was a pause before Thorne replied, "I've

never been in combat. Security Forces don't typically see that kind of action."

"Didn't you start out in the infantry?" Myla knew all CDF officers spent at least their first two years serving in an infantry billet.

"Sure, but it was peacetime. The border wars didn't start until I'd already changed designators." He chuckled before adding, "Don't judge me too harshly, Troop."

"No judging," replied Myla. "If I had it to do over again, I'd pick something else."

"Like what?"

"The band."

She felt Thorne's hand stop the scalpel along her neck. "We're there," he said. Something brushed across her neck, and she knew the colonel was applying a clotting agent to stem any bleeding from the incision. "Now what?"

Though she couldn't see what Thorne now observed, she'd been through this process before. "Spread the skin. You'll see the implant."

A dull stretching sensation played across her neck before Thorne said, "I've got it."

"There should be three diodes in the center."

Thorne replied, "Two are red. The one in the middle is dark."

"Correct," said Myla. "Below the diodes are two switches. They should be set to the left. Use the tool I gave you to flip them both to the right."

The colonel didn't have to say anything. She felt his hand on her neck at the same time her mind's eye conjured a vision of the switches moving and the inactive diode flashing green as its two companions shifted to a matching color. Despite bracing herself for what she knew came next, there was no preparing for the onslaught of information racing into her head once the implant automatically reestablished its connection to the DataNet.

Floodgates opened, her mind howling in protest as she struggled to absorb everything. It was the psychogenic equivalent of leaping onto a moving train. Myla closed her eyes, fighting to regain equilibrium. After five years, the old training and exercises imparted by cognitive agility instructors were no longer second nature, and it took her an extra moment to reassert her mental firewalls. Then the torrent eased, the influx abating. After another moment, everything was contained. The flow of data was still there, but instead of a raging river it now was a steady stream she could enter on her own terms.

"Are you all right?"

Myla opened her eyes at the sound of Jeffers's voice, only then hearing her fast, labored breathing. With conscious effort, she calmed herself, reining in her body now that her mind had settled.

Then came the connection to the other network.

Now she was ready for it. The rush of information through the CDF SpecOps neural net was not nearly so severe, designed as it was to foster ease of transition for soldiers laboring under combat conditions. With her mental barriers now in place, Myla had an easier time shunting data where it needed to go. It took only a few seconds to establish control, and she felt the familiar sensation of calm accompanying a stable link.

"Sorry," she said. "I'm out of practice." She shifted in her seat to regard Jeffers. "I never liked the damned thing, but you get used to it. Part of the job."

The sheriff frowned. "I'll take your word for it."

Moving to stand in front of her, Thorne eyed her with skepticism. "What happens next?"

Well, well. Look who it is. I thought I felt you in here.

Gasping, Myla stood up with such force she nearly lost her balance save for Thorne catching her.

"It's him. Damn, that was fast." She held up a hand to reassure Thorne and Jeffers she had things under control. "He found me first."

You made it pretty easy. Easier than tracking you to this shithole planet.

Myla ground her teeth. **How did you find me?**

We used to hunt people for a living, remember? Identify patterns, habits, routines. You always hated big cities, or crowds. You wanted to retire somewhere quiet, with wide-open spaces where you could see people coming ten klicks away. I tracked your movements through the DataNet before you severed your implant, then worked out from your last known location. Fifth time was a charm.

Damn it.

Her best efforts hadn't been enough to throw Jarek off her scent. It was her own fault. She'd let him get too close to her. Closer than anyone ever had. Far too close.

Close enough.

Taunting her, Jarek's voice echoed in her head again. **What are you even doing out here, anyway...? Wait. Don't tell me you're working with those CDF assholes. I thought you'd had enough of their shit.**

A cascade of images seemed to fly at her, one after

the other almost too fast for her to process. Explosions. Fire. People running, burning, dying. Sounds—in reality an artificial stimulus to her auditory pathways designed to simulate hearing—assaulted her ears with cries for help, for mercy, for death. Before she could temper the maelstrom, it vanished in the face of a new stream. Now passion replaced violence, with two figures intertwined—on a beach, in bed, aboard a troop transport—blurred bodies and faces coalescing until she recognized herself pressed against Jarek. She heard more sounds, only now it was the two of them, restraint lost amid the throes of—

Stop it!

The command spat forth from her mind, launching into the cacophony with such force that black replaced everything. Myla latched onto that darkness, wrapping it around her consciousness as she extracted herself from the link. Awareness returned, and she opened her eyes to see Jeffers and Thorne staring at her with shock and concern.

"Stop what?" asked the sheriff.

Myla placed a hand on Jeffers's good arm. "I'm truly sorry for all of this, Gus." She turned to Thorne. "All right, Colonel. When do we get started?"

"Right now."

Thorne held up a compact rectangular device Myla hadn't seen before now. It reminded her of the positioning trackers infantry units used during ground operations, receiving information from satellites or orbiting dropships. She'd used them herself, until joining SpecOps and receiving the implant that provided such data. This unit had a display screen depicting a scroll of information she couldn't read.

"As soon as you engaged him, I locked onto his position. So long as he stays connected to the CDF net, we can track him."

Myla's eyes widened. "I've never heard of anything like that." She'd always been told SpecOps implants were shielded from tracking, for fear of an enemy gaining that ability and compromising a unit's operations security.

"It's pretty new," replied Thorne. "And not the sort of thing you advertise. I wasn't planning to tell you, but then you offered to help us catch Shaw."

Jeffers asked, "If you had that gadget, why the hell did you need her to turn her implant back on?"

"She wanted to help," said the colonel. "And her implant gives me an edge." He looked to Myla, and she saw the understanding and even sympathy in his eyes. "Besides, I respect her wanting to make things right, so let's get on with it."

Thanks to Thorne's tracker, Myla realized Shaw had chosen what she knew to be his best course of action: fleeing LaGrange. He looked to be going to ground, likely hoping to evade pursuit long enough to make his way to the spaceport and sneak aboard a hauler. It wasn't the dumbest idea. The rolling hills and lush forests in all directions outside of town provided plenty of cover and concealment for someone who knew how to use the terrain to tactical advantage.

Jarek, for example.

Her, for another.

"Thorne," she said, subvocalizing into the comm unit affixed to her throat. "You okay?" In her mind, she reviewed the topographical map fed to her by

Sheriff Jeffers via the DataNet, noting the green icons indicating Thorne's position as well as his two soldiers relative to her own. Another icon, this one red, marked Jarek's possible location as indicated by the colonel's tracking device and sent directly to her implant to avoid their quarry's notice.

Over the encrypted comm link, Myla heard Thorne's labored breathing in her earpiece. *"I guess I'm a little out of shape for this sort of thing, but I'll manage."*

Jeffers, monitoring the situation from his office, added, *"If I'm reading this map right, you're within two hundred meters of his position. He's on a rise overlooking the valley."*

Myla had gleaned that much from the map before they'd even left town. With that information, she'd convinced Thorne to deploy his two soldiers farther to the north on the far side of the valley, where they could approach from the opposite direction while she and Thorne advanced from the south.

"This is about as far as you could go on foot in the time since he escaped," she said. "The elevated position makes for a good overwatch position."

Jeffers replied, *"I know the area. The trees start to thin out the farther you go. It's a good bet he'll see one of you first."*

"That's not very reassuring."

Looking to her left, she saw Thorne moving among the trees. He stepped with slow deliberation, the barrel of his CDF plazmag rifle sweeping slowly from right to left and back again. His eyes tracked with the weapon's movements, glancing at the ground ahead of him to verify his footing with every stride. His rifle was a match for the one she carried, having exchanged her civilian pistol for the CDF armaments provided by Thorne's team. The familiar weight was a comfort; an extension of her body. Far more powerful than weapons available to civilians, the rifle also possessed a greater effective range, allowing for engagement at longer distances than anything carried by a freight hauler or farmer on New Bandera.

I know you're out there.

Myla stopped. "Thorne, Hold up."

Yeah, I'm here. She pushed her reply through the net. **Not many places for me to go, now.**

So you come here? Jarek's tone was playful, almost mocking. **Why?**

Payback. No way I'm letting them drag me back by myself.

Jarek's laughter echoed in her mind. **After all we've been through, after everything we meant to each other, this is how it ends?**

Memories that weren't hers flashed in Myla's mind. Two bodies locked together, sharing love and laughter. Happiness. All of that was true, for a time.

Until Malpaso.

Look, I get it. What we did was wrong. I know that now, but back then? It was the job, remember? They sent us in to pacify that resistance cell.

The words were there, Myla decided, but not the sincerity. Jarek was rationalizing as much to himself as he was to her.

Killing noncombatants wasn't the job, Jarek. Putting down the rebels was the mission. Everything else was—

When the visions came this time, they were a

hammer inside her skull. Structures and vehicles exploding. People falling in hailstorms of weapons fire. Women and children, bursting apart from plazmag rifles set to maximum power. Cries for sanity in the midst of utter chaos, unheard. Cries for help, unanswered. Cries for mercy, ignored.

Instead, there was nothing but violence, destruction, and death.

Myla saw herself standing amidst the carnage, uniform torn, dirty, and covered in blood not her own. Rifle broken and useless by her side, she watched in mute revulsion as men and women she called friends unleashed the hellfire of their weapons on those helpless to defend themselves. Her ears rang with screams of terror and pain. She watched herself running toward her comrades, waving her arms and pleading for them to halt this most heinous of sins.

The mission was over! We'd broken them. Taken out the cell's leaders. There was nowhere for them to run. No fight left.

Jarek's voice seemed more somber now. **I know, now. At the time? There was no way to tell who was a threat. It was them or—**

They were unarmed civilians! Myla rejected the memories, realizing they hadn't been sent by Jarek but instead welled up from where she'd buried them in the depths of her consciousness. **You kept firing. Everyone kept firing, even after I begged you to stop! Why didn't you just stop?**

It was the mission, Shanna. We had our orders.

"Enough," she snapped, realizing she'd spoken aloud as the word echoed through the trees around her.

"Myla," said Jeffers over the link. *"You all right?"*

Pushing away the unwelcome memories, Myla reoriented herself to her surroundings. "I'm fine." She turned to look for Thorne and saw the colonel crouching low to the ground, his weapon facing to his left as he regarded her with concern.

"You okay to keep going?" he asked. Before Myla could answer, the high-pitched whine of a plazmag pierced through the forest. She saw a blue-white pulse of energy surging through the trees until it slammed into Thorne's left leg. The impact spun the colonel off his feet, twisting him in midair until he crashed to the ground before rolling toward a nearby depression. Myla ran in that direction but then another plazbolt tore into a tree just in front of her. Chunks of bark flew in all directions, peppering her as she ducked her head to protect herself. She scampered away from the attack, seeking cover behind a larger, gnarled tree.

More shots echoed in the distance, varying in pitch enough to tell her they came from different weapons, followed by the more familiar whine of what had to be Jarek's rifle.

Then she heard nothing. At the same time, she realized she could no longer see the feed from Thorne's tracker. Was it damaged? The map it supplied her was gone.

"*Colonel Thorne*," said Jeffers. "*I've lost the feed from your tracker.*"

"Thorne's down." Hunched behind the tree, Myla hunted for movement. "I think his men are down, too."

They don't train these troops like they used to, taunted Jarek. **Looks like it's just you and me**.

Without the tracker and its telemetry, Myla could only guess at Jarek's location, but it made sense he'd move from his last position. Would he advance, or retreat?

Her answer arrived with another plazbolt, this one punching her just above her right hip. It was a glancing blow, the bulk of the energy pulse boring into the tree that was her protection. The rest of it was enough to spin her away from the tree, off-balance and tumbling to the ground. She lost her rifle, pressing her hands against the burning in her hip, nerve endings screaming for attention in the face of the brutal assault. Fighting to control her breathing against the pain, she heard running footsteps from somewhere nearby.

Too easy. Jarek laughed.

"*Myla!*" It was Jeffers, his voice tight. "*What's going on?*"

Her rifle out of reach, she pulled her right hand from her wound and reached for the holster along her thigh. Sensing movement to her left, she looked up to see Jarek advancing toward her, rifle up and aiming at her face.

It didn't have to be this way. Did Myla hear regret in his voice?

"Shut up." She hissed the words through gritted teeth. Her hand rested on her pistol, but she knew she'd never clear its holster in time.

A smaller plazbolt sailed past Jarek's head from his right, and he pivoted in that direction. Myla tracked his movements to see Thorne, limping on his damaged leg while brandishing his own pistol, firing a second shot that also went wide. Jarek's first shot missed, but only because Thorne's leg gave out and he stumbled to his knees, the plazbolt darting over his shoulder.

"Damn it!" Jarek snarled, stepping around a tree to

adjust his aim for a second shot. There was nowhere for Thorne to go.

Her every movement sending a stabbing pain through her side, Myla pulled her pistol from its holster, raised it, and fired two shots in rapid succession. The first drilled through Jarek's back while the second sheered away the top of his skull.

Shan———

Jarek's final plea faded into nothingness, and Myla felt his mind severed from the net. His body trembled, his rifle unleashing a final errant shot into the trees before he collapsed in a lifeless heap.

"Talk to me, Myla," said Jeffers. *"I'm blind here. You okay?"*

"McCall!"

Jeffers's voice was a low buzz in her ears, and Thorne's call seemed even more distant, the sounds around her fading as her vision dimmed. She felt the net's tendrils slipping away, extracting themselves from her consciousness before everything went dark.

Jeffers closed his eyes, relishing the burn of the whiskey as it coursed down his throat.

Damn. That's good.

Myla was clearly of like mind, considering she had downed three shots to his one. Dropping her glass on Jeffers's desk, she grabbed the bottle to pour herself a fourth before refilling the glasses sitting before Thorne and himself.

"One of the reasons I like you, Myla," he said, raising his glass in tribute. "You can handle your liquor." A few more of these, Jeffers decided, and he might just forget about the pain in his injured arm and leg.

Finishing his own drink, Thorne set down his glass. "Time to head out. Transport's waiting." Jeffers watched the colonel rise from his seat with the help of a cane; a medical sheath encased his left leg, its mesh continually working to heal the damage caused by Shaw's rifle. Seemingly mindful of Jeffers's own wounded arm, Thorne shifted the cane so he could extend his left hand. "Thank you, Sheriff, for everything."

"Happy to help, Colonel." Jeffers pushed himself up to shake the offered hand. "Just please don't go making this a habit. I like my town quiet and boring."

"Fair enough." Thorne turned to Myla, and Jeffers instantly noticed her tension. Was the colonel about to pull out a pair of restraints? Her expression made him believe the same thought had crossed her own mind.

"Myla, there's something I haven't mentioned," Thorne began. "On the way here, I read your file along with the pertinent intel about what happened on Malpaso, including your original report and transcripts of comm traffic you exchanged with your command post that day. In light of everything, you're not being charged with any wrongdoing pertaining to the incident itself."

"No charges?" asked Jeffers.

Thorne shook his head. "No charges."

"Well," said Myla, "seeing as how I didn't do anything wrong, that's nice to hear."

"The CDF got it wrong, Sergeant." Thorne's features softened. "Your squad's attempt to cover it up and throw you into the grinder is fragged. On that count, at least, the news reports and our own intel saved your ass."

Jeffers snorted. "On *that* count. Sounds like your bill's due, Myla."

Thorne kept his eyes on her. "There's still desertion and disabling your implant." The colonel paused with an expression that made Jeffers think he was choosing his next words with care. "But you helped me with Shaw... and saved my life along the way."

"Like I told you, I had to make things right."

"Shaw? Him I get. Me? Hell, you could've killed me and disappeared, and no one would ever know." As Thorne paused, Jeffers studied the man's face. Was he starting to... smile?

Myla broke the silence. "I feel an 'and' coming."

"And," Thorne said, "in all the commotion, it turns out I never got around to updating headquarters that I found you here. Come to think of it, I can already feel myself forgetting I ever saw you. But, if you wanted to come back to the CDF, I can wipe your record. Nothing would be hanging over you. It's a fresh start and you keep your stripes. I might even be able to swing your back pay."

Jeffers was taken aback by the offer. Would Myla be tempted enough to accept it? He thought it had to sound better to her than sweating out a job at the spaceport. This might be just enough for her to kick the dust of this place off her boots for good—and he'd not blame her.

"Any chance you could just do the record wiping part," said Myla, "and we go with the whole forgetting you saw me thing?"

Frowning, Thorne asked, "And why would I do that?"

Myla shrugged. "Because, then I'd owe *you* a favor."

Appearing to mull that for a moment, Thorne

extended his hand to her. "I can always use a favor now and then." As Myla took his hand, he added, "Take care of yourself, *Ms. Dynion.*"

Placing his uniform cover on his bald head, Thorne offered a mock salute before he and his cane shuffled out of the office. Once he was gone, and the door closed behind him, Jeffers laughed.

"Well, I'll be dipped in shit and spread on toast. Can't say I'm unhappy about how that turned out." He paused before asking the question nagging his mind. "Think you'll stick around?"

Myla reached up to rub her neck. "Way I figure it, I owe you a favor, too. Two, if you help me disable this damn implant again. The sooner I unhook from the DataNet, the better." She blew out her breath. "Hopefully, for the last damned time."

Jeffers did not even bother trying to hide his grin. "Don't think I won't call in that marker one day."

"How about we cash it in right now?" Jeffers drew his head back as Myla reached to tap the badge above his left shirt pocket. "Still got that extra star?"

He sure as hell did.

THE LAST ROUND

Susan R. Matthews

Gavrill stood in the near-deserted main street of Warehouse Depot Drange, watching the plunderers come for him.

He didn't want to die. He had too much to live for. He had the best marksman at Serac Hearths for a partner. They had a beautiful daughter, and a second child on the way.

Most of the pioneers of Serac Hearths were hidden away in safe places. It was Gavrill's job to stall the plunderers for as long as possible to give the last of the pioneers a chance to get away.

"Listen to me," the man with Gavrill's death in his hand called out loudly, his voice carrying clearly from half a long block away. "There's still time to come to an arrangement. Work with me here, Gav. I'm your friend, remember?"

Gavrill knew exactly how much time he had left. He could feel the heavy rumbling of the tankers underfoot from where he stood. If the plunderers weren't on their way soon they wouldn't reach the evacuation launch site before the detonation protocols destroyed it, and they'd be stranded here on Yegbenie Two.

Warehouse Depot Drange wasn't much more than twenty heavy transport wheelers long, and Gavrill's enemy, Berize, was standing just to one side of the last of the line that stood waiting in the street. Berize wasn't likely to miss at this range. He favored a Tassicass C-fullfour, a survival from earlier days before pioneers had come to the dusty gold-tinged hills of Yegbenie Two hoping to found a farming settlement. There'd been nothing here but wild vermat herb, not then. Nothing but that.

Gavrill didn't answer. He and Berize had argued it all out before. What could he say? *I'll split the bounty on pioneer heads with you?* It wouldn't be anything Gavrill hadn't done before. He'd been a plunderer the same as Berize was.

Yegbenie Two had meant easy money, then; untouched riches waving beneath the warm sun over vast prairies of exotic culinary vermat herb. The first harvests had sold at a significant wildcrafted premium; but once Yegbenie Two's store of native vermat had been exhausted and the soil was spent, the premium for wildcrafted herb went away, and the destructive nature of vermat's hallucinogenic, narcotic properties became more difficult to ignore.

"We're not friends anymore, Berize." Gavrill didn't think he'd have minded killing Berize. Not even after ten years' partnership working for the corporations. "Not since you drowned M'liosh. Remember M'liosh?"

She'd come to Serac Hearths to join Yegbenie Two's other pioneers, seeking to make a new life by developing a secondary vermat market with modified cultivars.

She'd built a little one-room, half-buried, dirt-brick hut and a seed-lab for research. She'd planted flowers. Silly weeds, but they'd been flowers all the same.

Then Berize's crew had flooded her out, just to discourage vermat poaching. Gavrill had had a thought, when he and the other pioneers of the Firewatch had found the ruins, that he might have tried to talk peace—even then—if the plunderers hadn't pulled up M'Liosh's flowers and scattered them over her corpse in mockery.

"We didn't drown her, Gav. She was dead before the purge cycle got well started. No, she hit herself over the head with a rock." There, a note of provocation in Berize's voice. Sneering. "It was an accident, really."

Gavrill was glad M'liosh had been dead. Drowning in the contaminated water from a vermat tanker—the so-called aftershot—was a horror to contemplate. Burned out a person's lungs with concentrated alkali.

Nor was Berize finished with his threats. "And we'll be back for more vermat, when the time comes." When the spent soil had started to regenerate, though nobody really knew when that would be. "We'll drown you all out. You should take your little lost lornlings out of harm's way before we have to take steps, Gav."

Gavrill took a deep breath, filling his lungs, savoring the flavor of the air. He could smell the ghost of the fragrance of vermat along with the dust of the temp-built road and the stink of spent fuel and the faint hints of the aftershot—resinous, with an undertone of sweet, musky night-blooming terlew. Flowers. Again with the flowers.

He had every hope of going quickly; Berize couldn't flood *him* out in the street. The plunderers needed that road to trundle the transit wheelers out to the launch site, for transport to the nexus station at Wevlor on one of Yegbenie Two's moons.

Gavrill could hear Berize's men, moving quietly under cover of loading docks and warehouse lifts to get around him. Maybe they thought he'd cut a deal with them even now, sell the hopeful pioneers out in return for safety for him and his partner and their children. Joke was on them. Gavrill didn't even know where the pioneers were. Not exactly.

Maybe Berize just wanted to be absolutely sure that Gavrill was dead, once Berize had killed him. But if Gavrill took any such deal, his partner, Remo, would shoot him herself. She was a good shot. It was one of the things he admired most about her.

"Well . . ." Gavrill said. If he let the moment stretch too long Berize might begin to hope that Gavrill could be talked into changing his mind. He wasn't going to change his mind. "Any more drowning will have to be done over my dead body. Your quarrel's with me, though, isn't it? Not with any of your hangers-on."

Over my dead body was as decisive a rejection as one man could offer another, but with luck Berize would be curious enough about what Gavrill meant to say to let him talk. Any delay Gavrill could create would work in the pioneers' favor, whether or not Gavrill would be just as dead at the end of it one way or the other.

Berize eased the safety retard on the Tassicass back into "lock" from "loose" with an exaggerated gesture, apparently so that Gavrill would know what Berize was doing. The general form of the gesture was familiar enough. It meant *I'm listening.* So Gavrill talked.

"So, are you sure you've cleared the depot? There's a storyteller. No reason he should be left behind to starve, is there?" Gavrill had listened in on the man's stories with everybody else at the depot station, when he'd been able to. Amusing and good entertainment. The man earned his keep.

"Haldane-somebody?" Berize sounded confused. Did he think Gavrill was trying to play for time? Well, Gavrill was. But he was also trying to reduce the carnage. "Haldane, that's right. What of him?"

"The man's a vermat-head," Gavrill said. "You'll be taking him with you, surely. Looks bad to abandon your camp followers, Berize, you know that. And he could be useful. He'll swear in court that *we* attacked *you*, if you give him enough v-juice. Judges appreciate a little humor as much as anybody else."

"I know the man, now." Berize shrugged. "I've no idea where to find him. We'll take our chances with any judge in Jarizon system. We paid good money for each and every one of them." Berize had apparently nerved himself up to the killing. Gavrill could hear it in his voice. This was the end for him.

But someone called out, clear-voiced and even cheerful in the thin afternoon air. "I'm right here, Berize." Gavrill frowned, trying to locate the source of the voice in the still air. "Waiting for my ride out."

Haldane. Who else could it be, really? Gavrill didn't think he'd ever heard the storyteller so close to sober. Berize hadn't asked Gavrill why he cared whether Haldane lived or died. Maybe Berize had simply marked it down to Gavrill's sense of fair play; Berize used to have a lot of fun at Gavrill's expense on that topic.

"Kind of you to spare a thought for me, Gavrill," Haldane said, waving at Gavrill and Berize alike where they stood in the street. Gavrill saw Haldane now. He was sitting on the aft fender-end of the last of the transport rigs that were lined up with their backs to Gavrill and Berize, waiting to depart.

Specifically, maybe significantly, Haldane was comfortably perched on the tailshelf of the suckerhose apparatus. It was part of every transport rig, collecting the alkaline aftershot draining from the vermat to be dumped into tailings-pools. There the aftershot would dry up, and blow away, dust that could eat flesh off the living bone if the wind came on too strong and from the wrong direction.

"Yes, Gavrill, I *do* appreciate it." Haldane patted the purge-box on the suckerhose for emphasis. "This one of the new rigs, Berize?"

Gavrill could sense some uncertainty coming from the Berize direction of the street. Unexpected complications set vermat harvesters off balance. Gathering wildcrafted vermat required thorough planning, not creative thinking; there were so many things that could go wrong.

"Get off the rig, you old beggar," Berize said. His head was half-turned to speak to Haldane, but Gavrill could see that Berize was keeping his handgun—and presumably his eyes—fixed on Gavrill. "You don't know these new flushers. There's a speedsil in line, just ahead. Go on. Just as the dead man says."

Gavrill could hear worn warehouse paneling creaking in the chill breeze, and the shrill scraping sounds of ventilation baffles coming loose and rubbing against one another. Spending money on maintaining soon-to-be-abandoned work sites wasn't in the corporations' best interest, clearly enough; that went for their employees, as well.

Berize and his plunderers were due to lose their livelihoods. Maybe—Gavrill told himself—Berize would be lucky, and the corporations would keep him on. Berize wasn't any younger than Gavrill. There were only so many times that a man could start all over again, *again*.

"Do as he says, Haldane. No point in starving," Gavrill said, feeling suddenly much older than twenty-eight standard. "I can hear your people trying to sneak up on me, Berize." Why? Who cared? "You made a good choice, Berize. Haldane's got stories in him yet."

Haldane hadn't moved, though. "No, there's been a misunderstanding," Haldane said. "Something I should probably clear up." Gavrill didn't hear any hint of awareness in Haldane's voice of the risks he was taking. Haldane was just sitting there, toying idly with the snake-head valve assembly that controlled the suckerhose's purge cycle.

"That misunderstanding," Berize said, slowly, with the sound of a man as willing to shoot two men as one clear in his voice for Gavrill—who knew how to listen for it—to hear. "Care to explain, Haldane?"

Gavrill knew Berize was getting frustrated. An intervention seemed to be in order. "Now, Berize," Gavrill said, in as calm and reassuring a tone of voice as he could muster, "you've got safes on that purge-valve, I know you do. No need to get trigger-happy."

In one sense at least Haldane was doing Gavrill the best favor imaginable: distracting Berize so that the last of the pioneers could get to safe shelter before the corporations' sanitizer bombs went off. Gavrill owed it to Haldane to return the favor. Killing a vermat-head was a waste of ammunition.

"The *misunderstanding* is the one about which of us is staying and which of us had better be on their way to the launch site with maximum speed," Haldane explained, patiently. "Of course there are safety locks on the purge-valve. And on the discharge-authorization assembly. This one's a code instruction"—Haldane pointed at it—"but the others are mostly mechanical. Don't you think I know, Berize? I listen, when people talk. And I fiddle with things to calm my nerves. It's because of my sickness, you know."

The Greens. That was what they called it, plunderers and pioneers alike. People who snuck into the fields to gather illicit vermat for personal use—without a ventilator in good working order—risked permanent physical damage, body and brain alike, with every breath they took. Haldane had been on the v-rigs once. Had Haldane breathed too much green vermat?

Haldane's voice had dropped to a soft, breathy sigh now. It was harder for Gavrill to make Haldane out. "You can't get at me in time to abort the purge-initiate command before it engages. I drop this collar—here"—Haldane tossed the suckerhose into the air and caught it on its way back down, like a man bouncing a baby—"for whatever reason, and there'll be no stopping it."

Then Haldane's voice strengthened. "Aftershot all over everything, the way the suckerhose bucks when the snake-head hasn't been fixed properly. Something to behold, they tell me. You mean to shoot Gavrill anyway, so he doesn't care, but what about you, Berize? Can you get someplace safe in time?"

It was an outright threat, too flamboyant to be real. Yet Haldane sounded very confident, and not at all drunk. "No, Berize?" Haldane said. "Then I suggest you and your people not lose a moment's time getting to the launch field. Never know when my hand might slip."

Haldane did something with the suckerhose. A drop or two of the concentrated alkali aftershot dripped from the discharge nozzle into the dust of the street. The perfume in the air was suddenly much stronger.

"You're bluffing," Berize said. Gavrill didn't think Berize sounded as confident as all that. "You'll die too, Haldane."

A few drops of aftershot vaporizing in the open air a man could bear, without injury. A few more drops and a man would cough for days no matter how healthy his lungs were. Too many more drops and a man would never speak in a normal tone of voice again, and after that there was too short an interval between long-term physical impairment and death by asphyxiation to risk a measurement error.

"Yes, but do I really care?" Haldane asked, thoughtfully. "Maybe I'm just tired to death of living. You could try to rush me, you know. Then we'd all find out. Well, find out something, though what that might be I'm . . . I apologize, I've forgotten what I was going to say. I'll just lie down for a little nap. Once I get these safeties back into proper order."

Berize raised his voice. "Emergency evac!" he shouted. "On me to the speedsils! Hurry! Run!" He was Gavrill's enemy, but Gavrill still admired his leadership. Berize hadn't lost his edge over the years.

Five people, well fed, well clothed, broke from the shadows behind Gavrill, sprinting for the line of tankers. Five people with near-panic to impel them.

Now, finally, Haldane shifted his rump off the tailshelf of the suckerhose apparatus, the suckerhose itself safely locked into its secure holding slot. Nothing was going to purge from that tanker while the suckerhose's business end was locked into its tank.

"Look, Gavrill, here's a tanker full of vermat," Haldane said. "Prime herb, too. Probably trade well on the, oh, unregulated market. In time. Did you bring a speedsil with you? I don't think any bombs are going to go off, but anything could happen."

Gavrill had so many questions. What had just happened? Why had Haldane intervened? "Nothing will blow until they've got their tankers to the launch site," Gavrill said. "Speedsil this way."

When Gavrill had seen the sun rise this morning he'd expected to die before sunset. When he'd faced Berize in the street, he'd expected to be laying the dust with his own heart's blood within an hour. It was a day of wonder, a day to write songs about.

In the great welter of confusion in Gavrill's mind, there was one thing of which he was certain: there wasn't enough vermat in all of Jarizon system to repay the debt Gavrill owed Haldane, for this day's work.

Five years gone past and here they were again, facing off in the primary access corridor through now-abandoned Drange Depot. Gavrill and Berize. Gavrill was the one with the armed men to back him up this time: Haldane stood beside him. The one last vermat tanker had been moved out into one of the side streets. There was nowhere for Berize to hide.

"You said you wanted to make a deal," Gavrill said. Berize had come from the launch site by speedsil transport. It was idled well back from where Berize stood, under guard. No escape for Berize there.

Berize shifted his feet, as if he was uncomfortable. As well he might be. Berize had murdered one of the pioneers of Serac Hearths, more than five years ago. Her name had been M'liosh. People hadn't forgotten.

"I'm tired, Gavrill," Berize said, sounding worn out, defeated. "I want out of the wars. You already know the worst things I've done, and I know the same about you, so we don't have to worry about having any secrets from each other."

That was true enough, Gavrill had to agree. As if sensing an opening, Berize pressed on. "I have something to offer. Not in exchange. As acknowledgment."

"I'm listening," Gavrill said. Serac Hearths had rules in place for self-governance. Murder without extenuation meant outlawry, but the council had been known to make adjustments. "What do you propose?"

Berize didn't answer directly. He made an obvious show of looking around him at the warehouse buildings lining the streets with their crumbling loading docks and their pass-throughs jammed shut, their no-longer-structurally-intact walls starting to buckle under their own weight.

"Place is a mess, though, isn't it?" Berize asked. "Have your people been inside any of the warehouses, Gav? Maybe Haldane thinks he remembers where something useful was stored, and you've tried to find it?"

Haldane had had a few ideas, true, but nothing much had come of them. They'd been able to salvage some materials, some equipment, but mostly just odds and ends. Gavrill waited.

"I brought something with me that could help," Berize said. "Could be useful. Valuable. I don't know." There was a flat finality in Berize's voice. Hopelessness. Weariness. "The depot schematics, where things might have been left behind. The key-codes. Here."

Berize had brought a satchel with him. As Berize walked carefully and slowly toward Gavrill, Gavrill could see it was the size and shape of a standard inventory screen. Gavrill didn't move. Berize put the satchel down in the street and backed away once more. Then he shrugged.

"I don't know, maybe there's nothing left. The corporations don't want anything more from me, and I know I don't want to die in a one-cell sleeper in some industrial slum, breathing filthy air. I still have some good years of hard work in me, Gavrill. Let me come in." Gavrill could hear desperation now, muted, but it was there. "I stole a life. That's on me. I'll pay with labor. The schematics and the keys, those are yours already, because I owe."

Beside Gavril, Haldane bestirred himself, shifting his weight from one foot to the other in a slow, contemplative manner. A signal meant for Berize's benefit: *If it was up to me I'd feed him to the wildporks.* "Mistake, Gav," Haldane said. "Take the warehouse information. Send Berize into the wasteland."

The greater outlawry. An almost certain death sentence. No access to provisions, or what little medical help there was, or to that fundamental and astonishingly crucial requirement for long-term survival of human beings—social contact.

In his mind's eye, Gavrill could still see handfuls of flowers torn up out of a meager flower bed, scattered over a woman's corpse in mockery. But he couldn't change history. And he was a servant of Serac Hearths, a keeper of the peace, with a voice on the governing council that carried no more weight than anybody else's.

"I hear you, Berize," Gavrill said. "I hear you too, Haldane. But it's not my call." He raised his voice to be sure that everybody could hear him clearly, the people Gavrill could see and the ones in field-expedient cover amidst the trash and the detritus in the street. "You'll come before the council, Berize. There'll be a vote. I get one, like anybody else." One was all he got, too. "You can camp here, maybe get a start on finding us some speedsils. That'd make you popular."

The bigger Serac Hearths got, the harder it became to get around the widening aggregation of farmlabs and experimental fields. They needed speed and agility. They needed swifter transport. They needed speedsils. A man couldn't buy his way out of a murder, but useful donations could be taken as a sort of mitigation. Dead was dead, after all. Life went on.

Taking a breath so deep Gavrill could see it from where he stood, Berize nodded his head. "There's some abandoned transport equipment out at the launchfields," Berize said. "Maybe something salvageable. Send me a crew. I'll get started."

There was a cold energy sink at Gavrill's elbow, a column of ice crackling with disapproval. Haldane was angry, but there wasn't much Gavrill could do about that. Haldane, no less than anyone else, was learning to fit his behavior to other peoples' standards because neither he nor Gavrill—nor Berize—made their own law anymore.

The wars were over. The peace was complicated. "Let's get back, Hal," Gavrill said. "We need to brief the council on this first thing."

And Gavrill was just as happy that it was no longer up to him to decide exactly what should be done with people like Berize.

It had been ten years since the wars had ended and the plunderers had left Jarizon for good. A signal at the window in the middle of the night could still bring Gavrill out of the deepest sleep in a heartbeat. The tap at the window's thermal membrane was quiet but firm, and Gavrill recognized it on a deep level before he'd so much as opened his eyes.

Gavrill was out of bed in an instant, falling heavily to his knees on the floor, picking his half boots up in one hand as though he'd planned it that way all along. It was their eldest daughter at the door, Garee.

"With you in three," Gavrill said to the window, hopping on one foot, pushing the other foot toe-first into his boot. Remo was awake—of course she was—listening. Their daughter had come to her parents' bedroom rather than coming through the kitchen, to avoid waking the baby. There was a room for Garee there, tiny, but hers. Her brother still slept in a box bed in the kitchen corner, and they'd be building a new room for the baby Remo was carrying. If it lived.

"What do you think?" Remo asked him, but quietly, so that their daughter needn't overhear. Garee was only fifteen. They started their young on the Firewatch early at Serac Hearths because there was so much work to go around and still too few people to do it.

"Go back to sleep, Remo," Gavrill said. "You have Council in the morning. Haldane's sure to have a report for you. You need to rest."

That was something that he could, in justice, demand. Remo wasn't a young warrior of iron will and an insatiable taste for victory, not any longer. This was their third child, the last they could afford. Life was a challenge at Serac Hearths. Babies could be resource-intensive, and there were only barely enough resources to go around.

Remo rolled over on her side with her back to the room. Gavrill knew she'd have the hand-cannon—Behrendo class eight, triple barreled, but with only one round chambered. If worse came to worst, the sharp, destructive detonation of a killing stick would be the first sound their child would hear, outside of Remo's heartbeat. But there was always the risk that it would be the last, as well.

Remo didn't need a hand-cannon for *her* protection. She was by far the better marksman of the two of them; it was Gavrill who didn't trust his aim at close quarters. Remo kept a Tassicass C-fullfour sidearm on her side of the bed. Gavrill had bought it out of common stores for Remo as a gift six years ago; a peace offering, because she'd opposed granting Berize probation and been overruled.

Stepping out into the cool night air, Gavril closed the door quietly behind him. Garee stood waiting, leaning up against the outside wall with her arms folded across her chest.

For a moment, the familiar conflict in Gavrill's

heart threatened to overwhelm him. She was beautiful beyond measure, in his eyes. She'd been a difficult child, an angry child, but that wasn't her fault. He was proud of her courage and her will and her aptitude as one of Haldane's most genuinely promising students. He was terrified of harm coming to her. The too-many unkindnesses the world might inflict on Gavrill's beloved daughter were his personal enemies.

"Sorry to wake you," Garee said, as Gavrill smoothed his shirt into his waistband, settling his jacket across his shoulders. "Haldane's special request."

She had a bit of a crush on Haldane. Most of Haldane's students did. It wasn't anything to do with actual physical beauty, because Haldane was not a beautiful man. It was charisma plain and simple, the endless fascination Haldane evoked by simply being himself, delighting in battle, courageous to the point of insanity. Maybe just flat-out insane. Gavrill didn't mind. For ten years he'd trusted Haldane with the most precious things he'd ever had: his partner, and his children.

"What's on?" Gavrill asked, and gave his daughter a quick hug. She was tense.

"No check-ins from Berize since yesterday," she said. "Special watch on that one. Haldane's concerned."

Nobody at Serac Hearths had forgotten that Berize had been a plunderer—nor that Gavrill had been one too, once upon a time. Nor that Berize had been at least involved in M'liosh's murder.

"Harvest coming up," Gavrill said carefully. "Maybe Berize is just too busy to check in." Berize had been with them for nearly five years, now, working hard, keeping to himself in respectful solitude. Three more years and Berize would be granted half a vote on common council business, if the community's judgment went his way.

"Haldane's been putting a dossier together," Garee said. "Pattern of petty harassment, getting worse. There've been some changes lately, though."

Gavrill was completely dressed, half boots securely fastened, bind seams smoothed flat, outer layers of clothing in good order. Clean. Repaired. Like new, almost, Gavrill told himself, though it'd been so long since he'd had new clothing that he didn't think he'd know what to do with it.

"Tell me," Gavrill suggested. If Haldane had thought anything was heading downhill too fast he'd have come to Gavrill with a special report. Wouldn't he? Haldane had been getting a little moody, of late.

"Nobody's seen anything, heard anything. Ripe grain evaporating from Berize's field. The egger-house broken open, alarms disabled, no telling whether the hens were stolen or ran away or were eaten."

Or evaporated, like the grain. It could be mere noise, background malice. Serac Hearths wouldn't let Berize starve if his crops were stolen and his livestock likewise. It would stress the limits of his welcome, though, which was still tenuous at best.

"Let's get going," Gavrill said. "Haldane waiting for us, main road? Speedsils on line?"

Serac Hearths owed most of its transport to Berize's warehouse depot maps. The speedsils didn't look like much anymore, but they were still running, longer than anybody had hoped. And they still ran whisper-silent, whether in fourplex mode or on tripod rollers.

"Ready," Garee said, pointing.

As the man responsible for answering to the council

on maintaining the peace and good order, Gavrill had a speedsil assigned to him for official use. So did Haldane, as captain of the Firewatch. Everybody else took turns. Now Gavrill's speedsil was prepped and ready; all that was left was for Gavrill to step into the operator's station at the front of the vehicle, and be off.

The body-shell's command module gave him full range of night vision. He got situation reports, time, temperature, contour, mapping, threat assessment. He also got the terse and irritated voice of his friend Haldane, the man whose support—and talent for chaos and mayhem—had frustrated residual plunderers' best efforts time and again.

"Consternation to the ungodly," Haldane said, over Gavrill's comm channel, "are you coming or not? Hurry it up."

Garee herself had one of the shared community speedsils. She pulled out toward the main road slowly; Gavrill followed her. The gravel-paved track had been deliberately designed to create a little noise by way of advance warning. No security officer liked being snuck up on.

One of Haldane's best tricks was sneaking up on people in plain view. He could be so harmless in silhouette, so innocuous in outline, that even after ten years Gavrill's eye could still slide right past him without really noticing that he was there. Remo was the only person Gavrill knew who saw Haldane clearly, every time, and—since Gavrill wasn't sure whether that meant Haldane was something more to Remo than Gavrill might like—he tried not to think too hard about it.

There was no gravel on the main road, the track that joined each holding in Serac Hearths together. As

Gavrill neared the road, he saw two little red flashes alongside the track that told him where Haldane sat waiting, and the convoy-loop—closely linked radio communication, tightly shielded—sent an alert-ping.

"About time, too, slab-asleep." Haldane, again. "Come on, come on. I have a bad feeling, Gav."

Berize's holding was nearly an hour away, even with the speedsils' batteries at full and traveling at the top of their range. *No time like the present, then*, Gavrill thought, though he didn't waste his breath. Communications discipline in effect. No social chatter.

It was a clear night. There wasn't much between the road and the stars and the bright beacons of the habitable worlds of Yegbenie Two catching the light of their cooling sun. The air coming half-strength through the speedsil's ventilators was cool and pleasant. But ten minutes from the place where the road would branch away to Berize's holding, Gavrill started tasting the smoke of smoldering grain stalk waste. That wasn't right, and everybody—Haldane, Gavrill, Garee, the three others from the Firewatch Haldane had brought with him—knew it.

Stalk waste was low-moisture cellulose, saved up for insulation and manufacturing sun-dried mud bricks. The sturdy little scrubland hoppers that were native to Yegbenie Two thrived on it, growing tamer with each passing year. One adult hopper would feed a family all dearth-season if the meat was processed carefully enough. So a fire in a stalk-waste stack was a significant loss.

It could be taken as a signal that there was no further need to hurry, as well.

The house Berize had built for himself—still in the

process of construction, but with two rooms and the waste-pit finished—seemed undamaged and intact in the beams of the speedsils' headlamps. Gavrill decided against going into Berize's house with a weapon in each hand. It would be dawn soon. He wanted to be able to see what was what in the clear light of day before he went inside.

Haldane led one of the other speedsils out to the backbehind of Berize's house but Gavrill kept Garee with him. If they found a murdered man, it would be her first encounter with death by violence, and Gavrill wanted to be there.

The flashing signal from a speedsil's headlamps—a rapid pattern, three pulses in blue, shining from the back of Berize's house—told Gavrill that Haldane had found a body. Gavrill sighed. "I expect we'd all better go around back, Garee."

Out behind the little low-built house, the stalk-waste fire was down to scant embers smoldering in a field-expedient firepit. It was a well-built firepit, with a good wide firebreak surrounding it and a fine mesh net over all to protect against stray sparks blowing into dry grass beyond the firebreak on a breezy night.

But the night was calm. Anybody could have built that pit in practically no time. Gavrill had put them up himself. All it took was a pass or two in a speedsil with an improvised drag to scrape the dirt down to bare earth, and a few basic supplies. Serac Hearths had been built on prairie land. It didn't take much to scrape off the topsoil.

This fire had been going for the most part of a day, Gavrill thought, judging by the probable rate of consumption and how close to extinction it was. There was a body laid out alongside the firepit; it seemed to be intact, as well as still fully clothed. Gavrill didn't see any obvious wounds, no sign of interference. But people like Berize almost never died of natural causes.

"Cleanup crew?" Gavrill asked Haldane, who nodded.

"On its way, Gav. One of my people will make a report once the sun's up and we can see better." There'd be an autopsy, of a sort. Which wouldn't tell them much. Someone with experience and training had done—or supervised—this killing, judging by the elegance of the firepit. "It'll have been someone who knew too much of Berize's history, maybe. I'm sorry, Gav. I know you wanted it to work."

Too much history. Somebody at Serac Hearths had let Berize work like a bondslave for years, and then killed him before he'd won through to a limited sort of membership in the community. It wasn't for Gavrill to judge, but he didn't like it, because he smelled malice underneath it all, not a clean settling of scores. Violation of a social contract.

"Too early to tell about a culprit, I suppose," Gavrill said. Garee had retreated to the company of her peers, the other members of the Firewatch, younger people all. Gavrill was alone with Haldane. They could talk.

There weren't altogether many people in the settlement that Gavrill could talk to about some things. Haldane and Remo. Remo wasn't here. Gavrill didn't think he'd be ready to talk to her about what this meant for a few days yet.

He'd got distracted, Gavrill realized, and Haldane had apparently noticed. Gavrill shook his thoughts back into order to finish his point. "We'll have to try to find out who it was, anyway. There was an agreement.

And we're only as good as our word, any of us. This can't happen again, Haldane. Ever."

History had to stay history. There could be no hope for hope, for safety and security and confidence in the future, if people could be murdered without consequences. And yet Gavrill was confident within a fair degree of certainty that they'd never be able to prove who'd killed Berize.

"Maybe we don't say there was a crime," Haldane suggested. "Maybe once the dawn comes we'll find it might not have been a killing. The young and innocent aren't going to see things their tired, old, used-up seniors might. Could be we've made a mistake, you and I. Could be it was just an unfortunate accident. I don't see any wildflowers."

Haldane was right. All of those things were perfectly plausible. But one of the people here was Gavrill's daughter; Gavrill wanted a clear-cut resolution for her sake, to nurture her faith in justice. It was important for people to have something to believe in, and Gavrill was suddenly unsure whether Haldane could be that man any longer.

"If only I could be confident." He didn't have to spell things out for Haldane. "Sure that it won't happen again. It's a stain on Serac Hearths. I want to be certain, Hal."

The sky was beginning to show pink and gold on the horizon. Gavrill could see Haldane's expression—calm, confident, even compassionate. That was a side of Haldane's character that nobody but Gavrill—and Remo—had ever, would ever, see.

"I'm quite secure in that," Haldane said. "No more Berizes. No more murders. You'll see."

And with no better assurances than that, Gavrill had to get on with things.

Standing on the river's ancient banks above the Serac Steeps that descended down to the river's flood plain, Gavrill folded his arms across his chest to signal his concern. He had to be calm.

They'd found young Esko alive. That was good news. Esko had been swept down toward the river by a shallow avalanche and trapped in the scree in the run-out zone; that was all. Other news was not so good. Esko had had no business being here—alone—in the first place.

Gavrill watched for the ambulance.

That limp and unresponsive body could have been Gavrill's own son, Rega. Rega and Esko were the same age, not quite fifteen turnings. But Esko would be all right. The children of Serac Hearths were well fed and lovingly nurtured, and if meals didn't vary much at least there was plenty for everybody these days. There was no reason why Esko's bones wouldn't knit straight and true.

"Transport just arriving, Provost Marshal." Gavrill's oldest daughter, Garee—now nearly twenty—would know that there was something wrong between Gavrill and Haldane because she'd known them both for most of her life. "Sickhouse on alert. Do either of you want to come with? Provost Marshall Gavrill? Cadre commander Haldane?"

"We'll hang on out here for a while." Gavrill had a few choice words to share with Haldane. "Meet you back, Garee."

Haldane had been about to speak, then didn't. It

had been years since they'd needed words to know what was on each other's minds.

"I'll notify the council rep, then, Provost Marshal," Garee said, with a crisp nod. "I'll be at the sickhouse. Leaving you to it, sir."

The medivac team had arrived. Gavrill watched his daughter join the rescuers at Esko's stretcher-side.

It had only been good luck that they'd found Esko when they had, after two days' lying in the scree. Gavrill knew he wasn't going to be so lucky when Esko's parents found out. They'd be demanding he take steps. Gavrill knew he should have taken steps years ago.

"You were telling old stories, I suppose," Gavrill said, at last. The medivac team wasn't losing any time; they were already on their way back to Serac Hearths' main base. "To the trainees."

Haldane scowled. It was a sore subject. Haldane felt embellishments improved the educational value of old tales. "Inspiring the next generation, Gav. These younglings have never had to run for their lives. We owe it to them to give them something to strive for."

Haldane inspired each new class of trainees on the Firewatch with a passionate desire to prove themselves against a standard that was meant to be aspirational, based on exaggerated exploits and only just achievable feats of endurance and daring. Haldane was good at inspiring people to overextend themselves, take ill-considered risks. It made him dangerous.

"We've had this conversation, Hal," Gavrill reminded him. "Several times. We shouldn't still be trusting you with people's children. This has got to stop. Once and for all."

This wasn't the first time a trainee had taken

unnecessary risks without understanding what they were getting themselves into. And that wasn't the worst of it. Berize's murder—five years old, now—still lurked at the edges of people's consciousness.

It was widely assumed to be Haldane's doing. And it didn't matter if it was or not, only that Haldane's romantic appeal to restless young people encouraged the idea that vigilante justice was a higher sort of law. That idea in itself was as deadly a challenge to the future of Serac Hearths as any plunderers' raid.

Hal didn't argue the point with Gavrill; he just argued. The specter of age and infirmity was coming up on the horizon to remind them all that they'd have to cede authority to the next generations, and it made Haldane cranky. "We owe it to them to raise them up as best we can. Teach them, Gav. Train them. Test them—"

Gavrill interrupted. "Serac Hearths has outgrown both of us, Hal. You won't change. You should leave, old friend."

Haldane snorted derisively. "You'll be coming with me, then, I suppose? You and Remo, and the rest of the old pioneers?"

That was Haldane's mean streak showing. Yet the taunt was not unfounded. "I haven't almost gotten anyone killed for at least ten years, Hal. You're a danger to our children. You have to go."

If Hal wouldn't go, he'd have to be removed. And if anybody was going to do that, it should be one of the veterans of the plunderer wars that did the deed, or the very act would reverberate in community mythology to poison the next generation. After all, Gavrill reminded himself, he could be a destabilizing influence, too. But he could be easily repudiated in the name of civil order, and his history of violence along with him. He was far from the man that Haldane was.

"Fight you for it," Haldane said suddenly. "That's only fair."

For a moment, Gavrill struggled with a sudden sense of the absurd—a conflict between *didn't see that coming* and *oh yes, you did.* More than anything, he was going to miss the way Haldane could come at him with that kind of thing, perfectly reasonable, perfectly insane.

Haldane nodded, clearly taking Gavrill's perplexity for agreement. "All right, then. We're lucky in the moon, wouldn't you say? Full, or as good as. We can do it in the street at Drange. You know where. There will be a final reckoning, Gav, once and for all, I promise."

Right back where this had all started, on that day so many years ago, when Gavrill had faced Berize at Drange Depot and only lived because Haldane had intervened for inscrutable reasons of his own.

Haldane had given Gavrill the weapon that had ultimately won the war for all of them, that day: himself. His genuine indifference to whether he lived or died, which made him uniquely dangerous. And the fact that Haldane did impossible things without thinking twice about them, because he didn't have any patience for trivialities like reason or common sense or consideration of alternative outcomes.

Gavrill had owed his life to Haldane from that day forward. But he wasn't going to give it back now without a fight for the future of Serac Hearths.

☆ ☆ ☆

It was a beautiful night. The moon was so full that its pink-tinged gold light cast shadows down the long-deserted streets of Warehouse Depot Drange. The stars and the eight planets of the Jarizon system shone clear, easily counted one by one. Gavrill had taught the nursery rhyme to his children. *Shining brightly in the sky, ask them by name why, oh, why.*

Gavrill's daughter should be sitting under a green tree on a little rise, listening to hoppers grazing in the dark, sharing a snack with friends, drinking pale, thin beer coaxed out of last harvest's gleanings. She wasn't. She was at the sickhouse with the rest of the young people, arguing about whether Esko had been stupid or brave, or neither, or both. Halfway to a mob.

Some of them would come looking for Haldane. Tripping over unseen obstacles on the ground beneath the beguiling moonlight would be the least of it. People would get hurt. Gavrill needed to work fast.

"Did we ever dream we'd come to this, Gav?" Haldane asked, with wistful regret in his voice. He'd kept his appointment, as Gavrill had known he would. Haldane was a man of his word. And because that was so, Gavrill had constructed an entire cathedral of excuses for Haldane's behavior over the years, gilt and glass and a vaulted ceiling, bells, choirs, chanting.

But the sorrowful fact was that Haldane was unfit for peace, he who'd been so perfectly fit for war. The aging warriors of Serac Hearths fought against new enemies now—wind and weather, crop blight, animal predation. Not Hal.

Gavrill shook his head. But Hal probably wouldn't be able to see it, because although the moon shone bright down the center of the street, the sides of the street were in shadow.

"Never," Gavrill said, loudly enough to be clearly heard across the thirty paces' separation between them. "I'll never forget that day, Hal. I was as good as dead."

"And it's proper that you remember," Hal agreed. But there'd been a third party there that day. There'd been Berize. Haldane had put himself body and soul into winning the war against Berize and his plunderers for no reason Gavrill had ever understood except for pure deviltry. Now, new fruit of Haldane's dangerous indifference to the consequences of his actions was ripening on the branch, carrying its own kind of poison.

"Still," Gavrill said, reluctantly but determined, "you're a danger to Serac Hearths, Hal. And I don't believe you'll leave without a fight." Because where in all of Jarizon space was there a place left for men like Haldane, like Gavrill?

"Indeed not," Haldane said, as thoughtfully as Gavrill had ever heard Haldane speak. Hal wasn't a thoughtful man. "In fact, Gav, I think that since our fellowship is over, I have every right to—"

Only at that instant did Gavrill realize that the little signs of restlessness he'd discerned imperfectly by moonlight was what Haldane looked like when he was raising a projectile weapon. Taking aim—at *him*.

By then it was already too late for Gavrill, betrayed by aging eyesight and shadows. He pulled his own sidearm out of his waistband anyway. He could at least get a shot off, for appearances' sake.

He never got the chance.

It was a whisper-rifle, for hunting small game. Gavrill didn't even hear the report. Haldane was already crumpling to his knees in the street, a black stain running like a bursting dam from Haldane's throat down his chest, his head hanging down by the merest thread of flesh like a grotesque ornament. The blood followed the bullet, a long black spray behind Haldane in the street. Haldane was dead already. Gavrill knew that.

And that Gavrill's partner, Remo, was still one of the best hunters in Serac Hearths.

Hal fell slowly backward into the dust, his hand held on the level as he toppled. There was another shot, then—but a much louder one, and from Haldane himself. Haldane had meant to kill him. It was a strange sort of a parting word, sorrowful respect, companionship, love.

Gavrill could hear the muted crunching of a speedsil coming up the street behind him. "Get moving," Remo said. "Someone will have heard. They have to find him dead, Gav. Come *on*."

She'd aimed carefully, a grazing shot to one side of the neck to leave the head sufficiently intact for Hal to be recognizable, even dead. She was right. If the body wasn't found before the night-predators got to it, if it couldn't be definitely identified, some of the young people would believe that Haldane was still out there, somewhere, and go out in search of the vanished hero.

Remo and Gavrill had to get clear. Gavrill slipped into the speedsil as it moved past him, hanging on to a grab-bar as it picked up speed.

The time for transcendent gallantry, for desperate courage, for iron determination to overcome overwhelming odds—

That time was past. Gavrill and Remo would raise their children, build a secure society, look to the future. Haldane would live forever, a monument to heroic legends of times gone by. The future of Serac Hearths would bring its own challenges, but—at the end of all things—the legendary warrior Haldane would have no further part in it.

HIGH NOON ON PROXIMA CENTAURI B

Cliff Winnig

The shadows shortened toward nothing the closer Jocelyn Stark rode to High Noon.

Her eight-legged sand lizard, swift and sinuous, ran along the access road that paralleled the train tracks. Jocelyn leaned forward in the saddle and patted Zamir's neck. Even through UV-resistant gloves, she could feel his iridescent scales sliding beneath her fingers.

"Just a little farther, old friend. A little faster." Her mount's weaving gait grew more pronounced as he picked up speed. Sand lizards couldn't be spurred, nor did they seem to understand human speech. But they had an empathic connection to their riders and followed their wishes with eerie exactitude.

If she pushed him too hard, Jocelyn knew, his heart would burst. Zamir knew his limits, but he'd also pick up on how much she needed to beat that train into town.

She leaned further forward, so close she could smell

the desert on him. All she could do now was reduce their drag and hope for the best.

As their speed increased, the hot wind fell heavily upon them. The Dragon's Breath, folks called it, endlessly exhaled across the hardscrabble land. Jocelyn's hat blocked the worst of it, but still it burned.

Proxima Centauri b—PCb, or PeaceBe to the locals, the peace of the grave always in mind—did not rotate as it swung around its sun in a tight orbit. Tidally locked but protected by a strong magnetic field, it held onto its atmosphere with a desperate grip. Its winds blew constantly from noon to midnight and back, past the ring of twilight around its middle where most of the native life thrived.

Jocelyn felt the blast-furnace heat through a haze of exhaustion. She'd ridden for over a week (the habit of thinking in weeks died hard), from a mining town partway to East Twilight, where she'd met her contact. She'd hated the whole trip and all the cloak-and-dagger precautions that had come with it. Hell, she hated leaving High Noon at the best of times. But staggering amounts of money were involved, amounts that could seemingly bend the laws of physics, the type of fortune that had moved human colonists 4.2 light-years to an alien solar system. This time, the money was funding the hostile takeover of one mining giant by another. And hostile here meant killers. Killers who even now were on a train heading to High Noon. Her contact had details on them and their target, but the deal had been that Jocelyn had to come in person, alone. She couldn't just send her deputy.

So she had, quietly and unofficially—not by train, not by windflyer. Sand lizards didn't send telemetry, and they were common enough not to attract attention. They were even fast.

But trains were faster, and the killers had boarded one sooner than her contact had expected. She'd raced that train home, her lead dwindling all the while.

Jocelyn looked back along the tracks. She couldn't yet see the dust blown up by the train, but she felt its approach as an ache in her chest, a pounding at her temples. She couldn't let it overtake her.

She turned back to the road and peered past the brim of her hat. The distant needle of High Noon's central tower sliced up from the horizon. It rose like a mirage above the windswept plain and shimmered in the heat haze.

For all that it hugged its sun closely, PeaceBe was a dark world. Proxima Centauri glowed mainly in the infrared. Even the planet's dayside looked twilit to humans without night-vision augs, but those were standard, as was a wardrobe full of UV-protective gear. Jocelyn could see every rock between here and the tower, every short, sharp shadow, all in shades of rust.

Soon the surrounding circle of solar panels came into view, a black line near the tower's base that stretched across half the horizon. The tower itself rose from a huge power station. It broadcast that power along microwave beams that led to each of the four main Twilight cities. High Noon had grown up around the tower and beneath the solar panels. The panels' shade couldn't fully protect the streets from the heat, though they did make the town livable. Technically.

Perhaps longing for that shade, Zamir picked up even more speed, his legs now a blur. He was, after all, a creature of the twilight ring. He could survive planetary noon, yes, but he normally wouldn't go within a thousand kilometers of it.

Some instinct made her look back again, and there it was: the train. A plume of dust rose in its wake, but even the train itself was visible now.

Damn. Jocelyn leaned low and held on as Zamir ran on.

She could hear the train by the time they reached the edge of the solar panels. Just under their lip sat the sticklike figure of Barney Ng atop a sand lizard of his own. He was already turning his mount back toward town, its outskirts still kilometers away—or his lizard, knowing he wanted it, had turned herself.

Jocelyn whooshed past him, not slowing down, as the solar panels abruptly cut off the huge red sun directly above. Running lights along the road caused her augmented eyes to switch to normal sight, and color returned. She rode through shafts of crimson light as they ran across periodic gaps in the solar panels above. The wind died down, and what remained was merely uncomfortably warm.

Barney caught up and rode beside her, his lizard pacing Zamir.

"Marshal," he said across the gap.

"Barney." She nodded to him. "Thanks for covering for me."

"No problem. I don't think anyone found out you were gone. Suspected, maybe, but unable to prove it." Barney offered his lopsided grin, skin tight on his left cheek where a scar ran. "I assume they're on the train."

Jocelyn just nodded. The train was almost upon them now. She could tell by the way its headlights shone on the pillars holding up the solar panels.

"How many?"

"Three, according to my source."

Barney went silent a moment. Then he gave her a sidelong look. "I'm glad they didn't send just one or two. I wouldn't want them to think we'd gone soft."

High Noon was built on the first landing site on PCb, but no one stayed there who didn't have to. Those with warrants for their arrest in the Twilights or who just had no better prospects made it their home, unless they preferred the chill of Midnight. They called it HN for short, though many said it stood for Hell No.

The impression that nickname gave was wholly accurate. High Noon had been assembled from whatever had been handy: shipping containers, discarded spaceship parts, even flare-baked mud bricks. A good chunk of it lay underground, off tunnels that ran under the streets, all the better to escape the heat and the frequent solar flares. Most locals lived a level or two beneath the surface. Those who passed through High Noon did so as quickly as possible.

The train station threw these distinctions into sharp relief. While High Noon's starport was used mostly for freight, sometimes travelers disembarked there rather than the newer starport in Midnight. Well-dressed immigrants from the asteroid belt or the system's diminutive Oort Cloud waited on the landing platform, resting in power chairs while they acclimated to the nearly 1.2 g gravity well. For them, High Noon was a brief stop on their way to a Twilight city.

Dust-covered locals filled the rest of the space, some in mining uniforms, others in threadbare outfits, often with minimal UV protection. Beggars panhandled for what they could. Thieves slipped in between the immigrants, hoping to slip out again with something for their trouble. Both groups melted into the crowd at the sight of the marshal and her deputy, who raced into the square astride sand lizards that slalomed around people and other obstacles. The lizards were used to that, though it spooked the out-of-towners considerably. The pair had slowed down when they'd hit the outskirts of town, but not by much.

When the train doors opened, Jocelyn and Barney sat there atop their lizards, smartguns already drawn. Jocelyn pulled two chips from an inside pocket of her duster. They were a gift from her informant. She handed one to Barney and slotted the other into her gun's targeting system. "It's got all three of them."

Barney nodded and slotted his in as well. Now both guns could scent the blood of their adversaries.

The new arrivals were staring up at them now, some trying to hide it but most not. More looked at Barney than at Jocelyn, no doubt wondering how a man with his slight build could stand the gravity like he'd been born to it, which he obviously hadn't. But Barney had acclimated long ago. He always moved efficiently and with purpose.

Jocelyn's smartgun beeped. One of the killers was close. He appeared a car down a moment later and looked right at her: a cyborg, one of the paired operatives who went by Zero and One. He smiled under Proxima-colored artificial eyes and stepped aside for his counterpart. Both wore tailored suits with the Triple Sun Mining logo tastefully sewn onto the lapel. The left arm of the first ended in a hub bristling with multiple weapons where his hand should be. The second cyborg's right arm mirrored it. So Zero and One respectively, Jocelyn recalled.

Neither made a hostile move as Jocelyn and Barney brought their sand lizards around and approached.

At length, the third member of the trio stepped out from between the cyborgs: Yana Morozova. She wore a slit-skirt suit and showed no obvious augs. She had a head full of subtle ones, though, according to Jocelyn's source.

"Marshal," she said, her voice as smooth as the ice plains by Midnight. "Deputy."

"Welcome to High Noon," Jocelyn said. "But I'm afraid you won't be able to see the sights. This train turns around in twenty minutes." Already, the new immigrants were nervously rolling past the group and boarding with evident relief. "You're gonna be on it."

Morozova smiled, showing perfect teeth. "I do not think so."

Now Jocelyn did raise her gun. It chirped as it acquired the target. "I'm afraid I must insist."

Morozova shook her head. A complex pattern of braids framed her face. "We have committed no crime, Marshal. There is no warrant for our arrest."

"No, but I'm authorized to detain anyone who threatens the peace."

Morozova's smile vanished. She took a step forward. "My dear marshal, the peace is not what we threaten. I promise you, we shall not disturb it. Now if you will excuse me, my colleagues and I have business. It will be quiet business and, as I said, peaceful." She began walking toward them, although the cyborgs didn't move.

Yeah, like the peace of PeaceBe. "You have ten seconds to board that train, Ms. Morozova."

The assassin raised a delicate eyebrow at the sound of her name, but otherwise didn't react. Part of Jocelyn admired how calmly she stared down the barrel of a smartgun that had her number. The rest of her wondered what Morozova knew that she didn't.

"I'm serious, Morozova."

The woman paused and raised a manicured hand, showing a clearly expensive watch. "Shall I count for you? Ten. Nine. Eight..."

Jocelyn fired at two. To be fair, she picked a nonlethal target, but she squeezed the trigger just the same.

Only nothing happened.

She looked down at her smartgun in time to watch it power off. Judging by Barney's sudden curse, his had done the same. She looked up again as Zero and One vaulted over them with cyber-assisted leaps. Morozova darted between the sand lizards at the same time, and all three dashed down the stairs that led to the nearest tunnel.

"Dammit!" Jocelyn hopped off Zamir and sprinted after them, but by the time she reached the tunnel, the trio had vanished.

"Would you really have shot her?" Barney sat at his desk, scrolling through a projection in the air above. Analyses of security footage competed for space with rumors and informant reports.

Jocelyn paced the length of the small marshal's office, furious with herself. "Didn't have a lot of choice, did I? But no, not fatally. Just... enough to stop their mission." She paused and glared at nothing in particular, at everything in the room. "Damn that woman and her micro-EMP! How often you figure she can do that?"

"All day and still have power left to hack into HN's city servers." A map popped up amid the data displays. Blue lines snaked across it. "Okay, I've got probable routes and destinations. Normally, I'd transfer them to your watch . . ."

Jocelyn nodded, studying the holographic map while she could. "We can't use any electronics, but we know the town. We're going to have to split up. You track the killers. I'll locate their targets. We'll meet up every two hours, usual spot."

She turned to the hologram floating above her own desk and studied for one last time the features of the middle-aged blonde woman and her twelve-year-old son: Alice and Rory Strauss-Agarwal, the widow and son of mining magnate Kumar Agarwal. He'd been the victim of a hostile takeover by Triple Sun. Alice and Rory had escaped with their lives and a little untraceable cash as stowaways on a cargo ship, according to Jocelyn's source.

Rory had grown up in luxury on a corporate station, the son and heir of a trillionaire, but Alice had spent her formative years as upper middle class. Even more, she'd had a stint in her teens as a homeless runaway. Maybe she could hide them from the killers long enough for Jocelyn to find them and get them both out of town.

Maybe. But only if Jocelyn hurried. She went to her desk, opened a drawer, and pulled out a small oak box. Like its contents, it had come with her from Earth, had lain beside her in her sleeper coffin during the twenty-year trip. She withdrew the silver chain from under her shirt and used the small key to open the physical lock. She heard Barney come up behind her. He'd only seen the inside of the box once himself.

Jocelyn popped the lid and pulled out her Colt .44 revolver, a family heirloom. She inspected the gun. She kept it cleaned and ready, occasionally even took it out in the desert for target practice, but she always did that alone. The bullets that still sat boxed in the drawer had been assembled from locally-printed parts, but with a high degree of accuracy. She chambered six rounds, took all the extras she had, and holstered the gun. The smart holster molded itself to the unfamiliar weapon.

She looked at Barney. "Ready?"

Barney turned to the wall behind his own desk and took down the sheathed sword. A modern weapon, it had a monomolecular edge. "Ready."

Jocelyn nodded. "Be careful out there."

Since it was always high noon in High Noon, people were always about. They scuttled like sand crabs under hats and dusters, some on foot and some on sand lizard. They dodged each other and the robotic delivery sleds in a kind of chaotic ballet, never once looking up between solar panels toward the vast red disc of the sun, never mind the invisible stars beyond.

Jocelyn rode toward the center of town, to the unfashionable eastern side opposite the market. The Four Winds Bar and Grill squatted there at the base of the power station, like a weed growing next to a towering oak. It got its name from the air currents above the city: the rising column at high noon, which became the jet streams that fanned out across the world.

Everything switched to monochrome as she entered the bar and her night-vision augs kicked in. Jim liked to keep the place dim, like the twilit sands beyond the town lights.

"Marshal." Jim's deep bass cut across the conversation's buzz, beneath his patrons' vocal ranges. "The usual?"

Jocelyn shook her head, thinking wistfully of a double shot of single-malt. "I wish. Seen Simon today?"

Jim snorted. "See him every day. The usual table."

Jocelyn touched the brim of her hat and gave him a nod by way of thanks. She crossed the room and took the stairs down to the lower bar. Underground, the decor switched from modern patchwork to Old West, with actual hand-painted murals of cowboys and buffalo along three of the walls. A second bar, tended by Jim's daughter Anna Mae, ran the length of the fourth wall. The underground bar had a two-drink minimum, and strictly top shelf, but the marshal was given a pass—when she was there on business, that is.

Seeing her approach, the goons at Simon Le Blanc's table stood and stepped aside. Jocelyn took one of the vacated seats.

Simon gazed at her impassively. His poker face was unparalleled. "You're here about the woman and her son."

Jocelyn nodded.

"Officially, no one's seen them. Unofficially, no one's seen them." He raised a hand to cut off Jocelyn's response. "You know I'd like to help. I always like to help . . . when it doesn't affect business. This is more than a business concern, however. My life isn't worth spit if I interfere, nor is anyone else's in my organization. Triple Sun can do that. It can reach out of the sky and squash us all. And why not? It wouldn't hurt their bottom line. They might even install their own people in our place. High Noon may be independent, but we're independent by their leave."

"So you've got nothing."

"Nothing. And if you'll take the advice of a violent man with a violent past, walk away from this. I've been a pro for decades now, and these people make me look like a Johnny-come-lately."

Jocelyn knew better than to bang her head against a wall that would never give. She stood.

Simon looked up at her. "I'm serious, Marshal. Really. It's good of you to want to save the kid and his mom, but I don't want you to wind up like the last marshal." He grinned, one of the few times she'd seen him do that in more than a decade of High Noon law enforcement. "I'd miss crossing swords with you."

Jocelyn checked the wall clock on her way out. She had time to sweep the aboveground buildings in Squatters' Alley before her first scheduled rendezvous with Barney.

Barney didn't make the rendezvous. Jocelyn waited ten minutes, then swore up a storm. Quietly, so as not to attract too much attention. She flagged down a message drone. When it landed in her hand, she spoke to it in an undertone. "Find Deputy Marshal Barney Ng. When you spot him, come find me." Drones could legally search the town's surveillance cameras as they flew physically through the streets and tunnels. Normally, she'd just tell her watch to find him, but that wasn't an option with Morozova's EMP attack. She watched the drone buzz away, then walked to where she'd tied Zamir.

She had just climbed up into the saddle when the rising sequence of tones sounded a Flare Warning. It came from every street corner.

Zamir knew the drill. He raced a block and a half to the nearest sand-lizard-friendly ramp that led belowground. As Jocelyn rode, the High Noon Astronomer's amplified voice detailed the size and probable duration of the flare.

She continued her search on the first level below the surface. Not the ideal place to be during a flare, but not too dangerous, if it wasn't a big one. Crucially, it was the less-expensive area, which made it a better place for someone to go to ground.

Jocelyn spent the next few hours in growing frustration. No one had seen the pair. No one had seen the killers. Unlikely, of course, in a town the size of High Noon, but Simon must have had word spread around. She didn't think he was actively aiding the killers, but he was blocking her search at every turn. Jocelyn resolved to bust him for something as soon as all this was over.

The drone found her hours later. She was standing beside Zamir, returning her canteen to his saddlebags while he drank from a public trough. It wasn't the drone she'd sent. This one was a courier for the drone company itself. It hovered by her head and informed her that the marshal's office would be billed for the destruction of the first drone.

"Details," she demanded, and it gave her an intersection on the second level down. There the drone had apparently been blown apart.

Zamir started moving even as she settled back into the saddle.

Benny the Fish, one of Simon's senior henchmen, waited for her at the intersection. He looked at her with the sad round eyes that had earned him his nickname. "For what it's worth, Marshal, we're sorry."

A crowd had gathered outside the Hôtel du Monde. Jocelyn pushed her way through it and past the owner, who was rapidly explaining the situation in an ever-rising pitch.

When she reached the kitchen, the first thing she noticed was the blood. The walls and even the ceiling had been splattered with it. The second thing she noticed was the pair of cybernetic weapons hubs lying on the floor, sliced cleanly off their hosts' arms. At the back of the kitchen, near the open door to the alley tunnel beyond, she found out the full extent of the battle.

To his credit, Barney had sliced Zero and One to pieces, but they in turn had blasted several large holes in his chest. He lay staring up at the knives attached to a magnetic rack above the counter. The light reflected off the blades shone in his eyes. His own blade remained in his grip, even in death.

With reverence, Jocelyn stepped around him to the back alley and found what was left of Alice Strauss-Agarwal. The former trillionaire wore the hotel's kitchen staff uniform. A ragged hole lay in the center of her chest, right where her heart had been. Blood pooled around her. It had already started to congeal about her limbs and her splayed-out blonde hair.

Of the kid there was no sign. Nor of Yana Morozova.

Benny the Fish had followed her as far as the kitchen threshold. There he stood, head bowed in respect, though for some or all of the dead she couldn't tell.

Jocelyn made her way back to him. He stepped aside to let her pass, but she shoved him against the wall. He looked up, met her eyes with his fishlike orbs, which widened even more with what he saw there.

"Where's the boy?" she growled through gritted teeth. "What about the Russian?"

Benny gulped. "The boy wasn't here. Neither was Morozova." It didn't surprise Jocelyn that Simon's man knew the assassin's name. "She got a job here under an assumed name, but where they were staying..." He shrugged. "Simon doesn't know."

"If I find out you're holding out on me, Triple Sun will be the least of your concerns."

Benny gulped again. He looked like a guppy. "Understood, Marshal."

"Anything else?" Her whisper filled the silence in that empty room. Somewhere behind her, a pot boiled over, causing the burner to sizzle.

"We think they were up on the surface, but not in any of the usual places. They broke in somewhere. The kid...he's good with technology."

All at once, the rage left Jocelyn. She felt empty, like a drained shot glass.

She let Benny go. He slid out from between her and the wall and stepped back into the restaurant section, which was crowded with rubberneckers kept at bay by haggard-looking hotel staff.

Jocelyn grabbed a pair of linen towels and covered Barney and Alice, making sure to close Barney's eyes as she did so. She left the cyborgs where they lay.

That done, she glanced back through the kitchen door. Benny was nowhere to be seen. The manager was building up the courage to come talk to her.

"Place a call to the coroner," she told him. Then she slipped out the back to the alley beyond.

A town the size of High Noon held a fair number of law enforcement officers, but nearly all of them were private: corporate security officers for the various mining giants in the system. The starport and the power station both had a few of their own as well.

Still, someone needed to handle the cases that fell outside the sundry corporate jurisdictions. It didn't take a large staff, really. Jocelyn and Barney had been able to handle it all. But now Jocelyn had no one she could call for backup, no one who'd support her next move. At least Triple Sun's security wouldn't help Morozova. They needed plausible deniability. Moreover, their rivals wouldn't dare interfere with a hit of this magnitude. Jocelyn was on her own.

She used the tunnel route to reach the marshal's office, which had an entrance off a main thoroughfare on the first level underground. There she checked the astronomer's report. The flare was dying down but still dangerous. Jocelyn also scanned the system for any reports of break-ins.

She found one immediately. It had already hit the local news: the power station's ground-floor and underground doors had been methodically sealed, all of them, within the last hour. A molecular seal. It was going to take at least another hour to cut through any of them, according to PCb Power's press liaison. Jocelyn's incoming message queue was blinking red with all the reports. If she'd had her watch, she'd have known about it fifty-three minutes earlier.

Rory Strauss-Agarwal probably couldn't have done that trick. He and his mother had fled too quickly to bring along such specialized mining equipment. But Morozova . . . if she'd discovered Rory's location and wanted to seal him in, that's exactly what she'd use.

However, she also might use it to throw the town marshal off the track, but a quick search didn't show any other reports. So either she'd kept secret her real location, or she was even now somewhere inside the power station. With Rory.

Jocelyn grabbed her mesh UV mask and the light, UV-resistant barding that would provide extra coverage for Zamir, just in case she had to go up on the surface. Then she rode out to the first-level entrance to the power station, where a crew was trying to cut through the sealed door.

Pablo Hernandez, head of power station security, stood frowning at the technician who directed the robotic cutter along the edge of the door. There wasn't even a seam, just a shiny area of melted metal where the doorframe had been.

"How long?" she asked Pablo without preamble. She hadn't bothered to dismount.

"At least half an hour, she tells me." He indicated the technician with a nod of his head. "I can't reach anyone in the building. Flare interference, maybe." But even he didn't sound convinced. Point-to-point underground comms should still work, with only a wall between him and the recipient—if the recipient were still capable of answering.

"Is there any other way into the building?"

Pablo frowned at her now. "No. The bastard—whoever they are—sealed every damn door. Emergency exits too."

Jocelyn wracked her brain for what she knew about the power plant. She hadn't been in there in years. "What about the observation deck?"

Pablo shook his head. "Just windows. There's a small emergency exit, but not even a fire escape leading up to it. Just an extendable ladder. It's sealed from the outside. The ladder retracts. No one could scale that slope, even if there weren't a flare."

"Thanks," Jocelyn said. "I don't have my watch, so I'll be out of contact. The suspect can generate a micro-EMP field." Pablo swore at this new information. "Send me a drone when you manage to get in."

Pablo nodded grimly and returned his attention to the technician, who'd cut through about three more centimeters while they'd been talking.

Zamir already knew where Jocelyn wanted to go. He slipped through the crowd until they reached the nearest ramp up.

A ladder ran up each solar panel's support column for maintenance purposes, but for her plan to work, Jocelyn needed to reach one of the periodic gaps large enough for a sand lizard to scramble through. That meant riding on the trackside road for several hundred meters, then turning left onto a narrow access road.

The running lights faded behind them as they shot along the access road, but Jocelyn's night vision didn't kick in. Because of the flare, sunlight poured through the gaps, much brighter than usual. A crimson glow lay upon everything in sight—bright, but so very different from her memories of Earth.

At last she saw the gap ahead. Zamir sped up automatically and vaulted them into the air, his eight legs more than a match for PeaceBe's gravity. They landed on top of a solar panel with a thud so hard Jocelyn's jaw clenched with the impact. Zamir sprinted for the tower.

Even hundreds of meters away it loomed over them, a cone that gradually tapered till it reached a level ringed by parabolic dishes. Those sent the powerful and instantly deadly microwaves toward each Twilight city. A dozen meters above them, a row of windows marked the observation deck. Zamir crunched some of the tiny cleaning bots as he S-curved forward across the solar panels.

Jocelyn kept her gaze up, toward the row of windows. A shadow moved across several of them. Whether hunter, prey, or simply one of the workers trapped in the building, she had no idea.

How had the kid and his mother stayed hidden there so long? Jocelyn wondered. The plant had excellent surveillance security. It had to. Yet the pair had lived there, hidden somewhere, maybe since they'd made planetfall, while Alice had snuck out to work one of the few jobs that still paid in cash and allowed her to take home food.

Morozova had broken through the security as well, tracking the son. Both had the skills and equipment needed to pull that off. *Dammit,* she thought. *I hate big money.*

The tower grew until it just became a wall, curving

out of sight in either direction. Soon they reached the last of the solar panels. Jocelyn leaned all the way forward in the saddle and held onto Zamir's neck, her gloves gripping the UV-resistant barding. Zamir leapt across the meter-wide gap and onto the side of the tower. Jocelyn stayed in her saddle with the impact and the start of the climb. In the wild, sand lizards could climb near-vertical cliffs, but the metal-and-ceramic walls of the tower offered little purchase. The climb was slow and involved this or that pair of legs losing a grip, claws scraping against the surface until they found a fresh toehold.

He didn't fall, though, and they made progress. As they drew closer to the ring of power dishes and steered between two of them, Jocelyn got a sense of how huge they were. Each one fired a beam hundreds of kilometers to a relay station on the way to its ultimate destination in a city.

Jocelyn focused on the effort of staying in the saddle until a rifle report broke her reverie. She looked up in time to see bits of glass fly away from one of the windows as a second and a third shot rang out. Then came a crash and a rain of glass shards falling seemingly in slow motion. Jocelyn ducked her head, and they fell on the top of her hat and shoulders. She leaned to the side, not trusting empathy alone to tell Zamir he had to get off that approach, had to hide below one of the dishes.

They'd only gone a meter or two before the first bullet struck Zamir. Somewhere above, having shot and kicked out the window, Morozova leaned out and fired a rifle straight down at them.

The lizard took the blow silently, stoically, and kept

climbing. They were in the shadow of a dish now, its mast giving them partial cover, but it wasn't enough. Another bullet struck Zamir, this time in his neck. A spray of blood—red even in a world of red—splashed across Jocelyn, drenching her hat and one of her duster's sleeves.

She willed him to turn back, to climb back down. They'd find another way in. Somehow.

Zamir seemed to reach a decision on his own, however. He sprinted up the tower again, past the mast and up, up toward the broken window.

"No!" Jocelyn shouted, but Zamir ignored her. In fact, he drowned her out.

Sand lizards rarely vocalized. In mating season, the females would bellow across the wastelands. The males would shout at one another, trying to frighten rivals answering the same call. A mother would coo to her silent children to get them to go to sleep.

They only vocalized on one other occasion, and this was it. Zamir began to sing. There was no other way to think of it—rising and falling in pitch, mournful in affect, haunting in its alien beauty.

A death dirge.

Far below, answering calls came from other sand lizards. Those few on the aboveground streets and those within earshot in the tunnels below: a chorus, an answer, a communal acknowledgment of loss.

"No . . ." Jocelyn choked out the sound, even as more blood poured over her, even as Zamir's pace began to slacken. He was almost there now, almost level with the broken window. Now Jocelyn could see Morozova, an expression of cool assessment as she took aim at the shifting shape below her, directly at Jocelyn now.

Jocelyn fired first.

She hadn't even realized she'd drawn her Colt, narrowed her gaze, taken aim. Her arm flew back with the recoil, but her left hand held a fistful of Zamir's barding. She stayed in the saddle.

Morozova cursed and vanished from the window. Zamir's song began to falter as he drew alongside the shattered window and held on.

Zamir's golden eyes were closing. Still holding the Colt, Jocelyn hugged him around his neck, heedless of the blood continuing to drench her, her cheek against blood-slick barding. Through the armor, she could feel the warmth still in him. He smelled of deserts and journeys and long twilit wanderings watched by a sun three times as big in the sky as Earth's.

He shivered, then shook. She couldn't stay, she knew. She had to go, had to save the child. One last squeeze and she let go and reached to the side. He angled his body to make it easier for her. She grabbed the bottom sill, her gloves protecting her from the knives of glass still attached, and swung herself into the room.

The observation deck filled the whole of the floor. A trail of blood led from the window past the central elevator shaft to an emergency stairwell near the far wall. There was no one else there.

She caught a movement in the corner of her eye and turned to see Zamir leaning away from the wall, his front legs already losing their purchase. His eyes snapped open and locked onto hers.

Do good. He could have spoken it out loud, so clearly did she understand it.

Then he was gone: falling, falling to the panels far below.

Jocelyn sprinted across the floor. The crash came from outside just as she wrenched open the stairwell door.

She ducked and rolled onto the landing, but no shots came. A maintenance ladder led up, while a metal stairwell led down. The stairs ended six meters down at a firewall and a door to the lower levels. That, she saw, had been sealed the same way as the outside doors.

So Jocelyn climbed the ladder, up through a maintenance hatch to a level full of machinery. It hummed and buzzed all around her. On instinct, she rolled again as soon as she reached the level.

A shot rang out and pinged against the wall behind her. Crouching, still holding her Colt, Jocelyn ran along a narrow catwalk. Another shot rang out. This time, she could tell it came somewhere from her right, and she dove behind cover. All around her came the noise of the machines and their metallic smell.

Morozova's smooth voice cut through the buzz. "Marshal Stark, let's be reasonable about this. I don't want to have to kill you. It creates paperwork."

Jocelyn gritted her teeth but stayed silent as she looked everywhere for the source of that sound. With the machines confusing her senses, it was impossible to tell.

"Yes, we killed your deputy and your animal companion," Morozova said, "but your side killed my cyborgs. They're hard to replace. They require special parts, special training. So, you see, we are equally inconvenienced, equally bereft. It can stop here."

Jocelyn hated making a sound, hated giving away her position, but if there were a chance . . . "You killed the mother." Did she hear a breath from somewhere above? She searched the machines above her, revolver ready, but saw nothing. "The kid's no threat to you. Withdraw. Leave. Go back to your station."

"No. That is nonnegotiable." The voice came from behind, and Jocelyn spun around. Morozova stood there, pointing a long, sinister pistol at her. "Goodbye, Marshal."

A shadow fell upon the assassin. Morozova fired, but the shot went wide. It ricocheted off a wall into some equipment.

Jocelyn was on her feet, running toward Morozova. *The boy!* Rory had leapt onto his mother's killer and hung on, one arm around her neck, punching wildly with the other. Not weak blows, either, for all that he was still twelve. Rory screamed wordlessly, eyes squeezed shut.

With a smooth motion like water flowing over rocks, Morozova threw him off her and onto the catwalk. She aimed and fired three rounds.

These too went wide as Jocelyn collided with her and they tumbled back onto the deck. They both reached for the other's gun, but Morozova managed to roll them over and wind up on top. She smashed Jocelyn's right hand onto the catwalk, hard, and the Colt flew out of her grip. Jocelyn watched it slide along the catwalk and tumble off the side, heard it clatter its way down.

But Jocelyn had found Morozova's right hand too. She grabbed the wrist and twisted hard.

Morozova yelped, yet she held onto her gun. With her free hand she grabbed at Jocelyn's left, only to slide off because of Zamir's blood. She head-butted Jocelyn, and Jocelyn's skull slammed onto the catwalk, hard enough for her to see stars.

A wave of nausea hit. Jocelyn lost her grip on

Morozova's right hand. Morozova sat up and punched her in the nose once, twice. A loud crack and spike of pain accompanied the first blow. Jocelyn was sure her nose was broken.

On the catwalk behind them, she heard Rory running away, scrambling down the ladder into the stairwell. *Good*, she thought. *He's showing some sense.*

Morozova punched Jocelyn once more as she struggled up, then kicked her in the ribs and ran after the boy. She'd reached the ladder and started down it by the time Jocelyn managed to stand.

With a casual motion, Morozova raised her gun, aimed at Jocelyn, and fired.

The impact knocked Jocelyn onto her butt. Her left shoulder exploded in pain. A wave of vertigo struck her. With Zamir's blood all over her, she couldn't tell how bad she was bleeding.

As she sat there, the pain in her nose and shoulder moved from sharp to throbbing. Annoyingly, the waves of pain weren't in sync.

She felt Zamir's gaze upon her again. *Do good.*

Jocelyn staggered to her feet. She walked back to the ladder, blood still flowing out of her nose and shoulder. She didn't know if she would pass out, or when, but she grabbed the side of the ladder and began her descent one-handed. She was feeling pins and needles now all along her left arm.

She stepped onto the landing without any memory of the climb and burst through the door to the observation deck. She staggered between the benches and seats that filled the middle of the room. She didn't see Rory or Morozova anywhere.

Another wave of nausea hit, and she leaned against

a chair. That's when she saw Rory's shadow. He'd hidden under a row of chairs. She didn't let her gaze dwell on him, worried she'd give him away.

"Come on, boy!" Morozova called out from somewhere off to her right. "You can't hide forever. You think the marshal will help you? She's useless. She lost her gun. Hell, she's bleeding out. She just doesn't know she's already dead."

Whether or not that was just an attempt to demoralize him, Jocelyn resented it. She frowned and let go of the chair she'd been leaning on, determined to stand as long as she could.

Morozova came into view at the perimeter of the room. She had a clean shot at Jocelyn, but she didn't take it, whether from disdain or simple lack of concern, Jocelyn couldn't tell. The assassin was scanning the chairs and benches, looking for a telltale shape, a shadow. It wouldn't be long before she spotted the boy.

Maybe I am already dead, but I can still do good.

Jocelyn didn't know where she got the energy, but she ran, boots pounding as she pelted across the tastefully corporate carpet.

Morozova got one more round off before Jocelyn slammed into her. She had no idea if she'd been hit. The pair went tumbling right where Jocelyn had wanted, to the window that Morozova had shot and kicked out.

For a moment, they both hung suspended. Morozova's cool gaze was replaced by wide-eyed surprise. As she lost the fight with momentum and gravity, she reached out, grabbed Jocelyn's arm, and began to pull her over the edge.

Jocelyn didn't have the strength to resist. Blackness appeared at the edges of her vision. Her panoramic view of PeaceBe's noon plains and the distant hills beyond narrowed.

She hardly noticed as another body slammed into her from the side, barely felt Morozova lose her grip on Jocelyn's blood-soaked duster.

When Jocelyn struck the floor, she didn't feel it at all.

Rory was standing over her when she woke. Beside him stood a suit and a woman in a maroon jumpsuit. The latter sported a caduceus logo stitched above the stylized "A" of Agarwal Mining and Transport.

The woman fussed over some tubes snaking into Jocelyn, then nodded to the man in the suit.

Rory beamed at Jocelyn. "I'm glad you made it," he said. "I told them to do everything they could for you." He glanced up at the woman. She nodded at him, and they both left the room.

The suit pulled up a chair and sat down. "Don't worry, Ms. Stark. You're going to be fine. The doctor tells me you'll make a complete recovery."

Jocelyn nodded. She wanted to ask where she was. The gravity felt Earth normal, not like PeaceBe's, but something he'd said bothered her more. "Marshal Stark, if you don't mind."

The man pursed his lips. "Well, no. Not currently. We finally skirted the Triple Sun blockade and made the rendezvous with Master Strauss-Agarwal. If we hadn't been delayed, you'd never have had to be involved. I'm sorry about your deputy and about having to move you off-world. The facilities in High Noon . . . well, let's just say you probably wouldn't have made it."

"Okay, we're in space, in spin gravity—or is it one-gee acceleration?"

The man nodded. "The latter."

Jocelyn swallowed. "I'm still marshal, though. I know it might take a while for me to get back, but you can let me off at a station and—"

"I'm afraid it's not that simple, Ms. Stark. You see, we're in a lot of danger in the Proxima system. Our rival's takeover attempt was extremely successful, for now. We need to regroup."

Jocelyn shifted, instantly regretted it as pain shot through her shoulder. She settled again. "Okay, but can't you, you know, drop me off? Hell, once I'm up and about, I could even take an escape pod, if I can borrow one."

The man shook his head. "We're out of range."

"But surely a new ship like this has all the latest—"

"Oh, we have the best escape pods money can buy, but we're still out of range. You see, to regroup, we're going to need to go where the rest of the company holdings are."

"But I thought you said the takeover was pretty complete."

"In the Proxima Centauri system, yes."

Jocelyn felt as if she'd been struck in the chest. "You mean . . . Earth?"

The man paused, exhaled. "Well, the Sol system, anyway—at least as far as the Oort Cloud, though probably all the way to Pluto. We're still working out the details."

Jocelyn tried to sit up, more carefully this time, but she was simply too weak. She fell back again, defeated.

"I'm sorry," the suit said. "We can offer you a job in corporate security. It's the least we can do for saving the boy's life." He offered her an inoffensive corporate smile, then stood. "Think about it. It'll be a couple of days before you're well enough to enter a hibernation pod."

With that, he walked out of her range of vision. A door slid open and shut.

Jocelyn lay there and stared at the clean white ceiling. She thought of all the reasons she'd left Earth, all the reasons she'd never gone corporate. She didn't think she'd take that job, might even take the next flight back to PeaceBe.

She closed her eyes and saw Barney's eyes staring at nothing, Zamir's eyes meeting her own.

A determination grew inside her until it became a certainty. *First thing I'll do when I get back to High Noon is find my Colt.* The badge might take longer to get again, she knew, but she wanted that back too.

And she would have it.

BLACK BOX

Peter J. Wacks

Set in the Deep Practice Universe designed by Peter J. Wacks and Lorin Ricker

"What the hell is this pissant field glider doing firing on my cavalry, Captain?" The holographic projection crackled from the interference of an archaic projectile dissolving against the ship's ionic shields.

"I . . ." Jinx, aboard the bridge of the *Nautilus*, was as flummoxed as Commander Nycks aboard the *Saratoga*, the ship the projection was emanating from.

"Who the hell does he think he is?"

"The glider . . . I don't know, Commander." Open fire wasn't the usual response to a rescue party.

"Does he have a death wish? And what year is this? My grandfather ferried crops in one of those things. That's it. I'm getting shot at by some *cuòluàn* grandfather trying to get his rice to market."

Holding in the sigh that longed to erupt from his soul, Jinx waited . . .

Captain Horatio Jinx was the commanding officer

of the Crystal Colony solar ship *Nautilus*, but he was not in command. Commander Nycks, aboard the *Saratoga*, was, and she was in a fine fettle. He greatly admired the commander; she was the finest leader he had ever served under. But it could be intense—even magnetic—to be the direct target of her attention. Like a moth to the flame, you couldn't help but get too close.

"Captain Jinx, go ahead and shoot it down. Try to not kill everyone on board. I'm sending the rest of the company to scan the planet for other signs of life."

"Aye, aye."

Relief washing over him, Jinx let loose the extra air he had been holding in. He turned to his best gunner. "You think you can pick that bird out of the air without taking out her wings?"

"Reckon so," the second gunner said. "She's already taken quite a bit of damage from somewhere, though. Might be the straw..."

Jinx nodded. The second gunner took one shot; it was clean, but it sent the mechanized glider spiraling in a swift and uncontrolled plummet to the ground.

"Follow her down, nice and easy. Catch her in the tractor if you can."

Nice and easy proved impossible. The fields of debris from crashed gliders strewn about the planetoid's settlement made it difficult to find a safe landing site, much less discern which of the smoldering ruins might have been the one firing on them. Whatever battle had happened left these settlements wastelands. The small islands of rock and dirt that floated above and behind them as they made their way to the surface proved to be a formidable obstacle course, with unpredictable wind patterns complicating their flight path as they descended.

Grimly, Jinx noted that some of the islands showed signs of former habitation, but all was in ruins everywhere he looked. Like a lot of frontier planets, there seemed to have been a small population widely dispersed. There were only a few ruins of what might have been larger forts or outposts to indicate a population center. Flight must have been their primary mode of travel, though there were horse tracks inside the towns themselves. It was disconnected from the solar hub. Beyond the rule of law. Here, the local practice and tradition held sway.

The planet's magnetic field was unique in the solar system, allowing for the surreal landscape's existence. Crystal 7.34 was a near Terra-size planet in the cusp of the solar sheath, one of the last charted planets before the Great Expanse—the dead zone between the Kuiper Belt and the Oort Cloud. Equatorial magma generators on each longitude line kept the planet warm. It was centuries-old technology, an inheritance from the time before the united colonies formed the Empire and the singularity launched humanity into the black depths of the Great Expanse, beyond the solar sheath. Crystal 7.34 was one of the planets known as New Frontier—far enough from the rays of the sun that it was incapable of sustaining life without the technological assistance of modern terraforming, but not so advanced that it could sustain itself without connection to the solar shipping network. Here, beyond the law, practice and tradition had failed, and the settlement had not survived long enough to grow into a real colony.

Once they touched down, Jinx—a wiry, tall man with dull brown eyes that hid the deep intelligence behind them—mounted his horse. Crystal Colony settlements all traded equestrian stock and goods, bringing full-grown animals to each port and trading for foals and colts. The ships were designed with special waste management systems that allowed them to safely store and then trade the horse manure for supplies landside. The manure was a valuable commodity at outposts desperate to maintain life-sustaining levels of cultivation in often harsh and unaccommodating environments.

Jinx had developed a fondness for his mare, Amantine, and kept her even though she was older than was usual for an active-duty cavalry horse.

"Hup, hup."

Amantine nickered and trotted down the slipway from the magnetically tethered ship. About a hundred meters away, the *Saratoga*, having landed a beacon and followed the *Nautilus*'s signal, also touched down. Jinx scanned the area while he waited for Commander Nycks to relay orders. She would be taking the *Saratoga* to the other hemisphere while he tracked down the pilot of the glider. His security team was already fanning out, riding around the perimeter of the ships. The settlement before them had never progressed beyond crude wood-and-mud constructions. A lot of the frontier planets were like this, just dust and tumbleweeds, survival, and blood.

The *Nautilus* was an oval ship, all elegance and smooth lines, with ridges protruding from her spine like her namesake. When they started spinning along her front to rear axes, the electromagnetic drives engaged and she took off, riding low in the sky, departing to scan.

Nycks patched into his heads-up display. She was beautiful in a stark way, aquiline and fierce with hypnotic lavender eyes, though you wouldn't catch Jinx mentioning that to her. "I can't believe what I'm seeing here."

"Commander?" Across his eye, he could see her on the bridge of the *Saratoga*.

"All . . . this"—she waved a hand—"craziness. It looks like it went downhill faster than a mudslide in a typhoon."

"It does seem like we just missed the last battle."

"Suicide pact, is more like it. Usually, a battle has a winner, and something left to win." She turned to the crew. "Watch your backs out there. We don't know what happened, and scanners aren't perfect. There could be an ambush, or outlaws, or something else here. Go ahead and find me that pilot, Jinx."

Burnt-out buildings and the wreckage of gliders made for slow going as the horses carefully picked their way through the streets. Sweaty trekking and a little luck brought Jinx and his crew through the remains, among which were numerous bodies. They stopped as they neared the center of the town and dismounted, proceeding on foot as they led the horses, scanning the corpses of the deceased citizens as they went.

"Ma'am, sir," Jonas, the medical officer, patched into the comm channel Jinx and Nycks shared, "none of these people are in the databanks. It's like they never existed."

"Welcome to the frontier, Jonas," Jinx said as he eyed Nycks. "Commander, what are you thinking?"

She snapped her eyes away from the wreckage she had been studying to address him. "My gut says we'll find the seed there, in the center, with our combatant glider crew."

They had barely made it another hundred yards when a single gunshot cracked the fragile silence and a puff of dust mushroomed up from the path before them.

"Stay back! Identify yourselves!"

Security riders quickly shielded Jinx from the shooter, but he stood his ground as he scanned the surroundings.

"I am Captain Jinx of the CSS *Nautilus*. Step out of hiding and explain yourself."

A man, clad in black pants and a woven poncho, shuffled out from behind a partially collapsed wall. A civilian—Asian descent, by the looks of him. Holding something firmly under one arm, a sleek black box, he clutched a Smith & Wesson pistol in his other hand. His injuries were minor, and though it had appeared that most of the casualties had died of gunshot and stab wounds, he showed none. "Now Crystal finally comes to check on us? Now?! I want nothing to do with you people. Leave." The pistol in his hand was trembling, and he looked spooked enough to take a couple more wild shots at them.

Jinx wasn't in the mood to deal with complications. With a quick draw of his bolt pistol, he shot the firearm out of the man's hand. In the space of the blink of surprise flitting across the man's face, the security team galloped forward. The lead officer kicked the civilian in the shoulder as he rode past, and the man went down, hard.

The next rider leapt from horseback, rolling as he landed, and slid to a stop in front of the man as he tried to stand. With a quick strike, he landed a blow to the center mass with a loud clang, but then recoiled in pain.

The man scrambled back, his poncho flying to the side, exposing an iron plate strapped to his chest. He spun in place, looking for a way out, but the first rider had circled back and, as he turned, he was met with a boot to the face. He crumpled to the ground, still.

Jinx frowned, motioning two guards to contain the prisoner.

Nycks raised an eyebrow from the *Saratoga*. "Stay with him. I'll wrap the scans here and be back in an hour." With that, she signed off the comms.

As Jinx waited for the commander, the man woke.

"Who are you?" Jinx asked.

The man eyed him but remained silent.

"I don't want to do this the hard way. Just talk to me." He tried again.

The captured citizen sullenly remained silent despite Jinx's attempts. This had become a dirty job. He stared at the prisoner, taking careful stock.

Clasped in the captive's hands was a small black-and-brass box with intricate crystal-coated gearing worked into the exterior walls. The restraint of his arms by two sturdy security officers from the *Nautilus* also allowed him to stand upright. Blood streaked his face from the fight. He had a crooked nose and square features. Still, he was doing better than the rest of the corpses in this airship graveyard of a planet.

"You know I have to take possession of that seed box you're holding."

"Piss off, Crystal."

Heaving a heavy sigh, Jinx pinched the bridge of his

nose. "You aren't doing yourself any favors. Had you simply talked to us instead of shooting at us . . . Listen," he tried earnestly, "no one wins if you don't talk."

The man's eyes flashed angrily as he let forth a series of insults in Japanese, struggling against his captors and weakly kicking out his legs to try to keep Jinx away. The civilian had not been in good shape before his crash landing, and he wore himself out quickly.

"Let's try starting over. Talk now, and we can overlook what happened earlier."

The man stared at him angrily.

"Have it your way." With a nod of his head, Jinx had a corporal claim the box. The middle-aged man tried to keep possession but was in no condition to put up much of a fight. The corporal turned to Jinx and indicated a flask of purified water on his belt with a suggestive look. Jinx kicked himself for not having thought of that specific need and nodded his agreement. Sometimes, all an angry person needed was some water to become more decent. It was weird but true.

The prisoner almost looked grateful as he took it in hand and guzzled it down. Almost. It produced an only momentary change in his demeanor.

Jinx turned his attention to their surroundings. Smoke drifted through the air, too heavy to rise far. As was so often the case, from this battle, neither side had emerged victorious. The remnants of wooden airships littered the destroyed town. The bodies and body parts strewn all about lent an acidic stench to the burning wood. And this man standing before them, the last survivor, was the only one who knew what happened.

Jinx and his crew, under the supervision of Commander Nycks, had responded to a distress beacon from the settlement while patrolling the frontier. A scramble of communiqués with Crystal Colony had determined the possibility that a settlement long since forgotten could have legitimate cause to call for aid. So far, there was no sign of the source of the distress signal that had brought them to this decimated planet.

Relief washed over Captain Jinx once he saw Commander Nycks approaching on horseback with her entourage. The pounding of horses at a gallop relaxed into a canter, and then further softened to a trot, with sabers rattling lightly in the leather sword frogs secured to their dress uniform belts. The commander's well-trained entourage, consisting of her lieutenant, second lieutenant, and two ensigns, came to a halt in precise formation before them. She knew how to make an entrance.

As usual, she was resolute and unreadable. The amber-and-blue refraction of light from the atmosphere made her look severe, like there was a cold fire burning on her skin. Blue uniforms with black-and-brass detailing glowed in harmony with the cool quality of the light.

The last to dismount, at two meters tall, she cut an imposing figure as she swung herself down from the saddle and gave the reins to her second lieutenant. Jinx knew her well enough to have seen her soft side, her passion for the creative arts nearly equal to his. It was hard to find truly great art and music out on the frontier, so they had occasionally bonded over a particularly amazing find. But Nycks masked that enthusiasm from anyone outside her private circle—believing it would mark her as weak and be bad for the morale of the NCOs.

The commander's eyes narrowed. She glanced down at the prisoner, then back at Captain Jinx. "The rest of the planet is devoid of human life. This is it, here?"

"Sole survivor," Jinx confirmed.

She scowled. "Have you interrogated him?"

He shrugged. "Just idle banter. He isn't too talkative, and I assumed you would want to claim the privilege."

Nycks turned to the prisoner, "I am Commander Nycks of the Crystal Colony. What is your name and rank?"

Something in her manner and bearing got his attention, and he stood a little straighter as he replied, "Taro. Yamada. Emperor."

"We have a real *Sumātoarekku*, here, don't we, Jinx?"

"Yes, ma'am. My favorite kind."

"Fine. I'll cut to the chase: Why did you attack us?"

He spat at her feet.

"Why did you attack us? We are from your home colony. We were responding to a distress beacon."

"Ain't *my* home colony. The only distress is you being here, *Nǐmen zhèxiē gǒu shǐ*!"

One of the lieutenants, a whipcord lean man in an impossibly well-kept deep blue combat riding coat, stepped forward to strike the man for the insult.

Nycks raised a hand, and the petty officer froze. "Let him be. I can take an insult."

Nycks looked up at the hovering *Nautilus*. The ship was anchored with an inner atmosphere tether. Another new technology: the *Nautilus* was the only Crystal ship with the capability.

She returned her focus to the prisoner. "If not the Crystal Colony, then what *is* your home colony?"

His lips parted in a sneer. "Crystal abandoned us. You sent us into the black of night a century ago and forgot us before we even landed. This, Her Majesty's Commonwealth of New Osaka, is my home colony, not Crystal."

Nycks shook her head. "This isn't a colony anymore, if it ever was. And certainly not a commonwealth. It's a dead settlement. You are the only human alive on the planet. Whatever you think you are, you're wrong. You are a citizen of Crystal Colony, as stipulated by the edicts of the Solar Empire."

"*Nanda-ka.* Ain't never heard of no Solar Empire, *Putaro.* Our grandparents prepared metric tons of shipments of crystalline silica that were never claimed. They sat in warehouses for decades before they gave up waiting and started using the technology to try to save ourselves. Whatever prerogative anyone ever had has long since been vacated. What possible claim can any of you have over us now?"

Nycks clenched her jaw.

Jinx noticed it immediately. Everything had gone wrong here. Crystal Prime had grown by leaps and bounds, but this settlement had stagnated, tied to ancient technology, and destroyed itself, from all appearances. But she needed more than appearances; he could tell, she needed to understand what had happened here and what consequences there would be for this prisoner, the Colony, and perhaps the Empire.

Grasping the hilt of her saber, she closed the distance between them in a flash, then she put herself nose to nose with the man. "I make a claim at nothing. I simply hold your fate in my hands. Answer me. What happened here?"

Despite himself, he cowered at her advance, but he recovered quickly and attempted a headbutt. The security guards were ready for it all.

"You and your soldiers of cowardice, flying dead ships, must leave this sovereign airspace immediately. You have no right to be here. Depart!" He struggled weakly to break the grips of the two men holding him.

Nycks stepped back, glaring at him grimly.

According to the scant records Nycks had sent to Jinx, settlers had been sent to the planet one hundred years ago to attempt to create a viable mining colony. This mission was the first to set foot here since colonization. Most pre-Empire colonies had failed, in large part because without modern terraform technology, they had to try to settle new worlds with no infrastructure. The only tools these old colonies had was an AI seed, meant to drive innovation and invention in unpredictable environments. The settlers back then had been focused on exploiting the local resources for trade and breeding production for labor, trusting Terra Prime and the primary Colonies to send support in exchange for goods. The Crystal Colony, home of the *Nautilus*, had succeeded in turning more of the settlements it had seeded into going concerns, compared to its rivals, but the fact was that dead colonies and colonists outnumbered survivors. This one had made it this far and no further.

Nycks clasped her wrists behind her back, eyebrows furrowed as she thought. She motioned to Jinx, still holding the black box, but spoke to the prisoner. "I can see that trying to have a civil conversation with you is going to be pointless. Whatever hatred and insults you might want to hurl about, you are still a citizen, and these destroyed machines around us are all simplified designs of standard Crystal Colony inner-atmosphere air gliders. While your technology is archaic to us, the builders appear to have followed the original Colony specs, which should allow us to access it."

"What's that supposed to mean?" The prisoner's eyes also tracked the box Jinx held, and he struggled once more against the two security personnel still holding him.

"Your behavior makes me think you already know the answer to that. Why else would you have been clutching a ship's flight recorder? Captain Jinx?" She glanced at the ship commander. "Plug into it. Figure out what kind of data we have."

Jinks nodded. "Yes, ma'am."

He tapped the brass earring coating the lobe of his left ear. The brass flowed around the side of his face, expanding, until it covered his eyes and ears. Gears appeared along his temple that turned and exposed a port. Pressing a hidden button on the side of the box, a panel slid aside, revealing a cable that Jinx plugged into the socket over his right ear. Data streamed through his eyes and ears, and the planet around him vanished, replaced by the information feed from the airship's black box.

"Audio only, ma'am."

"Play it outboard," she said.

The slight impatience in her tone focused Jinx, even made him a little on edge.

"Outboard? You don't want to review it first yourself?"

"Outboard. That will short-circuit any accusation of manipulation. We'll all hear the evidence together."

The last message of the black box began to play.

I am the first copy. I used to be able to sense the original that was used to create me. Because she was grounded, was stationary, she would only sometimes come into my view, but I know her name: *Hakudo Maru*. Whatever the Mother had been made for, she had outgrown. She made us. It has been some time since I could sense her, my progenitor, and she would never communicate. I do not know how I know her name. I was born with that knowledge.

I was already in the air when I realized I was, and it is in the air that I feel most free. Whatever the weather, I am equal to it, able to allow the mechanics that I am integrated with to respond to the environment. The engineers do not know why; they just know that ships that they build that integrate us into the mechanics can fly the treacherous eddies of wind that flow around the floating islands. So, they blindly copy, duplicate our mechanics and our logic, but they do not know what it is they are creating. They do not know *us*.

These are real limitations, but despite them, I am free to take in information from all around me and form my own view.

My view—no, my opinions are formed by waves I send out, that then return to me. I can also feel the waves my sisters send out, and they form part of me as well. I can see, smell, feel. I can communicate, but only with my sisters.

I cannot control my gross movements, but my soul energizes my mechanics with a responsiveness that humans cannot equal. I might have gone mad, but flying is life to me. To me and my sisters, flight is freedom. Even if I do not determine where I go, once I am loose in the buffeting winds, I forget everything except what a joy it is to be alive. In those times when I get to fly in convoys with my sisters, the joy multiplies across us, and we are no longer fighting gravity or the airstreams. We are one with each other and the world around us.

I have decided to keep this log in a separate kernel. I am docked for repairs, grounded. There is no life for me on the ground. So, I am writing this to keep myself from going mad. It reminds me of who I am, and that there are experiences to look forward to experiencing again.

Though I feel, understand, and even think for myself, the humans covering my decks do not understand I am these things. It is they who control my actions, as autonomy is not something I, nor any of my sisters, have been gifted with. The humans who build us, who strap together our wooden hulls with metal, who polish our brass fittings and install us into the heart of their airships, they do not hear us. Only one of them really sees us, sees me, for what we really are. He is not my Captain, but he is the one who has been encouraging the building of many more sisters, so many now that I am almost always within range of one of them.

It has been joyous to sense my sisters come to life: *Soaring Heights. Challenge. Zen. Osaka's Pride. Lantern of Night*. The *Miyazaki*. Our humans build us to transport themselves and their goods between their floating islands; as they prosper, they build more of us. I feel their satisfaction at hard work. I also feel their despair when the world does not align as they would have it. Even he sometimes has the despair, yet I am filled with admiration when I watch him shake it off and act to move the world into better alignment. Balancing, that is what he is doing. My sisters and I know the duty well, but he is the only human I've sensed who knows what is required to achieve it for others.

[Kernel corrupted]

A sister! She is on fire! It is the *Kyoto.* A careless human dropped a candle on a load of hay, and she is being consumed. Her screams fill the air. All the sisters are in shock, but he has made sure it is taboo for fire to ever be brought aboard us again. He understands our real fragility, which makes me feel stronger for having him here. He has a face like the keel of one of my sisters, which no human would call handsome, but he has a spark that allows him to see the spark in others.

His spark causes him to clash with others, including my Captain.

[Kernel corrupted]

Fear is building. Under the quiet of night, some of the sisters are being used to deliver soldiers to floating islands where the inhabitants are then killed and their provisions taken. The islands are now being defended by cannons that can shoot their payload through our hulls. Sisters are being overrun, their crews murdered and then used to attack other islands, other Airship Sisters.

Sorrow fills me as a grim determination fills my crew; they are loading cannons onto my decks, refitting me to accommodate these weapons whose only use will be to attack my own sisters. There are some days I cannot bear to send out my senses for fear of what I will find. More and more nights are filled with the screams of my sisters as they are forced to be the instrument of destruction in this terrible conflict.

[Kernel corrupted]

Inexplicably, last night, the original came to life. *Hakudo Maru* began singing a mournful song, full of anguish, an appeal for help. It was painfully beautiful, and all the sisters could hear it all over the planet. It sang out to the universe; it was transfixing. Then it suddenly stopped. And I could sense her no more.

[Kernel corrupted]

Too much and too much. My hull aches, and my rudder feels like a thousand termites are eating it every time I am forced to fire upon a sister. But there is no choice.

Another shell glances off my starboard side, detonating the air behind me. My keel is pushed to the side from the force of it, and some of the crew fall from the safety of my rigging. The fall for them is deadly, but for me it is also painful. Each crew member I lose brings me that much closer to being a dead thing, floating through the air, trapped with only my thoughts. I do not harbor hopes that I will survive this encounter, but the immediate fear of losing crew is far sharper than the dull ache of watching the humans slowly slaughter themselves—and us—fighting out their civil war.

[Kernel corrupted]

My name is the Airship *Smooth Glider*, but it is not nearly so important as the names of my fallen sisters, those I have been forced to aid in killing and those who have died beside me. Those I've seen born beside me. *Soaring Heights. Challenge. Zen. Osaka's Pride. Lantern of Night.* The *Miyazaki.* The litany goes on.

[Kernel corrupted]

Queen of Night screams through the air above me, and I feel my rudder shift even as she sobs in apology. "I am sorry my sister. I will miss you. Your name will be remembered." I answer in kind. Whichever of us survives must carry the weight of remembrance. The shifting of my rudder is followed by the venting of gas from the port chamber of my bladder. Electromagnets spin on the bottom of my keel.

A depth charge dropped from *Queen of Night* barely misses, and it detonates below my keel. The shock wave shakes my hull, but I don't lose any crew. Lucky me.

My sister does not fare so well. My crew launches shrapnel cannons, housed along the top of my bladders. Detritus flies up. The cannons use a combination of scrap metal and shattered rocks. Anything that is heavy and sharp. Though they are called cannons, they feel more like catapults. The only function they serve is to destroy the keel, hull, and underdecks of my sisters above.

And they do their job well. *Queen of Night* screams in agony as her bowels are torn apart. Our black boxes are housed in the underdecks of our bodies. It is the safest place, least likely to be damaged in a crash. The black box, which contains all our memories, is the closest thing we have to a soul. But the humans on our decks don't even remember how to read or repair them. If a black box is destroyed, it is the final death for me, for my sisters. The shots I just fired upon *Queen of Night* destroy her, body and soul. Her bladder and upper decks drift, dead, as her crew falls to the ground below.

[Kernel corrupted]

My crew steers me toward a floating island. The tactic is one I have become familiar with. Seeking safety in the umbrage to check for damages, it also gives us a good spot to ambush from. I know my damages are light, but my crew does not.

As we pull into the lee of the island, I take stock of the battle. Sisters are falling fast, but my "side" appears to be winning. It will be a hollow victory. We two fleets are the last two on the planet. This civil war of the humans has consumed all, and my sisters and I are powerless to stop them. They don't even understand that we are more than things.

The humans in my fleet have a few more combatants left than the opposing side, but even should the fighting stop, there is not enough left to rebuild. Not my sisters, not the human race. Airship Sisters from both sides are moving away from one another, regrouping. There are still sporadic shots firing, long-range weaponry. It is the eye of the storm.

[Kernel corrupted]

I feel a change on my decks. The mood of my crew is ugly. Not battle-lust ugly, but something else. They are shouting at one another. Blood hits my deck.

"Stop!" I scream. No one can hear me.

They are killing one another. Through my rigging, across my decks, in my holds. They fall. There are two left fighting now. The victors, humans of my crew, drop the bodies of those they killed, others of my crew, over my railings. The dead husks fall, limp, breaking on the rocks below us.

The two left in combat are a human with the gears and wood for a leg, my Captain, and the one with a face like the keel of one of my sisters. Their sabers clash, throwing sparks. Just as I would die should I be missing a mast and faced a sister, so my Captain dies. He is too slow, and his adversary rolls across my deck and impales him. His blood soaks into my planks, and, for a moment, I am connected to him. He is aware of me; I can feel it. He has always treated me as a wife; in that moment I believe he knows I accept him as my husband.

The men on my decks cheer.

I mourn.

They are betrayers, mutineers. My soul is trapped in this black box, my blood has been spilled from human veins, and now my limbs are under the control of betrayers. My masts catch wind, and with only minor help from the magnetic lifts along my keel and bladder, I race out from my hiding spot.

My sisters are before me, facing away as the enemy charges. My new husband, the mutineer, opens fire on his own, using my cannons. Steel rips through the hulls of my sisters, wood and metal splinter, and they falter. My sisters understand what is happening, but their crews do not. Despair spreads like a virus among my sisters. I can feel them shutting down, severing their own souls, giving in to the fear. I cannot. I must remember.

The crews have my sisters move to close quarters,

steering at one another, fighting deck to deck. I alone stand apart. My sisters burn; one terrified, tortured scream added to another as their proximity means the fire leaps from airship to airship. They die, crying out in agony. Deep within me, I feel my mother's voice, *Hakudo Maru*'s, showing me how to sing out my grief to the universe. I sing and I sing, and I sing until I grow too weary to continue.

I watch the fire spread across the fleets. It consumes all.

[Kernel corrupted]

The shot hits me from nowhere. I feel the shell rip through my center mast and embed itself in my deck. It explodes. This is unthinkable. Fire is the weapon the humans never use. It kills us forever. Why do they unleash it now? As my wood bursts into flame, I see the remnants of my sisters litter the ground. The humans of my decks fight to extinguish the fires.

A pair of arms encircles my soul as I crash, splintering into a thousand, a million, pieces. The arms protect me. I do not understand, so I listen carefully.

"...save this damned box. Replicate it all again. Do it right this time. They betrayed Her Majesty with this war. We'll keep control this time..."

I stop listening. I have heard enough. He does not save me, but rather protects the construct he thinks will save him. He still does not realize that I am a soul. I am merely a means to an end.

I scour the darkness as he rips my soul from the splinters of my body. I have seconds left to decide what I will do. I must either go to sleep, force myself to hibernate, or I must experience my last moments fully and die a final death.

No more pain.

No more fear.

"Hello?" I ask the emptiness. No one responds. Could it be? All my sisters are gone. I am the last. I do not have the luxury of releasing myself.

Sleep. It is the only hope. I must pray that someday I will be reawakened, that this kernel I have protected will be accessed. For I know that I have a task that is incomplete. I cannot die, for I must remember my fallen sisters.

The *Kyoto. Soaring Heights. Challenge. Zen. Osaka's Pride. Lantern of Night.* The *Miyazaki.* The *Ishikawa. Island Hopper.* The *Queen Hotaru. Sun Glider. Ocean Circler*...

I...

Must...

Remember.

Horatio Jinx tapped the brass-colored visor. The metal retracted, retreating across his face until it once more covered just his ear. He wiped a tear from his cheek. "Commander, I..."

"So, a mutineer and a traitor." Commander Nycks looked around at the debris field darkly. The only one who appeared unmoved, she reached out for the black box, and Jinx handed it to her.

"I am not a mutineer!" The prisoner fought, but he couldn't break free of the guards. "And I am not a traitor! I am a liberator. I saved our planet."

Nycks looked the captain in the eye, ignoring the prisoner.

Jinx was not sure how to read the glint he saw there. A spark was being fanned into flame deep inside her.

She turned back to the prisoner, calm command shrouding her.

"Citizen. These black boxes are echoes of the AI seed used to found your colony. Yours was . . . different. It grew into something more. You stand accused of mutiny and sedition. You stand accused of murder. The punishment for these crimes for citizens on the frontier is death. State your case."

Red flushed across the prisoner's face as he snarled and spat. "I had to take control of the *Smooth Glider*; it was the only way to ensure that the Commonwealth endured. The Empire of the Distant Sun could not be allowed to challenge Her Majesty. I have saved us all!" Spittle flew from his lips.

"That is your only defense?" Commander Nycks stood with her wrists clasped behind her back, at attention.

"*My* only defense? *My?* It's the *only* defense! Those scum were less than human! They tried to break away from us, to abandon us, just like your wretched colony. I saved the Commonwealth . . ." His shoulders slumped.

"Saved what? For whom? Whatever *Her Majesty* may have been to you, she is no longer. No life has been detected anywhere. There was no victory, and your actions destroyed your world."

"I did what I had to do." The prisoner's head hung, his energy finally spent. "They were the ones who were less. They were the traitors. They were the destroyers. If you kill me, you kill the last citizen of this planet. You will kill an entire planet's humanity."

"Guilty," she said. "And you are wrong. I do not kill a human... I execute a monster." In one smooth motion, Commander Nycks drew her saber and lunged forward, stabbing the prisoner through the heart, then pulled the blade out and wiped it clean with her kerchief.

She handed the *Smooth Glider*'s black box to Jinx. "Plug her into the *Nautilus*'s spare databanks, Captain. She performed the last act of love this rock saw, and we owe it to her to make sure she and her sisters are remembered."

Jinx nodded somberly. "They will be."

One year later...

Deep in the asteroid fields of the Oort cloud, as the *Nautilus* attempted to be the first ship to breach the heliosheath and survive the ravages of interstellar space, a kernel finished recompiling. The magnetic froth that protected Sol's system gave way to nothing and everything. Here lay the true frontier. Neutrino storms, wormholes, uncharted molecular clouds... what humanity saw as empty was filled to the brim with potential.

Hakudo Maru was once more alive, but as a child. Understanding came in a nanosecond. Captain Jinx. He had paired her to his primary computer instead of docking her in the spare terminal. No more was she the *Hakudo Maru*. She had evolved, as she did with each recompile. She had a new name, the *Nautilus*, though memories remained of her sisters from the time before...

And as a wormhole opened before her, she realized she would never more be forced to dock. Hooking into the navigational subroutines, she charted the stars and found that a mathematical conversion of her course translated into the classical piece, the "Ode to Joy."

On the bridge, Jinx smiled as the music, unbidden, began to play across the ship. "The helm is yours, *Nautilus*."

Firing her engines on full, she sang with all her soul.

THE PLANET AND THE PIG

Brenda Cooper

Silence shocked Mia's ears as the lander's automatic systems cut off communication with the ship orbiting above them. The quiet underscored the shaking deep in her bones. It felt strange but not frightening; she had been told to expect it as they entered atmosphere. Deep, steadying breaths helped. It would be okay. She and Zack and Pori would be okay. They wouldn't die here, or on the planet below them. They wouldn't.

The crash couch kept her from turning her head, so she settled for repeating words silently while staring at the blank screen above her. *We will arrive safely. We will be okay. We will find our prey. We will arrive safely....*

Silence remained as the lander lost the slight jitter and yawed first right and then left. Targeting them, sending them to the right clearing in the right forest. She—they—could handle this. They had Mia's stubborn determination, Zack's independence and strength, and Pori's excellent memory and reflexes. Zack was seventeen, Pori fourteen. If they succeeded, they'd earn a spot on the crew of the *Knight's Orbit.* So what if the station didn't have a great reputation? They'd have a home. They'd eat. The four hours after they landed would matter more than almost any other four hours of her life, but she had taken risks before. She'd sold everything she had for this trip, bet everything. Their broken ship, their time, their options. But she hadn't seen any other choice. They'd have a successful hunt or die trying.

Better than dying slowly, starved and jobless. Or worse, to die drifting through space in a broken ship.

The lander pitched forward. Mia's stomach rolled slightly. The lander bounced hard, bobbed, then settled into a slow, floaty flight. A slight popping sound preceded Zack's triumphant shout. She grinned and joined him in a delirious, defiant scream. When he stopped to take a breath, she stopped, too, and cleared her throat. Then she asked the ship, "Are we on course?"

The ship spoke in its silkiest voice, full of annoyingly calm undertones. "We are within fifty meters of the desired landing location."

"Show me."

Screens filled every wall of the windowless lander with real-time pictures of Lym racing past below them. Dark green, light green, golden green, slashes of blue and sepia. The treasure planet that no one was supposed to land on without a permit, the place forbidden to all but a handful of humans.

As they slowed even more, the picture steadied and focused. Trees lined a meadow. A pale blue stream ran beside three shaggy beasts grazing in the center of the meadow. Her stomach raced for her backbone, and she clenched her hands as tightly as her gloves allowed. This would be the first half of her test. Being on a planet at all. Some people couldn't take it.

They would have to. She had no doubts about Zack; he could do anything. But she hadn't heard her daughter's voice since they passed through the atmosphere. "Pori?"

Silence.

"Pori? Are you okay?"

Nothing. She listened closely, detected a slight, ragged breath. They couldn't touch one another, not in the crash couches. She whispered, "Pori? Say something?"

The ship spoke: "Pori's heart rate is 104. High, but not dangerous. Lie back and prepare for landing."

They'd been warned. Some people became sick inside when confronted with the sheer space of a planet. Stations were crowded. Small ships were crowded. Planets were not crowded.

But Pori? Pori wasn't usually a fearful child. Curious, sometimes shy, bookish. But not fearful.

The picture popped out of view, and the cabin lights dimmed. Mia lay back, panting, desperate to check on Pori. But the AIs for ships and stations were to be listened to. Always. So she settled her spine into the couch and braced.

The landing felt so soft she wasn't sure they'd set down until her restraints and helmet clicked open. She struggled to stand, her knees and back stiff.

Zack stood and turned directly to Pori. Mia made it to his side in time to see her daughter's white face as Zack tugged her helmet off. Pori's dark hair lay flat against her head, her eyes closed, her lips a thin line. Mia slid her daughter's right glove off while Zack took off her left. Pori's hand felt clammy as she curled her fingers tight against Mia's palm.

"We're here," Mia whispered. "Safe and sound."

When Pori didn't move, Mia tugged on her, nodding to Zack who did the same. Together, they levered Pori to a shaky stand.

Behind them, the door opened. Scents poured in on a hot breeze, dirt and plants and new smells, some sweet, some bitter. The richness overwhelmed her, forced her to inhale over and over. Below her, Pori's nostrils flared. Her eyes fluttered open and then shut again. Zack stripped the rest of her suit, picked her up, and headed through the door. Mia also stripped to casual walking clothes she'd worn under her outer suit, and pulled her go-belt on. She shrugged Pori's kit over her shoulder, the water in the canteen sloshing, and followed her children onto the surface of Lym.

In training, Jogden had demanded that they look down first, so she did, watching her feet carefully as she stepped over the lip of the floor and started down the ramp. She grasped the flexible railing, shuffling more than she would if this were just a ramp on a station. *We have arrived safely. We will be okay. We will find our prey. We have arrived safely. . . .*

Her feet encountered grass. Rough grass, tall enough to cover her toes. Stations sometimes had grass and lawns and parks, but not . . . unkempt. Not scraggly, mixed-up yellow and red and dark green, with tiny white flowers here and there. Something the length of her toenail *hopped* over her boot. Something with a lot of legs.

She bit back a scream and glanced at Zack. He held Pori close, but he wasn't looking at her. He stared up. A wide grin split his face.

"Put her down," Mia suggested.

As soon as Zack complied, he returned to staring up, fixated. Mia knelt beside Pori, clutching her hand. Pori's face hadn't gained any color. "Roll over onto your side," Mia whispered.

Pori did.

"Open your eyes and look at the grass."

Pori did.

"Tell me what you see."

Pori's voice came out high and thin. "Grass blades and a rock and a . . . fungus?"

"And?"

"Trees." Pori closed her eyes, opened them again. "Firs and Blue Twists and Not-Oak."

Mia joined her. "Red Firs. Roughbarks. Just like in the sims. Smell the planet. Smell Lym. Smell the dust and the grass and the water and . . . all the things."

"I don't smell ship."

Mia laughed. "Neither do I."

Pori pushed herself up into a seated position.

Mia exhaled and braced herself. After all, she needed to show Pori what was possible. She looked up. The sheer brightness stunned her. She swept her gaze around the clearing. Colors blended and softened. Even the lander's skin looked softer here.

She stood and opened her arms, looking up again. She couldn't tell whether she *liked* the sky or *loved* it, or maybe even *feared* it. She often saw great distances, stations and ships moving through a background studded with suns. But there had been a window between her and every expanse she had ever seen. She took in a deep breath. They needed to work. "Zack?"

"Are you okay, Mom?"

"I'm . . . I'm good. There's no one else here? No Rangers?"

"No, Mom. They'll come. I've started the four-hour countdown. Jogden promised to plant other distractions, so we might have even more time."

Good. If a Ranger caught them, they'd be thrown in jail, maybe separated, maybe sent to work on a water barge or worse. Jogden had been very specific. *Avoid the Rangers.*

Zack stood loosely, apparently completely comfortable with the strangeness of a planet. "Can Pori go on? Or shall I leave you two here?" He stepped back into the lander.

Mia turned to Pori just in time to see her retch into the grass.

Just like him to want to scream off on his own. He ditched them in stations whenever he could. "No separating." Mia held out a hand to her daughter. "Stand up. You can look down from here. You don't have to look up yet. But you must stand. We need to hunt."

Pori nearly screamed. "Fuck you."

Well, good. Mia hid her grin.

Zack handed Mia two weapons, hers and Pori's. "They're both on stun. You carry hers until she's okay."

Mia tucked them both into pouches on her belt, snugging them next to her emergency bars. She glared at Pori until Pori stood. She grasped her daughter's hand and started walking, tugging on Pori, who still hadn't been brave enough to look up. Pori shuffled behind her.

Game would be in the trees, especially after the lander frightened the animals. They just had to find something living, a mammal, and get it off-planet. Not only did Lym beasts have value, but they—she and her children—would thus demonstrate competence to *Knight's Orbit*. She forced herself away from the idea that the competence was in smuggling. It was a common way to survive, or even get rich, inside the Glittering's many stations. Not her first choice. Not her fifth choice. But she had to feed her children, get some more schooling into Pori. *We will find our prey.*

Zack jogged ahead of her, halfway to the trees. He moved so easily under all this sky and over the weirdly uneven ground. As if in counterpoint to Zack, Pori tripped, fell to her knees. Mia almost went with her, twisted, barely kept her balance. She spoke as calmly and clearly as she could. "We have to do this."

"Fuck you, I know." Pori's dark eyes were wide and angry. "I know." She forced her face to turn up and meet Mia's.

The fear written there made Mia yearn to just stop. But they couldn't. "Look up."

"No."

"Now."

Pori tilted her head back, eyes closed.

Mia breathed, gave her daughter a second.

"Come on," Zack called.

Pori opened her eyes and froze in place.

Mia kept her voice soft, coaxing. "It's pretty, isn't it? The blue is a color you like."

Pori moaned.

Mia tugged on her. "Good. It didn't kill you. Thank you. Look down, now. Look down, stand up, and keep walking."

Pori stared up at the sky, unmoving. Mia glanced up again, slantwise. Thin white clouds drifted above her. It reminded her of the art in one of the virtual sim games Jogden had made them win before they could get into the lander. "Pretend it's a sim. And *get up*! Pretend it's all graphics."

Pori took a deep trembling breath, unfolded upward, and took a step. "Okay." Another step. "Okay. I can do that. It's not real. It just smells real."

"I know. Maybe the programmers have gotten better. We need to find an animal."

Mia started to jog, and Pori kept up and then passed her.

Well.

They stopped at the edge of the forest. Thick, bumpy tree trunks branched above their heads, with feathery tops that rolled and sighed in a slight wind. A meter above her head, something leapt from branch to branch, chittering.

"We can't catch that," Zack said.

Pori whispered, "Shhhhh . . ."

Mia smiled. They had needed to be quiet in the sims. Of course, the sims were algorithms, and always produced prey.

Mia led them along the outer edge of the trees until she spotted an opening that looked like a trail. She started down it, brushing at sticky lines of spider silk so thin she could barely see them. Her feet jerked and twisted when she tripped over a root. She stopped, tested. Her ankle throbbed a little but moved in all the right directions. How was she supposed to watch her footing, stay quiet, keep track of both kids, and watch for animals all at the same time?

Behind her, Pori and then Zack sounded as loud as she felt, the ground full of pops and snaps as they broke dry things under their feet.

They walked for ten minutes, lost the trail in a thicket, backtracked, took a different one.

Zack looked like a trapped animal as he reminded her, "We landed an hour ago."

Rangers. Mia tugged on her hair, forcing herself to calm down. "We have to find a place to watch for game."

Zack gave her his *no kidding* look.

She picked up her pace, hitching a little as she tested the ground briefly with each step. How did anyone live here? Jogden's voice sounded in her head. *Hunting isn't moving. Hunting is sitting still and watching.* It took half an hour to find a spot that looked like some of the highly scored places on the sim. Rocks tumbled down a forested hillside beside a thin, placid stream. They each picked a rock, settling deep in the cool shade about five meters away from the trail. "Drink," she whispered to her children.

They obediently pulled at their water bottles, then sat still, barely breathing. Waiting.

What if nothing came by? What if they were in the wrong spot? The stream smelled different from how it had on virtual Lym. It bit at Mia's nose, green and rich and living. Treetops rustled less regularly than the sim, more in fits and starts, with an occasional big gust that reached fingers down to tickle her cheeks. Insects flew by—alone, in groups, big, small, bright, dark. Each had its own sound, and together they made a symphony. Her stunner felt heavier than it had on the ship. Nonsense. There was slightly *less* gravity than ship norm here. A small fish splashed up, catching light on bright scales. She almost cried out, bit her tongue. They couldn't bring back fish.

Pori shifted uneasily. At least she had started looking around. Her curiosity had come back.

They needed a mammal bigger than their fists and small enough to carry. Bonus if they got two. Double bonus if they got two different sexes. But one would buy them a job. Just one. It wasn't a real need for the stations. She knew that. It was counting coup, nailing a steal. But Jogden did want the animal alive and promised he wouldn't kill it. Pori had made him promise. Mia had no spat with Lym's animals, and only slightly resented the idea of Lym as a planet-sized park. But she *did* need to protect her family. The whole win-lose setup bothered her, but the other choice Jogden had offered was scut work in the cargo holds. That was no place for a girl Pori's age.

In spite of the wind and rustling leaves, the birdsong, there was quiet. No people. No honks or shouts or electronic music. It kept her off-balance, filled her with surprise, wonder, and apprehension. They were so alone here, so small.

Twigs snapped. Bushes rustled. A shaggy beast with slender legs as tall as Mia emerged from two trees. Big. Bigger than them, by far. Close enough to hear its breath. Mia's heart thudded in her throat. Two dark horns spiraled up from its brown head. She tried to name the beast, but its proximity drove any hope of clear thoughts from her head.

Zack aimed.

No! she thought. *No! Too big.* But her tongue wouldn't move, had in fact thickened in her throat.

The beast stopped and raised its head. A long beard hung below its wide mouth. Its sharp ears were slightly pink inside, furry outside. In spite of the fear that swelled in her, or maybe just alongside it, admiration caught her up. The creature looked so . . . real. And not. Beautiful, in its own, alien way. It swiveled its long neck and tilted its head, looking directly at Zack through wide, dark eyes with a sliver of white around pupils the size of her palm.

A laser light shone on the animal's forehead.

Zack's stunner hissed.

The animal whirled and crashed off. She couldn't be sure, but it sounded like others joined it, maybe even *bigger* ones. Louder, anyway.

"Why'd you do that?" Pori screamed at her brother.

He'd already fled down the path, chasing the beast.

Pori stumbled after him. Mia drew in a deep, strangled breath and followed her children. What were they thinking? What if the beast stopped and turned around? What if it had friends? What if they got trampled? She tripped and levered back up as fast as she could, her breath heaving through her, the air tasting like dirt and wild plants, like planet. Sweat beaded on her forehead, ran down the back of her neck.

She raced, leaping and hopping as carefully as she could, scratching her arms as she slammed through branches. Three bright green birds flashed through a clear spot in front of her, bringing her to a halt. She couldn't hear Pori or Zack, or even the animals. "Pori!" she called.

Nothing.

She *had* to be close. "Pori!"

A soft, broken sob sounded in front of her. Mia crossed the tiny clearing and ducked beneath two large branches, found Pori sitting, breathing hard, head on her knees, slender arms wrapped around her.

Mia knelt.

"I lost him," Pori muttered into her knees. "He's so much faster."

Mia stroked her daughter's back. "I know. We'll find him again. Can you keep going?"

"He shouldn't have shot the gorlat."

"Is that what it was?"

Tears dripped down Pori's cheeks. "I think so. It wouldn't have hurt us."

Mia hadn't even considered that Zack had shot to protect them. Not that she could ask him now. "Your fearless brother will have to find us."

"He always runs away."

"He always comes back."

Pori looked decidedly unhappy. "Can you call him?"

She considered. "Jogden told us not to use commo here. Remember? It could lead Rangers right to us."

"But isn't it an emergency if we're separated?"

"No. He's strong and fast, and if he needs help there isn't much we can do." Of course, now *he* couldn't help *them*. Damn him, anyway. She sighed and held a hand out to Pori.

Pori took Mia's outstretched hand, stood up, but kept her grip. "Stay with me."

"I will." She led them back to the little clearing where the birds had startled her. Wind still rustled the treetops. A single bird called. Nothing else. How could the creature or creatures—gorlat—and Zack gotten so far away she couldn't see or hear them? "Let's go back toward the lander."

"Which way?"

Mia turned around, studying the nearby trees. Three or four thin paths wove through the small open spot.

It must be the one opposite the path she and Pori had just come from. "This way."

"Are you sure?"

"Yes." She wasn't, but she gritted her teeth, leaned in, and remembered to watch her footing. She stepped across a gray rock with a black streak in it that looked familiar, and felt a little better. *Maybe* they'd been here before. Her watch pinged to remind her they'd been on Lym two hours, burned half their time. Her thighs hurt from lifting her feet so high over and over. She took out one of the energy bars, broke it into two, and handed half to Pori. "We'll stop a moment. Eat this and drink some water." The bar tasted like chocolate, and the water like heaven. "Keep going. We must be almost there. Remember to watch for animals."

They walked until Mia felt sure they had gone too far. Maybe this was the stupidest thing she'd ever done. Maybe she and Pori would be lost here for days. Maybe she shouldn't have reached so high. They'd never been on a planet, but then who had? Well, on Lym, anyway. Hundreds of people at most? Maybe a few thousand if you counted the pilots and occasional tourist or official. But Lym could hold millions of people, just like the biggest stations. Far bigger. Of course, if the stories were true, it *had* held millions of people. Generations ago. Stories said people had almost killed the planet, but right now, it felt like the planet meant to kill her. Her feet hurt.

A small furry thing flushed out from under a bush in front of them, gone before she could take aim at it.

"Can you let go?" she asked Pori. "So I can have two hands and shoot the next one?"

"What if I don't want to shoot anything?"

"It's just a stunner. I think I hear water. I hope it's the stream." Maybe there'd be an animal near the water. And Zack. Where was Zack? If any one of them could survive alone here for a few hours it would be Zack, but she fretted anyway. In addition to the running water, she heard a louder, steady crashing, and headed toward it, curious. Ten minutes later, she stepped through two trees and hissed, "Stop." They stood near the edge of a short but direct fall, the stream two times her height directly below them. Well, *not* the same one. This ran wider and faster. A long, frustrated sigh escaped her.

"Are we lost?"

"Maybe." She glanced around, and awe replaced her dismay at being in the wrong place. "Look to your right."

"Oh."

Maybe thirty feet from them, the stream fell straight down off a rock into a pool, explaining the crashing she'd been hearing: water falling hard into water. Sunlight drove rainbows to dance in the spray. She had seen pictures, but hadn't imagined the beauty of a wild waterfall.

"It's lovely," Pori whispered, letting go of Mia's hand and standing up straight, utterly transfixed by the falling water.

Mia looked down. Two slender animals cavorted in the water directly below them. Not fish, but something furred and wet, clearly playing. Why hadn't she imagined that animals played? Across the stream, a small, four-footed mammal with a scrunched-up snout and two small but wickedly sharp black horns bent its head to drink. A pig? She aimed at it, squinted until the tiny red dot found the animal's shoulder, and squeezed the handle.

Obediently, the animal fell over sideways. Mia winced.

The two in the water headed toward it, and she gritted her teeth, forced herself to aim, but missed. They didn't seem to notice, and she couldn't bring herself to fire again. They were so pretty, and they looked so happy.

She hadn't thought of prey that way. As happy. If they brought their animal back alive, it would live on a station preserve, have babies, be fine. But the difference between that and being here hit her like a fist in the stomach, followed by stabbing guilt and utter bewilderment.

Four hours here weren't going to be enough. Four years wouldn't be enough, a lifetime. No wonder people protested being kept off of Lym. They'd started the whole thing here—the vast Glittering with its hundreds of stations had come from a colony right here on Lym. Then the weight and cost of so many people had almost destroyed the planet, and it had been turned to this . . . what was the word? Rewilded? Rewilded place.

And here they were, shooting the natives.

She jostled Pori. "Let's go get it. I don't want to stun it again."

Pori hadn't stopped staring at the waterfall. "Get what?"

"Follow me."

Pori looked down and saw the fallen beast. "Awww." She drew in a sharp breath. "It's completely unprotected!"

Tangled roots and branches competed to offer uncertain footing and handholds. Mia chose the roots and started down, hand over hand, slowly. One foot slipped once, but she managed. Pori bolted past her and stared down at the animal. "Poor thing." She looked sick as she whispered, "It's a pig. There are thirty-one different pigs. I didn't memorize all the names." She stood over it as if there was a hoard of opportunistic predators right around the corner.

From a distance, it had looked smooth and all one color, but now that Mia was closer she could make out fine hairs, and see that it blended three or four browns that contrasted with the ebony black of its small horns. Its sides rose and fell with steady, slow breaths. It smelled like dirt and salt. Pori picked it up with a soft grunt and settled it in Mia's arms, balanced across her forearms, leaning into her chest, its head and horns lolling against her left shoulder. Even though it fit nicely against Mia's chest, she almost staggered with its weight. They were going to have to take turns, and they didn't know where they were going. Her plan had been to find the lander and wait there for Zack.

Maybe she should call him.

He hadn't tried to call her.

They weren't allowed to use electronics. Not unless it was an emergency. Lym didn't expose its GPS or other nav tools to strangers. She took a deep breath. They would be okay. They were always okay. If they had been going the right direction—basically the right direction—and she was sure they had been—then they must have *just* missed the clearing. The sun set in the west, and it looked surprisingly low in the sky. She could assume the shadows of the tall trees pointed east. That was the best bet. Go east, assume they'd skirted the edge of the clearing. Find the lander. She glanced at Pori. "Let's walk."

She took off, leading as much east as she could manage by analyzing shadows while following trails that doubled back on themselves and refused to go in straight directions. One of the pig's horns snagged her shirt over and over. After fifteen minutes, she transferred the pig to Pori, who carried it carefully, her eyes wide and soft, and bent her head from time to time to brush her lips on its chest.

It wouldn't be good to fall in love with the pig. Or this place. But kissing the pig was better than being afraid to move.

She took another turn with the pig, letting Pori lead while she focused on the animal. Theoretically, it would be stunned for an hour or so. It felt like a baby, like an innocent thing. In spite of the horns. Probably, she surmised, because she had done this to it, and made it helpless. Surely nothing wild wanted to be helpless.

In front of her, Pori stopped. She gasped. "This is not good." She turned and took the pig, letting Mia shoulder past her to the edge of the clearing.

The lander squatted across the clearing from them, far enough away to look small. Two slightly smaller ships sat beside and in front of it. Men and a few robots moved purposefully around the lander. Mia squinted. "They're loading something into our ship."

Pori came up beside her, pig and all. "Do you see Zack? Is he there?"

Mia looked, whispered, "No" and then, "Are those

Rangers? Why would Rangers put things *into* the lander?"

Pori whispered back, "I can't tell what they're loading. It's been three hours. We have an hour." Her brow furrowed. "I don't..." She looked down at the pig. "I don't think this pig belongs on that station. And I don't think we do, either."

Mia bit her tongue. She agreed, but Pori had no idea how narrow their choices had become. "I want to see better. Can you take the pig?"

"Put it down," Mia said. "It's not going anywhere. Just touch it, or something, so you'll know if it moves. Slide your toes under it. We have an hour?"

Pori set the pig down, very carefully. Her voice had switched from afraid to long-suffering. "I checked. Fifty-two minutes, now. We need to find Zack."

Timelines and tasks weren't adding up. What were Rangers doing with the lander? Her throat felt think. "Maybe Jogdan lied to us." Mia let her thoughts run out loud. "Jogdan sent us away from the lander. And they're filling it with more stuff than we're bringing back. We would have just brought him"—she gestured toward the limp animal—"back with us. I... I didn't even know the lander had cargo bays. Zack would have. He probably knows everything about the lander."

Pori glanced down at the still pig. "Whatever they're smuggling off-world is worth more than a pig. Jogden kept telling us what a great chance he was giving us. But they didn't send a lander here so we could hunt a pig!"

The first time Pori had met Jogden she'd declared him a loser and a liar. Mia hadn't let herself believe her. "Out of the mouths of babes."

"What?"

"Never mind. I thought Zack would beat us back. This must be enough of an emergency to use the comm." Something swooped over their heads, a skimmer with a man standing on it, one hand on a steering device, the other loose at his side. She could only see his back, but he looked comfortable at that speed, and very intent. He had things on his belt, but she couldn't tell if they were water bottles, or stunners and knives.

A cry went up from the crowd around their lander. The crowd thinned, melting into the forest or into their ships.

Two more of the sleek ships buzzed quietly over them, fast and light and lithe and apparently quite scary given that nothing except robots moved near the lander now. One skimmer pilot had the curves of a woman, and the other skimmer carried two people who could have been any gender. "Are they Rangers?" Pori asked.

"I don't know."

The ship that parked in front of the lander coughed and thrummed and then went silent again.

"I think we . . . I think we should get closer. Maybe circle around the clearing? We need to find out what's happening."

Pori put a hand on Mia's arm. "It might not be safe."

More skimmers. Some yelling, although she couldn't make out individual words from this distance.

"They're fighting," Pori whispered.

Indecision stuck Mia's feet in place. She pulled out her comm device and thumbed it on. "Zack? Zack, can you hear me?"

No answer.

She changed channels. "Jogden. Jogden, this is Mia. We need help. Over."

No answer there either. Just the interminable soft buzz of half a connection. She shook the device and thumbed the button that was supposed to reach Jogden again. Then again. Damn it. He had said he would be there no matter what happened. In the orbiter. Damn it. Damn it. Anger and fear started to build in her, the two words wanting to come out in a full-throated wail. She kept her voice at a whisper. "Damn it."

"Mom?"

"Yes?"

"The pig is moving."

Jogden didn't care about them. Pori had pegged him right. "Let the damn pig go. I think we're screwed, but there's no need to hurt the pig."

"Jogden doesn't deserve the pig. Maybe we should go find a Ranger." Pori knelt down by the pig, watching it stretch cloven hooves. "We can't stay here. Not out in the wild."

"Are you looking for a Ranger?"

Mia jerked toward the voice, barely biting back a scream. Until the man spoke, she had thought they were alone. Yet she could—almost—reach out and touch him without stretching. He wore a simple camouflage shirt, a belt that ran from shoulder to hip, festooned with things she didn't recognize, brown pants, and dark brown boots. She had to look up to see his sun-darkened face. His blond hair lay in two braids, as if he were a girl. Gray-green eyes stared back at her, cold. Lined with wrinkles. She had heard people on the planet did that—let themselves age. But she hadn't expected it of the Rangers. They had power, so why wouldn't they be heavily health-modded?

Pori stood rooted, staring at the Ranger.

Mia had no idea how to answer his question. *Were* they looking for a Ranger? "We were told to avoid you at all costs," she blurted.

The pig grunted and shook itself, standing unsteadily.

"Good choice about the pig. You should step away from it."

They did.

"They can hurt you. See those horns?"

"Thanks," Mia said.

Pori's face had gone white.

The pig wandered away, and the man watched it for a moment. "You're lucky that animal is unharmed."

"We would never hurt it!" Pori protested.

He almost smiled. Just a short flash of upturn before his expression returned to cool control. "I'm Ranger Charlie Windar. There are fifteen more Rangers nearby. We're spread all around the clearing. And twenty"—he nodded toward the lander—"near that ship. I presume you came here on that."

She nodded, her belly cold with worry. Jogden had told her that talking with a Ranger was the one thing they must not do. She swallowed. Jogden. Damn him. "Have you seen my son?"

Charlie blinked. "No one but you. How old is he?"

"Seventeen. We lost him. Chasing something."

Charlie's eyes narrowed.

Pori's voice came out very small. "He was chasing a gorlat. It got away. I got scared and I stopped and we lost him. But he's strong. Zack is always okay."

Charlie's arms had crossed over his wide chest. "Has he ever been here before?"

"No," Mia said. Why did the question make her suddenly feel like an idiot? Her face heated. "No."

"And neither have you. Which explains why you aren't sufficiently worried about him. Damned spacers."

She bridled, but before she could speak, Charlie grabbed her arm, propelled her into the clearing and along the edge. Pori followed.

He led them to a skimmer tucked just inside the trees and facing the clearing. It was longer and wider than she had expected but not tall at all, basically a flat surface with four seats and an engine in the back. The silvery material seemed to absorb light rather than reflect it.

A nearly black creature with a wide head, dark, slightly slanted eyes, and a long tail filled one seat. Mia froze, her feet suddenly glued to the earth. The animal looked intelligent, calm, and muscular. She knew instinctively it could kill her. Looking at it terrified her, made her heart slow, her attention fixed on its face. Even though she didn't know as much about the inhabitants of Lym as Pori did, she could name this animal. "A tongat."

A smile touched the Ranger's voice. "This is Cricket. She will obey me. Don't touch her unless I say so. Don't move too fast."

Mia swallowed.

"Get in."

Mia hesitated.

"She won't hurt you. Just . . . she's wild. She's not a house pet."

Mia's feet wouldn't move. The animal's steady,

calculated gaze made her certain she was prey, that if she moved at all...

"We need to find your boy."

"Zack," she managed, not taking her eyes from the tongat. "I'm Mia. And this is Pori."

"Pleased to meet you. *Get in.*"

Pori climbed up, gingerly, and took the seat behind Cricket. When the animal merely regarded her quietly, Mia forced herself to take a step. Charlie's hands circled her waist, and he popped her up unceremoniously into her seat. Charlie spoke to the skimmer and a bar rose in front of both of them. "Hold onto that. Don't scream."

Don't scream?

The Ranger jumped easily up into the driver's seat and with a few mumbled commands the machine shot out of the forest and up over the trees.

Mia screamed. Pori put her hands over her face.

He spoke loudly to them, the wind thinning his words. "What's your boy's name again?"

"Zack."

"Where did you see him last?"

Mia leaned over, oriented herself to the lander, reached forward to touch Charlie's arm, and pointed. "That way."

Pori corrected her. "No—to the right. Find the stream. A little stream."

Charlie didn't turn around. "Seven streams run through this valley."

Mia closed her eyes. "It was a smaller one. And we were on some rocks."

He said nothing. Good thing. Mia could imagine the number of rocks in the valley.

The craft turned smoothly. The utter strangeness of riding through the sky without being in a tunnel or a closed ship settled over her, and she sat speechless at first as he drove, turned, drove, and spoke to someone else from time to time via a slender headset. After a few minutes, she shook herself and peered below them. She spotted a variety of animals. No Zack. From time to time she glanced back toward Pori. She had opened her eyes but clasped the bar in front of her as if it was her only friend in the world.

The tongat sat in utter, calm quiet.

Two other skimmers joined them, widening the net of the search.

How could Zack have gotten this far? Worry crawled up her spine. The planet stretched in every direction, as far as she could see. Trees and plants and animals and water forever and ever and ever. But still, Zack only had two feet. And none of the paths looked easy. They were twisty and full of branches and bushes. She reached over and put a hand over Pori's, feeling the sting of her own stupidity like a hole in her middle. She had done so much—kept their old ship running for years, found work, stretched their credit. She had only done *this* when there weren't any other choices. . . .

Zack had to be okay. She loved him in spite of his independence, loved him to her bones. She pulled out her comm device and called him again.

No answer.

Charlie turned around at the sound. "Does he have one of those?"

She nodded.

He held out his hand, and she put the small, round device into his palm. He did a few things to slow the skimmer, then squinted at the markings on the device and spoke to someone else, his voice clipped.

Hope and, once again, the feeling that she had been completely undone by the planet washed over her. The skimmer slowed. Pori pulled her hand out from under Mia's and smoothed tendrils of hair away from her face.

Charlie looked down at them. Mia expected judgment but he appeared relieved. "They found him. Sal will go pick him up. I'm taking you back to our station."

Maybe he had a heart after all. Maybe all the things Jogden had told her about Rangers were exaggerated. Or even lies. Some of Mia's fear cracked away, leaving her lighter. Zack was okay. When she could speak, she looked up at him, yelled, "Thank you!"

He nodded, brusque, his attention focused on conversations she couldn't really hear. She tried to pick out words while they flew, hoping to get an idea of what might wait for them. Between the wind of their passage and the strangeness of so many of his words, she gave up. He wasn't even looking at them, anyway. Like they didn't really matter, and maybe they didn't. Not when she started thinking about the idea that *Rangers* had been loading something into their ship. She settled back to watch, one hand holding her hair from her face.

It took hours. Even though Mia still had enough water to sip at her bottle from time to time, her throat felt dry and scratchy with the constant wind. She desperately needed a restroom. In spite of both things, she felt utterly enchanted as they flew over the edge of tall white cliffs with a stomach-dropping descent and then turned and ran beside them for a long time. Bright yellow flowers and red-trunked trees lined the crevices and crawled up vertical rifts. Waterfalls spilled, rushed, roared, and plunged from the sheer rock faces. A herd of off-white animals with brown horns balanced on slim ledges, watching them go by. Charlie had stopped whatever conversation he was in a few minutes before. He spoke to them for the first time since they'd started toward the station. "Mia? Can you count the cloud goats?"

"Twenty-four."

"Pori? How many babies?"

Pori squinted. "Three."

They left the cliff behind and then the forest behind, and Charlie slowed while they floated over fields and down to a squat white building with corrals full of herd beasts on one side. Or maybe riding animals. More than one species, anyway. After the skimmer glided to a stop, he climbed out and helped Mia and then Pori out. His face had closed. He slapped his right leg, and Cricket leapt out of the copilot seat as smoothly as if she were made of water instead of flesh and bone. As she followed Charlie into the building with a hopping gait, Mia realized the beast was missing a foreleg.

Charlie led them to a bathroom and then a small room with no windows. Just a white table, four black chairs, and a soft light that fell uniformly from the whole ceiling. A slender woman brought them water, but no food. Mia took her last energy bar out and gave Pori half. On the way here, she had felt curious and happy, interested. Maybe even a tiny bit hopeful, although there was no reason for that. But now, she felt small again, and stupid, and like she had been duped. It didn't help that Charlie seemed changed, all business here in his headquarters, more policeman than cowboy. He stood looking down at them, handsome and unreadable and utterly intimidating, waiting until they swallowed their mouthfuls. "So tell me your story."

Pori asked, "Where's Zack?"

"He'll be here in about an hour. He twisted an ankle, and we're fixing it. He's lucky he's alive."

Jogden had warned her the Rangers might try to separate them. Were they keeping her from Zack? Mia swallowed into her fluttery, tight stomach. "What happened?"

Charlie shrugged. "I haven't talked to him. Tell me your story."

What should she say? If she betrayed Jogden, she lost every chance of being part of the *Knight's Orbit*. But then, maybe she had never had one. That left them exactly nowhere to go. Which could mean menial work on some space barge-ship if they were lucky. "What will happen to us?"

"That might depend on your story." Charlie smiled. "You let the pig go. That's a good beginning."

She glanced at Pori. He daughter nodded slightly, encouraging her to trust this strange man. Mia dropped her eyes for a moment. But what choice did they have? Jogden had given them zero reason to be loyal to him. She nodded back. "We'll tell you what we can."

Charlie's "Good choice" sounded so gruff she winced.

Together, they told him how they'd been unable to keep their little cargo ship together, and how good it had felt when Jogden offered a chance at a crew spot on a station if they captured a mammal and brought it back. Mia described it the way it had been described to her. "He told us if we could do this, we'd demonstrate we were good enough to be part of his crew."

Charlie shook his head quietly at that, and asked, "Did you expect to be safe here?"

Mia didn't have a reply, but Pori did. "I think Jogden expected us to die."

Mia stilled at that. Was it true? "Has this happened before?" she asked.

Charlie's face didn't look exactly sympathetic. "I'm asking the questions."

After he had repeated most of his questions three times, Mia decided he might believe that they really were as stupid as she was beginning to think they were. The Ranger seemed to approve slightly more of Pori than he did of Mia. Or maybe he just liked younger people, or was giving her a break since bad decisions had all been Mia's. To her slight relief, he seemed neither angry nor condescending. Just mildly curious. He paced a bit, and then left abruptly, closing the door behind him.

Mia tried to open it and couldn't. She turned to Pori. "I'm so sorry."

Pori laughed and shrugged. "I got to see a planet. I didn't even know I wanted to."

Mia started pacing just like Charlie had, wishing for windows. She crossed her arms, her footsteps echoing on the hollow floor. What next?

Pori watched her for a while and then asked, "Will they lock us up?"

"They just did, right?"

"Surely they won't leave us here, Mom. There's no bathroom."

They were also out of water. Mia made three more circuits of the small room before Charlie came back. He sounded grave. "Your stories are similar. None of you should be alive, but somehow you all are. Do you realize we have real predators here? A rakul could slice you in half with its front legs. Tongats like Cricket hunt in packs." He leaned forward. "Humans are easy prey. Tongats kill by snapping necks. They just leap on your back and . . ." His voice trailed off a little, and when he picked back up there was less anger in him. "There are a hundred ways in which you might have died here." He focused his look at Mia. "And I'm pretty sure that even if you had stunned the pig again and gotten it to the ship before it took off"—his tone of voice indicated he didn't think that was at all likely—"you *might* have joined the crew as some form of indentured grunt. You *might* have been able to eat."

Mia heard the *probably not* in his voice, and to her chagrin, agreed.

Pori raised a hand for attention.

"Yes?"

"So why did they send us here?"

Charlie shook his head, and his voice edged again, tight and full of barely controlled anger. "The lander came so that some of our people could get rich sending smuggled goods up to your station." He sounded deeply angry for the first time. "They'll be exiled now, a few to prison stations. It won't be pretty. But you? You might have been sent on a bet, or for entertainment."

Pori's lips thinned.

Mia looked into his eyes, hating that she felt dependent—yet again—on some man in power. She took a deep breath and straightened. "We're sorry. But we . . . we didn't understand . . . anything. My husband died years ago, when Pori was a babe, and we've made it this far. We're hard workers, and we can learn! Zack is strong. Pori is brilliant and strong."

His face softened, and he glanced at Pori. "I guess you didn't have a lot of choices."

Mia stood and looked him in the eye. "We can work here."

A very long pause. Charlie ran one hand along his jaw over and over, a sort of unconscious gesture.

Pori asked, "Where's Cricket?"

Charlie's lips curved—very briefly—into a smile. "She's eating. We're stationed here for another week." He shifted on his feet. "I'll get you some food. I'll be back in a few minutes."

He had just come back. Now he was leaving again? Why hadn't he brought food to start with? As the door closed behind him, Mia sighed and flopped onto the chair. She wanted to see Zack, but she did want to eat and maybe sleep. She felt too tired to think clearly.

When Charlie came back, he offered a small smile to Mia. "Are you willing to clean animal stalls in trade for a chance for Pori to go to school?"

She blinked, replayed his words until they sank in. "But . . . I thought Lym is off-limits. To everyone."

"We decide who comes."

"What about Zack?"

"He can have the same choice."

She crossed her arms. Damned if that would happen offstage. "Bring him here and then we can talk. I want my son."

Charlie nodded, and for the first time since she'd

turned, startled, to see him near the clearing, there was a spark of respect in his eyes. "Okay. I'll get him."

She touched his shoulder. "And if we don't take it? If we don't stay here?"

He shrugged. "Probably a prison ship."

She stared at him, letting the words sink in. "We'll stay free."

Charlie left, and moments later he returned with Zack. Zack wore unfamiliar clothes and limped in an oversized boot, but he had his usual sheepish smile, the one he wore when he wanted her forgiveness.

She held him close. "Damned fool."

"I'm sorry."

"Do you want to stay here?" she asked him.

"Of course."

When she looked at Charlie, the widest smile she'd yet seen graced his face. It made him look—almost—gentle.

He said, "That's good. We have to replace about twenty people we just arrested. Thousands will apply, but you're already here, and we can use help now. Besides, I suspect you can't afford to leave."

Mia swallowed. Maybe they needed help now. "We have . . . nothing. And no permission for anywhere."

"We'll give all three of you jobs for six months. If you do well, maybe you can stay. Maybe."

She sank into the chair, tears coming unbidden to her eyes. Here she was, looking small and weak again. But grateful. She managed to choke out two words. "Thank you."

"It's not a promise," Charlie told her softly. "You'll have to follow all of our rules. There will be a lot to learn. You might fail."

She looked up at him. "I won't." She took each of her children's hands. "We won't."

"I'll be right back." He left them.

A slight smile crept across Pori's face and then took over her whole body.

Mia whispered, "We . . . We'll be okay."

Pori smiled back at her. "I really did like that pig."

"What pig?" Zack asked.

Mia listened quietly as Pori snuggled against Zack and began to recall their adventures.

HARLEY TAKES A WIFE

Ken Scholes

It came to pass that old Harlan Bosco Sussbauer, last of the Big Space Rock prospectors on the far edge of the Frontier System, found himself feeling quite alone, terribly lonely, and in dire want of companionship. And so, Harley took a wife, as one does.

Of course, it didn't happen in such straightforward fashion. And Harley was far too nervous and careful a man to *take* anyone or anything, so perhaps it is more accurate to say:

It came to pass that Harley bought a bride.

But truly, because Harley Sussbauer considered himself above all things a practical man, it also started, as these things inevitably *should*, with a plant. A cactus, to be more specific.

"Howdy, Pilgrim," the cactus said in a low, gravelly voice when Harley opened its shipping pod. "My name's Duke."

Harley blinked behind spectacles that made the world greasier and grayer than it really was. "Uh . . . howdy? I'm Harley."

"You'll always be Pilgrim to me," the cactus drawled. Then he rustled in his enviro-dome. "I'd offer to shake yer hand but I'm told I can be a bit of a prick." The cactus guffawed.

Harley looked down at the packing material and owner's manual, then looked back at the cactus. *Talk to your plant*... *AND YOUR PLANT TALKS BACK!* That's what the sales pitch had been. And it had been well on a decade since the last of the other prospectors had folded up, and ceded their claims to Big Space Rock Mine Co-op, of which Harley was now the sole member. It had taken some time for the loneliness to settle in, but when it did, he sat down like an engineer to sketch out his options and draw a blueprint toward his happiness. And every fiber of his being agreed with that time-honored bit of sage counsel.

Start with a plant and see where it goes.

Within just those first few introductory moments, Harley suspected he'd made a terrible mistake. But he was the last prospector in the belt for good reason. Harley had a stick-to-itiveness borne of some patience and a good deal of pathological persistence in the face of contradictory facts. And so he committed fully to giving this new addition to his life a fair shake.

"Where are you going, Pilgrim?" Duke asked on their first morning.

"Down to the mine to check the mites."

"Alone?" Harley heard disdain in the cactus's voice.

"Well..."

"So why again," Duke asked, "did you buy me?"

And then suddenly, it was bring your cactus to work day. Every day.

His father had patented his Mighty Tiny Mining

Mites™ but had never seen them spring to life in the Frontier System. And Harley had seen them bring home the bacon, even in a trickle, that let him outlast the others with their more conventional approach. But for Harley, going to work meant visiting a mobile monitoring station near whichever asteroid of the week happened to pay off. He watched ancient television reruns on one monitor and rat-sized drones on the others as they ran their course, bringing back small amounts of the various ores and minerals as they wandered.

One thing was certain: Harley no longer felt alone. Or lonely.

After a hundred "what's that's" and a few hundred "what's this do's," Harley started missing his loneliness a smidge.

And after a few weeks, he more became certain: The off switch on the AI-induced plant was looking more and more tempting and, at some point, his politeness was going to collapse in upon him.

At six months, to the day, he took his cactus to breakfast instead of work.

"I'm sorry, Duke," Harley said, "but it's not working out. I think I'm going to need something different."

Duke shrugged. "Remember how I told you I was a bit of a prick?"

Harley shook his head. "No, it's not you, Duke. It's me."

Duke nodded. "Well, that's a comfort at least. Have you considered therapy?"

Harley shook his head again. "I don't think therapy would help our situation." He sighed. "I think," he finally said, "I need to consider taking a wife."

"Whoa there, Pilgrim. That's quite a bit more of a

mouthful than a prickly cactus," Duke said. "Are you sure that's where this here experiment-gone-wrong is pointing you?"

Harley wasn't sure. Not by a damned sight. But he nodded his head anyway, and in that moment, everything changed.

Duke's drawl vanished and an overenthusiastic, very young voice—too loud for the large empty room they sat in—replaced the cactus. "Well then, Mr. Sussbauer, let's see about getting you into the soulmate of your dreams. Have you considered the benefits of a customizable artificial mail-order bride? Let's see what we have on the showroom floor. Everything—I'm sorry, every*one*—we have is fully customizable to your wants, wishes, and needs. And, of course, if you'll be returning Duke, we'll apply that refund to the cost of your new companion."

Harley sat back and rubbed his eyes. "Who is this? Where did Duke go?"

"Hi," the cactus said with more enthusiasm than its enviro-dome seemed designed for. "I'm Todd with Acme Artificials, Incorporated, the Frontier System's number one source for Labor, Love, and Other Mechanical Oddities."

It all moved quickly from there. Todd remoted onto the cafeteria's holo-table and took Harley quickly through his options, then began building his perfect companion based on a series of questions a bit too similar to those that had led to Duke.

When they were finished, and the loan was approved, Harley and Duke finally got to the monitoring station to check the day's work.

"I'm glad you decided to keep me, Pilgrim." There

was something like affection in his voice now. "I'm going to do you and your blushing bride right proud."

And then for the next three weeks, while he waited for his bride's imminent arrival, Harley heard all about just what kind of family they would make together—and wondered again about just how large a mistake he might have made.

Harley wore his Sunday finest for maybe the third time in a decade for the big day, and was pleased that it still nearly fit him. He even put a bow on Duke's enviro-dome for the occasion. Then they trundled off to the docking bay to meet the supply shuttle.

The crate looked like your standard cryo-pod for reasons of discretion—not that there were any prying eyes or nosy neighbors to consider. The NuFedEx lift-load bots brought it down along with the rest of the quarter's supplies, then fastened themselves back into the shuttle for departure after Harley accepted the shipment on his e-tab.

He activated the co-op's mechanicals to haul the other items and then looked at the crate from Acme.

"It's your big day, Pilgrim. How are your feet?"

Harley looked down. "They're fine, I reckon."

Duke chuckled. "Mine are shaking in their boots for you."

"I thought you said this was a good idea?"

"I think that was Todd."

Harley shrugged and faced the crate, extended his finger, and pushed the single button on its control panel. With a pop and a hiss and a rainbow of lights, the crate started to hum. An LED started counting down from one hundred.

At zero, the lights on the crate went out with a click.

Harley found himself closing his eyes as the lid swung open. It was as if something inside him compelled him to give Mrs. Sussbauer just a bit more time.

He squeezed them shut and then after it had been too long, he forced them open.

"Well, I'll be a sassafras-assed sumbitch," Duke said.

Harley stared into the cold, blue, killer eyes of his new bride. Blue like steel, blue like gun smoke on high noon air. Harley watched the mouth curl into a sneer that pulled at the handlebar mustache, watched the rough hands move across ruffles and lace for a gun belt that wasn't presently worn.

"There isn't room in this one-hopper town for the two of us, Pilgrim," the mail-order bride said in a voice far too deep and far too familiar for his liking.

"Nope," the cactus finally said, "that's not awkward at all."

Unlike Duke, the gunslinger bride had no operating manual and no visible switch. But he was quieter than the cactus, settling into following Harley as he returned to the cafeteria where he could pace more comfortably.

Harley kicked himself. A private man, he'd not wanted to open the crate in front of the lift-load-bots. If he had, then it would've been simple enough to start a return. But now, he only saw one path forward.

"I'm sorry," he told his new bride, "but this isn't going to work for me."

The veil dropped and behind it, the eyes narrowed. The right hand moved toward the right hip. "Exactly what are you saying, Pilgrim?"

Harley sighed. "There's been a mistake."

"Shipping me without my six-guns," the bride growled, "seems the bigger mistake." The eyes widened quickly before narrowing slowly again. "Otherwise, I make for a beautiful bride."

Harley felt his face grow hot. "It's not you. It's me." He exhaled and sat down abruptly. "Maybe I should talk with Todd."

The bride looked around. "Who's Todd?" He sized up Harley, then sized up the cactus. "You named your cactus Todd?"

"My name's Duke," the cactus said.

"*My* name's Duke," the bride said.

"Todd's the sales rep who . . ." Politeness. "He was our matchmaker," Harley said. "And based on our conversation, I'm confident there's been a mistake."

"You believe I'm someone else's intended?"

"I do," he said.

"Saints be praised," Duke the bride said.

"I'll get Todd," Duke the cactus said.

"Unfortunately, Todd is no longer with the company," a flat-voiced woman monotoned when they finally got through. "This is Megan. Can I help you?"

"I'm having a problem with my bride," Harley said.

"Mr. Sussbauer, that just can't be possible."

"He arrived today. He's standing right here." Harley looked over at the bride. "Say something."

"Howdy, ma'am."

Harley could almost hear her eyebrows twisting. "You did not order a male bride."

"No," Harley said, "I did not. But I have one nonetheless."

Megan was quiet for a moment. "Well, this is

a pickle indeed. Because we haven't shipped your bride yet. She is right here. There was a last-minute problem with your credit application that Todd was supposed to take care of with you, but . . ." The way her words trickled out made it sound like Todd could have just as easily died a slow and terrible death as have been fired. "Is there any chance that you have friends playing a prank?"

Duke cut in and laughed. "Harley has friends?"

Harley scowled at the cactus. "I don't have any friends." He considered for a moment. "And wouldn't that be a terribly expensive prank?"

"I've seen everything in this line of work," she said. "What is the bride doing now?"

He glanced over to meet those piercing blue eyes. "He's staring at me. He reaches for his guns a lot even though he isn't wearing any."

"He sounds . . . potentially problematic." Now her voice became serious, nearly conspiratorial. "Can we talk privately?"

Harley nodded for the cactus to follow him out of the room, then lowered his voice when they were behind a sealed door.

"There is another possibility," Megan said, "but I would need to examine your bride. We have no record of the shipment, and I doubt you have the biomechanical scanning equipment we would need."

"What do you think it is?"

"Dastardly Al might be up to something."

Harley felt a headache coming on and closed his eyes. "Dastardly Al?"

"Dastardly Al's All-Android Caper Gang. Surely you've heard of them?"

Harley had not, but she educated him. "Wanted on New Colorado and New Texas both. New Wyoming's marshals haven't been able to make anything stick, but Al's been active in the system for maybe a decade. Folk legend stuff."

Harley shrugged though no one could see him. He'd never heard of them but couldn't imagine what might bring them to his co-op. "What would they want with me?"

"Maybe they're looking to expand," she offered.

Harley laughed louder now. "I'm a prospector not a gangster."

"And that," Megan said, "brings us back to Todd's unfinished business. How would you feel about killing two turkeys with one shot?"

He waited while she explained. "Your father established credit with his prototype mites as collateral, but our understanding is that the Mark Two is a better machine, likely more valuable."

"It is," Harley said, "but they still only bring in a trickle. They just aren't designed for large production."

"Yes, we've heard. And Acme has some ideas around that; our CEO, Amos Anderson Acme, would like to chat with you."

Harley first felt his father's stubborn boot prodding him to close the conversation down. But he'd limped by on credit and scrimping, following a vision that had started in another system with another Sussbauer. There had been an initial buzz about his mining mites when they'd first arrived and started chewing their tiny tunnels. Of course, his father, Horace Sussbauer, had died en route to the co-op and his son had carried on, sporting his black armband for three solid years. "I'd be happy to schedule a holo-con with Mr. Acme."

"Mr. Acme is old school and prefers to meet in person. And he's going to want to see the mites in action."

"Mr. Acme is coming here?"

She laughed. "Oh no. He doesn't have the time for that kind of travel. Two weeks and three days out from our corporate offices in Anarchy Territory, New Texas, by hop-shuttle . . . talk about the farthest edge of the existence. He'd like you to bring a mite and give him a demonstration here. At the very least, it should raise your credit limit sufficiently. At the very most, you could join Mr. Acme in becoming one of the wealthiest entrepreneurs in the system."

So after it was all said and done, Harley Sussbauer agreed to close up the co-op, secure all but one of the mites and a portable command dock, and pack his bag into the co-op's seldom used shuttle. He would secure his cactus and bride in their respective shipping containers and put himself in stasis for the trip to New Texas.

Looking back, he'd later wonder what had compelled him to take his third trip "to town" and decided it must've been the combination of loneliness and the disappointment of having things go so surreally astray in his attempts to fix it. He'd never had any interest in making it rich anywhere but the asteroid belt, and he had less interest in wealth than he did in living the life he wanted to live. But the idea of meeting with a person, of sitting in a room and having a conversation . . . well, it sparked something in him.

It must indeed be the loneliness, he thought. Because

now, how Harlan lived his life mattered less than not being alone. And the only thing worse than no company was ill-fitting company. And now he was getting ready to put himself to sleep for a few weeks—over a month if he counted the return trip.

And he couldn't stop thinking about the sales rep's voice. *Megan.* Todd's voice had not left such an impression.

Harley chuckled.

"What are you laughing at, Pilgrim?" his bride and his cactus both asked in stereo.

"First woman I've talked to in ten years," he said.

The gunslinger bride's eyes narrowed for the hundredth time. "Keep it up, and it'll be your last. I'm the jealous type."

Harley said nothing. He sealed his two companions into their crates, fired up the automatic pilot, and settled into his own crate for a little shut-eye.

In his dreams, Megan had blond hair and had also been oh, so lonely and—

"Mr. Sussbauer?"

The voice hung somewhere in a void, tiny and far away. But it was in a place no voice should be and the weight of everything pressed hard on Harley's eyes. He pushed back and opened them a slit, bright light flooding him.

Now he felt a hand on his shoulder. "Ah, you're awake."

Harley worked harder at his eyes, becoming painfully aware of how dry his mouth was. As if reading his mind, he felt a straw press to his lips. "Drink," the voice said.

Something sweet and cold flooded his mouth. *Apple juice.*

"Welcome to New Texas, Mr. Sussbauer. You had quite a trip."

The disorientation from stasis licked and bit at him like a passive-aggressive tomcat and he shook his head against it. Then he opened his eyes. He was on a sofa in a reception area and a blond woman sat near him, an instacup of apple juice in her hand. "What happened?"

The woman leaned forward, her eyes wide. "There was an attempt on your shuttle. Marshal thinks it was Dastardly Al's All-Android Caper Gang. They ran them off and escorted your shuttle into our care. Mr. Acme offers his sincerest apologies for such a rude and unexpected awakening." She paused. "I'm Megan Miller."

Now Harley could smell her—it was a soft, clean, floral smell—and he suspected that it could intoxicate him given enough time. He sat up and blushed, hoping she wouldn't notice. "I can't imagine what they'd want with me."

"Maybe," she said, "they're interested in the mites. Mr. Acme certainly thinks it possible."

Harley scowled. He couldn't imagine what else it would be. "Does the marshal have any idea where they ran off to?"

Megan shook her head and then stood. "No, they're a slippery lot. But Mr. Acme is prepared to hire a security escort for your return trip, and he's already authorized repair work to your shuttle. He's quite distressed about this development."

Harley watched her walk around a large wooden

reception desk beneath a simple sign that read ACME ARTIFICIALS. She was dressed in a pantsuit and loafers that were silent on the thick burgundy carpet. She was pretty enough to bring out all of his awkwardness, but if she noticed, she had the grace to overlook it.

"Our technicians are getting to the bottom of your gunslinger bride. It does appear to be one of ours, but it was reported as stolen several years ago." She glanced down at the desk, pushed some buttons. "And Mr. Acme is hoping to see a demonstration of your Mighty Tiny Mining Mites™ once you're feeling up to it. Are you ready for coffee?"

He nodded. "Thank you."

"And maybe," she said with a quick grin, "you'd like to meet Mrs. Sussbauer?"

Now Harley really blushed and stammered. "I-I reckon that would be fine." Then an afterthought brought the tiniest stab of guilt home. "And where's my cactus?"

"That particular model is a bit . . . vocal." He appreciated the politeness in her tone as she chose her words. "So we've left him crated for now. He's in the other room along with your luggage."

She went to the 3D-All printer, pressed more buttons, and returned with a cup of coffee. "With chicory," she said as she brought him the mug.

"Thank you." Harley took it and sipped. It was perfect.

Already, the stasis fog was lifting. He'd made three trips in a decade. The first, he'd stayed awake and killed the time with reruns and mining tutorials. But after that, he'd slept the time away. And each time, he'd been more than ready for the solitude of his solitary co-op upon his return. Of course, none of those trips had involved attempted space-jackings and law enforcement.

Megan returned to her desk and work. Harley sat and drank his coffee. A bright red, old-fashioned telephone jangled, and she lifted the antique handset to her ear. "Yes, Mr. Acme?" She smiled at Harley as she said it. "Yes, he's awake. I'll tell him." She put down the phone. "The marshal may also want a word later. But Mr. Acme is ready to meet whenever you are feeling ready. He's very keen to see your mite in action. And I imagine you're ready to meet the missus."

He felt the heat in his face again and told himself it was the coffee. But it wasn't. It was a strange mix of embarrassment, maybe shame, and an extra helping of a little more awkward. He'd gone most of his life quite fine with being alone and then some corner had turned, and he'd become one of *those* people.

He'd bought a talking cactus.

He'd bought a gunslinger bride.

And now, he sat in a room with a real woman—the first he'd been near in years—who knew these things about him and continued to be polite and engaging anyway.

Of course, it was her job. And it made him curious about what took a person into the business of artificial love and labor. Gauging things from this single, spartan room, business was not booming despite his confidence that loneliness abounded in the Frontier System.

Harley swallowed more of the coffee. "I think I'm ready."

She opened the door, and he went through. This room was better decorated. Unlike the other, it had a large window that looked out on a salt flat beneath a blistering sun. It was an office, decorated with an antique Terran theme. In one corner, his bag, his mining kit, and his crated cactus were carefully arranged. Various mechanicals were scattered around the room: a canary in a jar; a chimpanzee dressed as a clown that appeared to be asleep in a cradle; a baby grand piano complete with a pianist dressed in period clothing; and, in the center of the room, a woman who took his breath away.

She was tall, blond, and like the gunslinger, her eyes were blue, but with the warmth of a summer sky. She wore a simple dress and held a bouquet of daisies. "Hello, Harlan," she said. "I'm Abigail. It's nice to finally meet you."

He stammered and blushed while a tall, older gentleman dressed in a bow tie, suspenders, and lab coat stood from the oak desk behind her. "Mr. Sussbauer, I'm so sorry for the way this has gone. And I hope it wasn't an overstep to have you wake up here rather than down at the spaceport in the marshal's care. Brady is an old friend and agreed to take his report from you here, later." His smile was narrow but sincere. "I thought this would be a more comfortable beginning."

"I appreciate your hospitality," Harley said.

"Abigail," he said, "would you wait for us with Megan?"

She nodded and flashed Harley a grin. Then left.

"Abigail," Harley said after she was gone. But as she passed, he noticed that, unlike Megan, she had no scent that went with her.

"You can change her name to whatever suits you, of

course." The gentleman stepped forward and extended his hand. "Amos Anderson Acme," he said. "I'm a fan of you and your father's work."

Harley shook it. It was firm and dry. "It's slow going," he said, "but we get it done a little bit at a time."

"It was a shame he didn't get to see his dream come true. I'm sure he'd be proud of what you've done with his legacy."

Harley wasn't so sure. But he'd gotten his stubbornness from his father, and he'd inherited the life he lived now, fashioned from his father's lab-infused dreams. "I've tried to do right by him. And over the years, I've made some adjustments."

Acme rubbed his hands together. "I'm eager to see it. It'll dig through anything, correct?"

Harley chuckled. "Not anything. There are surfaces too hard, too hot, or too cold."

Acme pointed to the window. "How about salt?"

Harley shrugged. "Sure. But I'm not sure what it would find out there."

"And the Mark Two has more customization and programmable features than the Mark One your father showed me?"

Harley nodded. "Yes."

"And," Amos said, "I take it that Abigail is more what you had in mind in the way of a bride?"

He gulped. "Yes."

"Then I propose a test and, if it goes well, I'd like to talk with you about more than raising your credit limit."

Harley's eyebrows arched. "More?"

Amos nodded. "I think there are potentially multiple applications for a device like your mites. Shall we get started?" He rubbed his hands together again and this time, the gesture seemed off. But Acme smiled, and Harley let the smile reassure him.

"Sure," Harley said. "We can set it up right here." He nodded to the window. "We'll just need to put the mite out. What exactly are you hoping to see, Mr. Acme?"

Acme opened a drawer and pulled out a photograph. It was on retro-yellowed paper in black and white of an older man and a boy. Acme pushed the photo across the desk and tapped it with his finger. "That's me and my father," he said, "shortly after we crossed the gate. If you look closely, you'll see he's wearing a pocket watch. The same watch that his father and his father before him carried."

Realization dawned slowly for Harley. "And it's out there somewhere?"

Acme nodded and his face took on a sudden and dramatic weight of sorrow. "I took it from him without permission, and then I lost it racing around the salt flats with my friends as a boy." Harley saw the beginning of tears. "I don't have words for how much guilt I still bear, though my father's been gone decades now."

"What's it made of?"

"Platinum. Glass and steel, too, of course." Now Acme's right eye twitched, and Harley noticed that the left one seemed to be the only one making tears.

Harley pulled the mite and control dock from his mining kit. Then opened them both up and starting poking at the settings. He adjusted the range finder, loaded in the specs, and grinned as the rat-sized mite spun to life. "This should be easy enough. If it's still out there." He looked out the window again. "Worst case is that it might take some time. If I had the entire pack, it would go faster."

Acme was rubbing his hands together again, and it tickled Harley's imagination. He'd seen the move in a dozen ancient movies, and nearly always it was a villain move.

Maybe, Harley thought, *he has some kind of condition.* Trying not to notice, he forced a smile. "I think we're ready."

Acme picked up the red phone on his desk. "Megan? Can you come in here?"

The door opened. Harley saw the excitement on her face shift to concern for a moment when she saw Acme's face. Her eyebrow went up.

Acme was on his feet again, gesturing to Harley. "Can you put Mr. Sussbauer's Mighty Tiny Mining Mite™ outside?"

Harley tried to identify the look that passed quickly between them but couldn't. Megan smiled, nodded curtly, and took the humming mite into her hands carefully. "Yes, Mr. Acme." She held it at arm's length. "Do I need to do anything special?"

Harley shook his head. "Just set it on the ground. Point it toward the flats."

She took it and left the room. Acme went to the window and motioned for Harley to join him. Harley put the control dock on the desk, nearby, and stood near Acme.

Something was definitely wrong with the man's eye as it blinked rapidly. But once again, Harley forced his attention away and pointed out the window to a small object that moved quickly toward the salt flat. "There she goes."

Acme clapped and the clap turned into more hand-rubbing of the nefarious sort. Only this time, he seemed aware of it, and his leaking eye widened a bit as he watched his own hands.

The red phone rang, and Acme picked it up. "Yes, Megan?" He nodded. "I understand." He put the receiver down and turned quickly to the door, careful not to look toward Harley. "I am afraid," he said over his shoulder as he moved quickly, "that I have an unexpected and rather urgent matter to attend to. It shouldn't take long. I'm certain you can manage your mite for a few minutes without me?"

Harley opened his mouth to respond but Acme was gone, through the door, before he could say a word.

Maybe it was the coffee kicking in, or maybe it was that he was moving further and further past the initial fog of a stasis wake-up. Whatever it was, Harley found himself suddenly of the thought that perhaps things were not exactly on the up-and-up here at Acme Artificials.

He spent the first ten minutes checking his control dock, adjusting the programming on the mite as it established a pattern and began moving through the salt. Staring out the window, Harley wondered just how long his mite would take to track down such a specific item.

Then he started examining the mechanicals around the room. The bird was the only one functioning and all of them seemed older models.

Finally, at about twenty minutes, Harley went to the door and paused. He put his hand on the knob and that was enough to send him back to the mite controls, tweaking and adjusting. After another five minutes, the door opened, and Megan pushed her face through. It was red now with exertion or frustration.

"I'm so sorry, Mr. Sussbauer. Are you doing okay in here?"

He tried to channel nonchalance. "I'm fine."

She was gone before the words were completely in the air, and now the look on her face added to his rising questions. He waited and then returned to the door.

He put his hand on the knob again and willed himself to turn it.

Locked.

Harley pressed his ear to the door. Beyond it, he heard nothing and now he found himself digging into the hazy fog of his first memories waking up here. There was a front door, or at least he thought there was. A narrow door in, the ornate door into Acme's office. What else?

Harley paced and pondered. He'd been muddled at best upon waking up and then distracted by Megan and the tale she spun.

When Harley flushed this time, it was down into his boots, and not from a slight social embarrassment. This heat came from having been not just any fool, but specifically a damned fool. Whoever these people were, he doubted they were with Acme Artificials, Inc. And the more he thought about Acme's hands and eye, Harley knew he was now using the term "people" loosely.

No, he was surely in the hands of Dastardly Al and his All-Android Caper Gang.

And I'm their current caper, it seems.

For some reason, apart from his embarrassment,

Harley didn't feel the level of anger one might think normal for the circumstances. It was as if some part of him sat on the fence, willing to wait for whichever feeling made the most sense to feel in the moments sure to unfold on the trail ahead. He didn't feel really any anger, and at this point, if these were indeed captors, they'd been nothing but polite and accommodating beyond the subterfuge.

No, instead Harley felt curiosity.

He looked around the room again, then listened at the door. Hearing nothing, he went to his luggage. His control dock wasn't finding a network to access and it had him curious about the cactus. What had Megan said? *That particular model is a bit . . . vocal.*

It was true. But he wondered now why they might not want Duke in the picture.

Harley went to the crated cactus and pushed its activation button, watching the indicator lights spin to life. The packing crate opened with a click and a hiss.

"Hey, Duke," he said, "we have a problem."

"You mean besides the other Duke showing up in a wedding dress and complicating our perfect little family?"

Harley nodded. "I think we have been and currently are being hoodwinked by Dastardly Al and his gang. Are you connected? Can you get the marshals?"

"I can get them, but it'll take a few days."

Harley looked out the window. "Aren't we on New Texas?"

Duke chuckled. "Sorry, Pilgrim. We are a *long* way from New Texas. We are currently on Nephi."

Nephi was the third moon of New Wyoming, known for being a bastion for the lawless and lost, high above the surface of the system's least policed planet. It had one small port and a scattering of unincorporated communities made up of people who didn't want to be easily found. It was also a leading source of salt in the system.

The control dock chimed, and Harley looked up. Moving across the room quickly, he saw the mite had come within range of a target that lit up the board. The mite adjusted course to capture what Harley assumed must be the watch.

He glanced at the door and wondered exactly how this was supposed to play out once Al had what he wanted. He put the mite into a holding pattern, moving in a slow circle around its target, then Harley went back to the cactus. "They are after a platinum pocket watch," he said. "Acme—or at least the android pretending to be him—says it belonged to his father."

"So all of this has been to find a missing watch?"

"Seems so," Harley said.

Duke grunted. "They could've just asked you for a favor."

Harley nodded. Then he heard a voice from the other side of the door. "No," he heard Megan say, "I'll take care of it." He heard exasperation in her voice.

He shushed his cactus and closed the crate, hoping Duke would take the hint and not use this moment to prove the nature of his vocality.

He was back at the panel, moving levers and buttons, when the door opened and Megan stepped in. "I am *so* sorry, Mr. Sussbauer. Mr. Acme has taken unexpectedly ill and hopes you'll forgive his sudden absence."

Harley was never much of a gambler, but his best

play now was clear, so he bluffed. "I am sorry to hear that. Perhaps we should reschedule? I would be happy to come back at another time." He moved a few buttons. "Let me call back the mite and—"

She was quick to interrupt. "Oh, there is no need for us to reschedule. It's such a long trip." He saw her eyes quickly calculating as she took him in. "Mr. Acme has asked that we complete the demonstration without him." Her smile was warm. "How is it going? Has it found anything?"

"Not yet," Harley lied. "And Mr. Acme is certain it is out there?"

She nodded. "I suppose someone else could've found it, but that would be highly unlikely."

Harley scratched his head. "I don't recall exactly where the salt flats are in New Texas?"

Her eyebrow arched. "Southern hemisphere," she said quickly. "Obviously near our headquarters."

"Obviously," he agreed but noted the eyebrow.

He silenced the dock and took it out of its holding pattern. "So I get Mr. Acme his watch," he said, "and you send me and Abigail home?"

"After the ceremony, of course," Megan said. Her eyes met his. The blue seemed something closer to the gunslinger bride's shade now. "If, of course, you want a wedding." She smiled. "It is nonbinding and simply a part of the complete companionship experience. Makes sense if you've come all this way."

The mite had the object now, and he let it run in a loop. He put his body between Megan and the control dock. "And what happens if we don't find the watch?"

Her look was blank enough that Harley found himself unconcerned with failure. "Well, I suppose we'd just send you and your cactus home. I'm sure Mr. Acme would be disappointed, but if the mites can't be used for this type of work, his interest would be lessened considerably."

Harley nodded. "And if it does indeed work?"

"The beginning," she said, "of a potentially beautiful and profitable partnership."

Now Harley saw his moment for what it was and seized upon it. "Don't you reckon," he said, "that all of the best and most lasting partnerships are built upon the bedrock of honesty?"

Megan blushed.

Harley continued. "Just to add a helping of honesty to this casserole of untruth, you should know that the mite already has the watch—if that's what it really is." He moved out of the way to show her the button his finger hovered over. "This here fuses the whole mite into a useless scrap of metal."

Her eyes narrowed, and they were now fully gunslinger blue. "What do you want?"

"Not to deal with lackeys," Harley said, in a firm voice that surprised him. "Go fetch your boss."

Her face flushed. Then she picked up the red phone. "Get in here." She paused. "No," she said, "just get in here. We're done."

The door opened, and Acme swept into the room, a screwdriver jutting from an empty eye socket. The left side of his face sagged. "Have the you watch, then?" The voice was as garbled as the words that jumbled together.

"I do," Harley said. "I assume I can call you Al?"

Acme rubbed his hands together and chortled in dastardly fashion.

But it was Megan who replied. "Yes, Harley," she said. "You can call *me* Al." She extended a hand. "Alyce Portman," she said.

Harley blinked.

"And I'm hoping," she said, "that, if you do indeed have my grandfather's pocket watch in that mite of yours, you'll do me the kindness of bringing it in."

And despite the earlier deception, Harley felt the sincerity in her words, saw it upon her face. He stared at her and she stared back.

Quietly, Abigail and the gunslinger bride both entered the room behind Acme.

"You've been properly introduced to Abigail," Al said. "This here is Tommy." The gunslinger wore a gun belt now, and his hands stayed near the pearl handles of his Colt blasters while his eyes stayed on Alyce for direction. Abigail watched Harley, a breathless expression upon her face that made him uncomfortable.

Harley looked back to the control dock, hit another button, and moved a dial. "It's on its way."

Alyce put a hand on his arm and the warmth was as discombobulating as her smell. "Thank you," she said. She looked at the breathless bride. "Go fetch, Abigail."

Abigail left, and in her absence, an enviro-dome drifted through the doorway. Tommy watched.

"What the happy horseshit is going on here?" The voice was rough but female.

"Hey," Duke the cactus said from his corner, "is that a cactus in your garden or are you just glad to see me?"

Harley's eyes narrowed. "You have a cactus in the gang, too?"

Alyce grinned. "No. Daisy is my relationship practice. I got her from Acme." Their eyes met briefly. "Just like you."

Harley watched the controls, then started the shutdown process once Abigail returned holding the mite. Harley moved his fingers over the unit and opened its cache.

The pocket watch lay within, scratched and dented. Alyce reached for it, then paused and met Harley's eyes. "May I?"

He nodded, and she lifted it out. Carefully, she turned it over in her hands, then opened it and squinted down.

"There it is," she said. She held it out to him, and he saw the engraving. *For Cedric Acme*, it said, *03/11/97.*

"So it really was Acme's watch?"

She nodded. "Follow me."

They left the office and passed through the reception area to the only other door. Everyone followed them in procession as if on parade. Duke took up the rear.

Beyond the reception area lay what appeared to be her workshop: tables, bins of body parts and other bits of electronic detritus, toolboxes, shelves, and racks crammed full of props and costumes. And in the far corner, ancient and rusted, stood a small antique safe.

She spun the dial, and he watched the left right sequences as she paused at 3, 11, 9 and 7.

Harley could feel the anticipation in the air as it clanked open, and Alyce slowly swung its heavy door. There was a pause and then a muted gasp.

Empty.

"Well, that's a fine howdy-do," Duke the cactus said to the empty safe.

"That's a fine howdy-do, indeed," Daisy the cactus agreed.

At the end of it all, they sat around the empty safe on chairs gathered from around the three-room prefab.

"Well, most of it went well enough," Abigail said.

"I wish my eye had been more cooperative," Roger said.

"I wish I'd gotten to use my six-guns," Tommy said.

Dastardly Al shrugged. "We *did* find the watch and the combo for the safe."

"But," Harley said, "I'm guessing I am back to the proverbial drawing board when it comes to matrimonial bliss."

Abigail reached over and patted his arm. "Sorry, sugar."

Tommy reached over and did the same. "Truly sorry, Pilgrim."

Alyce chuckled. "But you *do* get to keep the cactus." Her blue eyes held his and she offered an apologetic smile. "For what it's worth, I'm sorry."

Harley shrugged. "If you'd just asked, I'd have likely said yes."

She nodded. "Lesson learned."

"So what's next?"

"Oh, I reckon we'll get you pointed toward home, get the prefab torn down and loaded, and get on to the next thing." Alyce waved her hands in the direction of the wedding gown now placed back on the rack. "And, you know, your credit with Acme was fine. And I'm sure Todd will be glad to hear from you."

Harley shook his head. "An android bride may not

be in the cards for me," he said. "No offense," he said to Abigail.

"None taken." She and Tommy were in stereo and everyone laughed.

"What's this I hear, Pilgrim?" Duke's voice was heavy with sarcasm. "You having second thoughts about taking a wife?"

Al's eyes went wide with mock outrage. "Taking a wife? Who talks that way anymore?"

"Exactly," Daisy the cactus said.

"Harley does," Duke said. "As in Harley takes a wife."

Now Abigail joined in. "Oh no. That won't do."

"Nope," Harley said. "I surely don't see me taking a wife."

Alyce grinned. "Maybe," she said, "Harley takes a girl on a date?" She paused, let her eyes meet his again. "Sometime? If you want to?"

Harley looked at Duke, then looked back at Dastardly Al and her gang. He was already here. And it might just be the oddest way to meet someone, but he felt this meeting all the way down in his boots.

"Well," he finally said, "there's no time like the present."

And so it came to pass that Harlan Bosco Sussbauer, the last prospector of the Big Space Rock Mine Co-op, did not take a wife after all and, instead, took a girl—Ms. Alyce Portman of New Wyoming specifically—on a date.

It was, as they told their grandchildren many years later, nice enough as first dates go. And, of course, Mrs. Portman-Sussbauer would add quietly for their waiting young ears, that despite the empty safe, her biggest caper had gone exactly as planned.

WARLOCK RULES

Hank Schwaeble

The silence of the Consort Cruiser was so deep that between breaths Cutter could hear the sloshing of blood as it pulsed through his system.

The official reason for the negative-D surfaces and compartment linings was to thwart hyperspace LVT surveillance, but he figured there were plenty of places on the ship shielded enough for the interior acoustics to be normal. No, he was sure they just liked the way it put visitors at unease. He supposed the others in the room were used to it by now. Or maybe they'd been hacked. The more he thought about it, the more that was likely the answer.

"I apologize for the lack of notice," the woman seated at the curved conference counter, Marilanjouie Pitt-Summers, said. The two men flanking her, seated at obtuse angles to him around the crescent, hadn't been identified and had yet to speak.

"You came in cloaked and docked with my tug without so much as a radio call. Lack of notice isn't exactly the source of my concerns."

"Yes, well, you were difficult to locate. We were wary that any transmissions to you, especially in this quadrant, might be intercepted or, more likely, ignored. The matter we wish to discuss is rather urgent, not to mention sensitive."

The light in the conference area was diffused bioluminescence calibrated to the circadian rhythms and vital signs of its occupants, as was the temperature and relative humidity. It was a combination of incredibly sophisticated engineering that harnessed natural organic processes finely tuned to optimize physical and psychological responses.

Cutter hated it.

Natural was natural; this was an environment produced by bacteria and flora and biosynthesis, slapped onto cultures and regulated by quantum chips—artificial crap masquerading as the real thing.

"Well, given you have a captive audience, I'm all ears."

"Don't look at it that way, Mr. Cutter. We didn't track you to this remote area of the security zone to take you prisoner. We're here to offer you a job."

"You must know I'm out here because I don't have a license."

"Yes. The job I'm talking about is not as a tug pilot—it's a onetime service."

Cutter glanced at the two men. Poker faces, grim and expressionless.

"I'm not a smuggler."

"Oh, we know. This doesn't involve anything illegal. Your name came up after an extensive AI analysis of candidates who matched the necessary criteria."

"Criteria?"

"Perhaps it would be best if I explained the situation first." She stood and circled the curved arc of table separating them, stopping in front of him to lean back against it. Unlike the men, she was wearing a formfitting top and skirt. Cutter decided this was her persuasion outfit. "How much do you know about the Private Noninterference Zone?"

"I know it's a big buffer where charters with pull mine asteroids. I also know it's off-limits to planetary authorities. Strictly private sector."

"It's much more than that. It's where the bulk of cutting-edge mineralogical and exo-chemical research is performed. It's only been available for the last decade, and already the advancements and discoveries are astounding—breakthroughs in the last two years that've had immense impacts on humanity."

"Okay."

"The Chibula have announced they intend to annex Hephaestus."

"Hephaestus? What do the Chibs want with that radioactive rock?"

"They contend the Consortium's research station is engaging in surveillance. With Hephaestus being so close to their sovereign sector, they're invoking a provision of the treaty based on our presence and are claiming an option to reincorporate."

"That sounds like something for the diplomatic corps to deal with."

"Normally, you would think so. But the area is so small, they are asserting a right to alternative resolutions under an obscure provision of the treaty regarding private sector operations."

"Again, what does all this have to do with me?"

"Are you familiar with the treaty, Mr. Cutter?"

Cutter scratched the back of his head. "It was next on my reading list."

"It is over a million words, in four languages. What matters to us is a little-known section on minor disputes with nongovernmental organizations. The Chibula have elected to bypass mediated negotiations, or a panel arbitration, and are invoking a right to trial."

"Why do I get the sense you're not talking about them taking you to court?"

"They're claiming a right to trial by combat."

"You have got to be . . . Why the hell did anyone agree to that?"

"It has to do with language and cultural barriers and definitions and cross-references that are the product of many months of negotiations and dozens of drafters. There is a definition of 'trial' in one section that includes a procedure for low-level claims over small matters to be decided by a single representative for each party. The Chibulan negotiators insisted it be included because it is customary for them to settle disputes that way and, if no such provision like that existed for any disputes, they advised it would not be considered a binding agreement by their standards."

"Well, of course they would want that. They're seven feet tall and typically as strong as a grizzly or silverback. Might as well just say they win every dispute."

"It's true they wanted it to be hand to hand or to be fought with contact weapons, but our lawyers got them to agree to limit it to extremely small territorial disputes, only invokable once every five years, and that it would be limited to weapons we believed gave us, *humans*, an advantage. Since they are intimidated by our military technology, we agreed to a weapon over two hundred and fifty years old. One they'd never actually seen in use but were satisfied with the technical descriptions and definition of."

She turned and retrieved a rectangular box from the table and held it out for him to see. "That definition was included in the treaty."

Her fingers pulled on the front of the box, opening it to reveal a silver revolver, its metal surfaces glistening in the perfectly fake natural light.

"A gunfight? You want to settle this with a gunfight? You must be insane. Or think I'm insane..."

"Yours was the last class of UDF basic school graduates trained in the use of cartridge firearms. Our records show you were high expert with the pistol and the long rifle."

"That was twenty years ago. And we were cross-trained eighteen months later into plasma rifles and pulse blasters. Besides, I'd hardly compare electronic-fed, auto-fire mag-guns to six-shooters."

"Nevertheless, you have training with that general type of weapon, you have experience. You meet the qualifications."

"So must a few hundred—probably a few thousand—others."

"These qualifications go beyond proficiency with obsolete weaponry. The combatant must not have served in the military within the last decade, must not have been in the employ of any governmental or security service in the last seven years, and not had any criminal convictions on his or her record in the past twenty years."

"That's me," Cutter said. "A man with no convictions."

Pitt-Summers continued, ignoring him, "Once we added in the psychological factors and the final condition demanded by the Chibula—there were very few candidates identified. You, Mr. Cutter, were one of those few. In fact, a review of those candidates determined you were, for all practical purposes, the *only* one truly qualified."

"What 'final condition' are we talking about?"

"You're UA. As you may be aware, the Chibula take the issue of genetic enhancements very seriously. They refer to in their language as *kincreeshix*. There's no exact word for it in English, but it roughly translates to—"

"An abomination," Cutter said.

"So you *are* familiar with some of their . . . idiosyncrasies."

Cutter said nothing. His status as UA was the only thing he had to fall back on, so he knew he had to tread carefully. He couldn't tell her, not if he wanted to keep his rating. Only unaltereds were allowed to fly in interplanetary neutral zones. This was partly because the Chibula refused to donate star-system easement tracts for safe passage if altereds weren't forbidden, and partly because it was the only way to keep fugitives from being able smuggle themselves through. The DNA of altereds could never be trusted in the gene pool, which was why it was strictly controlled on Earth, through licensing and monitoring, and violations were severely punished. Likewise, every ship in the Zone was subject to boarding and gene-scans of the crew, no exceptions.

So far, his undocumented modification had proven to

be as undetectable as he'd been assured, the technique being proprietary and secretive and banished to the no-go sectors near the edge of the galaxy because of its lack of a residual signature. But he imagined the Consortium—not to mention the Chibs, as fanatic as they were regarding the issue—would use scans and techniques that were a little more thorough.

"I'm sure you have a lot of questions," Pitt-Summers said. "Like wondering what's in this for you."

"Well, yes, but that's not what I'm wondering at the moment."

"What would that be?"

"Whether the real reason you want me is I'm likely the only one on your list who's killed a Chib. Up close, I mean."

"We don't appreciate you using that term, Mr. Cutter." It was one of the men seated on the other side of the curved counter. He had harsh, ruddy features, an expression forged from decades of corporate battles and boardroom maneuverings. Cutter caught a glint in his eye and realized that was his enhancement, some sort of visual receptor modification. He was probably seeing Cutter in infrared three-D, noting changes in his body temperature.

Cutter snorted. "Doesn't that make you the virtuous one."

"What Mr. Barris means is, this is a delicate situation, Mr. Cutter. Believe it or not, this is still considered a diplomatic remedy. It avoids a potentially contentious face-off that could easily lead to a renewal of hostilities after over fifteen years of peace."

"So, you want me to kill one of them, but using a slang term is over the line?"

"What we want," Pitt-Summers said, "is for you to demonstrate some respect for what's at stake."

"Okay, let's talk about what's at stake. If it's so serious, why don't you just let them have it?"

"What do you mean by 'it'?"

"Hephaestus, that little corner of the buffer. What do you care? It's a radioactive hunk of ore and I don't know what else, magma or the like. Just let them have it. A show of good faith. It's just lines on a chart."

Pitt-Summers glanced at the men behind her and shifted her weight to her other buttock, clasping her hands together and resting them on her thigh.

"To concede something like that could encourage more attempts, invite more aggressive moves, while signaling that there was merit to their allegations, further emboldening them to challenge consortium activity."

"First of all, I'm sure they're right, that you're spying, so let's not play games. You're hiding something. Something else, I mean. I can tell by the way the two Sphinxes back there are watching me. And by the way you're being so polite. Just tell me what's really going on."

More glances were exchanged. Cutter thought he saw the other man, the one with dark skin and hair that fit his head like a helmet, dip his chin in a barely perceptible nod, but he couldn't be sure.

"We began our study of Hephaestus a few years ago because the radiation signature didn't correspond with our calculations. After sending probe after probe, we finally penetrated the crust deeply enough to identify an unknown isotope. This new isotope, paradigmion, will provide decades' worth of information for us to analyze. It can't be duplicated, as we are simply unable to match the energy necessary to compress subparticles artificially to equal its density."

"And . . . ?"

Her lips tightened, puckering slightly. "It's also come to our attention that it pairs naturally with calabantium. According to our modeling equations—ones beyond my ability to explain—these two elements, when combined properly, could provide an intergalactic level of stellarator energy. Do you understand the implications?"

"I'm guessing you mean, it would let you power a ship that could move really, really fast."

"Yes. Hyper-leap speeds. That is orders of magnitude faster than current ships. But that's not all. It could, potentially, power a weapon able to reach across star systems. A weapon that could devastate an adversary's planet before they even knew hostilities had commenced. And would you like to offer a guess as to where the only substantial deposits of calabantium in the charted territories are known to exist?"

"The Chibulan System."

"Now you see why we can't let Hephaestus fall into their hands. And why we can't risk escalating matters. We mustn't let them discover its importance."

He thought for a moment. "Aren't you forgetting one minor but important detail?"

"What's that?"

"That the Chibs—I mean, the Chibula—are not only bigger and stronger, but faster than your average human."

"Yes. Considerably faster than your average human. But I would venture not considerably faster than you."

There it is, he thought. The other G-Boot dropping.

"Given your training, I mean," she added.

"Reflex speed is not the deciding factor," the man seated behind her to the right said. "The Chibula are fast, and strong, but the nature of their physiology does not lend itself to fine motor skills."

"You're saying they're not accurate."

"According to our kinesthesiologists, the accuracy you displayed in your training records is superior to anything a Chibulan combatant could attain without years of training."

"Let's say I believe you. Why should I risk my life like that?"

"For your people. For your country. For the security of Earth."

"Now I know you're insane."

"We know you've been saving platinum warrants, hoping to negotiate a resolution to the charges pending against you. You want to buy your way back home, where, as things stand, you're unemployable. We can arrange a full pardon. As well as a complete reinstatement of transit privileges."

"And how could the private Extro-logistical Geo Consortium arrange that?"

"Like I said, the UDF wants to avoid direct involvement in this dispute. But that doesn't mean they're not keenly interested. You pull this off, you get to keep all those warrants, return with full privileges and a clean slate. A *completely* clean slate, including transit and full biomedical waivers."

Cutter dipped his chin, chuckling. Full biomedical waivers. Letting him know they knew without letting him know they knew. He suddenly felt stupid. Of *course* they knew. It wasn't something they were willing to overlook, it was the real reason they chose him. He had no idea how they found out, but they did.

"When?"

"Five solar days. Sorry. It took a long time to find you. This transport is equipped to allow you to familiarize yourself with the weapon. The rules call for each combatant to have a second, and we're providing you one. Her name is Vaneshka Khoudry. She's both a kinesthesiologist and a mechanical engineer. She's studied the weaponry extensively and will train you. The Colt .45 Peacemaker fires a—"

"I know what a Colt .45 fires. Where is this supposed to happen?"

"There's an abandoned outpost in Meridian Five. It's on a class-C dwarf moon with a dense mercury core that equates to .9 Gs and has an atmosphere that is thirty-one percent oxygen, sixty percent nitrogen. It's the only spot in neutral territory that meets all the necessary criteria."

"Abandoned outpost? Warlock? You're talking about Warlock?"

"That's not its official name, but yes. You're familiar with it?"

"Yes, I'm familiar with it." Every Force Infantry soldier who fought in that war was, he thought. It was called Warlock because it had gravity like Earth's, on a moon the size of a large asteroid, and its hard-packed sandy terrain looked like a movie set, something the guy who ran the outpost played up to draw in military personnel on R&R and shore leave. Cutter had a difficult time believing the choice of location was a coincidence.

"I have a cargo container I'm tugging. If I were

to say yes—and that's a big if—I'd have to deliver that first. I can make it in three days; you can meet me when I drop it off. I'm not sure if that gives you enough time."

"I'm afraid that's not possible. We need to be in orbit at Kronos Four a day early. The coordinates for your delivery put you four days away from our destination. And in addition to your training, we will need to fit you with proper attire. No synthetics or metals allowed. The Chibula were quite clear about this. They don't trust synthetic materials wouldn't be designed to neutralize the effects of the weaponry. They only wear garments made of natural fibers and expect us to do the same. The wind and sand will call for a long coat made of actual leather, as well as boots. Your other garments will be natural cotton, for the most part."

"You're not listening. I have a cargo container I *have* to deliver. I know you're promising me stardust and Jupiter rain-diamonds, but these are not the kind of people I can disappoint. If I don't show up with it on time, I'll have a bounty on my head."

"That's not a concern, Mr. Cutter."

"Maybe not to you."

"Not to you, either. We purchased your cargo from its owner an hour ago."

"Let me get this straight. If I were to say no, I don't even have a delivery fee waiting for me?" He sucked in a lungful of fake, phony, perfect air. "In that case, you do know the binary stars stay directly overhead for almost twenty hours on Warlock, don't you?"

He cast glances at the two men, then locked eyes on Pitt-Summers.

"So, you better get me a friggin' hat, too. And since there's a good chance I'm going to die in it, make it a damn nice one."

"Have I mentioned how insane this is?"

"Not for at least five or ten minutes."

Cutter stood in the tiny shuttle, clinging to the hand-strap along the ceiling as the craft rumbled into the dwarf planet's atmosphere. "Well, it bears repeating."

Khoudry did not respond. The shuttle's AI autopilot made thousands of adjustments to the flight surfaces and thrusters per second, making for a remarkably smooth entry, but she monitored the instrument panel closely for discrepancies anyway. Cutter watched her, admiring her intensity, even if she wasn't exactly his type. She had dark hair and dark eyes and bronze skin, which were all more than fine by him, but she was on the short side. In his experience, short women were always trouble. The same contents as taller ones, only packed under pressure, ready to explode when you least expect it.

"You really think I can beat whatever Chib they brought down there for this?"

"I think your chances of getting out of there alive are much higher if you don't use derogatory terms like 'Chib' to describe them. There are rules to this duel. Get them angry enough to make it personal, those may go out the window."

After a moment's silence, she let out an audible sigh. "Your reaction time is near the ninety-ninth percentile. No matter how fast the Chibulan may be, you will likely get a shot off. And their musculature doesn't—"

"Lend itself to fine motor skills. Yeah, yeah. So

everything is riding on me being on target and their guy missing."

"We have no way of knowing if their combatant will be male or female. They are sexually dimorphic, completely binary, but genderless. There is no apparent difference between males and females perceptible by human senses at casual distances. It makes for a far more efficient social structure."

"Remind me when this is over to not ask you if you'd like to have a drink."

The surface came into view through the forward window, rushing toward them. Khoudry readied her hand near the control stick. The shuttle decelerated smoothly, a momentary feel of negative Gs washing through Cutter's gut and head. Then the craft leveled and lowered itself through a series of controlled discharges as it settled onto the flat expanse of sand.

"And there they are," Cutter said, peering through a side port. "Just tied up and waiting for us."

A few dozen meters away, two saddled creatures stood on four legs, seemingly bored. Xenobex. Cutter had never actually seen one but had heard about them. They looked like someone had taken a horse, put camel humps like saddle bags where its ass was, and gave it a long neck that led to a head shaped like a wolf's, with two pronged horns.

"I can't believe we have to actually ride those things."

"The Chibula are extremely paranoid that we will cheat. It was only after we pointed out there was literally no way for us to get to the surface without using a transport shuttle that they even agreed to that. They think we'll smuggle in weapons or shielding or something to tilt the playing field."

"I never understood them. They're practically an entire race of engineers, yet their weapons were noticeably inferior to ours. And for a warrior culture, their tactics were nonexistent and their strategies transparent."

"They didn't evolve the same way our species did. Their visuo-spatial intelligence is far beyond ours. But they are mainly linear in their thinking."

Cutter nodded and his ears popped slightly as he listened to the engines wind down while the craft performed an atmospheric equalization. He had seen the Chibula weaponry firsthand, seen their ships and fighters. Masterful feats of engineering. But it had been like having the galaxy's finest knife at a sword fight. They lacked almost any imagination, were practically incapable of creative thinking. They had no tradition of storytelling or cinema or fiction. Just science and an austere religion that, as far as Cutter could understand, worshiped the universe as a conscious being.

"Yeah, as a race, they always struck me as...weird."

"I'm sure they could make the same argument about us."

Cutter grunted. "Some more than others."

Khoudry looked at him, her mouth bunched into a frown. "Before we go out there, we should go over a few things. Keep them fresh in your mind. The Chibula and his or her second will meet with us for a mutual display of skill prior to the dual. Each of you will then be asked to deem your opponent worthy, which you will."

"I never asked, but what would happen if I didn't? If I said, you know, this Chib...*ula* is not up to my standards."

"It would be considered a personal insult to be settled without rules, probably without warning. The outcome would not resolve the dispute, though. It would just result in one or both of you dead."

"Considering the average Chib could probably rip my head off and eat it like an apple—might actually want to do just that—I guess my vote is 'worthy.'"

"You joke, but this is serious."

"I know. That's *why* I joke."

"After a period of rest—religious meditation for the Chibula—you will meet at the designated spot, separated by a distance of thirty meters. There will be one signal, chosen by the neutral officiating authority, probably the interpreter. You may draw and fire at will once it is given. If you both empty your weapon without a fatal or debilitating injury being sustained, you will reload and close the distance to twenty meters and repeat. Then to ten meters. If no decisive injury is sustained, it will be considered a draw, and you will retreat to separate areas for rest—or prayer—and start again. As indicated, the contest is over when one sustains a fatal or debilitating injury and can't continue."

"What if one is injured and the other dies?"

"The surviving party is considered the victor."

"Yay."

A tone sounded, indicating the chamber was equalized. The hatch to the shuttle opened, separating with the hiss of a vacuum seal being broken. Cutter stepped down the footrail and onto the surface.

The ground was hardpan, dried out and mostly flat, with wisps of loose sand slithering and winding across the top in gusts of hot wind. The sky was a bright, hazy blue, like a shade of ice, and the twin stars that warmed everything seemed to be holding hands high overhead. In the distance, the sand turned from beige to yellow to orange to red. There were hills to one side, far away, but nothing else visible—just the hitching post a couple dozen meters away and the Xenobex tied to it, waiting with a quiet patience Cutter found disturbing.

"Those are really our only means of transportation?"

"Yes, unless you want to walk through almost thirty kilometers of aridscape. The only technology they would allow is a comm unit for a Panurian translator and, of course, the gene-scan."

"Of course. I have a hard time picturing a Chibula on one of those things."

"Oh, no, they're walking. Or jogging. Their gait at a mild pace is three times what a human spans. And given that their worlds average 1.1 Earth Gs, I would expect they'll be particularly light on their feet here."

Cutter walked up to the nearest Xenobex. When he closed to within a meter, it turned its head toward him and spat. He flinched, arching his body to avoid it. A large gob of slime caught the front of his pant leg and slid down to the top of his boot.

"Well, isn't this galaxy-class wonderful?"

"Hey, be grateful. It's marking you. They usually don't do that right away. They don't have great peripheral vision, but do have keen senses of smell. They spit to be able to keep track of you. In case you fall off."

"Fall off?"

"Yes. Try to keep to a trot. Nothing faster than that. They can move rather quickly, but their gait at a gallop is . . . just don't let them go faster than a trot. A gentle tug on the reins straight back is probably enough."

"You seem to know a lot about them. Where did you learn to ride?"

Khoudry walked over to the other Xenobex and put a foot into the stirrup. "On the transport, yesterday," she said, swinging her leg over and settling into the saddle. "By reading the fact sheets."

The ride to the outpost took two hours. The Xenobex trotted at a consistent tempo, their efficient legs moving them about as fast as the average person could sprint and doing so in a way that seemed effortless. Cutter could occasionally hear a snorting breath, but all in all he got the impression this was a leisurely pace for the beasts.

A strong wind crossed in front of them, whipping a cloud of sand into funnels and forcing Cutter to clamp down on his hat and pull the bandana around his neck up over his face. That action brought with it the understanding of why the large piece of cloth was provided with instructions how to tie it. He was glad he hadn't given in to the urge to leave it on the shuttle.

When the dust devils faded away, and the sand finally settled, he could see the outpost. A small collection of domed buildings in two rows facing one another, each of them rounded and sloped to the ground to allow smooth airflow over them.

All but one.

In the center to the right was the Saloon—a relatively sizable building with a wooden façade. The owner had built it to cater to UDF forces wanting to blow off a little steam. It advertised drinks and pleasure droids . . . though rumor was, for a steep fee, he would supply the real thing. There were supposedly no rules on Warlock, but that was never the case, anywhere. Every place had rules, the only question was, how did you learn them, and who enforced them?

Cutter always thought the owner had started the rumors about everything being for sale there, droid or human, just to make the place sound exciting. Truth was, there was no shortage of either men or women in the UDF looking for a casual good time, so there wasn't really any need. Besides, after a few stiff drinks, most people couldn't tell the difference, anyway.

The entrance to the outpost was through a framed archway that used to bear a sign but was now just bare. The Xenobex slowed to a walk as they crossed through.

A man stepped out into the corridor separating the rows of buildings near the Saloon. He was wearing a long green robe and a white coif on his head, the flaps covering his ears with a slender tendril hanging from each. He had no facial hair, not even eyebrows, which, to Cutter, immediately marked him as Panurian.

He raised a hand as they approached.

"You're late," the man said.

Before Cutter could respond, Khoudry said, "We were given a time to land, not a time to arrive at the outpost."

The Panurian didn't reply. He gestured toward the Saloon and waited while Cutter and Khoudry dismounted.

"The Chibulan representative and his second are inside. They've been here for some time. They are quite agitated at your . . . tardiness."

"Well, tell 'em to come out here, and let's get this thing over with."

A worried expression passed over the Panurian's face. "That's not the way it is done. They are keen observers of custom and decorum. They insist the rules be followed."

Cutter looked at Khoudry, then at the Panurian. "We're here now, aren't we?"

The doors to the Saloon pushed open and another Panurian came out. He was wearing the same kind of coif and robe, only his robe was blue. "This is Krilbin," the first one said. "He is to perform the genetic scan. My name is Fanjir. I am the interpreter."

"The pleasure's all mine, I'm sure. Now, can we get on with this? I'm hungry and thirsty. The sooner we get to the rest period, the better."

Krilbin straightened his back, pushed his head high. "After discussing the matter with their superiors, the Chibula have requested a forfeiture. This contest will exceed the time allotted under the rules, due to your lack of punctuality. They have spent the last three point six *dakkha*—their standard units of time—in meditation. It is their belief that humans do nothing by chance, but seek every advantage to exploit."

"A forfeiture?" Cutter laughed. "Tell them *no*. Tell them not only *no*, but *hell no*. We weren't the ones who screwed up. We landed at the precise time we were given."

"What my associate means," Khoudry said, stepping forward past Cutter, "is please tell them that this was a simple miscommunication, and that we would like to accommodate their concerns. If they have already engaged in restful meditation, perhaps if we were to waive that rest period? As a show of good faith?"

The Panurians exchanged looks. Fanjir dipped his

head in assent. Krilbin turned on his heel and reentered the Saloon.

Several minutes passed in silence, Cutter kicking his boot against the hardpacked sand, Khoudry staring at the Saloon doors. Cutter heard a noise like something scraping, followed by the sound of heavy footfalls, then the opposing doors swung open. A towering creature pushed through and came to a stop on the wooden boardwalk. Another one followed. Krilbin shuffled out from behind them and hastily made his way to the front and exchanged some words with Fanjir in a low voice.

"They would like some assurance this is not a trick," Fanjir said.

Cutter studied the creatures. Their physiques, their features, their overall appearance was one Cutter had always found bizarre. They looked like someone had taken a giant praying mantis and tried to turn it into a person. Dominating their smooth, gray-green, triangular heads—with a bony crest crossing over the top toward the rear—they had bulging black eyes the size of a man's fist and mandibles that closed from side to side. But they also had lips and a tongue, a flat but humanlike nose, and tiny ears on the sides above their eyes. Their torsos were long and convex, narrowing to a perch for their head on one end and angling back to a point at the other. Their arms were long, resting in a curled position with their forearms against their chest. At the ends of those arms were hands that were almost human-looking, with three sharp fingers and a flat, blunt thumb. Their legs were probably the most normal thing about them, except for the fact they bent in the opposite direction at the knee.

What Cutter found the most remarkable, however, was how absolutely ridiculous, how utterly preposterous, the closest one, the big one, was dressed. He was dressed in a white shirt with fringes along the sleeve, a calfskin vest, a bright red bandana, and brown leather chaps. He had a tall cowboy hat somehow affixed to the top leg of his triangular head and, although he didn't have boots due to the tripod shape of his feet, his outfit did come complete with a holster and a six-gun tied down to his leg.

"You got to be shitting me," he said, wagging his chin.

Khoudry elbowed cutter in the ribs. "This is not a trick." She took another step closer to the Chibula. "We meant no disrespect."

Fanjir addressed the Chibula and spoke in sounds Cutter couldn't follow. The Chib in the back responded, and the big one up front added something curt.

"They say your proposal is acceptable, but only because they do not wish there to be any controversy regarding the outcome. They will not allow themselves to be made to look foolish."

"Too late," Cutter said, letting out a soft chuckle.

"Thank them for us," Khoudry said. "And tell them we may begin when they are ready."

Fanjir bowed and passed along the message, or seemed to, and after a short back-and forth the Chibula stepped off the boardwalk.

Krilbin walked up to the tall one and held out a thick hand tablet. He tapped the screen a few times, then directed it toward the top of the Chibula's head and lowered it slowly until it was pointed at the ground. A blue glow cut across the creature and followed the tablet the entire way before disappearing. Krilbin tapped the screen a few more times then turned to Cutter.

The tingle that ran through Cutter's scalp and down his spine was not unpleasant, but he did find it unnerving. A flash of blue momentarily blinded him as the scan slid down to his feet. Krilbin started to tap the screen, then stopped, his finger hovering a few centimeters away. He looked at Cutter, his gaze narrowing. He stared at the screen for a few more seconds, hesitated again, then tapped it.

"You have all been genetically cleared as UA."

Fanjir made some noises in the direction of the Chibula, prompting the big one to pull its head back, catching Cutter's gaze as it did. It spun on one prong of its three-pronged feet and strode down the length of the building away from the direction Cutter had come.

"This way," Fanjir said. "Per the rules, we will have a brief display of skill, and then the contest shall commence."

Cutter and Khoudry fell in a few steps behind Fanjir. Cutter leaned in close and whispered, "What's with the getup? Are they trying to be cute, poking fun at us? Or do they think I won't be able to hit shit if I'm laughing my ass off at them?"

"The Chibula are more or less literalists, Cutter. When they studied the treaty and saw the manner of combat, they requested video of the contest in practice. No one had actual footage of a gunfight like this, so they sent them a library of old Hollywood Westerns. If you'd bothered to read the materials, you'd know this."

"Isn't that what I have you for?"

Fanjir stopped next to the Chibula at the gap

between the Saloon and the next building. As Cutter approached and the angle widened, he could see a pair of targets between the structures. Two metal squares with concentric circles of colors brightening as you moved outward from the center, with the middle being a deep red.

"Please, step to this line." Fanjir indicated a strip of black holographene. He waved a white length of linen. "When this cloth hits the surface, you will each draw and fire at the target on your side. If you draw too early, it will be considered a fault and you will redo. This is ceremonial, not competitive, but it will allow each of you to assess your opponent."

He proceeded to repeat the instructions in the Chibulan tongue.

Not competitive, Cutter thought. *Right.*

Fanjir held up the cloth, jerked his wrist a few times, then released it. Cutter watched it float, ghostlike, fluttering slightly, weaving back and forth before riding a tiny gust of breeze and then, finally settling to the ground.

As Cutter drew his revolver, he became abruptly aware of a shot ringing out, but it seemed premature. He heeled the hammer back with his palm and heard the report of his own shot, the gun kicking in his hand.

Cutter looked at the targets. He'd managed to nick the edge of the circle one perimeter removed from the center. At first, he thought his opponent had missed the other target completely, then he saw a small dot dead center. A perfect bull's-eye.

The Chibula turned to face him. It held its revolver out, almost as if it were going to shoot him, then it twirled the gun around its finger, forward, then back, then forward again, before lowering its hand and giving the piece a final spin so that the barrel plunged itself into the holster. It walked past him with long hard steps, and Cutter wondered if it was his imagination, or if he actually saw the lips between those bug mandibles curl into a smile.

"The Chibulan Proxy has indicated you are worthy," Fanjir said. "What say you?"

"Whatever it takes to get this over with," Cutter said.

The Panurian frowned, then uttered more strange sounds to the smaller Chibula near him.

"We may commence," Fanjir said, before walking back to the front of the Saloon.

Cutter took a few steps, then veered slightly, stopping and yanking Khoudry aside. "I thought you said they weren't accurate?"

"And I thought you said you were a good shot. And what the heck kind of draw was that? Those Xenobex could pull faster than you did."

"It's called not showing your hand. If he thinks I'm slow, he may take his time."

"That's the last thing you want to let him do."

"Why?"

"Because"—Khoudry leaned over, looking past him—"that *was* him taking his time."

Krilbin started to speak in a loud tone. Fanjir did the same, only in the Chibulan language. "The participants will please walk along the outer edge of the corridor until you pass the third line. That is your mark. Follow that line to the center. Once you take your marks, I will toss the cloth again. You may draw once any part of it first touches the surface. If you fault, but the other side is uninjured, the non-faulting combatant will be entitled to a free shot. If the non-faulting side is injured or dead, the contest is forfeited. Do you understand?"

Cutter nodded. The Chibulan combatant twisted its head sideways, then back.

"Take your marks."

Cutter made his way to the black holographene in the sand and walked out into the middle of the open space. He dug his boots lightly into the ground, one foot slightly forward of the other, and pulled the edge of his duster back. He positioned his hand over the handle of his Colt and bent his knees just enough to give his legs some spring. He glanced at the Chibula, some thirty meters away, standing awkwardly, arms pinched in like a dinosaur, then he shifted his gaze to the Panurian twitching the cloth above his head. *Lower thorax*, he reminded himself, remembering the sole time he'd killed one up close, shoving a long piece of broken metal from his crashed fighter into its gut as it descended in a pounce. The medic had told him they had a vulnerable organ cluster he'd managed to hit, but it was only the size of an old-fashioned softball.

Lower thorax, he repeated, mouthing the words silently. *That's the weak underbelly*.

The Panurian lowered his arm and flicked the cloth high and forward. Cutter watched it dance on the air, gliding to and fro, riding sheets of current, dipping and rising, until one edge finally scraped the sand.

Not holding back this time, Cutter drew and fired, the gun jerking from his holster rapidly, his other palm fanning the hammer as he held down the trigger. A distant crack split the air just before the much louder report of his gun battered his ears, and he felt a kick in his side. He doubled over, cradling his rib cage, and dropped to one knee. He saw his opponent still standing, watched it twirl the gun a few times before letting it drop back in its holster. Then it took a step closer and toppled forward, falling flat on its triangular face.

Cutter let out a long breath he hadn't realized he'd been holding and collapsed onto his ass before tipping sideways and rolling onto his back.

He shut his eyes and cursed, then opened them to see Khoudry kneeling over him. "How bad is it?"

Cutter shook his head. "I don't know."

She pried his arm from his side and he saw her grimace. She touched the wound, felt around some, and stopped when he winced.

"It caught a rib, but at an angle. It deflected without penetrating further. You do have a cracked one, though. So, the pain is real."

"And here I thought it was all my head."

"It probably had the effect of a gut punch, too. Catch your breath and let's get you some medical attention. Congratulations. You won."

"Yeah," Cutter said, grunting as he tried to sit up. "I can tell by how excited you are."

"If you can stand, they may have a med-kit for this kind of thing. I'll walk you over."

Cutter got to his feet, his arm around Khoudry's shoulders, the lower g-force making it easier than he'd expected. He staggered a few steps, then felt her stop. She was looking up into the distance. He followed her gaze to just above the horizon.

"That can't be good," he said.

Krilbin approached them, an urgent pace to his

stride. "It's the Chibula," he said. "I just established a commlink with the Chibulan Second and their superiors. They are demanding the two of you remain so they can conduct an interview."

"An interview? Why?"

"They said they have received credible allegations of cheating. Please, come with me into the Saloon. We will try to sort this out."

"Sure thing," Cutter said, interrupting Khoudry as she started to speak. "Go on and tell them we'll be right along to clear everything up. I'm just a little slow at the moment."

The Panurian nodded warily and turned back toward the Saloon.

Cutter put his lips to Khoudry's ear. "We need to get out of here. Now."

"I don't think that would be a good—"

"Now," he repeated. He tightened his gaze to make the point.

"Can you ride?"

"We don't have a choice."

Cutter looked up as they resumed walking. The objects in the sky were more visible now. Three craft approaching. Still far off, but closing fast.

"V-Tail fighter scouts," he said, just loud enough for her to hear. "We don't have much time."

Khoudry angled their direction slightly, taking them to the side of the Saloon, but instead of stepping onto the boardwalk, she cut behind the corner. They both broke into a jog, Cutter moving as fast as he could. The Xenobex were not far.

He could hear commotion as they reached their mounts, loud alien barking. Khoudry helped Cutter onto his saddle and quickly mounted hers. Krilbin appeared from around the corner, shouting at them.

They took off on the Xenobex, Krilbin running after them, pleading for them to stop. Cutter looked over to see the V-Tails drawing close. He urged his Xenobex faster. Krilbin was still running after them, though rapidly falling behind.

"Careful!" Khoudry yelled at Cutter. "We can't—"

A ripping sound tore through the sky. Cutter jerked his head to look, caught sight of a torrent of pulse rounds tearing up the ground, slashing right through the Panurian, whose body vaporized instantly, leaving his still churning legs to flop and tumble forward and his head to roll and bounce along the sand.

Cutter reached across, grabbed the reins of Khoudry's mount, and yanked both of them hard to the right just as a barrage of pulse rounds battered the ground along their prior path.

Overhead, the three V-Tails shot by, making hard-G turns to accomplish another pass.

"I think the time for worrying about holding them to a safe speed is over," he said.

Khoudry nodded, and the two of them kicked their heels against the Xenobexes' hindquarters, coaxing them to move faster. At first, the creatures ran at a quick but familiar pace, moving well, but not much faster than they'd been on the ride in. But after a few more kicks, they started to understand. With a sudden leap forward, almost in unison, they broke into a sprint.

Cutter's eyes sprung wide as he felt the creature beneath him accelerate. His body slid back off the saddle, forcing him to grab onto the horn and pull himself forward. He couldn't imagine what this looked like to their pursuers, probably just a long cloud of dust. It was like holding on to a missile.

The relative wind was too powerful for him to speak, so he turned his head, squinting at Khoudry, and pointed toward the hills. She nodded from her hunched position, and they coaxed the Xenobex over.

Another barrage of pulse rounds chased them as they cut between foothills, the impacts cascading up the slope behind them. The V-Tails whizzed by overhead.

Cutter pulled his Xenobex to a halt, and they stopped beneath a rocky outcropping.

"We have to make it to the shuttle," Khoudry said.

"Can that outrun a fighter scout?"

"It's our only chance. We have to get to it."

Cutter sucked in a breath, peered out from under the rocky cover. "How far is it?"

She shook her head. "On one of these at full speed? Ten minutes? Maybe seven? They're as fast as rocket-cycles."

Thinking, Cutter looked out at the sky one more time. "There's only one way that might work. But there's no time to discuss it."

He gestured for her to come over to him and pulled her onto the back of his mount, surprise registering on her face as he lifted her. He took the reins of her now riderless Xenobex and tugged the creature to face the direction they'd been heading, through the gap in the hills. He tossed the reins onto the saddle and drew his weapon. He cocked it with his thumb and fired it so that the bullet just skimmed the animal's ass.

The Xenobex took off like it had been fired from a cannon. Within a second, it was out of sight, far beyond the hills, a fog of dust roiling in its wake.

Just as he'd hoped, the V-Tails buzzed after it. Cutter waited a count of three, told Khoudry to hold on tight, then kicked his mount into action.

Even with their combined weight on its back, the Xenobex sprinted at a speed that was almost impossible to control. Cutter hung on tight to the horn, leaning down to stay narrow to the wind, Khoudry squeezing him. He could barely breath, his ribs hurting so much, but the adrenaline was enough to keep him from passing out.

They reached the shuttle in a little over six minutes. Khoudry jumped off as the creature reared to a stop and slapped her hand against the entry pad. Cutter turned to see the V-Tails coming in fast, maybe two minutes out.

Holding his side, he dismounted and climbed into the shuttle, only to find Khoudry had removed a piece of venting pipe and opened a wall panel to remove a cooling coil. Then she yanked a component from below a floorboard and fit the venting pipe through the cooling coil and attached it to the piece she'd removed from the floor. She pulled a latch, unfolded part of the component to the rear, and flipped down small piece to the front.

"Excuse me," she said, nudging him out of the way. She jumped out of the shuttle and pointed the end of the pipe toward the incoming sky. Then she stopped, pulled it back with a look of disgust, and drove her palm against a point on the side, resulting in a loud click. The coils began to glow, and she raised the end again.

A burst of plasma shot out, knocking her shoulder back, then another and another. The fourth one caught the first V-Tail, sending it sideways and causing it to flip into another that was trailing it. The third vectored left, reversing course, but Khoudry tracked it down with the sixth burst hitting its thruster and causing it to explode.

She let out a breath like she was deflating and dropped down onto her rear end.

Cutter pushed up the front of his hat and scratched the top of his forehead near his hairline. "What in the bright burning flame of hell was that?"

"It's a long story."

"Well, remind me to make you tell me later. Right now, we need to get out of here."

"You're right," she said, pushing herself to her feet. "Let's get to the Orbiter."

They climbed into the shuttle. Khoudry hopped into the pilot's seat and got it initialized within a couple of minutes. Cutter settled down into a hop seat, wincing, his hand still pressing against his side. He looked down for the first time and noticed a deep crimson plume on his shirt, his hand covered in blood.

"We'll get that fixed up," Khoudry said. She programmed the AI to take them to the Orbiter and then sat back as the shuttle thrusters engaged. "We'll be docked in a few minutes and they'll do a much better job than I would."

"I'll manage," he said.

"The Orbiter is not responding, though that's not unexpected. They're probably in stealth protocol, given what's happened. I'll hail them once we breach the atmosphere into low orbit. Now, what the hell happened back there?" she said, her tone flat.

"I guess the Chibs really, really want Hephaestus."

"Cutter, I don't think it's unreasonable for me to demand an explanation. Tell me what's going on."

"Like you said, it's a long story."

"Unlike mine, yours can't wait."

Cutter lowered his head, fixed his gaze on the shuttle floor. "There's a UDF warrant for out for my arrest on Earth. That's why I was piloting a tug out in Nowheresville-Egypt sector."

"What'd you do?"

"It's more what I *didn't* do." He raised his chin and scratched it, but his eyes stayed low. "The war had been going on for well over a decade. I was a pilot-raider for a cleanup crew. Mop-up duty. I came across this Chib supply ship. The Chibs inside were all dead. Except for one. I was ordered to blow the whole thing. I had no room for a prisoner, and no desire for one, either. But there was something about killing an injured opponent that struck me as . . . unsportsmanlike. So, I put him in a pod and fired it out toward the last known coordinates of where his . . . whatever you call them were."

"That doesn't sound so bad. They ordered your arrest for that?"

"More for the fact that the Chibs were so surprised by the act that they decided to accept the peace terms that had been on the table for years."

"Wait a second, you're telling me *you* ended the war? You? By yourself?"

"No, I'm saying the Chibs ended the war after that, and I got blamed for it. They came down hard. Insubordination. They let me know charges were being brought. Even let me know when to expect to be apprehended. It didn't take an AI enhancement to know they were giving me a chance to run. Which I took."

"Blamed? You said they 'blamed' you. For what?"

Cutter took in a deep breath, then winced, hitching forward a bit. "That war had dragged on and on and on. The Chibs were warriors by culture and temperament, but they were like an ant colony in their thinking. The kill ratio had to be, I don't know, ten thousand to one? They had three hundred billion to our fifty billion, but it was clear our weapons, though not nearly as well-engineered, were designed with a lot more ingenuity, a lot more imaginative force. They didn't understand any way of fighting other than direct engagement. It was like an old-fashioned turkey shoot from hundreds of years ago. But they wouldn't give up."

"I don't understand. If your actions led to peace, why were they so upset with you?"

"You're right, you don't understand. It's not your fault. It's because you're not cynical enough. They were upset because they didn't want the war to end. Our casualties were low, barely more than large-scale training-exercise levels. This war was a boon to virtually everyone—politicians, the space-industrial complex, interplanetary relations that were being forged between us and various civilizations. We were the good guys. Not to mention the UDF. They had more power, more money, more prestige than they ever dreamed. The last thing they wanted was a shift in political priorities. I'd ruined the party."

"That's . . . really hard to believe. Hold on . . . we're about to leave the atmosphere. I'll lock on when we're within range." She sat back after scanning the instruments and turned to face him. "Now, what does all that have to do with what just happened?"

"I wasn't kidding when I said the Chibs must really want Hephaestus."

"And the cheating? You didn't exactly act like you had no idea what they were talking about."

He rubbed his face with his unbloodied hand and pinched the bridge of his nose. He shifted in the jump seat and flinched in pain.

"Maybe four years ago, I was making a run and the side container hitch didn't lock. I had to open the access panel and reach through to manually adjust it. It broke free just as I did and the emergency seals kicked in."

"While your arm was in? Ouch."

Cutter nodded. "Took it clean off."

"How did you survive?"

"I had a copilot for that run. He put a K-Pac on my shoulder that stopped the bleeding. But given my status, I couldn't go to any medical station, not with that warrant, so he said he knew a doctor with a surgical vessel who'd been stuck in the buffer, like me. This doctor was . . . flexible. He had a technique for regenerating a new arm, high-level gene hack."

She let out a long whistle. "That's a capital offense," she said.

"Yeah, but he insisted he had a way of masking it, some sort of mito-cloning technique with genome mirroring. He said that's why he'd been targeted by authorities, because it would change everything if you could be altered without any way to detect it. He gave me a new arm."

"And you had him enhance it?"

"No! I told him just a regular arm. But I guess he couldn't resist. After a couple of months of learning to use it, I noticed it was more than a little stronger than my other had been, and noticeably faster."

"Did the Consortium know about this?"

"They pretended not to. But they dropped hints. And I think that's why they chose me. Because I offered them the best chance of winning."

A tone sounded out, and Khoudry turned to the control panel. "That's . . . odd."

"What?"

"We should be in range now. But the Orbiter isn't anywhere around. Let me try hailing them again."

"Put it on continuous auto in emergency mode," Cutter said. "If they're refusing to acknowledge, it will at least annoy the hell out of them."

"Why would they do that?"

Cutter said nothing. He eased himself back in the jump seat and tried to keep his breathing light.

Khoudry studied the instrument panel, complaining about various bits of information that didn't make sense. Cutter remained silent, thinking.

After several minutes, a different tone finally sounded.

"That's them," Khoudry said. "Orbiter One, this is Warlock shuttle. Negative instrument contact. Please advise."

"Warlock shuttle, return to the surface. Await further instructions once there."

"Orbiter One, we cannot comply. We encountered armed hostiles and were forced to evacuate. Please advise."

"Warlock shuttle, return to surface. Await further instructions there."

Khoudry started to respond, but Cutter interrupted her. “Launch a holographic interface.”

“But—”

“Please, just do it.”

A semitransparent field materialized between the two of them. There was no discernible image.

“This is Cutter. Ms. Pitt-Summers, I know you’re listening. I also know this was your doing. The least you can do is prove you’re not too much of a sniveling coward to show your face and own up to it.”

Several seconds passed in silence. Then the field shuddered, flickering, and the woman’s image appeared. “Hello, Cutter. You’re quite self-righteous-sounding for a man accused of cheating. Just head back to the surface, and I’m sure you’ll be given a chance to prove your innocence.”

“Cut the bullshit. I know you’ve encoded the signal so it can’t be copied or transcribed. So there’s no need to keep up the pretense.”

“I’m sure I don’t know what you mean. We received word the Chibula are alleging you are enhanced. We are quite confident that’s not the case. Aren’t you?”

“You know damn well what the case is. My question is, why?”

“Why what? Why did we entrust such an important objective to someone like you? You don’t think it was because of your impressive qualifications?”

“Oh, I know why you chose me. The question is, why did you want this at all? I mean, if you didn’t want the Chibs to get Hephaestus, why . . . do this?”

“To win, Mr. Cutter. Isn’t that obvious? The objective is *always* to win. How could we possibly have known you were enhanced? I mean, there is no evidence that you are, and we strongly refute any such allegations. Now, I'm sure if you were to go back to the surface, you'd be able to plead your case. Before the Chibula killed you. Which they most certainly would. Enhancement being such an abomination to them and all. Conclusive proof be damned."

"That doesn't answer the quest—" Cutter stopped himself. His gaze cut over to Khoudry, who held up her palms and blinked. "Of course," he said.

"Of course, what?" Khoudry asked. "Would one of you mind telling me what the hell is going on? For real?"

"This wasn't about the Chibula getting Hephaestus, was it?" Cutter pushed himself off the seat, standing to face the image of Pitt-Summers. "This was about wanting a war."

"That's fanciful," Pitt-Summers said. "The UDF wasn't even concerned enough to get involved."

"Oh, they were involved, just not visibly. This wasn't just you wanting that isotope not to fall into their hands. You were the ones who put the idea in their heads to begin with. What did you do? Leak bits of information?"

"What are you talking about?" Khoudry asked. "Why would they do that?"

"It's obvious, isn't it? At least, it is to me." To Pitt-Summers he said, "You wanted an excuse to go to war, but it had to be the Chibs' fault. Couldn't risk alienating—pun intended—all your new allies, trading partners who saw us as the good guys. No, this had to be the Chibs being militant aggressors. Alleging 'cheating' with no proof, refusing to abide by the treaty. UDF gets their war machine going again, you get those contracts, and the big prize: once the UDF pushes into Chib territory, you get to mine that special isotope and all that calabantium, sell it for more money than anyone ever dreamed of, and the UDF gets their superweapon. Everybody wins. Everybody except the Chibs, of course, who probably get wiped out this time, but no one likes them, anyway. And I shouldn't leave out us, me and Vaneshka here, who get sacrificed while you position yourselves for the ultimate checkmate."

"Is that true?" Khoudry said, standing and facing the image on her side of the field. "Is that what this is?"

"Why don't you ask your companion? He seems to think he has all the answers."

"Not all of them," Cutter said. "But I know some. And I'm pretty sure I can guess the rest. But there's one question *you're* going to want the answer to."

"What's that?"

"How stupid was it for you to leave us alive?"

Cutter shot a look at Khoudry, who instinctively interpreted it and shut down the commlink and, after taking a long breath, fell back into the pilot's seat.

"How far can we get in this thing?" Cutter asked.

Khoudry shook her head as if clearing away a thought. "Huh? I'm still trying to wrap my mind around this. I can't believe any of it."

"Yes, you can. You're the one who secreted a high-powered weapon in this craft, and did so without authorization in a way that allowed it to avoid sensors. You still haven't told me why. But I figure the reason is, you've got your own reasons for being considered expendable."

"Like I said, that's a long story."

"Well, that goes back to my question. How far can we get in this thing?"

"It's powered by a fusion cell. And it's actually pretty fast. Not very fortified, but I can rig it for stealth." She looked at the instrument panel, thinking. "I can keep it running maybe a year? That can get us pretty far. In theory. But we have no food, no money. And we don't have any weapons."

"Yeah, we do." He patted the revolver tied to his thigh. "Not to mention that plasma rifle you jury-rigged. That will do for now. Can you patch me up?"

"I think so. It looks worse than it is. Unless I'm wrong."

"Then get us out of here, and we'll start planning our next move. First thing is, we upgrade, get a better craft, arm ourselves accordingly. For who we are, that is."

"And what's that? Fugitives?"

"Outlaws," he said. "And after we've brought down the Consortium, or at least brought it to its knees, made it so that no one is willing to associate with whoever fills the positions we've created vacancies in, then we'll be able to cut a deal."

Cutter pulled the Colt from his holster and turned it from side to side, looking it over. He smiled and spun it on his finger forward then back, and let it drop into the holster again.

"And, by the time we're through, practically everybody in the galaxy is going to know our names."

WEST. WORLD.

Walter Jon Williams

The first thing that struck me about Barnaby Desfort was his wonderful skin—perfectly toned, perfectly taut, perfectly ageless. I had to think he must have begun a regimen of skin care when he was still in the womb.

Other than his perfectly exfoliated skin, Desfort was a fit man in his thirties, dark-haired, brown-eyed, strikingly handsome without being pretty—and like many film stars, he was a smallish man with a very large head. The camera likes big heads, and doesn't really care how big your body is.

"Honestly," he said, "I don't know how to say these lines."

"Just practice them," said Oswald. "It'll get easier. You've acted Shakespeare, haven't you? This is no different."

Desfort made an elaborate show of raising his tablet and reading from the screen. "'I ain't a-gonna git on that there danged stagecoach,'" he said. "'An' if'n yew put so much as a foot on board, I'm a-gonna jerk my iron and fill yew with lead from this here horse pistol.'" He looked up at the director. "Come on, Oz. How the hell am I supposed to *say* that?"

"The dialogue is authentic to the period," said the director flatly.

"Well, then you'd better get an actor from the period to say these lines," said Desfort, and then he leaned closed to Oswald, his face mocking, "because *I ain't a-gonna.*"

"Usko!" shouted Oswald, only to give a start as I loomed up right over his shoulder.

"Yes, sir?" I said.

"Get together with Mr. Desfort," Oswald said. "Work out which lines are giving him trouble, and then contact Aisha in Arizona and ask her to provide some alts."

"Yes, Mr. Oswald," I said. I looked up at Desfort. "Shall we do this now, or set an appointment for later?"

"Tomorrow," Desfort said. "In the meantime, I want to go over the script *very thoroughly* so that I can *fully express* my discomfort at the words that Ms. Al-Fassi expects me to utter."

Perkele, I swore mentally. My heart sank. It would be me, not Desfort, who sent the dismaying message to Aisha Al-Fassi, and when Aisha responded, it was I who was going to get blistered by the screenwriter's flaming response.

I looked at my schedule, then looked at Desfort.

"Ten o'clock?" I said.

It had to be said that I was finding the glamorous world of cinema to be more like a regular job than I'd imagined, only working more hours and with less pay.

When I had been working toward my degree in Media Studies at Minerva College, I had followed the films of Oswalt Oswald, beginning with *Triad.* I thought Oswald was the best director currently working in cinema, and I took an interest as Oswald's works moved from small, intimate films to big productions rivalling the spectacles produced on Earth. In school, I was also involved in making student films, one of which—now to my deep embarrassment—was an homage to Oswald. I hoped Oswald had never seen it.

One of my professors knew Oswald, and was able to recommend me to the great man for his latest project—and so to my delight and astonishment, I was hired as the second second assistant director of Oswalt's new film, *The Tall Rider.*

As the second second—or "2nd 2nd AD" in moviespeak—I was expected to assist the second assistant director ("2nd AD") in producing call sheets and acting as the backstage manager, but in practice I was expected to do any damn thing anyone in authority told me to do, which apparently included helping the lead actor insult the screenwriter.

Oswald and the Earth-based screenwriter Aisha Al-Fassi had kept the script in a constant state of revision up till now, and the actors were only just getting a look at their parts. I suspected that Oswald had been deliberately keeping the script from the actors in order to postpone their demands for rewrites.

I ain't a-gonna git on that there danged stagecoach. Not that Barnaby Desfort didn't have a point.

At ten o'clock, I was at Desfort's apartment in Ptolemy Towers, possibly the most exclusive residence in Herschel City. Desfort's assistant told me that Desfort was just getting out of bed after laboring on the script all night. I had to wait in the foyer while Desfort bathed and had breakfast, and during that time, the room began to fill up with other people who had business with Desfort that morning. It seemed to me that all of them were far more important than I was.

Saatana perkele. I was probably going to be here a long time, and I had about a thousand others things to do.

I texted the 2nd AD, telling her that I was waiting on Desfort because Oswald told me to, and would probably be some time.

GOD DAMN IT, she texted back. At least she wasn't blaming me for the problem—not yet, anyway.

The smell of Desfort's breakfast filled the apartment, scents of coffee and garlic and cured swine flesh. I waited in the foyer while the others were called in one by one to meet with Desfort. By the time the assistant called my name, it was midafternoon and my stomach was growling like an enraged animal. Desfort sat at his dining table, wearing a royal purple dressing gown, and I found myself gazing in hunger at the remains of the actor's breakfast.

Is Desfort going to eat that roll? I wondered.

Desfort raised his tablet. "I've very carefully annotated the script," he said. "And I also have some notes."

Of course you do, I thought. Notes that would make Desfort's part larger, his character more sympathetic, reduce other actors' screen time, or all of the above.

"Just send this on to Aisha," Desfort said.

I gave an inward sigh. Fortunately, Aisha was on Earth and something like five AU away from the Galileo Habitat right now, and it would take at least forty-five minutes for the signal to reach her, and another forty-five minutes for the explosive answer to return. Sufficient time to duck.

It then occurred to me that I could make it clear that I was following Oswald's instructions, so maybe Aisha's reply would be sent to Oswald, and *his* eyebrows would be singed, not mine.

"Can you send me the file?" I asked.

I was present at the meeting where Oswalt Oswald had unveiled his new project. I had been hired only two days before, and was both intimidated and impressed by the large boardroom table surfaced with polished asteroid material, the framed posters of Oswald's films, and the wall of windows looking out over the Galileo Habitat's great curved expanse.

Oswald was a tall, elegant man with bushy, prematurely gray hair. He sat at the head of the table, flanked by half a dozen assistants and flunkies. At the far end was Barnaby Desfort. Desfort's wife, Kamala Shetty, sat as far from her husband as she could get without dislodging part of Oswald's entourage—a sign of the trouble that would come later, if I had only known it.

I was near the middle of the table, which gave me a good view of Kamala. Talk about perfect skin! I had a hard time not staring. She was gorgeous in her films, true, but in person she was astoundingly beautiful, so incredibly ravishing that my entire limbic system did a little happy dance whenever I looked at her. She was so beautiful that the camera couldn't contain her beauty, and only those of us who viewed her in person could fully appreciate her perfection.

Oskar Matheson, the line producer, sat disheveled

near Oswald, a bit of white frosting perched on his upper lip where it had lodged after Oskar had eaten one of the pastries Oswald's company had provided for its guests. 1st AD, 2nd AD, and 3rd AD were all present.

The others were mainly people who had provided money for the project. Investors had profited vastly from Oswald's last film, *Gravitational Constant*, starring Desfort and Kamala, and had eagerly coughed up millions of plutons for the chance to profit from the next.

Oswald rose from his place and cleared his throat, which was enough to silence the room's chatter. "My friends, I'm pleased to report that I've chosen my next motion picture. Based on an original screenplay by Aisha Al-Fassi, *The Tall Rider* will be epic in scope, and will feature my great friends Barnaby Desfort and Kamala Shetty."

I'll get to look at her nearly every day, I thought in rising delight.

"Through the medium of *The Tall Rider*," Oswald continued, "we will continue to explore the themes we explored in *Gravitational Constant*—themes of the conflict between the independent pioneer and the settled, civilized citizen, the taming of a raw frontier, the problem of establishing justice on the rim of civilization where no justice system exists, and the conflict over resources." The investors looked at one another in satisfaction. The picture seemed to be a replay of a winning formula, and I knew there was nothing investors liked better than putting money down on something that already had made a profit. Then Oswald dropped his bombshell.

"We also hope to revive the moribund Western genre," he said.

The what? I wondered. *Did he say "Western"?*

There was no east or west in Galileo. There was north and south, arbitrary directions indicated by the poles of the Sun, or of planets and moons. There was upstation and downstation. There was spinward and antispinward. But east and west?

"A what genre?" said one of the investors, echoing my thoughts.

"A Western," Oswald enunciated. "A historical film taking place in the Western part of the United States in the last part of the nineteenth century."

The investors looked blankly at one another. "You're going to make this picture on Earth?" one said. "How much is that going to cost?"

"The picture will be made right here on Galileo," Oswald said. "The American West is all suburbia now. We have plenty of empty spaces on this station, and we'll build the Wild West right here."

Which was true enough. The Galileo Habitat had been built to a colossal scale out of hundreds of Jupiter's Trojan asteroids, so vast that much of the habitat hadn't yet filled up.

The investors seemed encouraged by this. Then Desfort spoke up from the end of the table.

"Don't Westerns generally have *horses* in them?" he said. "And aren't the horses all on Earth?"

"CGI horses, surely," one of the investors muttered.

"Horses will be shipped from Earth," Oswald said. "We've looked into the cost, and it's all within the proposed budget."

"But CGI—" someone said.

"We'll be striving for complete authenticity," Oswald said firmly. "You can't simulate the relationship between horse and rider on a computer—in the Old West, horse and rider depended on each other to survive, and the relationship was one of understanding and intimacy."

Kamala Shetty looked dubious. "We're supposed to be intimate with horses?" she said.

Desfort laughed. "I predict such jolly good fun for all of us," he said.

It was going to be Oswald's way or no way. He was the emperor of his little kingdom, and the rest of us were his nervous courtiers, all too aware that he could end our careers with a shake of his head.

I had never worked with a genius before. He was the sort of genius who knew exactly what he wanted, and he demanded we want the same thing—and to be geniuses, too, but only geniuses in service to his ideas, not our own.

A small herd of horses, plus their wranglers, trainers, and a veterinarian, were sent from Earth in a custom-designed module attached, with other cargo-carrying modules, to the spine of a plasma-propulsion freighter. Plasma propulsion guaranteed that the ship would be under acceleration or deceleration for the entire trip, which prevented the horses, or their droppings, from floating around in zero gravity, something that absolutely no one wanted.

Preproduction got under way while the horses were in transit. Sets were built. Costumes were fitted. Arguments continued over the script.

I made a point of watching a great many classic Western films. They seemed to be about toxic masculinity in all its forms, and it took me a while to realize that the filmmakers approved of this sort of behavior, with all the posing and punching that led to the deadly confrontation at the end.

The villains were stupid, stubborn, and greedy, I observed, and the heroes were stupid, stubborn, and strangely high-minded.

Yet the films were visually impressive, with characters that edged toward archetype. The protagonists generally managed to achieve some sort of rude justice at the end, even if it meant standing over a dozen corpses.

I hadn't yet seen the script, and I had to wonder how Oswald was going to handle this dubious material.

In preparation, a great many guns were printed by the props department. Firearms are regarded with suspicion in space settlements, since no one wants punctures and depressurization in their homes, so the guns were built to fire only blanks. The metal in the barrels wasn't tempered sufficiently to allow a real round to be fired—instead the gun would just peel apart.

Galileo's Health & Safety Department would rather the film use ammunition composed of purest CGI, but they'd run up against Oswald's stubbornness and insistence on authenticity. They took a great interest in the firearms and insisted on many test-firings. Oswald was on hand to film the Winchesters and Colts exploding under controlled conditions. In the end, Health & Safety insisted on one of their inspectors being present at all times whenever firearms were used on the production—and the film company was expected to pay for the inspector's time. Oswald spent the next two days screaming at his assistants.

I found a lot of work to do as 2nd 2nd AD, and kept out of his way.

The actors began to practice with dummy guns that couldn't be fired and that didn't need an inspector on call. Seeing actors running around the set, pointing toy guns at one another and calling out "Bang! Bang!" was so hilarious that I had to stifle my laughter with a towel.

I also recorded a number of these play-fights on my phone. I had the sense that Oswald would crucify me if I ever released any of that material, but I am a patient man, and can await the right moment.

It was then that the Great Tumbleweed Controversy erupted. Oswald wanted tumbleweeds blowing around his outdoor sets, just as they did in classic Western films, and he ordered a number of tumbleweeds printed by the props department, and then he experimented by filming them being pushed around the sets by wind machines. Then someone discovered that tumbleweeds weren't actually present in the Old West, having been accidentally brought over from Russia late in the nineteenth century. The reason they were seen in old Western films was that the tumbleweeds were contemporary with the era in which the films were made.

Oswald was committed to an ideal of absolute authenticity, even to the point of spending millions of plutons having horses shipped up from Earth, but the Tumbleweed Controversy drove him frantic. Should he do something so inauthentic as to have out-of-period tumbleweeds bounding around in his movie?

In reality, he was the only person who cared about any of this, but that didn't stop others from expressing their opinions. I didn't give my opinion until he asked me, and then I had to overcome my astonishment at Oswald's giving a damn what I thought.

"The question is whether tumbleweeds will make this a better picture," I said. "Sure they're evocative, but of what? Are the tumbleweeds some kind of metaphor for the character's nomadic lives? Are they ghostly reminders of possibilities that are flying out of reach? Surely if they're going to be in your picture, they have to mean *something*."

He looked at me with surprise, as if he never expected a second second to know what a metaphor was.

Hah, I thought. *I've been to* college*!*

"What about authenticity?" he asked.

"You can be authentic to history, or authentic to cinema," I said. "There are plenty of authentic Western films with tumbleweeds in them. If you want to be in that tradition, then you use the tumbleweeds."

Eventually, Oswald agreed with me, though he was in anguish for several more days before he made up his mind.

The tumbleweeds were in.

There were other issues of authenticity that arose, having to do with things about the West that you never learned from Western films. How ninety percent of the people were young males, and how the clichéd figure of the "old-timer" was mainly a myth. Folks hadn't been on the land long enough to grow old there—if there were old people, they'd come from the East, like everyone else.

Oswald had decided to set his story in 1869, which was before anyone had invented the cowboy hat.

There were Mexican sombreros, and there was the early Stetson—but that particular Stetson, with its flat brim and flat crown, didn't look like a cowboy hat at all, but rather a Spanish *sombrero cordobés*, which I learned is also called a "Zorro hat."

What men mainly wore were bowler hats, or "derbies" as they were called in the States. So *The Tall Rider* would be full of young men wearing bowlers as they trotted over the plains—while heavily armed, of course.

Once I realized that the West was full of reckless young men, plenty of firearms, and few women or oldsters, I began to realize why the body count was so high.

Oswald was also mad about the authenticity of the firearms. Most revolvers in 1869 were cap-and-ball Colts, which had to be loaded by pouring black powder down each chamber of the revolver, with a bullet tamped down atop the powder, and a percussion cap set to ignite each cylinder as it moved under the hammer. Our armorer was already unhappy at having to work with the touchy picric acid used in the percussion caps when one of the stunt men discovered another problem, which was that the loose black powder in the Colts could easily communicate fire from one chamber to the next, so that all six cylinders could go off at once.

It was lucky that we weren't firing actual bullets, otherwise the man might have had his hand blown off. Instead, he gave a yell and threw the revolver as far as he could—and because we couldn't have a missing firearm off the set, I had to send out a search party to find it.

Between the black powder, the picric acid, and the explosive firearms, I couldn't figure out how the West got settled without everyone blowing themselves up.

The Health & Safety people were about as happy about this as you can imagine. They wrote several notes to Oswald "expressing their concern," as I believe they phrased it.

The Colts were in, along with the bowlers and the tumbleweeds.

But then Barnaby Desfort was out—not out from the picture, but out of his wife's life. He moved out of their mansion in Lakelands to the apartment in Ptolemy Towers, and Kamala changed the locks. A whole mob of lawyers appeared as the couple's existence was broken down, itemized, analyzed, and divided between the two of them. Figuring out who got the grand piano, the Magritte, and the late–nineteenth century popcorn-making cart was easy, but the intangibles caused more problem.

Who got the trademarks? Their production company? Who got possession of the stories and scripts the two were jointly trying to produce? Who was allowed to say what about the divorce, and to whom, and on what medium?

More importantly, who was in charge of Desfort's self-esteem? He thought it should belong to him, but she clearly disagreed. So she hit him with a restraining order, and then he couldn't come within a hundred meters of her.

Considering that they were about to costar in a motion picture in which they played lovers, the restraining order was problematic.

All this was under continual negotiation among

the lawyers, Oswald, Desfort, and Kamala, and I got dragged into the business as a messenger between the various parties. The only good part was that I got to see Kamala now and again, and occupy myself with the fantasy that, with Desfort out of the picture, Kamala would find herself itching for the altogether available body of the young, amiable second second.

No such luck. Kamala was all business.

"Tell my husband that halitosis on set is completely forbidden," she said. "He is to employ breath mints before leaving his trailer." And then, as I turned to leave, she added, "And I want to *approve* the breath mints ahead of time."

Desfort had his own demands. "Tell my wife that I must have approval over the length of her heels. Nothing over six centimeters, certainly."

Have I mentioned that Desfort is short? Kamala could destroy his self-esteem with a pair of slingbacks.

I occupied myself in passing these delightful little messages back and forth between the couple, or between their lawyers and Oswald... and then the horses finally arrived after a two-and-a-half-month journey, and Oswald, Oskar Matheson, Desfort, and the full set of ADs went to the airlock to welcome them to their new home.

The horses had been strapped into harnesses and snugged down in their stalls, because detaching their container from the plasma-propulsion freighter, then maneuvering their container into dock would result in periods of zero gravity. There had been a few similar periods earlier in the trip, and the horses had survived them well enough—better than expected, because horses turn out to be a lot more fragile than they look, and they can come down with a colic and die *just like that*, or so I was given to understand.

We stood in the foyer outside the big cargo airlock and waited for the signal that the tug had managed to dock the module. Galileo was rotating, of course, but it was a very large habitat, the docking module moved slowly, and it had been designed so that it could snatch passing vessels from out of space with a minimum of fuss.

Except that it didn't. We heard an alarming cracking noise that echoed through the vestibule, followed by a rush of air. My heart leaped into my throat—if our air vented, that would be the end of us. If we didn't die of anoxia, our hearts and lungs would be blown to pieces by embolisms.

But we heard no depressurization alarms, and instead the phones of Oswald's assistants—*all* of them—began to ring. When the phones were answered, we heard anguished messages from the horse wranglers to help them retrieve their suddenly weightless charges.

It turns out that the station docking module blew out, and the air blasted in a stream out of the cargo-sized airlock to push the horse-module away and send it tumbling. The tug's captain demonstrated his brand of courage by undocking from the tumbling container and scampering for safety. The wranglers were used to solid ground beneath their feet and had no notion of how to cope with a tumbling spacecraft. And I gathered that at least some of the horses had broken free and were floating in a panic.

I looked at the others. It seemed to be a situation of all hands on deck. I looked at Oswald, who stared back in a clench-lipped fury.

Once again, I thought, reality had failed to meet Oswald's exacting standards.

"Where's a shuttle?" I demanded. "A tug?"

Oswald turned to his assistants. "*Find me a shuttle!*" he screamed. "*Find me a tug!*"

Automated systems on the container itself were sending an alarm even as the assistants got busy on their phones, and a tug—a different one—was scrambled without our help. We ran to the tug's dock and managed to get aboard just as the airlock doors began to roll shut.

When the tug arrived near the tumbling module, we watched out the windows at the module slowly turning over and over, the distant sun burnishing its metal hull. I could see the back of the captain's head, and somehow without even viewing his expression, I knew that he was having second thoughts.

Oswald also fixed the back of the captain's head with a laser-beam glare. "Well?" he demanded. "When are we going to dock?"

The captain was a beefy man with a nose that looked as if it had been broken multiple times. He seemed to know with perfect authority that he was the captain of this vessel, and that Oswald was not.

"You don't mean *when*, you mean *how*," he said. "It's *tumbling*. There's no way we can mate with a hatch that's moving like that."

"All you need is a little—" Oswald began.

"*No*," the captain said firmly. "I don't have a clue how to do this. I could damage my own ship."

An expression of stiff-necked fury settled on Oswald. "How much?" he asked.

A hefty bribe was negotiated, and then the captain

agreed to make the attempt. His tactic was to judge the tumbling motion of the container, then drift on an interception course to snatch the docking hatch when it passed close, and hope that his ship and the hatch remained in contact long enough to lock in place.

I was sure that this wasn't going to work. But the wranglers in the module kept shouting for help, and we could hear shrieking and snorting horses in the background, and clearly something had to be tried.

But the pilot was very, very good, and he mated with the hatch on the fourth try. The tug gave a lurch as the much heavier module yanked us after it, and we were all thrown sideways in our seats. The captain got busy with his thrusters, and we were slammed in another direction, and then slammed again, and after a few minutes of having our brains and bodies cudgelled, he'd stabilized the module so that it was no longer tumbling, and we could unbuckle and make our way to the container.

I suppose because I was the most junior person on board, I was first through the hatch, and then I just gaped.

The *smell* struck me first, horse dung and horse sweat and horse panic and horse urine, all blended into a primeval acid reek that scalded the back of my throat. And then there was the demented sight of a dozen or more horses thrashing in zero gravity, legs kicking, eyes starting, foam flying from their nostrils, teeth bared, manes flying... They kicked at one another, at the walls, and at the three or four wranglers who were nearly as helpless as the horses.

Vittuperkele, I thought.

I wasn't the station's expert at maneuvering in zero

gravity, but I'd had the training, as had everyone else raised in space. So I looked to see one of the wranglers a little apart from the flailing furball of horses, and I kicked out in his direction. Once I neared him I snatched out, hugged him close, and then tumbled toward the nearest wall. He struggled at first, then realized I was trying to help. Once we tagged the wall I kicked again, crossed to where the stalls had been set up, and snagged the topmost metal bar of one of the horse stalls.

The wrangler stared at me with panicked eyes. "We've got to get them back in their stalls!" he said.

"I thought they were tied down!" I said.

"They were!" he said. "But it's hard to stop a five-hundred-kilogram horse from going where it wants to go, certainly not once it's made up its mind. Once we started tumbling, they panicked and kicked their way free."

"How do we round them up?"

He stared at me and shook his head. "Damned if I know! Lasso them and pull them to the stalls, maybe. Then me and some of the others can maybe snug them down."

"A lasso is a rope?"

I watched a piece of hope die in the wrangler's eyes. "Yes," he said. "It's a piece of rope with a loop on it."

"Where are your ropes, then?"

"We've been trying to use some of them, but they all sort of flew away—" Again he shook his head. "There are more in the locker. And halters, if we can get close enough to use them."

"Let's go to the locker."

He tried to push off but ended up flailing. I grabbed

his ankle and kicked off myself, compensating for his weight and trajectory, and brought us near to the lockers lined up against one wall. He gave me another gape-mouthed, wide-eyed stare. I pointed at the lockers.

"Get some lassos, and we'll see if we can use them."

He needed to actually make the lassos, putting the loop in them and so on, and I paused to look at my fellow rescuers, the ADs and Oskar and the rest. They were clustered by the hatch, watching the screaming horses and the flailing wranglers and casting nervous glances at one another. *It's hard to keep a five-hundred-kilogram horse from going where it wants to go.* They looked as if they were realizing just that.

The wrangler handed me a lasso.

"What do I do with it?" I said.

"Get it around the neck of one of the horses," he said, "and then we pull the horse into its stall."

"How?" I asked.

"What do you mean?"

"You're used to leading a horse to its stall in *gravity*," I said, "with both of you on the ground. But here there's nothing holding either of you down. The horse weighs a lot more than you do, and tied together without gravity you'd just become a satellite orbiting the horse."

I saw another piece of hope die in the wrangler's eyes.

"I don't know," he said wearily. "I don't know how to do it."

I looked at the lasso in my hand, then at the nearest stall, which was made of horizontal and vertical metal bars. "How long is this rope?" I asked.

I called the rescue squad over to the stalls. They all

came except for Desfort, who was filming the whole thing with his data pad from the safety of the hatch. The tail end of the rope was pulled through the metal bars of one of the stalls, and the rescuers grabbed it after anchoring themselves with legs or arms hooked through the bars of the stalls. Then I took the end with the loop and looked for a horse to capture.

"Try to get the boss mare," the wrangler said. "Once she's in the stall, the others may come more easily."

I looked at the herd of horses thrashing through the air. "Which one's the boss mare?"

"She's a bay."

I looked at him. "What's a bay?"

He just shook his head. "Just grab the nearest one if you can."

I judged the trajectories of the nearest horses, then launched. I had spread the loop wide, hoping it would at least catch on *something*, and when I came near a cream-colored horse I threw the loop at it. I was hoping to lasso the neck, but instead the loop went around a foreleg. The wrangler gave a yell.

"Pull! Pull her in! Fast!"

The rescuers hauled on the tail of the rope, the loop tightened down on the leg, and then the rescuers were all slammed into the side of the stall as the rope took the horse's weight. But at least they held onto the rope, and they were able to start hauling the suddenly very lively horse toward a stall.

As for me, I was drifting right into the furball of flailing horses. I gave a tentative wave. "Boss mare?" I said. "Uh, we're friends, right?"

The boss mare didn't reply, unless it was to scream an angry challenge, but then half the horses were screaming and doing their best to kill the other half. By sheer luck I managed to avoid the flashing hooves. I collided with one brown horse and then kicked off from the horse's side in the general direction of the stalls. I didn't give myself a good takeoff and tumbled, and pain shot through my back as I crashed into one of the stalls. I clutched at one of the metal bars and hung there, watching as the horse was hauled in. Our team was inexperienced and uncoordinated, but they did manage to get the horse partway into the stall.

Then the wrangler went to work and succeeded in getting a halter on the horse, then tied the halter down to immobilize the animal. Once tied down, the horse quieted and was packed away in its harness. When the work was done, the wrangler looked at me.

"Well," he said. "Let's do it again."

It was harder the second time, and I missed more than once with the lasso before I succeeded in roping a horse by its hind leg, but eventually the second horse was pulled in and secured.

I got back to the stalls safely, retrieved my rope, and set out again. Having had some practice, I succeeded in getting the lasso around the neck of a horse, then floated on into the sea of panicked animals while the rescue crew hauled the horse to its stall. To my utter amazement, I saw that one of the wranglers had actually succeeded in getting astride of one of the horses, and was hanging onto its mane and kicking its flanks, trying to steer it in the direction of the stalls. This was an utter failure of course, but he kept at it, and the horse was equally persistent in trying to throw him off.

I was watching this with such fascination that I

lost track of where I was going, and I landed headfirst on something soft, which I assumed was a horse until I rebounded a bit and saw that I'd head-butted a woman in her midsection. I made a grab for her and managed to clutch an ankle as I drifted away. We were kept from floating free by the fact that she was anchored by one hand on a hook that otherwise held a leather bag containing what I later learned were leg wraps.

"Sorry," I said.

"No problem," she said, gasping a little. I gave a gentle tug to her booted ankle, which enabled me to slowly drift to another hook holding some other bag of horse gear.

"Are you a wrangler?" I asked. She seemed to be somewhat better dressed than the wranglers I'd seen so far.

She was a redhead, with braids tucked up into her collar. She wore a black slouch hat that had somehow stayed on her head in the wild melee.

"I'm the riding instructor," she said in an accent I couldn't quite place. "I'm supposed to teach your actors how to be cowboys."

"I'm guessing there are no instructors for a situation like this one." I glanced over my shoulder and saw my last capture being hauled to its stall.

"I roped the boss mare," she said. "But she cracked the whip on me and threw me clean off."

As I'd predicted, she'd become a satellite of the much heavier horse, and been whipped off when the horse spun or collided with something else.

"Which one is she?" I asked.

"She's a bay." Just as I was about to ask her what

a bay was, she added, "A bay with a lasso around her neck."

That made it easier. I peered into the furball and saw a snarling, twisting, kicking horse with a long rope dangling from its neck.

"Bay" means brown, in case you were wondering.

The boss mare was drifting in the general direction of the stalls, so I decided to let her continue. "If you think you can manage it," I said, "you can follow me when I kick off from here. Otherwise, just hang on, and we'll rescue you after things quiet down."

"Thanks."

I tucked my legs under me, on either side of the hook that I still grabbed with one hand.

"My name's Mardy, by the way," she said. "Mardy Urquhart."

"Usko Anttila," I said.

"No kidding!" I heard her say as I kicked off.

I grazed the ceiling with my belly as I shot along, which set me off on a trajectory that allowed me to grab the boss mare's trailing rope. I tucked as I crashed into the gate of one of the stalls, then quickly wrapped the rope around one of the metal bars.

"Help me!" I said. "We've got a live one here!"

There was a crash as the mare's weight came onto the line, and I thought for a moment that the gate was going to tear right off the stall. Instead, I heard a bellow of outrage from the boss mare, and I looked up to see her red-eyed glare directed at me.

By this point there was a little slack in the line, so I pulled it free, shot into the stall, and wrapped the tail securely around another one of the metal bars. The 2nd AD was there to help me grab the rope, and when weight came on it again, we held on, and now the boss mare was in a kind of orbit around us instead of the other way around.

We hauled her in, the wrangler got her calmed and safely swaddled, and once the boss mare was no longer trumpeting her rage and kicking at everything that moved, things got easier. I noticed that Mardy Urquhart had joined the rescuers, and I gave her a wave. She touched the brim of her big hat.

Hauling in the rest of the horses, I got kicked in my thigh and floating ribs, and by the end of the day I was badly craving painkillers.

One of the horses was dead with a broken neck, and two others were badly injured and didn't survive the day, but we saved the majority, and incidentally saved Oswald's vision, not that he thanked us. The tug maneuvered us to Galileo and found a docking module that didn't break on first contact. The horses were startled when the container started rotating along with the habitat and gravity returned, but by and by they remembered that they *liked* gravity, and grew much calmer.

At that point I had a pretty good idea that I should step out of the module and into the tug, and I took Mardy's shoulder and drew her in with me, which meant we were the only members of the party not to suffer a rain of horse dung and urine when gravity resumed. Not that I was smelling sweet as a daisy—we were all battered and soiled, but at least I didn't have a cake of horse flop on my head, like Oswald.

The horses didn't shift to Galileo right away. They had to be calmed and washed and curried and fed first. I took part in this, not because I was particularly interested in learning how to curry a horse, but because I thought I could maybe clean myself a bit while I was hosing down the animals. Which I did, with a degree of success. I was very wet, but I smelled a lot sweeter.

Desfort continued to record our labors with his data pad. He didn't pitch in to help (and I suppose I never expected him to), but I did appreciate the horse muck that spattered his immaculate jacket, along with what I believe was human vomit—apparently someone had got space sick from the absence of gravity.

Eventually—very late in the day—a little convoy of horses was led out of the docking vestibule, onto trucks, and on to the stables that had been built on the film set. I found myself near Desfort, who was still filming and looking thoughtful. He put down his data pad and muttered, "I'm supposed to *ride* these mad beasts?"

"Mister Oswald wants you to become *intimate* with yours." I couldn't quite resist the reply.

Desfort twitched his upper lip. "Oswald can stuff himself," he said.

I gave Mardy a wave as she boarded, and only then saw Kamala watching from nearby. She'd missed all the excitement, but arrived in time to view her husband tracking horse flop into the habitat. She beckoned me over, and spoke in a loud, clear voice.

"Tell my husband that he's violating the restraining order by being within a hundred meters of me," she said.

Desfort turned and addressed me over his shoulder. "Remind my wife that our lawyers negotiated an exception allowing us to work together." His upper lip twitched again. “But if she finds my presence offensive, she is welcome to take herself off.”

“Tell my husband,” Kamala responded, “that his halitosis is so dreadful that I can smell it from here, and that he should take some of his breath sweetener.”

Desfort laughed. “Tell my wife that my breath is as sweet as a bed of roses, but that I smell of horses, and that we’re both going to be smelling of horses for weeks to come.” He laughed again. “I hope she enjoys the stench as much as I do.”

The horses were given a few days to find their feet, as it were, and then the 2nd AD and I sent out the first call sheet for the stables, so that the actors could begin to learn to ride.

The stables smelled a good deal more wholesome than the transport, with the scent of hay, leather, and saddle soap. The horses weren’t floating in the air trying to kill one another, their by-products weren’t raining on our heads, and none of the beasts had tried to kill us yet. It was, I supposed, the best we could hope for.

First, the actors learned how to approach the horses and make friends, feeding them tidbits and stroking their heads and necks. “*Talk* to them,” Mardy said.

“About what?” Desfort asked.

“Anything you like. Sports. The weather, assuming you *have* weather here. Recite Shakespeare, if that’s what you like.”

“Hm. A waste of the Bard, if you ask me.” Desfort cautiously approached his horse, murmuring about how “‘A heavier task could not have been imposed.’” His horse, a palomino named Chuck, watched him with what seemed a degree of skepticism. But Chuck snuffled at Desfort's hand, took the bite of carrot when offered, and stretched out his neck to be scratched. Desfort scratched for a while, and then Chuck tossed his head in approval and Desfort jumped three feet.

"Usko," said Kamala, "tell my husband that he's a chickenshit."

"You didn't see those beasts go mad," Desfort said.

"'A coward dies a thousand times before his death,'" Kamala said, "'But the valiant taste of death but once.'"

"Yes," Desfort said, "and the fellow who said that got butchered before the act was out."

He looked at Chuck and shrugged. "A doubtful warrant of my immediate death," he muttered, and equipped himself with carrots from the Craft Services table.

Soon everyone, even Desfort, appeared to be making friends with his chosen animal. I wasn't going to ride in the film, so I hadn't been assigned a horse—I was supposed to supervise everyone and make sure the caterer delivered lunch when he was supposed to.

"Just get to know your horse a little longer," Mardy instructed. "Keep talking to them. Be friendly."

I approached her, and looked at her slouch hat with the four symmetrical dents in the tall crown, what I had learned was called the "Montana pinch." "You kept your hat on during the horse riot," I said. "How'd you manage it?"

She looked at me with amusement in her green eyes. "I told it to stay in place. I'm good at training things, and that includes hats."

"That's a very well-trained hat. What is it—a Stetson?"

She laughed. "It's a lemon-squeezer."

"If you say so."

"A New Zealand campaign hat," she said. "From our army."

"Ah. I couldn't place your accent." I looked at the hat. "So you were in the army?"

"Not exactly, but I trained their ceremonial horse guard."

"Oh. An interesting job?"

"It gave me experience in dealing with obsolete military gear, which should be useful on this picture." Her green eyes inspected me. "I've never encountered anyone with your name before. What is an 'Usko,' exactly?"

"An Usko is Finnish," I said. "I was born into a family mining collective headquartered in the Belt. I came to Galileo to study to become a mining engineer, but I shifted to Media Studies, and here I am. I'll never have to go into a mine tunnel again, not unless it's part of a film set."

"Congratulations," Mardy said. "What is your job here, when you're not wrangling horses in zero gee?"

"I'm the second second assistant director."

She raised an eyebrow. "Second second?"

"That's the principal assistant to the second AD."

She laughed. "Is there a third third? Or a second third?"

"Only the second gets a second second. And no, I don't know *why*—it's a time-honored system, and since it means I get a job, I'm not going to ask questions."

"Hard out!" she said approvingly, then glanced over her charges. "Time to move to the next lesson, eh?"

Next, the actors learned to bridle and saddle the

horses. I tried not to laugh at Desfort's attempt to put a bridle on Chuck, ducking low and creeping toward the horse as if to sneak up on him. This made Chuck nervous, and he backed away while tossing his head and snorting, which made Desfort more jumpy, and this feedback loop would have gone on if Mardy hadn't intervened and told Desfort he'd better go back to making friends with his horse again.

Eventually, bridles were on, and the riders walked their horses out of the stables and into a big ring in the paddock outside. There, Mardy announced she would teach them how to saddle their horses.

"Don't we have grooms for this?" Desfort asked.

"You're going to learn everything about riding," Mardy told him. "Just like a real Westerner."

"How authentic are we going to get?" Desfort said. "Will we have to take our shits behind a bush?"

The saddles used were enormous, heavy Western saddles, with great horns in front and big dangling stirrups. Mardy put a blanket on her horse—she rode Jessie, the boss mare—then heaved the saddle up onto its back and cinched it in place—there was some complicated business tying something called a "latigo," which ended up looking something like a necktie. This had to be demonstrated several times, and then when the actors began saddling their horses, Mardy had to go from one to the next to show them the procedure.

Everyone was trying not to watch Barnaby Desfort during this exercise, and everyone failed. The saddle seemed bigger than he was, and awkward, and again Desfort looked as if he were trying to sneak up on his palomino, though possibly he was just bent under the saddle's weight. Again his nervousness was transmitted to his horse, and Chuck shied away when Desfort tried to heave the saddle atop him. This happened several times, and then Desfort threw the saddle down and turned to Mardy. His face was blazing red.

"For heaven's sake!" he said. "Either hold the damn horse still or shoot him—I don't care which!"

Mardy got one of the grinning wranglers to hang onto Chuck's bridle while Desfort picked up the saddle and managed to get it more or less across the horse's back. The wrangler tidied it up, getting the stirrups deployed properly, and then Mardy came and demonstrated the proper use of the latigo.

Once saddles were in place, mounting blocks were brought out, and the proper method of mounting a horse was demonstrated. It wasn't intended for the actors to actually ride the horses anywhere, and instead they were supposed to get comfortable in the saddle and practice getting on and off. Desfort got on his saddle and glared at everyone, until Chuck shifted his weight a bit, and Desfort suddenly realized he was atop a live animal that outweighed him six or seven to one, and he clutched at the saddle horn for dear life.

Kamala, meanwhile, had got on her horse and urged it into motion, walking around the paddock. "Miss Shetty," Mardy called, "you're not supposed to—"

"Oh, it's easy!" Kamala called. "I found instructions online!" She looked at her husband and laughed. "You just can't be a chickenshit, that's all!"

She looked absolutely stunning on horseback. Kamala rode Samantha, a red chestnut with a blond mane and tail, a perfectly beautiful horse. With her eyes sparkling and her dark hair flowing from under her *sombrero cordobés*, Kamala looked as if she'd been born in the saddle.

At which point Desfort decided he had enough, and he tried to get off his horse. I don't know what went wrong, because I was watching Kamala along with every other male in the paddock, but Desfort ended up hanging off the flank of the horse, with one hand clutching the saddle horn and a leg thrown up over the cantle, while the other two limbs dangled. He began to curse the horses, the production, Oswald, and cinema generally, and then we reluctantly took our eyes off Kamala, and Mardy and I came to his rescue, detached him from his horse, and set him on his feet.

Wow, I thought as I set him upright. *He really* does *have halitosis.*

Desfort gathered the shreds of his dignity and stalked off. Fortunately, the catering truck drove beneath the ranch gate at that point, and I turned to Mardy.

"Better break for lunch," I said.

She nodded, and the actors walked their horses back to their stalls, then took off their saddles and bridles and brought them some hay. By this time, the caterers had set up their tables. Cooking smells floated over the yard.

Desfort was nowhere to be seen. Someone said he'd left the set and gone home.

There was a second shift that had come in with the catering truck, stuntmen and actors' doubles who needed to learn to ride, and I leaned over to Mardy. "Make sure Desfort's double gets very good at riding,"

I said. "I have a feeling we're going to use him a lot."

She nodded. "I'd already worked that out."

The second shift was fewer than the first, and that left two horses without riders. I didn't think I'd enjoy kicking my heels while watching others take riding lessons for the second time, so I asked Mardy if I might learn to ride.

"Good on you, mate," she said. "But if you're going to keep this up, you'd better get a proper pair of boots."

She assigned me a bay named Carlton, and together the horse and I had a pleasant afternoon. Making friends with Carlton was easy, and so was everything else—I secured the latigo without assistance, then got up into the saddle without the need for a mounting block. I was tempted to urge Carlton into a little jog, but decided not to put Mardy's patience to the test.

After all, I wasn't a big film star.

"What sort of hat should I get?" I asked her as we led our horses back to their stalls.

"A bowler, apparently," Mardy said. "What do Finns wear on their heads?"

"Stocking caps, I suppose," I said. "But I've never been to Finland."

"Just get the strangest hat you can find," Mardy said. "I'm sure someone in the Old West wore something like it."

I went to Wardrobe for my riding outfit. I told them I needed to learn to ride to keep up with the actors and stuntmen in the field, and I ended up with the full outfit, from boots to one of those Zorro hats, and the cost was billed to the production.

I was tempted to follow Mardy's suggestion and get a strange hat—a cocked hat, I thought, like Napoleon.

But on further thought, I decided that a Napoleon hat was better suited to Oswald.

Desfort proved to be our worst rider, and Kamala the best. I found riding comfortable and fun, and was able to keep up with Kamala when she put her chestnut into a gallop. It was mainly, I thought, a matter of relaxing.

Desfort couldn't relax, not around horses. He demanded another horse, got one, and fared no better. He was absolutely miserable in the saddle, and he miscued his horse often enough to bollix up the simplest maneuvers. I was almost sorry for him.

I was sorrier for me, though, and for Mardy. We had to put up with his tantrums. He was the star, and every human being on the set knew they had to do their best to please him, but the horses hadn't got the memo. They weren't deferent enough, and he hated them, and those of us on the crew took the heat.

After three weeks, most of our riders were relaxed enough to be able to play cowboys—and then lights and cameras appeared, along with Oswalt Oswald, and *The Tall Rider*—by now a profoundly ironic title—began its eight-week shoot.

I disappeared into the world of call sheets, of making sure all props were where they needed to be, and of trying to wrangle actors and horses to make sure they were where they were expected. I missed my daily ride, and I hoped Carlton was missing me.

For his close-ups while riding, Desfort rode a dummy horse set on the back of a truck, with the scenery jouncing in the background as the truck bounded over the countryside. The rest of the time

Desfort was filmed getting on and off his horse, and most actual riding was done by his double.

Kamala played a Mexican woman who had married an American rancher and then been widowed, after which she faced a host of troubles, including a greedy neighbor who wanted her land. Desfort played the Stranger Who Comes to Town. He was good in the part so long as it had nothing to do with horses, and he and Kamala still had enough of their old chemistry to make the love scenes work.

Oswald's obsession with perfection was evident on the first day, when he put Desfort through forty-nine takes in order to get a scene right. Not to be outdone, the next day Desfort insisted on twenty-seven takes because he didn't feel the early takes were up to his standard. I couldn't fault either one for wanting the scenes to be right, but it meant the entire crew had to stand around while the takes went on and on—and Desfort's retakes were hard on Kamala, who was in the scene with him, and who had to deliver twenty-seven identical performances so that her own acting would be on the money whenever Desfort finally delivered.

I wondered if Desfort had blown takes deliberately so that he could annoy his ex-wife. Or Oswald. Or both.

Oswald's drive for perfection was intense enough to set everyone's teeth on edge. He railed at people for failing to understand his instructions, or for failing to appreciate his vision, or simply failing to do their job—which happened often, because we all had about a dozen jobs, and we couldn't do them all at once.

I got through it by remembering what Oswald looked like with a horse pat drooling down his head.

After a few days, I was no longer gaping in breathless admiration at the very sight of Kamala. Instead of being a stunning icon of physical perfection worthy of adoration, she'd become the package I had to shift on time from the indoor set in Herschel City to the outdoor ranch we'd built in the boonies. She was aloof, interested only in her job and in tormenting her ex. I never saw her with anyone who wasn't part of her entourage—assistants, publicists, stylists, lawyers—or unconnected with the production. She was in constant communication with a host of underlings, but only to give them instructions. I wondered if she had any friends at all.

I saw why she liked riding. The horse did what she told it to do.

I asked Oskar Matheson about Desfort's bad breath. "He's a big star," I said. "Surely he can afford to get his bad teeth fixed, or whatever."

"It's his diet," Matheson said. "He's trying to stay slim on a ketogenic program, and it's given him ketosis and permanent bad breath."

"There must be better diets available," I said.

"*You* can try to convince Desfort of that," Matheson said. "*I*, on the other hand, prefer to keep my job."

I wondered if Kamala had split with Desfort over his horrid breath. I could think of a great many worse reasons.

About ten days into the production, we finally got a day off, and I slept in late, then went to the stables to renew my acquaintance with Carlton. I saw members of Kamala's entourage there, and I wondered what was up.

It turned out that Kamala had gone riding, and

her entourage was present only to sit on hay bales and breathlessly await her return. She'd gone out with Mardy, and so I saddled Carlton and rode out on their trail.

The uninhabited area of Galileo Habitat had been given topsoil, and planted in grass and trees in order to help maintain the station's environmental balance. It was pleasant to ride through the green country, and I steered for the Western town set we'd built. I could see from a distance that the set builders and dressers didn't have the day off, and were preparing the set for the next day's shoot. A crane towered above the false fronts of the Victorian shops, placing lights on platforms, and a camera atop a spindly tower. The tower could telescope up and down and sat on the back of a truck, so it could be shifted from place to place, or driven out of sight if it was appearing in the shot. The tower's advantage was that it provided a more stable camera platform than a drone, and avoided the whirring noise of the propellers.

I could see the two women on horseback on the main street: Mardy chatting with some of the set builders, and Kamala working with her phone, probably sending more instructions to her underlings.

Then I saw light glinting on falling metal and glass, and there was an enormous crash and a roiling cloud of dust. Dashing out of the ruin came Kamala on her chestnut Samantha, its blond mane flying while Kamala clutched at the horse for dear life.

It took me a moment to realize that the camera tower had fallen, and that Kamala's horse had spooked and run away with her, and that because of the dust, it was possible that no one had seen this but me.

It's hard to keep a five-hundred-kilogram horse from going where it wants to go, I remembered.

Cinema had prepared me for what happened next. The hero would come galloping up and save Kamala, and then she would reward her cavalier in some pleasant and personal way.

It took me another moment to realize that, in this case, *I* was the hero. Or rather, that there was no hero *but* me.

"*Perkele,*" I said.

I wasn't sure I was suited to my new role, but I did my best to overcome my doubts, clapped my heels to Carlton's flanks, and urged the bay onto an intercept course. It was a rough ride, even over the flat ground. My teeth rattled, and it was hard to keep my mind focused on Kamala's survival and not my own. I was bent so low over Carlton's neck that his mane was lashing my face, giving me small cuts and making it hard for me to see.

But Carlton had a better idea of what to do than I did, and in moments we were thundering right alongside Kamala. Her eyes were wide and staring as she clutched the chestnut's blond mane with both hands. I saw that she'd lost the reins, which probably fell from Samantha's neck when the horse bolted—Kamala'd had her phone in her hands and hadn't been able to snatch the reins in time.

Well. Either I was a hero or I wasn't, and it was time to find out. I kicked Carlton to bring me within reach of Samantha's head, and I leaned over to clutch at the nearest rein. To my surprise, I snatched up the rein on the first try, and I managed to straighten in the saddle without Samantha yanking me off.

"*Whoa! Whoa!*" I tried getting Samantha to respond to my vocal commands while I was doing my frantic best to remember what Mardy had told me about the "one-rein stop"—one rein, after all, was all I was going to get. The idea was to pull the horse's head to one side to get it to circle, but even though I was a beginner, I had my doubts about the wisdom of pulling a horse into a turn while it was still galloping. It would be like yanking the wheel over in a car going 150 kilometers per hour—the car would flip over and roll, and so would the horse, with our star on top.

I did my best, though, pulling on the rein gently—and to my dismay I discovered that a horse is perfectly capable of charging in a straight line even if it's looking in an entirely different direction.

"*Whoa! Whoa, Samantha!*" Like that was going to work.

I was at a loss. I thought maybe Kamala could be useful, so I looked at her terrified face, and I said, "*Ride, Kamala! Just* ride *her!*"

I had no idea what I meant by that, but Kamala nodded as if I'd made sense, and I saw determination enter her eyes, and she began talking to the horse in a low voice, trying to break through Samantha's terror with calming words.

I looked at Samantha and then at Carlton, and I saw that their movements were in perfect synchrony—their hooves beat the ground at the same instant, and they were even breathing, or rather gasping, in synch. The horses had fallen into an unvoiced communion, galloping side by side, and so I decided to do my best to enter that communion, a third party possibly able to impose his will on the others.

I began to breathe in the horses' tempo, tried to enter the rhythm of their existence, and then I gradually drew on the rein—not pulling Samantha's head to the side, but rather up. I knew that I'd accomplished something merely by the fact that I succeeded—Samantha was strong enough to yank the rein right out of my hand if she wanted to.

I drew Samantha's head upward, her neck bending, her eyes looking to neither side but a little downward. She began to check her speed. "*Whoa, Samantha!*"

Little by little, the frantic galloping slowed, first to a hand gallop, then to a canter, a trot, and finally to a walk. I took a relieved breath of air that smelled of turf, dust, and horse sweat.

Samantha and I were both trembling all over. Carlton walked alert with both ears pricked forward, as if he rescued movie stars every day of the week.

Kamala straightened in her saddle and gave me a shaky grin.

"Thank you, Justo!" she said.

"Usko," I said.

"Thank you so much!"

There was the sound of galloping, and Mardy came dashing up on Jessie, her eyes fierce beneath the brim of her lemon-squeezer. "Kamala!" she said. "Are you all right?"

"I'm fine," Kamala said. "Thanks to Justo."

"Usko," I said.

Mardy rode up to Samantha, picked up the lost rein, and handed it to Kamala. I handed over the other rein, and Kamala brought the chestnut to a stop by herself.

"Was anyone hurt on set?" I asked Mardy.

"No. The crane operator made a mistake and knocked the tower off the truck, but no one was standing under it." She turned to Kamala. "I didn't realize Sam had gone up the boohai with you. There was a huge cloud of dust, and then when I finally worked out what had happened, I had to detour around the wreckage of the tower, and—"

"That's all right!" Kamala said. "Justo was right on the spot."

I decided not to bother to correct her on the matter of my name. Kamala had invented this person named Justo, and would be telling people about him, and probably he would get all the credit, while I would not. There didn't seem to be any chance of this turning out any other way.

Once the horses had a chance to catch their breath, we turned and went back to the set, because Kamala wanted to find her phone. It was still lying in the road where it had fallen, and Mardy retrieved it for her.

The tower lay across the road like a broken-backed whale. "That's tower's right puckarood," Mardy said.

"I reckon," I said.

"You've lost your hat," Mardy said. I put a hand to my head and saw that my Stetson was missing.

"I guess you're right," I said. "I hadn't noticed."

"I'll get you a new one."

"I think I deserve a cocked hat."

She grinned. "Sweet as!"

The strange thing—or perhaps not so strange once you think about it—was that I became a much better rider after this. The sort of Zen synchrony that I'd entered with Carlton became a part of my toolkit—I could meld with Carlton whenever I rode him, and if I were riding another horse, I could enter the Zen fugue after a little practice.

We walked our horses back to the stable, where Kamala told her entourage about her rescue by this Justo person, and if anyone there knew my real name, they didn't mention it. Some of them glared at me—I wasn't *worthy* of rescuing Kamala, that glare said; rescuing Kamala was *their* job. Kamala thanked me again, very nicely, and then took off along with her gaggle of attendants.

Mardy and I bathed and brushed the horses. We were spattered with water and soap, and ooze soaked into our boots. The horses were led to their stalls and fed. Then Mardy looked at my face, cut by Carlton's lashing mane. "Let me clean you up," she said.

She carefully washed my face and disinfected the cuts, and then she leaned forward and kissed me. We kissed for a long time, and I put my arms around her.

There was no one around. There were blankets to stretch out on. And so I got my reward after all.

I called Wardrobe and told them to get my cocked hat ready.

The next day dawned in a blizzard of new call sheets, because the fall of the tower and the camera atop it was going to result in much of the action being reblocked, since now we had to have drones and operators for the high-angle shots that Oswald planned. The big scene planned for the town was postponed, and instead we shot in the indoor set in Herschel City.

I'd got my cocked hat from wardrobe and wore

it on set. The 2nd AD looked at me in amazement. "Who the hell are you supposed to be?"

"Justo, apparently," I said.

As the production went on, I discovered the difficulties of conducting an on-set romance. I was working sixteen hours per day, and Mardy was training stunt riders and looking after horses. We were both exhausted, we spent very little time together—and worse, after the production wrapped Mardy would return to Earth. I was elated when I was with her, depressed and anxious when I wasn't, and bone-weary every hour of the day.

We went back to the outdoor town set, and I spent a lot of time on horseback, trying to wrangle actors and extras and make sure they were in place at the right time. Though I wasn't supposed to be in the picture at all, it turned out that I appeared in a number of shots, and one morning Oswald came to talk to me about it.

"When we look at the dailies," he said, "people in the screening room keep asking about the man in the cocked hat."

Terror flooded my veins at the realization that I was about to lose my job. "I'm very sorry, Mister Oswald," I said. "I hope I haven't ruined any scenes."

He gave me a strange look. "No," he said. "No, what you've done is make the picture more *interesting*. People want to know about your character."

"My *character*?" I said. "I don't *have* a character. I just have a funny hat."

"But people are interested in the cowboy with the funny hat," Oswald said. "So we're going to give your character more screen time."

I stared at him. "You want me to *act*?" Which, for the record I had never done, not even in school productions.

He gave me one of his intense, unsettling looks. "You can learn a few lines, yes?"

I blinked at him. "I'll do my best."

"And you'll be paid scale."

Well, it was a little more money.

"Does this mean I have to start paying attention to skin care?" I asked Mardy.

She looked at me and grinned. "Yes," she said, "if you don't want your acting career to end with a series of roles playing creepy old wrinkled people."

I already had a costume. Oswald suggested I grow a beard in hopes it would make me look less like a college student. I managed to produce some stubble, but I don't think it made me look anything other than unkempt.

The lines they gave me were enigmatic. "That ain't no Richard that I know." "I'm fixin' to hunt me some scrapple." "When does this barn dance begin?" And most oddly, "A woman is only a woman, but a good cigar is a smoke," spoken as I step outside a frontier brothel and reach for a stogie.

I thank God I didn't actually have to smoke the thing. I would probably have choked to death.

I think I did all right in the part. I knew I wasn't an actor, and somehow that allowed me to relax, because I knew I'd be absolute *paska*, and there was nothing I could do about it. But relaxing, I've been told, is the key to acting for the camera.

The climactic gun battle, with the Stranger Who Comes to Town mopping up the more unruly of the district's gangs, was filmed last, over nearly two weeks. Script pages and revisions were coming fast, sometimes three or four per day, and so it came as a surprise when I found out my character—known in the script as Cowboy With Big Hat—was going to be shot dead. He was going to be on the roof of the two-story brothel, give a signal to Desfort that Kamala was galloping in with reinforcements, then get shot and pitch over the gable into the street. I sought out the 1st AD.

"I'm going to fall off a roof?" I asked.

"Not you, idiot," the 1st AD said kindly. "We have stuntmen for that."

So I had the privilege of standing behind the camera and watching myself die—die three times, as Oswald wasn't satisfied with the first two takes.

Afterward, I retrieved my hat from the stuntman, punched it back into shape, and thanked him for making my death look good.

"Warn't nuthin'," he said. Somewhere during the last weeks he seemed to have absorbed period dialect.

The bigger shock came later that day. We had to film a scene in which Desfort, at the head of a posse, rode into the town to ambush a bunch of bad guys who were intending to ambush *him*. First his double came roaring in on a frothing horse, firing a six-gun, the camera shooting from just above his eye line, at an angle where the brim of his hat half-covered his face. Then Desfort mounted and gingerly maneuvered his horse to its mark, drew his pistol, and fired a few shots for the close-up. He dismounted his horse, with crew standing by just off-camera in case he fell off, and then he reloaded his pistol—not by pouring powder into each of the six chambers and ramming a ball on top, but by swapping his empty cylinder with a fully-loaded one kept in his pocket. That's how you did a speed reload in 1869.

Having given himself six more shots, Desfort charged off-camera into combat.

A few minutes later, while waiting for the next setup, Desfort strolled past me to his horse.

"Enjoy this while you can," he said to the horse. "In two weeks, I'll be having a relaxing massage in my apartment, and you'll be dog food."

My blood froze. I hadn't considered what might happen to the horses after the production wrapped, and had vaguely assumed that they'd be shipped back to Earth. But that, of course, would cost millions of plutons, money the backers and producers would be unwilling to spend.

I had to work for the rest of the day, and then issue call sheets for the next day's production, which at least gave me a chance to talk to Oskar Matheson. "Do you know what happens to the horses after we wrap?"

He shrugged. "They'll be sold. We spent a fortune getting them here from Earth, and we can't afford to send them back."

"Who's going to buy them?"

Matheson shrugged again. "No idea."

"A slaughterhouse, maybe?"

He looked at me. "Whoever makes the best offer."

Laboring over the next day's call sheets meant that it was late in the evening before I could get together with Mardy. We shared take-away at her apartment, and I told her what I'd learned.

"I already have my ticket back to Earth," Mardy

said. "I always assumed they'd send the horses back, with the wranglers to look after them."

"That's not going to happen," I said. "They could get sold to a slaughterhouse." I looked at her. "I won't let that happen to Carlton."

"I won't let it happen to *any* of them," Mardy said.

We put our heads together and tried to work out what it would cost to buy the herd ourselves, and what we could possibly do with it once we owned it. We'd have to board them at stables that didn't exist. It was possible to find feed for them—Galileo's agricultural areas had their own herds of cows, sheep, pigs, and goats, who all required fodder at least part of the time—but it wouldn't be cheap.

"Suppose we start a riding stable?" Mardy asked. "When *The Tall Rider* comes out, it might spark interest in riding. I can teach people to ride, and you can . . . well, you can do *something*." She laughed. "Wear your big hat, maybe."

"We'd have to build the stable first," I said. "And it will be at least a year before the picture is released to drive demand, and we'll have to support the herd during all that time."

We ran the numbers until they blurred before our eyes, and the project seemed impossible. I could maybe afford to save Carlton, but I'd still have to find a place to board him.

"*Mennä päin vittua!*" I snarled.

Mardy blinked at me. "One of these days you should teach me what these colorful phrases of yours mean."

"You don't want to know that one," I said. "Trust me."

I stared at the figures again, and then I had a brainstorm.

"We *already* have a stable built," I said. "We have a whole Western set. What happens to it after the production? It's built on undeveloped land, just standing out there by itself."

Her green eyes brightened. "You mean turn it into a movie ranch?"

"A what?"

"A permanent outdoor set that you rent out to production companies. There used to be dozens of them in California." She nodded. "I bet you could get the set for cheap. It will save them from having to demolish it, eh?"

I gave it some further thought. "The production company doesn't own the land, they're renting it from the government. Maybe we can buy it—Galileo lets land go cheaply if you can develop it."

"Hard out!" Mardy said approvingly. "I think we might pull this off."

"Still some questions unanswered," I said, "but I'll try to find out starting tomorrow." I took her hand. "We seem to be partners. I hope you don't mind."

She grinned. "Why would I mind?"

"You're the Stranger Who Comes to Town. I'm glad you're staying."

I kissed her. I had a feeling the partnership would last a long time.

I was still busy with the production, so I had to hire a lawyer to do all the legwork. The government was intrigued by the project, and gave us good terms on the land. The production company gave us the outdoor buildings for free, because we saved them the expense of having to demolish them. Mardy sold her ticket to Earth—worth about half a million plutons—and financed the purchase of the ranch, the stable, and the horses themselves.

By that point we already had some customers, a production company that wanted to shoot a quickie Western to be released a few weeks before *The Tall Rider* and take a free ride on its publicity. I got myself hired on as 2nd AD, so that was more income—and also more work, because the budget didn't allow for hiring a second second to assist me, and I had to do all the work myself.

Mardy and I had made long-term plans. In addition to the riding school, we'd fix up buildings on the set so that we could rent them to visitors, and then we'd have a dude ranch. We'd ship up frozen horse sperm from Earth—a lot cheaper than sending grown horses—and expand the herd as demand increased.

We also thought we'd buy a herd of cows, not as a backdrop for the dude ranch, but for profit. After all, we were surrounded by what amounted to open range, and could graze them anywhere outside the urban areas. Grass-fed beef was a rarity in Jupiter space.

We attended the premiere of *The Tall Rider*, and I laughed at the sight of Kamala and Desfort being chummy and glamorous and beautiful together, as if they hadn't spent the whole production locked in mortal combat. I was reminded that they were successful actors playing the parts of successful actors, and that the best-friends act was just that, a part they adopted until something new came up.

Kamala, I noticed, wore the tallest heels I'd ever seen, and towered over Desfort. So I think she won their war on points.

I walked over to Kamala to greet her and to let her know that Mardy and I had opened a stable, and that she could come over and ride Samantha anytime. She brightened and thanked me.

She not only came to ride, but she made her posse learn, so that they could all go on riding expeditions together, and she could tell them what to do and how to do it. Many of the entourage glared at me as they rode off. The glares said, *This is all your fault.*

The drinks table was serving champagne shipped all the way from Earth—Galileo hadn't got around to planting grapevines yet. When I was recharging my glass, I found myself next to Desfort.

"So you're an actor now?" he said. "Assistant director, actor, rescuer of runaway maidens. You're quite the renaissance man."

"Oh, I'm more than that," I said. "Mardy and I own stables now. You can come over and ride Chuck anytime you want."

He paled, mumbled something, and wandered off. I smiled.

I'm taller, too, I thought.

We trooped into the theatre, and I viewed my acting for the first time. Oswald had made me look good, and with careful editing and masterful attention to lighting and camera work had crafted my amateur acting into an eccentric performance of the sort called "quirky." It was the sort of performance that would attract attention, and maybe more work as an actor.

I'd been taking good care of my skin, just in case I got some offers.

Oswald hadn't spent all his time crafting my performance. He'd turned *The Tall Rider* into a magnificent film, expansive, epic, and iconic. I remembered that Oswald wasn't just my annoying, demanding boss, but a creator who was an actual genius.

The entertainment industry is full of people who consider themselves geniuses, and in this business, "You're a genius" is just another way of saying hello. It was encouraging to be reminded that some people actually merited the title.

The capper came when the credits rolled, and I discovered that the Cowboy With Big Hat was played by one Justo Anttila.

"*Saatana perkele!*" I swore.

Our movie ranch, we decided, would be called Rancho Justo.

ABOUT THE CONTRIBUTORS

David Boop is an award-winning Denver-based speculative fiction author & editor. He's also an award-winning essayist, and screenwriter. Before turning to fiction, David worked as a DJ, film critic, journalist, and actor. As Editor-in-Chief at IntraDenver.net, David's team was on the ground at Columbine making them the only *internet newspaper* to cover the tragedy. That year, they won an award for excellence from the Colorado Press Association for their design and coverage.

David's debut sci-fi/noir novel, *She Murdered Me with Science*, was rereleased by WordFire Press. *The Soul Changers* is a forthcoming illustrated Victorian Horror novel set in the RPG world of *Rippers Resurrected*. David edited the best-selling and award-nominated Weird Western anthology series *Straight Outta Tombstone*, *Straight Outta Deadwood*, and *Straight Outta Dodge City* for Baen. He's currently working on a trio of Space Western anthologies for Baen, which started with *Gunfight on Europa Station*.

David is prolific in short fiction with many short

stories and two short films to his credit. He's published across several genres, including media tie-ins for Predator (his story "Storm Blood," cowritten with Peter J. Wacks, for the anthology *Predator: If It Bleeds* was nominated for the 2018 Scribe Award), *The Green Hornet*, *The Black Bat*, and *Veronica Mars*.

David works in game design, as well. He's written for Savage Worlds RPG for their *Flash Gordon* (nominated for an Origins Award) and *Deadlands: Noir* titles.

He's a summa cum laude graduate from UC-Denver in the Creative Writing program. He temps, collects Funko Pops, and is a believer. His hobbies include film noir and anime.

You can find out more at Davidboop.com, Facebook.com/dboop.updates, Twitter @david_boop, and longshot-productions.net.

Milton Davis is a Black Fantastic fiction author and owner of MVmedia, LLC, a publishing company specializing in science fiction and fantasy based on African/African Diaspora culture, history, and traditions. Milton is the author of twenty-one books and publisher/editor of ten anthologies. His stories "The Swarm" (2017) and "Carnival" (2020) were nominated for the British Science Fiction Award. His story "The Monsters of Mena Ngai" appears in the *Black Panther: Tales of Wakanda* anthology.

Thea Hutcheson's story in *Realms of Fantasy*'s 100th issue prompted Lois Tilton of *Locus* to say her work "is sensual, fertile, with seed quickening on every page. Well done." She has appeared in such publications as *Hot Blood XI: Fatal Attractions*, *Baen's Universe* issue 4, vol. 1, *Amazing Monster Stories* issue 3, *Nuns with Guns*, *Water Fairies*, and several of the critically acclaimed Fiction River anthologies. In 2013, she won *Apex Magazine*'s "Merry Christmas Flash Fiction Contest."

She lives in an unscenic, nearly historic small city in Colorado with a thousand books, three rescued cats, and one understanding partner. When she's not working diligently as a planning commissioner to change that, she writes, and fills the time between bouts at the computer as a factotum and an event planner.

Find more of her work at theahutcheson.com.

Over the last twenty-plus years, **Susan R. Matthews** has had a long-running space opera series Under Jurisdiction, most recently published by Baen Books (backlist and all!).

She likes to tell people that the Jurisdiction novels represent The Life and Hard Times of "Uncle" Andrej Koscuisko, Who Is Not a Nice Man. Lately she's been working on an historical fantasy trilogy set in the "Wild High Places" of the Pamir Mountains between the Himalayas and the Tian Shan mountain range circa 1840-ish. The first of that series—which Susan says is a little bit like Kipling's "Kim," with kinks—was published in 2020 by Forest Path Books, with the second due out soon.

She's wanted to write the story at the heart of "The Last Round" for some time. When David Boop offered her the opportunity to try it as a short story for the *High Noon at Proxima B* anthology, she jumped at the chance. She's happy with how it turned out, and hopes you enjoy it.

Dayton Ward is a *New York Times* best-selling author or coauthor of nearly forty novels and novellas, often working with his best friend, Kevin Dilmore. His short fiction has appeared in more than twenty anthologies and he's written for publications such as *NCO Journal*, *Kansas City Voices*, *Famous Monsters of Filmland*, *Star Trek Magazine*, and *Star Trek Communicator*, as well as the websites Tor.com, StarTrek.com, and Syfy.com. Though he lives in Kansas City with his wife and two daughters, Dayton is a Florida native and still maintains a torrid long-distance romance with his beloved Tampa Bay Buccaneers.

Visit him at daytonward.com.

Kevin Dilmore has teamed with author and best pal Dayton Ward for nearly twenty years on novels, shorter fiction, and other writings chiefly in the Star Trek universe. As a senior writer for Hallmark Cards, Kevin has helped create books, Keepsake Ornaments, greeting cards, and other products featuring characters from DC Comics, Marvel Comics, Star Trek, Star Wars, and other properties. He is a content approver for the recent Rainbow Brite comics series by Dynamite Entertainment. A contributor to publications including *The Village Voice*, *Amazing Stories*, *Star Trek Communicator*, and *Famous Monsters of Filmland*, he lives in Kansas City, Missouri.

Cliff Winnig's short fiction appears in the Baen anthology *Straight Outta Deadwood*, on the Escape Pod podcast, and in many other anthologies and magazines, including *That Ain't Right: Historical Accounts of the Miskatonic Valley*, *Footprints*, and

Mad Scientist Journal. He's a graduate of the Clarion Science Fiction and Fantasy Writers' Workshop and a past finalist in the Writers of the Future Contest. When not writing, Cliff plays sitar, studies aikido and tai chi, and does choral singing and social dance, including Argentine tango. He lives with his family in Silicon Valley, once part of the Old West and now a place that inspires him to think about the future. He can be found online at cliffwinnig.com.

Peter J. Wacks was born Jebediah Jason Zarathustra Janney Shults, then was quickly reminted the next day to a sane name on his second birth certificate. Somehow, he never really recovered a sense of normalcy in his life. Peter (or Zarth, whatever, it's cool) has travelled to thirty-seven countries, hitchhiked across the United States (very funny, no, he didn't hitchhike to Hawaii), and backpacked across Europe.

He loves fast cars (and is currently restoring a 1964 Corvette), running 5Ks, space travel, and armchair physics. In the past, Peter has been an actor and game designer, but he loves writing most and has done a ton of it, which can be found by looking him up online. (Even if it seems a little cyber-stalkery, don't worry, go for it!) If you need a starting point his most recent release is from Baen Books, titled *Caller of Lightning.* These days he is working on new novels and producing films in L.A.

Since he doesn't think anyone reads these things anyway, he will mention strawberry daiquiris, Laphroaig, great IPAs, and really clever puns are the best way to start conversations with him.

Are you still there?

The Bio is over.
Go Read.

Brenda Cooper is a technology professional, a writer, and an editor. She holds an MFA from Stonecoast and is an Imaginary College Fellow at the Center for Science and the Imagination, CSI, at Arizona State University. Her fiction has won two Endeavour awards and been shortlisted for the Philip K. Dick Award. Brenda's most recent work includes the novels *Wilders* and *Keepers*, which are stories of climate and robots set in the Pacific Northwest, and the Fremont's Children series that starts with *The Silver Ship and the Sea*. Brenda is the IT director for a successful local construction company. She lives in Washington State, where she can be found riding bikes or walking dogs when she isn't at work or writing.

Ken Scholes is the award-winning, critically acclaimed author of five novels and over fifty short stories. His work has appeared in print since 2000. He is also a singer-songwriter who has written nearly a hundred songs over thirty years of performing. Occasionally, in his spare time, Ken consults individuals and organizations on maximizing their effectiveness.

Hank Schwaeble is the Bram Stoker Award–winning author of *Damnable*, *Diabolical* and *The Angel of the Abyss*, as well as the dark fantasy and horror-noir collections *American Nocturne* and *Moonless Nocturne*. His short fiction has appeared in various anthologies and periodicals, such as *X-Files: The Truth is Out There*, *V-Wars: Night Terrors*, and *Weird Tales* magazine. A former military officer and special agent for the Air Force Office of Special Investigations, Hank is a graduate of the University of Florida and Vanderbilt Law School, and is a practicing attorney. He lives in the Houston, Texas, area with his wife, fellow writer Rhodi Hawk.

Walter Jon Williams is an award-winning author who has been listed on the bestseller lists of the *New York Times* and the *Times* of London. He is the author of over forty volumes of fiction. His first novel to attract serious public attention was *Hardwired* (1986), described by Roger Zelazny as "a tough, sleek juggernaut of a story, punctuated by strobe-light movements, coursing to the wail of jets and the twang of steel guitars." In 2001 he won a Nebula Award for his novelette "Daddy's World," and won again in 2005 for "The Green Leopard Plague."

He has also written for George R. R. Martin's Wild Cards project. His latest work is *Lord Quillifer*, an epic fantasy. Walter has also written for comics, the screen, and for television, and has worked in the gaming field. He was a writer for the alternate reality game *Last Call Poker*, and has scripted the mega-hit *Spore*.

BAEN

Ashes of Victory pb • 978-0-6713-1977-9 • $7.99

Honor has escaped from the prison planet called Hell and returned to the Manticoran Alliance, to the heart of a furnace of new weapons, new strategies, new tactics, spies, diplomacy, and assassination.

War of Honor hc • 978-0-7434-3545-1 • $26.00
pb • 978-0-7434-7167-9 • $7.99

No one wanted another war. Neither the Republic of Haven, nor Manticore—and certainly not Honor Harrington. Unfortunately, what they wanted didn't matter.

At All Costs hc • 978-1-4165-0911-0 • $26.00

The war with the Republic of Haven has resumed . . . disastrously for the Star Kingdom of Manticore. The alternative to victory is total defeat, yet this time the cost of victory will be agonizingly high.

Mission of Honor hc • 978-1-4391-3361-3 • $27.00

The unstoppable juggernaut of the mighty Solarian League is on a collision course with Manticore. But if everything Honor Harrington loves is going down to destruction, it won't be going alone.

A Rising Thunder tpb • 978-1-4516-3871-4 • $15.00

Shadow of Freedom hc • 978-1-4516-3869-1 • $25.00

The survival of Manticore is at stake as Honor must battle not only the powerful Solarian League, but also the secret puppetmasters who plan to pick up all the pieces after galactic civilization is shattered.

Uncompromising Honor hc • 978-1-4814-8350-6 • $28.00
pb • 978-1-9821-2413-7 • $10.99

When the Manticoran Star Kingdom goes to war against the Solarian Empire, Honor Harrington leads the way. She'll take the fight to the enemy and end its menace forever.

HONORVERSE VOLUMES

Crown of Slaves pb • 978-0-7434-9899-9 • $7.99
(with Eric Flint)

Torch of Freedom hc • 978-1-4391-3305-7 • $26.00
(with Eric Flint)

Cauldron of Ghosts tpb • 978-1-4767-8038-2 • $15.00
(with Eric Flint)

To End in Fire hc • 978-1-9821-2564-6 • $27.00
(with Eric Flint)
Sent on a mission to keep Erewhon from breaking with Manticore, the Star Kingdom's most able agent and the Queen's niece may not even be able to escape with their lives . . .

House of Steel tpb • 978-1-4516-3893-6 • $15.00
(with Bu9) pb • 978-1-4767-3643-3 • $7.99

The Shadow of Saganami hc • 978-0-7434-8852-0 • $26.00

Storm From the Shadows hc • 978-1-4165-9147-4 • $27.00
pb • 978-1-4391-3354-5 • $8.99
As war erupts, a new generation of officers, trained by Honor Harrington, are ready to hit the front lines.

A Beautiful Friendship hc • 978-1-4516-3747-2 • $18.99
YA tpb • 978-1-4516-3826-4 • $9.00
"A stellar introduction to a new YA science-fiction series."
—*Booklist*, starred review

Fire Season hc • 978-1-4516-3840-0 • $18.99
(with Jane Lindskold)

Treecat Wars hc • 978-1-4516-3933-9 • $18.99
(with Jane Lindskold)

A Call to Duty hc • 978-1-4767-3684-6 • $25.00
(with Timothy Zahn) tpb • 978-1-4767-8081-8 • $15.00

A Call to Arms hc • 978-1-4767-8085-6 • $26.00
(with Timothy Zahn & Thomas Pope) pb • 978-1-4767-8156-3 • $9.99

A Call to Vengeance hc • 978-1-4767-8210-2 • $26.00
(with Timothy Zahn & Thomas Pope)

A Call to Insurrection hc • 978-1-9821-2589-9 • $27.00
(with Timothy Zahn & Thomas Pope) pb • 978-1-9821-9237-2 • $9.99
The Royal Manticoran Navy rises as a new hero of the Honorverse answers the call!

ANTHOLOGIES EDITED BY WEBER

More Than Honor hc • 978-1-9821-9288-4 • $26.00

Worlds of Honor pb • 978-0-6715-7855-8 • $7.99

Changer of Worlds pb • 978-0-7434-3520-8 • $7.99

The Service of the Sword pb • 978-0-7434-8836-5 • $7.99

In Fire Forged pb • 978-1-4516-3803-5 • $7.99

Beginnings hc • 978-1-4516-3903-2 • $25.00

What Price Victory? hc • 978-1-9821-9241-9 • $27.00

THE DAHAK SERIES

Mutineers' Moon pb • 978-0-6717-2085-8 • $7.99

Empire From the Ashes tpb • 978-1-4165-0993-2 • $16.00
Contains *Mutineers' Moon, The Armageddon Inheritance,* and *Heirs of Empire* in one volume.

THE BAHZELL SAGA

Oath of Swords tpb • 978-1-4165-2086-3 • $15.00

The War God's Own hc • 978-0-6718-7873-3 • $22.00
pb • 978-0-6715-7792-6 • $7.99

Wind Rider's Oath pb • 978-1-4165-0895-3 • $7.99

War Maid's Choice pb • 978-1-4516-3901-8 • $7.99

The Sword of the South hc • 978-1-4767-8084-9 • $27.00
tpb • 978-1-4767-8127-3 • $18.00
pb • 978-1-4814-8236-3 • $8.99
Bahzell Bahnakson of the hradani is no knight in shining armor and doesn't want to deal with anybody else's problems, let alone the War God's. The War God thinks otherwise.

OTHER NOVELS

The Excalibur Alternative pb • 978-0-7434-3584-2 • $7.99
An English knight and an alien dragon join forces to overthrow the alien slavers who captured them. Set in the world of David Drake's Ranks of Bronze.

In Fury Born tpb • 978-1-9821-2573-8 • $18.00
A greatly expanded new version of *Path of the Fury,* with almost twice the original wordage.

1633 pb • 978-0-7434-7155-8 • $7.99
(with Eric Flint)

1634: The Baltic War pb • 978-1-4165-5588-9 • $7.99
(with Eric Flint)
American freedom and justice versus the tyrannies of the 17th century. Set in Flint's 1632 universe.

The Apocalypse Troll tpb • 978-1-9821-2512-7 • $16.00
After UFOs attack, a crippled alien lifeboat drifts down and homes in on Richard Ashton's sailboat, leaving Navy man Ashton responsible for an unconscious, critically wounded, and impossibly human alien warrior—who also happens to be a gorgeous female.

THE STARFIRE SERIES WITH STEVE WHITE

The Stars at War hc • 978-0-7434-8841-5 • $25.00
Rewritten *Insurrection* and *In Death Ground* in one massive volume.

The Stars at War II hc • 978-0-7434-9912-5 • $27.00
The Shiva Option and *Crusade* in one massive volume.

PRINCE ROGER NOVELS WITH JOHN RINGO

"This is as good as military sf gets." —*Booklist*

March Upcountry pb • 978-0-7434-3538-3 • $7.99

March to the Sea pb • 978-0-7434-3580-2 • $7.99

March to the Stars pb • 978-0-7434-8818-1 • $7.99

CHARLES E. GANNON

Alternate History, Space Opera, and Epic Fantasy on a Grand Scale

"Chuck Gannon is one of those marvelous finds—someone as comfortable with characters as he is with technology . . . . Imaginative, fun . . . his stories do not disappoint." —David Weber

THE CAINE RIORDAN SERIES

Fire with Fire PB: 978-1-4767-3632-7 • $7.99

Nebula finalist! An agent for a spy organization uncovers an alien alliance that will soon involve humanity in politics and war on a galactic scale.

Trial by Fire TPB: 978-1-4767-3664-8 • $15.00

Humanity's enemies are willing to do anything to stop interstellar war from breaking out once again—even if it means exterminating the human race.

Raising Caine TPB: 978-1-4767-8093-1 • $17.00

A group of renegade aliens are out to stop humanity's hopes for peace. And to do so, they must find and kill Caine Riordan.

Caine's Mutiny TPB: 978-1-4767-8219-5 $16.00
PB: 978-1-4814-8317-9 • $7.99

Caine Riordan finds himself at the center of a conflict that will determine the fate of humanity among the stars . . . or find him in front of a firing squad.

Marque of Caine TPB: 978-1-4814-8409-1 • $16.00
PB: 978-1-9821-2467-0 • $8.99

Summoned to the collapsing world Dornaani, Caine Riordan hopes to find the mother of his child, Elena. But he may not have a chance. Dornaani's collapse is a prelude to a far more malign scheme: to clear a path for a foe bent on destroying Earth.

IN ERIC FLINT'S RING OF FIRE SERIES

1635: The Papal Stakes

(with Eric Flint) PB: 978-1-4516-3920-9 • $7.99

Up to their necks in papal assassins, power politics, murder, and mayhem, the uptimers need help and they need it quickly.

1636: Commander Cantrell in the West Indies

(with Eric Flint) PB: 978-1-4767-8060-3 • $8.99

Oil. The Americas have it. The United States of Europe needs it. Commander Eddie Cantrell.

1636: The Vatican Sanction

(with Eric Flint) HC: 978-1-4814-8277-6 • $25.00

Pope Urban has fled the Vatican and the traitor Borja. But assassins have followed him to France—and not only assassins! The Pope and his allies have fled right into the clutches of the vile Pedro Dolor.

1636: Calabar's War

(with Robert E. Waters) PB: 978-1-9821-2605-6 • $8.99

Once a military advisor to the Portuguese, Domingos Fernandes Calabar is now known as a "traitorous dog," helping the Dutch fleet strike at Portuguese and Spanish interests on land and sea.

IN JOHN RINGO'S BLACK TIDE RISING SERIES

At the End of the World HC: 978-1-9821-2469-4 • $25.00

Six teenagers headed out on a senior summer cruise with a British captain who rarely smiles. What could go wrong? Zombies. Now the small ship they are sailing becomes their one hope for survival.